THE WITCHES OF WYLDEDEN
CHRONICLES

THE MARK OF ONE UNENDING

ALEX CLIFFORD

THE MARK OF ONE UNENDING

BOOK TWO OF THE WITCHES OF WYLDEDEN CHRONICLES

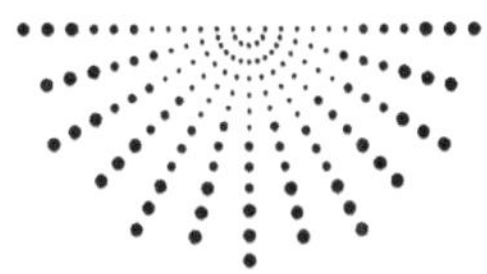

ALEX CLIFFORD

Nir
Ahrenhale
QIRI
North Mountains
Northern Spine
TERVEDA
Dvsarn
The Vein
Pirevia
VERTLYN
Womb
Heart Lake
Soul Lake
Orhn
Treppa
ANFAR
Southern Spine
Wyldeden
Dividing River
BERNT
Hyrsch
Belden
OFORD

PART I

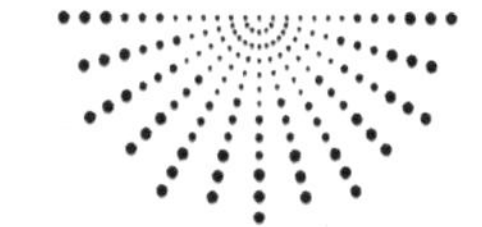

THE RISE OF CHAOS

CHAPTER ONE

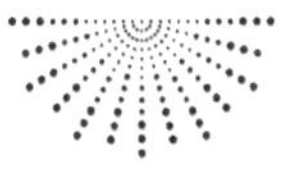

EAON

WITH A CHISEL AND MALLET, EAON FINISHED CARVING THE spellmark into the last fencepost surrounding the Copeland farm. Sweat curled the mousy hair behind his ears, the summer heat leaving his shirt damp and lips dry. He ought to have gone inside hours ago for water, but Eaon couldn't bring himself to face the others yet. Nor could he bring himself to jump the fence and drink from the Narrow River trickling a few short paces away, sure that if he left the property he would just keep going. Keep running as far and as fast as possible until he found a place where he couldn't hurt anybody.

Again.

The morning had been a disaster. He should know better by now than to push himself when he was in one of his moods.

The spellmarks he had been gradually etching into every flat surface on the farm required more concentration than he could muster today, but he wasn't comfortable lazing around either, so Eaon had asked William if there was something else he could help with. Something to burn off the restless urgency humming through his body. He hadn't slept in days, yet he was not tired.

Cinn often worked the land with the humans, and though Eaon had never been blessed enough to be taught how to do it in Wyldeden, William had encouraged him to go with them. His thoughts bounced around too quickly to hang on to one for long, but as Eaon had followed them into the small cornfield, he had admired the humans. Most didn't believe in the Spirits and all of them were without blessings, and yet they farmed and gardened and crafted—they survived—despite it. And their lives, for the most part, had always seemed so full in a way Eaon never imagined his own could be. Seeing the pride humans took in their work had given Eaon hope that, if they could be happy with such a magic-less existence, then perhaps he could be, too.

For a moment, he'd almost felt it. Standing in that cornfield, he almost believed he could be happy here with the Copelands, with Cinn and Siobhan, making up a strange little family.

And then he'd ruined it.

The summer heat had gone to his head, thoughts of Wyldeden, of his family, of Dearmead, dancing dizzily until Eaon could barely stand. Which was when the crop around him had begun to wilt.

Cinn had barely gotten to him in time to stop Eaon's surge from killing William, taking the brunt of that destructive force directly.

Again.

Eaon knew he needed to leave, but not before he did what he had promised. So despite his scattered state, he'd spent the rest of the day carving the last spellmarks. And it was almost done. A now familiar ache weighed down every single one of Eaon's bones as he drew the last line until he collapsed in the grass.

Eavha had made the spell seem simple, but it required an exorbitant amount of focus. To cast The Barring Mark of Things Unwanted, a witch had to keep a clear image of what was unwanted in their mind as they drew, or in this case, carved it. For Eavha, it had involved thinking about rogue witches. For Eaon, it was much less tangible. Any creature with ill intentions toward anyone living on the land would not be able to pass the ring of marks Eaon had drawn without experiencing debilitating pain.

Again, when Eavha had cast it she had used earth and salt and blood to bind her Terra magic to the mark. But Eaon was not using a Terra-blessing.

Reaching into his pocket as he blinked back the red spotting his vision, Eaon retrieved what was left of the sparrow bone he'd procured from the forest. Sitting up, he pricked his now scar-peppered finger with it, soaking the pointed edge of bone in blood before grinding it into dust against the carving.

"Eaon!"

Flinching, Eaon dropped the bone. Sticking his bleeding finger in his mouth, he glanced over his shoulder to the old farmer marching toward him.

"I'm just finishing the marks. Then I'll go," Eaon promised.

William paused a short distance away, crossing his large arms, a heavy frown creasing his brow. While the man's hair was mostly black, the stubble covering the lower half of his face was entirely gray, reflecting his age in a way that Eaon's body never would.

"Go where?"

"Not sure yet. Maybe home."

William didn't need to know that Eaon wasn't entirely sure Wyldeden was his home anymore. Things had been well enough when he'd left, but when he lay awake at night, night after night after night, it became too easy to convince himself that their acceptance of him was fake. How, even if he went back and became a teacher, or to labor for Eavha, the clan would never look at him without the hard edge of suspicion and disgust.

"I thought you planned to stay for the summer festival."

Eaon frowned, picking up the bone and returning to crushing it against the open wounds in the fence post.

"That was before this morning. I'm too dangerous to keep around."

"Ah."

William watched Eaon work in silence for a while, letting him finish the magic. The aura of the mark didn't affect him the way it affected Eaon, or Cinn, or the Wyldeden travelers that occasionally stopped by with supplies. The humans said they got a sense that something was *off* whenever witches were around but they didn't feel the magic, so William didn't experience any of the nauseating effects of the spell being completed. Unlike Eaon, who leaned over and heaved into the grass.

With a sigh, William crouched down and handed Eaon a canteen of water. Eaon nodded for the man to put it down on the grass so he could pick it up without risking physical contact.

"Cinn said you haven't been sleeping."

Rat. He only knew that because he didn't sleep either. Eaon didn't acknowledge the statement as he drained the canteen.

"What is it you need of me before I go?" he asked instead.

William turned his head, frowning even deeper. "I wanted to show you something, but if you need rest—"

"I don't." Eaon used the fencepost to pull himself to his feet, slipping his hands into his gloves and retrieving his staff from where he'd left it in the grass.

The intricately carved oak hummed at his touch.

It might not have been a wand like those made in Bernt, but it did a good enough job at channelling Eaon's magic to get him by. He'd forgotten it this morning when he'd gone to help with the crops. A mistake he wouldn't make again.

William watched Eaon as he swayed where he stood. His mind wouldn't rest, but his body wouldn't tolerate the neglect much longer. But the farmer must have decided he was well enough, because he nodded and led the way back toward the separate cottages on the estate.

The little stone building Eaon had relegated himself to was the farthest from the main house where the humans stayed, both structures warded with the marks Eaon had studied in the Pirevian prison during the spring. Back then, they had kept his magic from spilling out beyond the bars of Prince Nevan's cage. Now, it was the best protection he could offer the humans against any accidental surges. He had tried drawing them directly on his skin, but he'd passed out from the pain before he'd gotten two of the series done.

The second cottage had an odd annex attached that Eaon had never bothered to investigate, but that was where the farmer was leading him now.

Pushing open the heavy wooden door, William stood back to let Eaon take in the pottery shed. Barrels of clay were stacked in the dark corner, tables full of tools lining the wall, while in the middle of the room was the turning table and an old stool. On the opposite wall was a simple kiln, shelves laden with pottery surrounding it.

If Eaon was being entirely honest, the pieces were terrible. The ones with prime mantel space were some of the most misshapen pieces of work he had ever seen, which was a considerable statement after witnessing the messes made during clay classes in elementary school.

"This is our backup plan," William explained. "Sometimes when a crop goes sideways, we take things to town, or to the other villages, even into the city if we have to, to make up the losses."

"Clever." Eaon nodded.

"Would you like to have a crack?"

Eaon frowned at the turn of phrase, unfamiliar with it but able to guess what the farmer was asking.

"I'm afraid I was never any good at pottery."

He had tried. Everybody in his class took a test to see if there was a Terra-blessing in them that responded to clay. It was one of the final tests Eaon had taken before being declared too poorly blessed to be useful to the clan as anything but a laborer.

"Can't be any worse than Cinn," William said with a grimace, lifting his chin toward the malformed lumps on the shelves.

"No, perhaps not." Eaon turned his face to hide the bubble of amusement rising in his chest. But as the farmer's words sank in, the bubble burst. "If you want me to pay for the damages I can find a more efficient way."

"No, Eaon, that's not what this is about." William sighed, running a hand over the back of his head. "Just . . . sit. Do you know how to use this stuff?"

"I do," Eaon admitted, taking a careful seat on the rickety stool.

William grabbed a lump of soft clay from a barrel and brought it to the table, along with a pail of water. "Great. I've got a few things to do, but muck around for a while."

"I don't understand."

"Just . . ." William held out his hands, struggling for the right words.

"Have a crack?" Eaon suggested.

"Yeah." William shrugged. "I'll be back in a bit."

William left Eaon in the stuffy pottery shed with nothing but silence for company. Not wanting to offend the farmer, Eaon let his staff rest against the wall and shucked off his gloves again. Once his foot was moving on the peddle, the silence was replaced with a hypnotic spinning rhythm.

Despite the shame of the morning and the bitterness beneath his tongue as memories of his humiliation the last time he was behind a turning table whispered at the back of his mind, it felt good to have cool, wet clay sliding under his hands again. It wasn't as clean or soft as what he had used in Wyldeden, but nothing anywhere in Nir would be.

With his head and heart slowing, Eaon let the rhythm of the peddling, the spin of the table, absorb him.

CHAPTER TWO

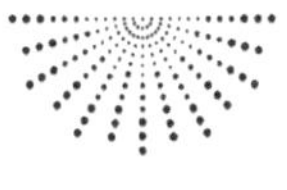

EAON

WHEN THE SUN WAS LOW ON THE HORIZON, SARAH CAME TO retrieve him for dinner. Eaon loathed to step away from the turning table, but his body was threatening to riot if he didn't feed it and let it rest soon.

"Let me clean up and I'll be right in. Thank you." Eaon smiled, the way he always did whenever Sarah was around.

After washing his hands and pulling his gloves back on, Eaon made his way back to the cottage to change out of his sweat-soaked shirt and into something that didn't stink. Cinn stood by the hearth, rummaging through his laundry for the same thing.

The kinner had changed during the month they had been back at the farm. He had to have grown at least another foot taller, able to look Eaon directly in the eye now, while all the farm work and endless hearty meals had given his wiry frame some strength. His black hair was cut short enough that he didn't have to worry about tangles, but the biggest difference was the softness of Cinn's face. There was an easiness about him, a happiness that only came from believing that he was truly safe now.

Yet, that Cinn slept as little as Eaon did these days gave away his lingering fear.

"I know you don't want to hear it," Eaon began, "but I'm sorry about this morning."

Cinn pulled a fresh linen shirt over his head and tucked it into his pants. {For the love of all things holy, stop apologizing.}

When they had first arrived back at the Copeland farm, Cinn had been more than happy to give up his old room for Siobhan and stay with Eaon in the cottage. The little house only had one bedroom, one bed, but Cinn insisted he liked sleeping in front of the fireplace even when it wasn't lit. Blankets and pillows were strewn messily over the feather-stuffed couch in the middle of the room, Cinn's clothes in haphazard piles on the floor beside it.

"I should go."

{Don't be dumb.}

"I could have killed them."

{You didn't. I was there.}

"What if you hadn't been?"

Cinn gave Eaon an exasperated look. Then turned his head, as if listening to something distant. Chewing his lip, he gave Eaon a once over before walking to the cabinet beneath the only window in the room. The sills were laden with shiny rocks, speckled eggshells and twigs that were oddly twisted, while tiny animals and flowers made of folded paper—Siobhan's handiwork—were strung on twine and dangling in front of the glass. All Cinn's little things that he liked, scattered about where he could see them.

Eaon left them alone for the most part, but every now and then Cinn would bring something in that was a little *off* and Eaon would move it around the room until it felt better. There were a few chunks of raw crystal that he would have preferred were cleansed as well, but that was another thing he had never learned how to do.

Cinn's most prized possessions, however, were still kept in his trinket box. A paper fox and the turquoise stone he had first found upon their return to the farm had been added to the collection.

It was this box that Cinn went to, rifling through it carefully until he pulled out a leaf. Eaon had seen it before; a green leaf that had clung to the branch of a tree all winter, through hail and snow and storms, refusing to brown. Cinn had explained one night when they both couldn't sleep that he had watched that leaf all winter, waiting, and that the day it finally let go he had raced across the orchard to catch it. It had never touched the ground.

Holding it delicately, Cinn brought it over and pushed it against Eaon's chest.

His whole body trembled. Being touched was such a scarcity these days that every brush of Cinn's fingers, every elbow in the side or stomp on the foot thrilled Eaon into palpitations.

Swallowing, he looked down at the leaf. "You're not trying to give me another one of your treasures, are you?"

Cinn nodded.

"I can't."

Cinn nodded again, pushing harder.

Eaon wasn't about to start an argument over a leaf. Not when he was ravenous and dinner was waiting. So he took it carefully. "Thank you."

He couldn't pretend he understood why Cinn kept giving him things, and Cinn had never explained what each gift meant; the button he'd given him in the spring was strung beside the willow amulet Eavha had gotten him, tied around his neck with a piece of twine.

To keep the leaf safe, Eaon found a scrap of cloth he'd meant to mend a shirt with and carefully folded it over, placing the package in his pocket.

William watched Eaon carefully as he sat down at the dining table. The wrinkles on the man's hands and the gray at both the Copelands' temples might have given away their age, but it was an age that didn't touch the alertness in William's deep brown eyes, nor the kindness in Sarah's.

Conversation quieted and, despite them having done this for him every night since his arrival, Eaon blushed. Bowing his head, he rushed through a quiet Terranian prayer, making a point to apologize for the ruination of the crop and asking for a good harvest next season. Once he'd raised his head, Sarah began serving the salad.

"How was the pottery shed?" William asked.

Eaon gave the farmer a grateful smile. "Surprisingly enjoyable."

"Make anything good?"

"You'll have to be the judge of that. Though I can say it's better than Cinn's."

Cinn pouted. {Take it easy. I had a tremor.}

"Sure you did." Eaon chuckled, passing the slices of lemon to Siobhan a moment before she was about to ask for them. Perhaps it was a strange pregnancy craving, but she put lemon on everything.

{Shithead.}

Sarah scowled as she slopped salad onto Cinn's plate. "Language."

Cinn grimaced, giving Eaon a filthy glare. {Why did you have to teach them that?}

"So we could scold you for using bad manners at the dinner table," Sarah continued, sitting down with her own plate. Then she turned her frown to Eaon and clicked her tongue. "I told you to leave your shirts for me and I'll mend them for you."

Confused, Eaon looked down at himself. There was a tear in the seam beneath his arm. Most of his clothes had become ragged over the past few weeks as he'd fumbled around the farm, making an idiot of himself. Patching them was on his list of things to do when he had the concentration to do so. Or even remembered to do so.

"Oh, I can do it. I just . . . haven't."

"Well, the offer stands, sweetheart."

The endearment sat on his chest uncomfortably. Sweetheart. Petal. Terms of affection he'd heard directed at his sister, but never to him.

Conversation drifted to Siobhan's concerns that the demi-kin she was waiting for hadn't arrived yet, and William's suggestions about how they might get information. Despite her concerns, the energy at the table was content.

Yet, Eaon ached.

Maybe, once, he could have learned to be happy here. He could have defected from Wyldeden and lived among the humans where even the speck of Terra magic in his blood made him slightly better at farming and gardening than average. But that was before the curse.

Before the Lover had tainted him. Every second he lingered was another moment he was putting this family in danger.

When the meal was over, William and Cinn took the dishes to the sink to clean up. Eaon picked up his staff and rose from the table.

"You're not staying tonight?" Siobhan asked.

She and Eaon often took turns telling stories after dinner, and it was supposed to be his night.

"I left some things unfinished in the shed. Do you mind?"

"No, no. Go ahead."

With a nod of thanks, he walked back into the silent night, too aware of the eyes following after him.

Back in the shed, leaving the door ajar for fresh air, Eaon took a seat at the table once more. He would leave in the morning, but for now, working in the pottery shed kept him calm. It felt good to make something instead of always destroying. This table, turning out pots and mugs and bowls for the Copelands to sell at the markets—it was the most useful he had ever felt.

Outside the door the farm had turned black, stars on full display in the clear night sky. Flickering shadows danced over the table as the candles burned low but, elbow deep in clay, Eaon was too engrossed in the vase he was turning to consider changing them.

"Psst."

Eaon stilled and looked up at the door. Cinn stood there in a light shirt and his undershorts, bleary eyed and frowning.

{It's late. Come in.}

"I'm not tired and I have all these ideas. William and Sarah will make a fortune if I can get the details right."

{Eaon. Come inside.}

He meant to argue, but bursts of color streaked through the sky above Cinn's head, connecting the stars. The light dusted the fields in glitter like gold, the scent of wheat and hay swelling until the urge to roll in the grass for hours was hard to resist. Eaon grinned, even though a part of him knew none of it was real. Not that it mattered right then, with Cinn standing in the doorway in all his languid grace.

"You're really beautiful."

Cinn raised an eyebrow. {Okay, it's definitely time for a tonic.}

"What? No, I'm fine. Can I not appreciate the world for a moment?"

Stepping inside, Cinn tugged on Eaon's filthy sleeve.

{Appreciating the world is fine when you're not delirious. Come and get cleaned up. Sarah and I made tarts for dessert and I kept some for you.}

Cinn did make exceptional tarts.

"Alright. Okay," Eaon agreed.

Waiting as Eaon cleaned up and grabbed his staff, Cinn blew out the candles before leading him by the arm back to their house. A plate of miniature pastries was on the cabinet beneath the window, and while Eaon picked one to enjoy, Cinn crouched down to pull out the box of tonics Eavha routinely sent via traveler. Selecting one labeled *Sleep*, Cinn passed it to Eaon, who begrudgingly drank it down. It hadn't worked the past few days, but it was worth a try.

"You know, I am more than capable of looking after myself," Eaon grumbled as he handed back the vial, watching Cinn put it in the little bag they would send back with the next traveler.

Cinn lifted an eyebrow, sliding Eaon a dubious look. {Get some sleep.}

Scoffing, Eaon made a sign he hadn't taught the Copelands.

The near-silent chuckle Cinn smothered was answered by the weary meow of the farm cat who Cinn had, for unknown reasons, named Puddles.

Leaving Eaon to finish his tart, Cinn shuffled back to the couch and curled up beside the tabby, whispering a meow back to it and stroking its long tail. The cat purred and meowed again, stretching until it was hanging off the couch.

Eaon shook his head as Cinn continued to engage in some imaginary conversation with the creature. At least Puddles had stopped hissing and spitting every time Eaon entered the room.

"Goodnight," he said, leaving them be and making his way to the bedroom.

Collapsing on the bed, Eaon ran his hands through his floppy hair. The earth-stained lines of his palms reminded him that he'd forgotten his gloves in the shed. With a sigh, he leaned over and picked up a second pair that the Copelands had gotten him as a gift on one of the human holidays. He wouldn't risk leaving his hands bare, even in sleep. As for washing them, washing himself . . . tomorrow. His head was getting heavy, mind quieting like it hadn't done for weeks. The tonic was hitting him harder than usual and a slight panic swelled and died in his chest as he realized he might actually fall asleep.

CHAPTER THREE

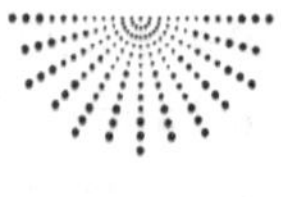

EAON

THE SUNRISE BROUGHT WITH IT ONE OF THE WORST HEADACHES Eaon had suffered in a long time. The light was sandpaper behind his eyelids, the pressure inside his skull enough to keep him from opening them. In the next room, the tap for the bath was running, which meant Cinn was up. Rolling his tongue in his mouth until his dry lips could part, Eaon called out to him.

The creak of his bedroom door opening was torture.

"Can you get something for my headache," he begged softly.

The door creaked again, followed by footsteps trotting down the hall.

After taking the tonic for pain that Cinn brought him, Eaon pulled the blanket over his head and waited while Cinn took a bath. Slowly, the pressure eased until he was well enough to sit up.

Squinting against the daylight as he shuffled into the living room, he went directly to the pitcher of water Cinn kept by the couch and drank his fill. Though it hurt his head, the sun's warmth eased the tension in his neck as he stretched and pulled at the tight muscles there.

That's when he felt it.

Like a cold finger down the back of his spine, curling around the base of his skull, the sensation of an unwanted presence brushing against the warded boundary was impossible to ignore.

Eyes snapping open, Eaon grabbed his staff and gave a sharp two-toned whistle to warn Cinn. Water sloshed onto the tiles as Cinn hurtled from the bath, still dripping and soaking the fresh clothes he pulled on as he ran into the room, color bleaching from his sun-kissed face.

Eaon peered out the window, but whatever had come was outside his line of sight. Creeping to the door, his bare feet a whisper over wood, he turned the handle.

Cinn hissed, making Eaon glance back.

{Let me go first. Just in case.}

{I'm just as immortal as you,} Eaon signed back furiously.

He had told Cinn about his time in the void, including the Lover's promise not to claim him until something or another was finished. He didn't exactly remember.

{We don't know that. Move.}

Cinn pushed Eaon out of the way and opened the door. Eaon scowled, following only a step behind. His first glance was toward the main house. Movement in the windows told him the Copelands were awake.

A sharp gasp.

Cinn shoved Eaon back, scrambling over himself to shut the door again. Clamping a hand over Eaon's mouth before he could ask what was wrong, Cinn dragged him to the floor, breaths coming too fast as sweat broke across his skin.

{What?} Eaon signed.

Only after he was sure Eaon wasn't going to talk aloud did Cinn let him go. His hands shook as he signed, {Witches. At the fence.}

Lowering Cinn's head to his knees the way Eavha had taught him to do during a panic attack, Eaon crawled back to the door and pushed it open a fraction. Enough to poke his head around the corner.

Standing by the fence, studying the marks he had carved into the posts, were two figures dressed in black tunics, golden sparrow crests embroidered on their chests. One male, one female, both carrying swords at their hips, daggers across their chests, open and waiting shackles dangling from their belts. The male witch paced along the fence line, running a hand across the invisible boundary.

{The wards are working,} Eaon told Cinn. {I'm going to go and deal with them.}

Cinn shook his head, damp hair plastered across his still-paling face, eyes glistening. Eaon's chest ached seeing him so scared again.

{It will be fine,} he insisted.

As he stood, Cinn grabbed Eaon's wrists to hold him back.

"Stop it, Cinn," Eaon urged as he pulled himself free. "Let me deal with them."

But Cinn wasn't listening, trying to grab Eaon's wrists again, his staff, his ankle—anything to keep him from leaving. Managing to wrangle himself free, stumbling out the doorway where Cinn wouldn't follow, Eaon looked back with pity as Cinn covered his face and buried his head back between his knees. No words would calm him, so Eaon didn't try.

Leaving the cottage door ajar, Eaon strode toward the fence. Within a few steps, both the Sparrow witches' heads snapped up in his direction.

"Can I help you?" Eaon called out, hostility lacing every word.

For the first time in a while, he roused his magic on purpose, letting the sharp, bitter scent of necrosis waft off him as it thrummed hungrily in his veins.

"Is this your place?" one of them asked.

"What business is it of yours?"

The two witches kept their hands on their hilts as they looked Eaon over. Twice.

"You're Returned, but you are not Sparrow," the other witch noted, narrowing his eyes.

"I'm going to ask you one more time before this becomes a much less civilized conversation," Eaon warned. "What. Do. You. Want."

The female lifted her chin, incensed. "We are here for the kinner. Our intelligence is reliable so do not bother denying he is here. Surrender him immediately."

Her flash of teeth was anything but friendly and a shudder ran down Eaon's spine. Not at the threat, not because his magic was roiling in anticipation beneath his skin, but because it was clear the princess of Hyrsch had not heeded his warning. When nobody had shown up at the farm after the first week, Eaon had thought they would be safe. Whatever reason for this delay, he doubted it was good. That the Sparrows had come meant he would have to do something.

Taking a step closer, poisonously calm, Eaon kept his voice low. "I warned you people what would happen if you did not leave him alone."

Readying himself, Eaon raised his staff off the ground.

"I wouldn't," the male warned him, watching Eaon's hands. "We are not alone. Put the wand down before an arrow pierces your skull."

Resisting the sneer pulling at his lip, Eaon dropped his staff. He didn't need it. Not at this proximity.

Just them. Eaon stroked the magic blistering his spine with cold.

All around him, the wards began to sing. A faint snap, and ten arrows split the air to burrow beside Eaon's bare feet.

A warning.

He hadn't studied weaponry enough to be able to tell how far each arrow had traveled, the exact position of the archer. Dearmead might have been able to, but Eaon was a far cry from being him.

Clenching his teeth, Eaon took another breath to steady the magic clawing to get out. There were precautions that needed to be taken first.

"Alright. I'll get him."

Stepping over the arrows, he reached for his staff. Another arrow scratched the skin on the back of his hand. Either very accurate or a close miss.

"Leave it." The Sparrow witches watched him warily.

Fine.

Eaon left his staff and stalked toward the farmhouse. Inside, the Copelands had formed a shield around Siobhan, watching the exchange through the kitchen window. Could an arrow pierce glass?

"They're here for Cinn," Eaon explained through gritted teeth. "Is the cellar still prepared?"

Just like the outside of the house, Eaon had put extra warding in the cellar. It was the best protection he could offer in case of an emergency. In case of what was about to come.

"Yes." Sarah nodded, pale and trembling.

"Cinn will come and get you when it's over. I'm sorry."

"Do not apologize, Eaon," William said sternly. "Thank you. Thank you for protecting him. And us."

Leave these three, Eaon pleaded as the farmer shepherded the others down the hall, but his blessing was beyond listening to him now.

Shaking from the effort of containing it, Eaon's breath hitched as he waited for the cellar door to close. Then he took a single step outside.

And was immediately barraged with a volley of arrows.

The sensation was too familiar. Eaon couldn't breathe.

Peeling his eyes open, he could feel the shafts of wood spearing his lungs. Cold stiffened his body, but his blessing had no hand in it. As blood pooled beneath him, the force that had always clawed to get out shriveled into a tiny kernel somewhere deep inside.

Darkness threatened to steal his vision as Eaon turned his head toward the still-open cottage door. Cinn's face was twisted in terrified rage, crouching in the doorway and poised to run, glancing between Eaon and the fence where the Sparrow witches were still held back by wards that would not break, even in death. The archers had revealed themselves, circling the farm like hyenas. If Cinn stepped out, they would shoot him too. And what then?

{Wait,} Eaon managed the simplest sign.

Closing his eyes, he drew on his dormant blessing. His fingers twitched uselessly, feeling for something, anything, he could use. Everything was so dry.

In his pocket.

Barely holding onto consciousness, Eaon managed to pull Cinn's green leaf from his pocket and fed what little Terra magic he had into it.

One word. He only had the energy for one word.

Help.

A heartbeat passed before Terra accepted the offering, carrying the leaf away.

CHAPTER FOUR

KAELEAN

KAELEAN DIDN'T HEAR A SINGLE PROTEST THE ELDERS HURLED AT her. As soon as the messenger barged into the temple with Eaon's name on his lips, Kaelean was already racing toward the Boab. For Eaon to be calling for help, it was serious.

Striding across the bridge, she kept stumbling over the length of her stupid—

"—fucking dress!" she hissed.

Shredding her gown, she bit her fingertip until it bled and drew hasty spellmarks on her face. The lupanis was faster than she was, and though she'd sworn to never absorb another form, she suddenly wished she had taken something even faster. If she ran at full speed without stopping, it would still take her almost two days to reach the human farm.

Ignoring the stares of witches offended to see their high priestess naked, Kaelean shifted and charged through the portal to Anfar.

———

She sensed the wards surrounding the human farm long before she came within visual distance of it. It wasn't Eaon's fault that he'd practically put out a beacon to his location—there was a fine line between casting a spell powerful enough for your needs and casting something too pungent, and Eaon had never learned to walk that line.

Exhaustion had slowed her down the past few hours, limbs burning from two days without rest, but as she scented the Sparrow witches surrounding the farm she knew she would demand more from herself this day. She'd rip herself and the whole Mother-made world to shreds if Eaon or Cinn were hurt.

It went against all her instincts, but she couldn't help that she loved their stupid faces. After last time, she'd vowed to never form another coven. Yet here she was. Whether they liked it or not, they were hers now.

The Sparrows were chipping away at the posts surrounding the farm. Some were sleeping on the ground while others cooked over a small fire. Eaon's spell might have been excessive, but it worked. Those heretics weren't getting through any time soon.

Or at all.

Slowing, she counted her enemies. Ten, eleven, twelve. Four necromancers and eight Returned.

Her stalking came to a stop as she took a moment to catch her breath.

This would not be an easy fight. Despite her thick-scaled skin, the claws and teeth she knew could crush bone and rip apart stone, she trembled like the thirteen-year-old witchling she'd been the last time she'd faced off against Sparrows. Nevan didn't count. He barely counted as a witch at all.

Quietly, she backed away. This was not a fight for the lupanis.

Shifting back into a witch, Kaelean knelt in the dirt and bowed her head, threading her fingers under the earth. It warmed beneath her palms, particles rising to brush her lips as she muttered a spell. The Terra-blessing in her soul rumbled, shuddering its way down her arms, through her hands and into the ground.

Spirit of the earth, from thee I am descendent and to thee I give my all. Terra, keeper of our foundation, bless me once more. Take my enemies.

She lifted her head just high enough to watch the Sparrows

standing up, panicking as the soil softened beneath their feet. No matter how they scrambled, it swallowed them to their knees. Their thighs.

"Witch!" one shouted, pointing in her direction.

Kaelean hissed and rolled to the side as an arrow loosed, splitting the hair by her ear. The ground solidified as she broke her hold, leaving the Sparrows trapped.

Ducking behind a tree, she drove her hands back into the earth.

Take my enemies.

The ground cracked, the sound of a mountain being cleaved in two. Shouts of warning as the earth opened up were followed by silver-tipped arrows thudding into the tree Kaelean hid behind, unable to find their target. Spears of magic weren't far behind. The tree groaned, rivaling the earth in its complaints as the rot took hold.

Swearing, Kaelean raced for the next thick-trunked conifer, but another dark, cold spear of power had it crumpling to one side before she could reach it.

Gritting her teeth, she fled through the forest. She needed a new approach.

"Fucking Sparrows," she spat, leaping into the branches of a nearby pine.

She was far enough that the deadly magic couldn't reach her, but hers couldn't get to them, either. Silently, she stalked her way back from above, hoping the camouflage would provide an advantage.

A number of Sparrow witches were aiming arrows at the surrounding bushes, searching for her. Others were digging furiously at their trapped legs.

She had a minute at most before they began to free themselves.

Through the branches, her sharp vision spotted a prone figure lying outside the farmer's house, arrows sticking out of their body.

White hot rage obliterated any sense of self-preservation she had.

Not again.

She would not lose anyone else.

Shifting again, readying her claws, she leaped from the tree.

Her full weight pummeled into one of the arrow-wielding witches, snapping his spine in two before she threw herself at the next, ripping his throat out before he even had time to turn. She slashed for the next archer, cutting the female's belly open in one swipe. An arrow found its mark in Kaelean's flank, the silver tip shredding her scales like cobwebs. Snarling through the sharp bite of pain, she took a limping dive for the last archer, locking her jaw around his arm and pulling it clean off his body.

A spear of deadly cold hit her in the gut, and she fell, gasping. The scales on her belly began rotting, flaking off like sunburnt skin. But only in that one spot.

Dragging herself up, she rolled and ducked as a second and third spear shot for her, the chilling tingle of her sensitive neck frill the only warning of the magic's approach.

Luckily for her, the Returned were not half as powerful as the quarry they'd found with the kinner.

As another spear of deadly magic passed by, she realized she was too big a target. So she began to shrink, the arrow falling from her side as she did.

Her mouse form was the same brown as the dried leaves coating the forest floor, and as she burrowed under a pile of them, bursts of aimless power hit nothing but already decayed brush. Only three of her four tiny feet worked as she dug down into the earth, tunneling until she hoped she was deep enough. If she was wrong, the earth would mound as she grew and her position would be evident. But she was nine hundred and fifty years old; she wasn't often wrong.

Pulling in what little air she could fit into her rodent lungs, she returned to her natural form. The pressure was crushing, but even in Oford the earth acknowledged Terra's blessing, softening just enough to not kill her. No air, no light, but safe in the ground that responded to her every whim, she offered her will to Terra once again.

Take. My. Enemies.

The earth around her began to churn.

As soon as the magic took hold, she changed once more into the mouse to escape the pressure. Not for the first time, she wished she could cast from a different form, but only a witch's body was designed to host blessings.

Clawing to the surface, she waited until the ground went still. One final change, sucking in deep lungfuls of air, she rolled to the side and sprung to all fours, ready to fight again.

There was no need.

All that was left of the Sparrow witches was an axe buried in a fence post.

The ward created by Eaon's magic brushed over her harmlessly as Kaelean stumbled over the threshold. By the farmhouse, Cinn knelt over the body. He'd grown since she had last seen him but Kaelean would know that gangly form anywhere. A stack of knives and broken arrows, a mallet, a meat pulverizer, and a bundle of sharpened sticks lay in neat piles beside him, as if he had been preparing for battle. A bloody stain had blossomed across his shirt, though there were no wounds to be seen.

Unlike the corpse Cinn was pointlessly packing the wounds of.

Eaon's skin had gone a shade of gray she knew meant he was long gone, his eyelids and lips the blue of bloodless veins. The bundles of torn cloth stuffed in the entry wounds were soaked in dark witch blood that had stopped running some time ago.

From the moment she had learned he had followed his sister into Anfar against Lorelei's wishes, the instinct that drove her to form coven after coven had reared its annoying head again. Even after the centuries of pain she had endured from losing them all, the urge had not been subdued.

And now, here she was again, her heart torn to pieces.

"Is he actually dead this time?"

Cinn snarled, flinching back. He wouldn't have heard her approach. Taking his blood-stained hands away from Eaon's wounds, he signed, {The Lover promised not to take him.}

Glad she had asked Bodhi to teach her more sign language, Kaelean blinked, suppressing her surprise. She hadn't asked Eaon about his second encounter with the Lover, High Spirit of Death, but she'd thought he would have told her something like that.

"Does his magic linger?"

Swallowing deeply, Cinn shook his head.

Leaving them, she stalked into the house and gathered a handful of salt and herbs. Taking them outside and collecting one of the knives Cinn had stockpiled, she dropped to her knees and scooped a bowl in the earth to mix the ingredients together, dipping her fingers into her still-bleeding leg wound until she made a paste.

Covered in dirt and blood, Kaelean drew Marks of Concentration on her sternum and closed her eyes.

"Mother, hear my call," she prayed aloud, feeling her body slip into a weightless state.

The realms of the Spirits existed everywhere together, like pages of a closed book pressed atop each other. A witch only had to learn how to open the book to be able to flick between them. The temples made it easier, but Kaelean knew that if she shouted loudly enough, Mother would come to her wherever she was.

The magic she had once stolen burbled in her belly as she peeled open the book of realms, sweat beading down her back as she pushed herself against the Mother's page.

"Mother, hear my call."

Like plunging into a hot spring, her body fell apart, soul slipping into the realm of creation. Mother's workshop was pure starlight, all heat and brightness. There was nothing tangible to see, but she could feel the matter of all things filling the space with an energy unlike anything else. It was life. It was everything that had ever been made, and everything that ever might be.

Not many could find their way to this particular page, and certainly no others who had managed had ever taken a bite from it.

What do you want, thief?

A voice that was not a voice, everywhere and nowhere. Lilting and soft, as if in perpetual harmony, even when the words were scathing.

"So, I'm still not forgiven?" Kaelean smirked, quickly losing it as the deity became a blistering pillar of rage. "I'll get to the point, then. Is he truly gone?"

A perfume of nectar and honey blossomed around her, Mother's bristling presence leering over the scattered particles of Kaelean's existence.

What will you give me for this information?

Nasty spirit. Always bargaining. No better than the damned fae.

"Nothing. But I won't take anything, either," Kaelean promised.

The heat became suffocating. *Impudent child.*

"Has Eaon truly passed or not?"

I wish I'd never made you.

"Has. Eaon. Passed?"

Not for the first time, Kaelean pondered whether Mother would, or even could, smite her where she knelt or if that was solely the domain of her Lover, Death.

No, Mother hissed. *He is in between. My lover will not take him yet. Heal the body and Death will push him back.*

Perfect.

Without another word, Kaelean retreated. Heat scorched her flesh as her soul returned, crammed back into a form that felt much too frail.

Opening her eyes, she once again knelt on the hard soil of the Copelands' farm. Cinn was still watching her.

"He can be revived," she told him. "But not here. I will take him to a healer in Wyldeden."

A muscle in Cinn's jaw ticked as he looked back down to Eaon's ghastly pallor.

"More Sparrows will come for you once they realize their comrades have gone missing. The wards will hold, but . . . you should come with me too."

Cinn's shoulders dropped. {I . . . you will be counting this on how many life . . . I owe you.}

Kaelean missed some of the signs, but caught enough to get the gist of what he was saying.

"Consider this one a freebie."

He scoffed, but as he got to his feet and looked to the house, defeat marred his expression.

{They will never be safe here again, will they?}

For all their bickering, Cinn was hers too. Which meant so were the Copelands.

"Pack your bag, kinner. And tell the humans to pack one too. You're all coming to Wyldeden with me."

CHAPTER FIVE

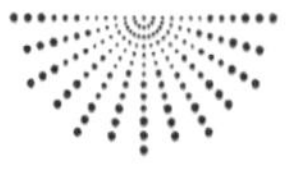

KAELEAN

WHILE CINN RETRIEVED THE HUMANS FROM THE CELLAR, KAELEAN took a couple of bedsheets hanging over an outdoor clothesline. One she tore to shreds, packing and tying strips around the wound in her thigh.

"Always the leg," she muttered to herself, grunting as she pulled the bandages tight.

She managed to wrestle Eaon's body onto the second sheet, twisting the edges and tying knots to make him easier to carry. Pulling her gaze away from his gray face was painful; he had called for help, and yet again she had been too late.

"Oh my gods, she's naked."

Kaelean looked up to see the humans exiting their house, carrying large packs. It was the farmer woman who had spoken, covering her eyes as her face bloomed red, while the man made a point of not looking at her at all. The third human was unexpected. Black hair tied low, youthful yet shrewd, this human was unlike the others. Breathing deeply, sticking her tongue between her teeth, Kaelean scented the hormones swamping the young one's body and reeled back.

At the same time, the pregnant woman went wide-eyed as she asked, "Cinn, is that her?"

Cinn nodded, and the woman lowered her gaze as she curtseyed in that awkward way human's often did. "Your Highness. Or . . . I'm sorry, I don't know what to call witch priestesses. But Eaon told us about you."

Kaelean tilted her head as the two farmers exchanged wary glances. They clearly remembered her bursting into their kitchen all those months ago, and no doubt what Eaon had told them was less than flattering, but eventually they bowed their heads for her too.

"Calling me Kaelean is fine," she grunted as she struggled to her feet.

Nobody offered a hand to help her, nor did they hear her answer as they noticed Eaon on the ground.

"Oh!" Sarah covered her mouth, grabbing a hold of her husband. William swore and turned away.

"He will be fine," Kaelean assured them, nodding toward their packs. "Cinn explained that we must leave?"

"He did," William said, crouching by Eaon and tucking the sheet around him tighter. "We've always been ready to leave if it came to it. Just need to stop at the neighbors on the way. They will take the animals and keep the place ready for us when we return."

"I'm staying," the pregnant one declared.

Kaelean bristled. "Absolutely not. The Sparrows will return—"

"I must wait. There are people coming to meet me—"

"Then leave a note. But you cannot stay. Not in your condition."

The pregnant woman only crossed her arms and set her feet. "My *condition* has no impact on my ability to defend myself."

"Against witches of death?" Kaelean challenged, lifting her brow.

"The wards still work, do they not?"

"If they think the kinner is here they will eventually find a way to break through them. They will find you and *convince* you to tell them where he has gone. So I do not care who is supposed to meet you, you will come with me."

{Why do you care so much?} Cinn asked, though he of all people ought to be on her side.

"The baby must be protected," she explained, looking down to the human's belly where the looseness of her dress hid any evidence that she had begun to swell.

"It's hardly a baby yet," she scoffed, but her hand moved to rest against her stomach.

"It is a gift from the Mother, and you would be foolish to do anything to risk it. She may not bless you again if you offend her," Kaelean warned, shaking her head. "So you will leave a note and come with me, or I will send a patrol of guardians to take you by force."

{Kaelean!} Cinn gestured angrily, but she ignored him.

The human woman raised her chin. "Eaon told us about the tantrums you throw when you don't get your way. Hardly high priestess behavior, don't you think?"

"You are an exceptional time waster," Kaelean growled, then turned to the farmers. "Eaon is safe to touch until he is revived. I am injured. Would you mind carrying him?"

William nodded.

{Let me get my . . . and I'll help you,} Cinn signed, then jogged toward the small cottage nearby.

When he returned, Sarah and Siobhan took two packs each while William and Cinn carried Eaon in the makeshift stretcher. Kaelean retrieved Eaon's staff and used it as a crutch as she limped back into the forest.

Kaelean blamed the humans for the agonizing pace as they traveled toward the Dividing River, but her wound was just as guilty for slowing them down. Not to mention the exhaustion cramping every muscle in her body. She'd run a nine-day journey in only two, defeated twelve Sparrow witches, and convened with the Mother, all on no sleep or food.

As night fell, she gratefully lowered herself to the ground and closed her eyes. By some kindness of the Lover, Eaon's body had not started to rot, so William and Cinn put the stretcher down carefully and covered him with a blanket from the packs. Siobhan immediately began retrieving dry logs to make a fire while William and Sarah removed an array of metal poles, a kettle, and sacks of vegetables from another of their packs.

Cinn did exactly what Kaelean expected him to do; he stood guard, hand on the hilt of the small blade at his hip. What was curious was the way he kept glancing at his own pack. Sniffing, Kaelean picked up on a familiar scent that bristled the hair at the nape of her neck.

"Tell me you did not bring what I think you did."

Color bloomed across Cinn's cheeks.

Ignoring the strain in her back, she moved, intending to check, but Cinn darted for it first, shielding it with his body.

"You have to be kidding me," Kaelean growled at him.

The color in his face deepened.

"Cinn?" Sarah asked, looking between him and Kaelean nervously.

Carefully, Cinn opened his pack and pulled out a canvas sack. From within, he pulled out the farm cat. It was stiff and startled, clinging to Cinn's shoulder as it peered around the campsite.

"Cinn!" Sarah put a hand to her mouth, laughter wrinkling her eyes.

William turned his face up to the moon and sighed deeply before throwing more kindling on the pile.

The cat finally noticed Kaelean, their eyes meeting across the camp. It hissed, and Kaelean returned it. During the long autumn she'd spent in fox form watching Cinn in the barn, making sure he was keeping it together, she and that damned cat had fought over mice relentlessly.

Cinn pressed his face into the cat's fur and stroked its head soothingly.

"You're not bringing that thing to Wyldeden. We don't allow predators."

Cinn turned his back and resumed watching the forest.

"We'll make sure it doesn't cause trouble," William promised, a grimace plastered across his weary face. Sarah, too, pleaded silently.

Pathetic.

"Fine." Kaelean rolled her eyes.

William rubbed Sarah's back affectionately as the human woman smiled fondly at Cinn. Preparing camp, Siobhan pulled out a second blanket and spread it over the layer of pine needles on the forest floor.

"You are not as bothered by the forest as I expected," Kaelean admitted.

"I grew up on a farm," Siobhan explained, sitting down and taking off her shoes to rub her feet. "My cousins and I would camp in the woods all the time. It was kind of a badge of honor, in a way. Proving we were brave enough to live among the forest folk."

Brave. And stupid. She was lucky not to have been eaten by ratki or a shtryg. But from her pack, Siobhan pulled out a collection of silver and iron weapons along with a jar of salt, a string of rowanberries and a pouch of gold coins. She certainly seemed prepared.

"Before I met Sarah and settled down," William started as he assembled the metal poles into a makeshift spit, "I used to smuggle demi-kin out of Kerveda. I'm used to camping. And Sarah? Well, she's just tough as nails."

The older woman gave him a coy smile as she filled the kettle with tea leaves and water from her canteen, hanging it over the campfire William was now trying to light with two stones.

Kaelean raised her brow, impressed. Of all the humans she had ever come to spend time with, these three seemed to be among the most sensible. Sarah carried a second waterskin over to where Kaelean had collapsed.

"Would you like something to wear?"

"I am not bothered," Kaelean answered, taking the water with a grateful nod. "Tomorrow we will reach the river. It is not an easy crossing."

{Eaon and I made a raft,} said Cinn, having put the cat down. It paced beside his legs, rubbing against his boots. {It should still be in good . . . Might take two trips to . . . everybody across though.}

Kaelean raised her eyebrows again. She had wondered how they crossed the river when the two of them had left Wyldeden, but it made sense Eaon would have a way. She sometimes forgot he had traveled from a young age without blessings and would probably be more savvy than most at getting around.

"I can carry a couple of you as the lupanis," Kaelean offered.

There was the smallest smirk on his face as he signed. {I'd rather swim.}

Kaelean returned it.

By the time they had eaten, Kaelean was ready to faint. Her eyelids grew heavy, body sagging against the ground as the small fire crackled and popped. They were drawing too much attention.

Cinn would stay up, she knew, but still, she felt responsible for protecting them. The beasts and the fae knew to keep away from her, but if she were sleeping . . .

Siobhan sat on the opposite side of the fire from Cinn, facing the darkness, two knives in her hands. She had the posture and focus of someone who had spent many nights awake, keeping vigil.

Regardless, with all the energy she had left, Kaelean fixed the spellmarks on her face and shifted again into the lupanis form. Perhaps just the presence of it would help.

It would have to do. She could deny sleep no longer.

CHAPTER SIX

KAELEAN

THE SMELL OF COOKING MEATS WOKE HER. HER REPTILIAN SKIN kept her cool as the summer sun rose high in the sky, but the pain in her leg had worsened. Peeling open her heavy eyelids, she checked the seeping wound before looking at the camp.

A duo of cawkers lay dead over a nearby boulder while a third roasted over the still burning fire. Carnivorous birdlike beasts of limited intelligence, named after the sound they made while mating, the creatures were half the height of a human and unafraid of a challenging meal. William plucked the one still feathered while Sarah carved the meat off the one already cooked. Dress soaked in blood, Siobhan ate greedily from the leg Sarah handed her while Cinn cleaned their weapons in the grass.

What in the Mother-made world had she slept through?

When the humans noticed her watching them, she was surprised by the hostility with which they glared at her. Despite her sluggishness, Kaelean rallied her blessing and shifted back, limping closer to the fire.

"Were we attacked or did you hunt?"

"They were watching, but we took no chances," Siobhan answered around the bones between her teeth. "Cinn said we should let you rest."

"Cinn is too kind," Sarah said coldly.

Curiously, Kaelean looked to the kinner, who was feeding strips of meat to the cat while the tips of his ears burned red. William stayed silent, but the ferocity with which he yanked feathers from the cawker told her all she needed to know. Eaon must have used some discretion when telling them about this past spring, but Cinn had clearly been more honest during the night.

"Should we discuss it, or should we just eat and move on?" she offered.

There was nothing new about being distrusted; about being given only begrudged respect for her position because they feared her power. If the humans wanted to express their unhappiness with the choices Kaelean had made that had hurt Cinn, she would let them. She was not deluded enough to think her actions had been acceptable, and yet she would not do any of it differently. That was the difference between her and the Sparrows, or so she told herself. They all walked the fine line between right and wrong, but while the Sparrows deemed all lives disposable for the sake of the cause, Kaelean grieved those she destroyed in her wake.

To her surprise, it was Siobhan who stood up, tossing her bone into the fire before stepping close enough to keep her words inaudible to the others.

The farmers stilled, watching carefully. There was a rage in Siobhan's hardened face that Kaelean didn't understand.

"You played us. The other rebels in the city and I. Tricked us into doing your dirty work for you. Getting him free, just so you could drag him across the country and lock him in a different cell. People died for his freedom. My closest friend was tortured to death and staked on the palace gate for months for it."

Ah.

"Don't misplace your anger," Kaelean said softly. "All I did was confirm the rumors that he existed and told you where to find him. Was your little rebellion not already searching anyway? The rest of what happened to your friend was the Sparrow bitch's doing."

"Don't worry, I have enough anger to go around. Because what happened to Cinn afterward is on you," Siobhan countered. "He is proof that the Kinner are real. He is hope that they will return and reclaim our cities from the Sparrows. And if you ever do anything to risk him again, I will bring the entire force of the Hyrschan rebellion to your precious boab and burn it to the ground."

Kaelean's hands curled into fists, tilting her head as the threat awoke something feral. Again, her nostrils flared at the scent of the hormones flooding the human's body. Only that managed to calm her.

"Take comfort," Kaelean lowered her voice as she let the violence shine on her face anyway, "in the knowledge that the kinner has managed to squirm his way into the very small circle of things I care about. I would not willingly put him in danger again."

She had not suggested a formal coven because she knew neither Eaon nor Cinn would accept her, but it had not stopped the bond forming in her own heart.

Siobhan narrowed her eyes further, but gave a short nod and stepped back.

Shifting his gaze between the two of them and his shoes, Cinn approached the fire to take the cawker from the spit. He winced at the sizzle of burning flesh, face reddening as he shucked off the meat, spiked the last bird, and put it back over the fire. Within seconds, the burns were healing.

"I don't think I'll ever get used to that," William muttered, taking over the carving so Sarah could eat.

Kaelean shook her head. "No, neither will I."

On the way to the Dividing River they passed a tall witch-hazel tree, and Kaelean paused to strip some flowers from a low-reaching branch. Along with a handful of other herbs she'd been collecting on the way, she managed to mix together a rough poultice to smear on the wound. Hopefully it would stave off further infection before she could get to a healer.

The torrent of the river was faster than usual, the ice from the mountains melting in the summer heat and rushing for the ocean. Crossing was foolish, and even as the lupanis, Kaelean had struggled with the current. Sheer will had gotten her over, but now that the urgency had passed she was not as confident.

They wandered upstream until they found the hidden raft Eaon and Cinn had used to ferry across before, and seeing it only annoyed her all over again. How had anyone ever thought travelers were "useless" when they were resourceful enough to make something like that? The raft was narrow but long, made of fallen branches and forest debris, packed with mud and bound with vines. It also had knee-high walls to stop beasts and fae from sliding aboard to steal them into the water. Only just wide enough to lay Eaon along the bottom, there was room for two people to stand at the ends with long branches they could use to steer the structure through the river. It reminded Kaelean of the canoes the river clan witches used in the north.

"You said you could swim?" William asked her.

She had said that. With her leg aching so incessantly she was not at her fittest, yet the humans would be safer with her in the water to scare away anything too curious.

"I can." The declaration was as much for herself as for them. Gritting her teeth, she limped to the riverbed and ran her finger through the mud to refresh the spellmarks on her face that would help her change form.

"What are you thinking?" Sarah asked William, wringing her hands as she eyed the deafening river.

"We'll take Eaon across first. Then there should be room for the other two to sit for a second trip."

Kaelean looked to Cinn. "I could take you and Eaon on my back. Do it in one go."

She had meant it as a joke, but the kinner scratched his chin as he looked between the humans and the river. He knew what was in there. Knew that he and Eaon would live if something came for them, but the humans would not. It said a lot for how much he cared for them that he nodded.

{Are you sure? Your leg—}

"Barely a scratch," she assured him before letting her body turn to clay.

Once formed again, Cinn moved Eaon onto her back and perched over the top of him, pinning him down tightly with his own body. William, Sarah and Siobhan pushed the raft into the river and quickly clambered aboard, dumping the packs and the sack with their ridiculous cat inside between them. Siobhan stood with her weapons out, watching the water as if she too knew what lived beneath.

Waiting to make sure the humans could handle the raft, Kaelean watched them slowly wrestle against the current before easing herself into the water. As entertaining as it was to scare the shit out of Cinn, now was not the time. The weight of Eaon's body on her back lifted as they submerged, but Cinn adjusted himself to keep him caught between the two of them. She swam slowly, keeping to the side of the raft and ignoring the stiffness growing in her leg.

When she got back to Wyldeden, she didn't care what treaties she had to break or the risk involved, she was ordering a damn bridge to be built.

They managed to cross the river without trouble, but as she climbed ashore it became clear that Cinn was not okay. Pulling Eaon off her back, he lay him down gently on the soil, eyes rimmed with red as he pushed the soaked hair off Eaon's gray face and tucked the sheet tighter around him. His lips moved, but no sound came out as he repeated the same word over and over.

Sorry.

Sorry.

Sorry.

Kaelean shivered as she returned to her witch form and helped the humans pull the raft to shore, covering it with enough foliage to protect it from the weather. Sarah's own eyes were welling as she saw Cinn.

"He will be fine," Kaelean began, but the woman ignored her and went to kneel beside Cinn, sliding an arm over his shaking shoulders. William and Siobhan grabbed the packs, giving her a filthy glare as they strode past to sit with the others.

Kaelean rolled her eyes. It wasn't much farther until they reached Anfar, so after adjusting her bandage she plucked a leaf from the closest shrub and whispered instructions for the Wyldeden scouts at the border.

Fragile laughter swelled from the others, including Cinn, who wiped his face on his sleeve. With a grateful nod, he grabbed one end of Eaon's stretcher while Sarah took the packs, freeing up William to carry the other.

Kaelean had made her bed with the humans and she didn't see the point in forcing any further conversation. Her leg was more manageable as a lupanis, so she shifted once more and strode ahead into the forest.

Even if the humans couldn't sense the intrinsic magic of the Anfar forest or the wards surrounding it, the scout, healer and three guardians waiting stoically among the trees made it obvious where the boundary was.

Kaelean had stayed in her lupanis form the entire journey to this point, but, as soon as she saw Yvette, she sagged and began to shift.

"I'm surprised you let us meet you here, since you seem intent on doing everything yourself," the new elder healer scolded, immediately dropping to one knee to untie the ragged bandage around Kaelean's thigh.

The humans slowed, staring at the gathering of witches. Being face to face with one hadn't disturbed them much, but now they were outnumbered. Their discomfort and inability to understand the conversation anymore made Kaelean smirk with satisfaction.

"Are we really taking these humans to Wyldeden?" one of the guardians asked, appraising the trio.

"Is that . . . Eaon Nemuse?" another asked in trepidation.

"Yes," Kaelean huffed, hissing as Yvette put something on the wound that immediately began to burn.

"Hold still," she scolded again, though her eyes darted to the corpse wrapped in linen.

"The Mother said if we can repair the body, her Lover will return his soul to it," Kaelean explained. "And the humans are under my protection until this business with the Sparrows is sorted out."

The witches exchanged glances, but nobody argued. Two of the guardians stepped forward to take Eaon but hesitated as Cinn snarled. Only after Kaelean nodded in assurance did he let go, exchanging Eaon for his damned cat. The other guardian and the scout took the packs from the women, who sagged in relief at their lessened load.

"Come," the scout commanded in Nirnish.

The guardians watched the humans as they ventured into lands no human had been allowed to step foot in for a millennium. Judging by the spooked expressions on their faces, the Copelands no doubt sensed that something about the trees, the ground, the air, was vastly different from what they were used to.

"Should I send for Eavha?" Yvette asked quietly as she finished treating the wound and slipped an arm around Kaelean's waist, taking some of the pressure off as they walked.

"No. I will tell her what had happened when we get home. The healers at the clinic will be able to repair the body."

"They are not necromancers like she is."

"Eaon is not gone the way he should be. Treat the wounds as if he were alive and he will return."

Yvette grimaced but didn't argue. The clan had accepted Eavha back without too many complaints, but the magic she had once displayed still frightened them. And that fear was nothing compared to what she knew they still harbored for Eaon.

A deep sense of relief washed through Kaelean as they reached the Boab. Soon, she could rest.

Intruders. Trespassers, the witchmark on the tree whispered as the humans approached. *Not of Anfar. Not of Wyldeden.*

The shadows of Terra's guardians loomed. Not even Kaelean entirely understood what they were; not beast, not spirit, not anything tangible. Yet, they were sentient, and she knew that if the humans tried to cross into Terra's realm, into Wyldeden, without permission, the shadows would take them.

Easy, she soothed them. *Friends.*

Trespassers.

Friends.

Trespassers!

Friends!

At thirteen, when she had first torn open the bridge between Nir and Terra's realm, the shadows had been there. Had come for her. But like everything else that had ever dared to face Kaelean Caesarea, she had conquered them. From the moment she had tied her blood to the witchmark, the shadows had no choice but to accept her as a part of their realm.

TRESPASSERS!

FRIENDS!

The ground rumbled as she pushed back at the shadows, her magic plunging into the earth in response to her frustration. Siobhan screamed, clinging to Sarah and William, who were equally panicked. The witches simply waited. Cinn glared at her.

But as the shadows backed down, she was able to soothe the earth into stillness once more.

"It's safe to pass through now," Kaelean told them.

"Safe?" Sarah asked, frowning as she squeezed Siobhan's hand.

"Do you think any old wanderer is allowed to enter Terra's realm? You'd be lost to the void had I not convinced Terra's guardians you had permission."

The humans paled. Cinn glared harder. She smirked at him before waving a hand impatiently.

"Onwards."

Anfar was warm in the summer, even under the smothering canopy that left them breathing thick humidity, but as they crossed through the Great Boab the air turned immaculate. Despite their fear, all three humans stopped in stunned silence as they took in the rolling plains and quartz towers surrounding the lake. Yvette left as some of Kaelean's acolytes approached, the elder healer leading the guardians carrying Eaon toward the clinic.

As the acolytes draped Kaelean's filthy shoulders in a robe of deep green, she stepped up behind Siobhan and leaned in close.

"Threaten this place, these people, again," she whispered in her ear, that feral thing that lived inside her snarling once more at the memory, "and not even your condition will protect you from the full might of *me*."

Fear soaked Siobhan's scent, but Kaelean turned to face all the humans, bowing deeply.

"Welcome to Wyldeden. My home, and for as long as you need it, yours."

CHAPTER SEVEN

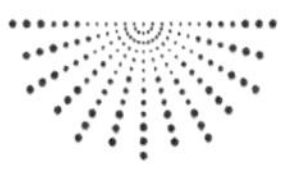

EAON

He couldn't breathe.

Eyes like stars stared out of the darkness.

Skin burning, he ran a hand over his chest to find three suckling leeches.

Stop fighting it.

Yomra's words echoed through the void.

The stars winked out as he began to sink into oblivion.

He surfaced in the clinic.

Gasping, Eaon lurched up from the bed. Cinn grabbed his shoulder, squeezing his hand tightly.

It was dark, but not like the void. A candle burned low on the nightstand while the moonlight filtered through the windows, illuminating healers doing their nightly rounds. Praying aloud to Sanni, they burned sage over the occupied beds. Yvette rose from a nearby desk, dark circles under her eyes.

"Sorry," Eaon panted, the bone-deep cold making him shiver. "Was I surging? I'm sorry."

Cinn pushed his shoulder until Eaon lay back down.

{It's okay. Go back to sleep.}

"Are you alright?"

Cinn blinked and turned to look at the elder healer, who came over with a vial of milky liquid.

"Drink this," she said, holding the vial to his lips. "You need more rest."

"It's not worth it if I'm surging. Cinn shouldn't have to sit here—"

Cinn pinched his ear and scowled. {Go. To. Sleep.}

A cramp spasmed through his core, radiating through his chest and eliciting a pained gasp. "What's happening?"

"I gave you something to speed up the healing. You don't want to be awake while it works. Take the sleeping tonic, Eaon," Yvette warned him.

Grimacing, he gave Cinn an apologetic glance before parting his lips and letting Yvette pour the tonic down.

Eaon could not stop shaking. No matter how many blankets the healers placed over him, the cold of that eternal void lingered. Now that he was properly awake, it was worse. The sun beaming through the windows could not touch him while the weight and restriction of being in a physical form again smothered him.

Still sitting on a stool beside the bed, Cinn held his hand and absorbed the wafts of magic spilling out as Eaon struggled with his third return. It was clear now why dying without the Lover's embrace waiting on the other side was such an intrinsic fear among those who understood Balance. His memories of the void were a haze, and yet Eaon was absolutely sure he never wanted to go back.

"Wh-what h-happ-happened?" Eaon asked, teeth chattering so hard he could barely speak. Pulling the blankets higher required too much from his still-aching body, but he would not whine. He was alive. He did not get to complain about it.

Letting go of Eaon's hand for a moment, Cinn explained to the best of his ability what had happened over the days it took for Kaelean to arrive at the farm. Cinn had waited, just as Eaon had told him. The wards had held. The humans were now in Wyldeden, William and Sarah happily finding themselves a place among the clan, farming and gardening alongside witches who had welcomed them kindly. Siobhan had offered to work, but Kaelean wouldn't allow it, insisting the spy relay all she knew about the princess and the rebellions working in secret throughout the city instead.

Aisling had been warned not to come after Cinn and had chosen to ignore it. There would be consequences. Eaon would lay waste to the entire Sparrow Coven himself as soon as he stopped trembling quite so badly.

"Wh-where's Eavha?" he asked.

Cinn's eyes darkened in a way Eaon had never seen before.

Wincing, Eaon forced himself to sit up. Even if she was not technically a healer anymore, Eavha would have been here, insisting on overseeing Eaon's recovery herself.

"Cinn, where is she?"

"Lay back down before you injure yourself again," Kaelean's sharp voice snapped from the window beside his bed. Eaon turned to stare as the high priestess climbed through the open arch as casually as if she had entered via the door. "Weeks it's taken to heal you. Yvette will have a mental breakdown if all the prayer and work she's put in is wasted."

Eaon's throat bobbed as he lay back down. Standing tall, Kaelean wore knee length pants and a cashmere blouse tied around the waist with a strip of intricately woven leather, her volumes of brownish-red hair bundled messily atop her head.

"You're welcome by the way." She smirked, but there was no amusement in her beast-like eyes as she assessed the state of him. Only rage and concern flickering like black fire.

She had come for him. For both of them. He wasn't sure why he was so surprised. Wasn't sure why her anger on his behalf made him so uncomfortable.

"Th-thank you," he told her sincerely, a shudder running through him as he tried to speak. "But please, Kaelean. Where is-is Eavha? Is she okay?"

"She is fine. She's running errands for me."

"Does she know I'm here?"

"I sent a whispering leaf to update her on the situation. She is very worried and sent back instructions to help the healers restore your body. She would be here if she could."

None of that explained the hatred pouring out of Cinn as he leveled a glare at Kaelean, fists clenched at his sides.

Kaelean noticed, straightening her shoulders. "There is so much to do here in Wyldeden that I could not leave. So I sent Eavha to Imsa on my behalf."

"With the other clans?" Eaon raised his brow, imagining Eavha's glee at being able to flaunt her new status around.

"No, we hosted that a while ago. I meant Imsa in Hyrsch."

Eaon's heart fell into his stomach. Vision spotting, the cold stilled, then swelled beneath his skin. Cinn grabbed a hold of both Eaon's hands, grimacing as the magic ripped into him. It was only his pain that made Eaon reel it back in, gritting his teeth against the familiar claws in his spine.

"You sent my sister to Hyrsch," he hissed.

"Give her some credit, Eaon. She is a capable witch and she is not alone. I sent our best guardians and Milnova with her."

Dearmead. He had asked Dearmead to look after her.

Nausea rolled in his stomach.

Kaelean nodded, reading the name in Eaon's face. "Yes. When Eavha insisted on going despite his protests, he went with her too."

Eaon closed his eyes.

"Oh, stop looking at me like that," Kaelean snapped at Cinn. "Did I not make it clear that I detest the Sparrows almost as much as you do? But between what little information I could get out of Aadya and the persistent warnings coming from the princess, I had reason enough to be concerned."

The storm brewing under Eaon's skin roared and his eyes flew open once more.

"What did you say about Aadya?"

Kaelean grimaced, looking down to Eaon. "All she did was carry on about her oh-so-powerful master. How he was coming and there was nothing we could do to stop him, blah, blah, blah. I'd be stupid not to take the threats of a Morvish witch seriously, so . . . I sent her and her coven to Imsa as well. The princess may have more luck getting information out of them than I did."

Cinn stiffened, the color draining from his face. Without even a glance in Eaon's direction, he dropped both hands and fled the clinic.

Kaelean groaned, watching him go. "I'll deal with that later."

Eaon clenched his fists and focused on breathing. Eavha and Dearmead, escorting the coven that had almost killed them a few months ago, in the hands of the princess who had almost broken Cinn beyond repair. His magic roiled, feeding on the panic that worsened the shakes still plaguing him. Despite them, Eaon threw back the blankets. They made no difference anyway; the cold came from within.

"Where do you think you're going?" Kaelean snapped, stepping in front of him as Eaon sat upright in the bed, trying to gather the strength to stand. He wore clean undershorts and a shirt of bandages around his chest, but that wasn't going to deter him.

"To Hyrsch."

"Absolutely not."

"You can't stop me."

"You were dead a few hours ago!"

"And now I'm not!"

Eaon held back a whine as he forced himself to his feet, but his knees buckled. Immortal, at least for a while, but clearly he was no kinner. Cinn never had this much trouble after healing.

Collapsing back on the hard clinic mattress, he took a few deep breaths before reaching for where his staff leaned against the wall. Using it as a crutch, he pushed himself up once more.

"You need time to rest, Eaon."

"Shut up."

Kaelean's nostrils flared, fists clenching at her sides. For a moment, Eaon had forgotten she wasn't some rogue witch anymore; that he spoke to the high priestess. That she had the power to punish him for such disrespect.

Perhaps with his blessing he could defend himself, but it didn't stop his shoulders from caving in. Didn't stop the blinking as he struggled to maintain eye contact.

As if scenting his fear, Kaelean stepped back and relaxed her fists, but her eyes remained cold and hard as they silently commanded him to sit back down.

He did not.

"I wouldn't have sent them if I thought they couldn't handle it. It is Imsa. They will be safe. The second I get word they are not, I will take you to Hyrsch myself. I will cover you with enough witchmarks to level the entire fucking territory."

He met her gaze once more, reading the utter sincerity of that promise.

"Sorry to interrupt, High Priestess," Yvette said as she approached, placing a tray of salves and bandages on the bedside table. "I need to check Eaon's wounds."

Sucking in a breath, Eaon sat down and clutched his staff, urging his blessing to settle.

"I'll leave you be." Kaelean gave Eaon one more warning look before striding from the clinic.

Yvette watched her leave, then looked around with a frown. "Where is the kinner?"

"He . . . needed a moment."

"Well, I can't touch you. Can you remove your own bandages?"

"Sure. Just give me a second." His magic was calming, but he didn't dare let go of his staff yet.

Shuffling her feet, Yvette asked stiffly, "How are you feeling?"

The question reminded him of the cold lingering in his bones. A harsh shiver had him pulling the blankets back over his lap.

"All things considered, I can't complain." A small smile graced his lips, but his head was still spinning.

Eavha. Dearmead. Aadya. Hyrsch.

Eventually, he calmed enough to lay his staff across the bed, untying the knot above his sternum to slowly unwrap the bandages. There were no powerful healers left in Wyldeden, but the lesser-blessed and medicalists had done their best to restore Eaon's body. His chest, abdomen and back were flecked with wounds that would scar.

Handing Eaon a cloth, she instructed him on how to clean his own wounds.

"Cinn was doing this?" Eaon asked, wincing as his sore muscles protested the movement.

"He was here the whole time while we put your insides back together," she said, preparing a poultice. "Most of the healers were too spooked to work on you. Kaelean said your magic was dormant, but you weren't rotting and that kind of defiance of nature makes people wary. But Cinn helped me. We weren't sure when you would be well enough to return so he did most of the physical work."

Eaon swallowed the lump in his throat. "That's fair."

When he was finished cleaning himself, the healer donned a pair of cotton gloves and picked up a soft-bristled brush. "This isn't going to be pleasant."

Eaon grabbed his staff and put his head down, preparing himself as the healer scooped up some of the mixture she'd prepared and slathered it onto his back. It stung, the brush scratching his already tender flesh.

"You know," Yvette said, trying to distract him. "The Lover did you a kindness keeping you in limbo until most of the healing was done. You wouldn't have wanted to wake up any earlier."

"Mm," Eaon mumbled, squeezing his eyes closed.

Breathe. He just had to breathe.

"And your sister was a great help. She sent back very thorough instructions on what she would do if she were here."

"Of course she did," Eaon hissed, but inside he smiled. Of course she did.

By the time Yvette was done and Eaon had rewrapped his bandages, the weight of his body had become so much that he had no choice but to lay back down.

"Do you need anything? Some water?" the healer asked.

"No, thank you," he sighed breathily. "Just rest."

"No doubt you'll be hungry soon. I'll come back then."

Eaon nodded, tucking his staff into his side. Pulling the blankets over himself, he had enough energy to worry that Cinn had not returned.

CHAPTER EIGHT

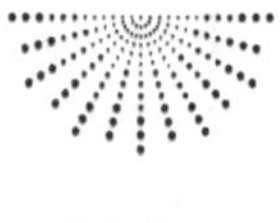

EAON

THE HEALERS WERE RELIEVED WHEN, A FEW DAYS LATER, EAON WAS able to leave the clinic. His chest still ached when he breathed too deeply but he was well enough to continue applying the salves himself. Not that he would have to; Cinn had come back with his tail between his legs and insisted on helping Eaon with everything.

Deep in thought, Cinn let Eaon lean on him as they made their way along the mossy paths winding through the city, white marble and amethyst spires shooting toward the ever-blue sky. Nothing obvious was different about Wyldeden, yet everything was. The laborers rushing between buildings with their arms full of supplies, or carrying pails of water, or trailing after their charges, walked a little straighter, a little lighter, their eyes bright as they smiled to one another. The dipping of chins from the bakers and jewelers and stonemasons as laborers walked past. Not just acknowledgment, but respect. Apology.

Eavha's absence tainted Eaon's satisfaction, as did knowing Dearmead was in Hyrsch, in danger, because of him. A different kind of danger than the kind Pirevia had posed, but danger all the same. The kind that had brought the shadows back to Cinn's eyes.

The high priestess's estate came into view as the two of them crested a hill, Eaon leaning heavily on his staff and breathing hard. It was one of the few places in Wyldeden he'd never been before, but

Cinn had. The kinner led him through a garden of roses and foxgloves, the mossy paths glittering with chips of precious stones, until they reached a circle of houses. Each had a dainty fence containing a themed garden, the stone walls polished to an impossible shine.

"This is where you've been staying?" Eaon asked, looking around at the dozen other houses. The one Cinn approached had a rosemary and seaside daisy garden, the smell of the herbs overpowering.

Cinn nodded, then pointed to the house beside his.

"The Copelands?"

Cinn nodded again, shoulders dropping.

Inside, the ceiling was covered in ivy and wisteria, glass bulbs of glowing buds held in pendants of willow. Delicately carved furniture and richly colored wool rugs reminded Eaon almost painfully of the rooms he'd frequented in his own home back when there had been enough of them to warrant such extravagancies. As the Nemuse numbers had dwindled they'd been forced to surrender their belongings in exchange for more important things. He didn't miss any of it, per se—not even the majority of his family, to be entirely honest—but there was a lingering sense of home attached to such luxury that he ached for.

Eaon stopped walking as soon as the door closed behind them, keeping his grip on Cinn's arm to pull the kinner to a halt.

"I know what you're thinking," Eaon started.

Cinn raised an eyebrow.

"You're blaming yourself for the Copelands having to leave their farm."

A muscle in Cinn's jaw twitched, eyes averting. Eaon knew he was right, because he too blamed himself. He had made mistakes dealing with the Sparrow witches. If he'd been smarter, or faster, or more in control of his magic, this whole thing could have been avoided. But deep down, he also knew that blaming himself was as unfair as letting Cinn do so.

"It's not your fault. It's not my fault. It's *her* fault."

He knew better than to say the princess's name.

Cinn closed his eyes, shoulders dropping even farther with an invisible weight. {I never should have gone back.}

"I'm going to fix this." Eaon stepped closer, tipping Cinn's chin up. "I'll do whatever it takes. I'll burn the world down to make sure you can go home and never have to worry about anything ever again."

Cinn's throat bobbed, his mottled blue-green eyes shining like glass. {I appreciate that. I do. But I don't think even death would stop her. And I don't know if I should keep thinking of the Copelands' as my home.}

It was Eaon's turn to raise his eyebrows.

{I love them. I love Belden. But look at what I brought to their door. And I can't keep running away, it will only put more people in danger. What if she comes here next? I never let myself think about it, but . . . I have family in Hyrsch, Eaon. I didn't want to risk them, but what if she knows about them? What if she has them? And now Eavha is there, and I don't know what to do. Maybe I should be on my own, so nobody else can get hurt.}

Cinn's trembling hands moved so quickly Eaon had trouble keeping up. Clasping them in his own, Eaon pulled them against his chest.

"Breathe."

A knock on the door interrupted them.

Through the gap in the door as she opened it, Selina peeked inside. The freckles spattering her pink nose reflected the amber in her widening eyes.

"Oh, Mother bless us, it's true." She covered her mouth as she pushed all the way inside, auburn hair swinging in its ponytail as she rushed across the room. "I can't believe you really came back from the dead again."

"For what it's worth, I don't recommend it." Eaon smiled, lowering his and Cinn's joined hands but refusing to let go just yet. Not until they stopped shaking.

Selina bit her lip, watching the motion. "I'm interrupting. I'm so sorry. You probably need to rest, too. Can I get you anything? Something to read?"

"No, I'm fine," Eaon assured her, then switched to Nirnish for Cinn as he said, "Do you remember Selina?"

He gave a small nod and extricated his hands. Pulling out a chair, he pointed to Eaon and Selina. {Sit. I'll make tea.}

"I can ask her to come back later."

{No. I don't want to talk about it anymore.}

Eaon sighed, scratching his chin. Sitting down was probably a good idea anyway; the walk from the clinic had left his lungs raw. To Selina, he asked, "You want to stay for some tea?"

Hesitantly, she took a second chair from the little table and glanced between the two males.

"Are you and him . . ."

Eaon shook his head.

Leaning forward, Selina glanced over at him again. "Why in Nir not?"

"He's barely twenty."

"So? There's twelve years between me and my boyfriend."

Eaon rolled his eyes. "Okay, firstly, you're forty-eight. Which makes him thirty-six. It's different."

"Forty-seven."

"Whatever. Secondly, since when do you actually admit you have a boyfriend?"

Selina pursed her lips, crossing her ankles beneath her long skirt. This kind of banter was familiar, though he was used to having it with her in their shared office back at the elementary school. Before, Eaon had thought she was just curious and kind, but she had called him a friend at his quarter-century birthday celebration. Sitting at this table with her now, gossiping like a couple of nosy neighbors, Eaon couldn't help but smile.

"Since we made it official during the inter-clan Imsa the other week," Selina said, slipping a stray piece of wispy hair behind her ear. "But that's beside the point. We're talking about you."

"Why?"

"He's cute."

"So?"

"You like him."

"Selina, it's been so long that I'd like anything I could touch without killing right now. We're just friends." Eaon grimaced, tucking his hands under his arms. "Besides, he's never seemed interested."

"That's your self-esteem talking."

Eaon narrowed his eyes. "No, actually, I'm rather aware when someone is interested in me."

"Have you asked him?" she pried.

"Don't be ridiculous."

Selina scoffed. "You know, for someone who speaks so many languages I thought you'd be a better communicator."

Eaon scowled, then reached quickly to pull out a third chair as Cinn brought over a pot of tea, placing it between him and Selina.

Shaking his head, Cinn signed, {No thanks. I'm tired.}

Eaon frowned. {Are you alright? I can translate for you.}

{Just tired.} Cinn forced a pathetic smile on his face for Selina before shuffling toward the bedroom where, through the doorway, Eaon could see Puddles purring on the thick blankets.

"Is he okay?" Selina asked as Cinn closed the door.

"No." Eaon sighed. "Not even close."

***

Over tea, Selina told Eaon in more detail about how an elder had been appointed to represent the laborers. The camps for unassigned laborers had been shut down, new homes being built for them along the northern river instead. Selina had played a role in seeing the training system completely overhauled, while a number of keepers had formed a task force to investigate crimes against laborers. The new elder had been filing constant petitions, already having won access to communal supplies for their own use and the right to rest days. Little things, but they meant self-sufficiency. Meant freedom. Meant everything.

In return, Eaon told Selina about the Copeland farm. About William and Sarah and Siobhan, who had welcomed him without hesitation, teaching him how humans worked the land without magic and despite their ever-changing weather. Admitted that his skill with fundamental magic was still embarrassingly poor, mostly because he was too wary to try much around the humans.

"I can help you with that," Selina offered.

"Thank you, but it's not safe for you either," he pointed out.

"We're talking about fundamentals. Basic spellmarks. You said you managed The Barring Mark of Things Unwanted okay, and that's archaic high-level stuff. I could never pull that off without putting myself in a coma."

"I promised Cinn I would do it, so I did it. But the rest of it . . ."

"I'll help you," Selina repeated.

A breeze blew through the window carrying an oak leaf right to the table. Eaon picked it up and held it to his ear. Then groaned loudly.

"What's wrong?" Selina asked.

"Kaelean's inviting us for dinner."

"Oh, wow. At the pavilion? That's a real honor, Eaon." Her eyes had widened to fill her pointed face. Eaon had forgotten that most people in Wyldeden only knew Kaelean as their high priestess.

"Yeah, it is, I suppose."

"Do you have clothes?" she asked, appraising the plain pants and shirt the healers had given him to wear. "I could find something before the stalls close."

"It's okay, I don't think I'll go," Eaon said, shaking his head.

"You can't be serious. Of course you're going!"

"I'm tired and Cinn's in a mood. Even on a good day, things never end well between the two of them." Rubbing his thumbs across his brow, Eaon recalled Cinn and Kaelean brawling in Vertlyn, coinciding flares of temper ending with her trying to bury him alive.

"Do you really think ignoring her will end well either?" Selina countered.

Which was a very good point. Kaelean would likely show up in his bedroom in the middle of the night if they didn't go.

"Cinn!" he shouted, massaging his temples.

Selina flinched. "Shush. He's sleeping."

"He's not. I guarantee it."

The bedroom door opened. Cinn stood there holding his cat to his chest with one arm. With his free hand, he signed, {You okay?}

"Kaelean wants us for dinner."

The shadows in Cinn's eyes grew deeper before he turned around and slammed the door. There was a moment of silence and Eaon held up a hand, lowering fingers until he reached zero. A loud thump echoed from behind Cinn's door.

"Wow," Selina whispered. "He's so quiet, I didn't think he'd be the type to throw a tantrum."

Eaon snorted, but kept his eyes on the door as concern burrowed deeper in his gut. "He's earned as many tantrums as he wants."

"Yes, I've heard a little about where he's from," she added softly.

Taking a steadying breath, Eaon turned back to Selina. "Thank you for stopping by."

"Anytime. I mean it," she said, smiling widely as she stood and began collecting the tea dishes.

"Leave it. I'll clean up."

"No. It's not your job anymore. Go and rest before dinner while I wash these," she insisted, taking them to the kitchen.

It wasn't his job anymore.

The fact of it hit him quite suddenly. He didn't have a clan role.

Before he could dwell too much on how untethered he felt in this place that had never felt like home, Eaon went to bathe.

CHAPTER NINE

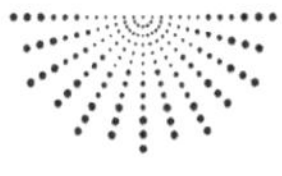

EAON

THE PAVILION WHERE THE ELDERS USUALLY DINED WAS EXACTLY THE
way Cinn had described it. Vines and flowers cascaded down pillars of
white marble, tables laden with food prepared by some of the best
cooks in Wyldeden. There were no elders tonight, though.

Kaelean sat at the head of the table dressed in an unusual shade of
red that complimented the tones in her hair, haltered around her neck
and cinched at the waist with braided twine. Every time Eaon saw her
in something other than wolf furs was a shock. To her right sat
Siobhan, nibbling on a fruit platter while farther down the table Sarah
and William whispered to each other.

All four of them perked up as Eaon and Cinn climbed the stairs
and took seats across from the Copelands, Cinn keeping as far from
Kaelean as possible.

"You're late," Kaelean said with a scowl, black eyes locking on
Eaon. "And I'm too tired to shout down the table all night. Come
closer. I want to talk more about what is happening to the south."

Eaon sighed, plucking a piece of seared pineapple from a platter
before shifting down the table.

A laborer lingering nearby whistled, and from the nearby kitchens
others emerged carrying large bowls of noodle salads, roast beetroots
and assorted breadsticks with swathes of cheese. Smiling at Kaelean,

the laborers placed the food down before hurrying back to the kitchens. Not one of them bowed, and Kaelean did not seem to notice.

Eaon did.

Then he noticed Lorelei, face twisted with bitterness as she carried a tray of baked potatoes slathered with butter, cream, chives and garlic. With her chin raised, she tossed her tray down on the table. For a moment, it looked like she wanted to spit on the food, but with an indignant huff she turned and stalked away.

Kaelean ignored her.

As they always did, the humans waited patiently while Kaelean, Selina and Eaon thanked Terra for the plentiful bounty her land provided them, then thanked the Mother for the company they shared tonight. Sunset gilded the pavilion in subtle pinks and golds, the thousand glow-worms and luminescent flowers twinkling to life.

"I must say, I've never had potatoes so wonderful," Sarah commented as she took one from the platter and moved it to her plate.

"Our gardeners are very blessed," Kaelean agreed. "Wine?"

{It's strong,} Cinn warned them. It was the first indication he was paying attention to the evening at all.

"Oh, we're alright with water, thank you," Sarah declined. William took a little.

"Kaelean and I have been talking most of the day," Siobhan started as she shoveled potato and bread into her mouth. "With what happened at the farm, it might be wise to send additional guardians to support Eavha during Imsa. I can get word to the rebels and make sure she's protected from within as well."

Taking a deep breath, Eaon repeated, "I'm going."

A beat of silence before Siobhan cleared her throat. "Sending you to Hyrsch is a monumentally bad idea."

"I don't care. I'm going to Hyrsch and I'm going to kill the princess."

William choked on his wine. Clapping his back, Sarah looked to Cinn, who had gone somewhere else in his head again.

"You will do no such thing," Kaelean warned. "Not until Imsa is over."

"You can't—"

"*Eaon*." Kaelean raised her voice as she interrupted him. "This clan is not ready for war against the Sparrow Coven."

"Then I go wild and do it without ties to this clan."

Kaelean visibly flinched. "You're still Eavha's brother, and she is Wyldeden."

"I'll renounce my last name."

"You will do no such—" Kaelean started, but Eaon leveled a glare that rivaled even her own ferocity.

"Look at him," Eaon hissed in Terranian so as not to embarrass Cinn. "You cared enough to come running when we were in danger of being taken, but every day she goes unpunished for what she did to him is a day he suffers. Look at him."

Livid, Kaelean held his gaze for a moment before glancing across the table to where Cinn was completely vacant, staring at his empty plate like it was the only thing in the world.

"After Imsa," Kaelean repeated coldly.

"Look, I want the bitch dead too," Siobhan joined in, unconcerned by Kaelean and Eaon's unintelligible bickering. "But there are serious repercussions for the demi-kin if the princess dies."

"Are we really sitting here discussing whether or not to kill someone? This is hardly dinner conversation," Sarah chided, though the worry lines ran deep on either side of her mouth. Standing up, she reached over the table to pile food on Cinn's plate. "Cinn, sweetheart, grab a potato. They're delicious."

"What's so important about this Imsa?" Eaon asked, again in Terranian, so Cinn didn't have to listen anymore.

"Despite our warnings, the princess sent multiple letters insisting she had urgent business to discuss that will affect this clan in the near future. It wasn't something I could ignore in good conscience. Eavha is there to find out what exactly the princess knows and, after discussing it with the other clans, we agreed that she might have more luck getting through to Aadya. Let the princess do what she does best, and let Eavha do her job. Once it's all said and done, we will discuss a strategy for vengeance that does not involve bringing the entire Sparrow Coven down on our heads."

It irritated Eaon to no end that Kaelean had a good point. The part of him that wanted Aisling's blood soaking his hands was not as strong as the part that understood the logic of waiting. Not as strong as the part of him that balked at his own sanguinary impulses.

"Alright, fine," he conceded. "But I'm still going. Not to kill the princess, but to watch out for my sister."

"That is why Dearmead is with her." Kaelean waved a hand as she cut into a steaming potato.

"I'm still the Head of House. It's *my* responsibility to take care of her," Eaon snapped. It was a role he had never wanted, but one he took seriously.

He expected Kaelean to laugh at him, but she didn't. She leaned back in her seat and cocked her head, the cold shrewdness of those black beady eyes sending a chill down Eaon's spine.

"I see," she said. Then she turned to where Cinn had not moved to eat his food. Straightening her shoulders, she lifted her chin before switching to Nirnish. "I will only allow you to go to Hyrsch if Cinn goes with you."

The table went silent. A cold hatred washed over Eaon at the audacity she had to even ask such a thing of Cinn. A rage that was echoed in the expressions of everyone else sitting at the table.

Slowly, Cinn rose. Grabbing a potato in his fist, he turned and flung it at Kaelean's head.

For reasons Eaon could not begin to understand, Kaelean did not move, letting the potato smack her in the face, smearing butter and mash down her dress as it fell.

The argument on the tip of Eaon's tongue as to why Kaelean was a revolting hag for even suggesting it died at the sight. Across from him, Siobhan had covered her mouth to hide the malicious laughter brimming in her eyes. An amusement that was not mirrored in the watching laborers, who'd gone pale as they peered out the kitchen doorway. Even Lorelei looked queasy.

With a single finger, Kaelean wiped a clean line from her chin to her cheek and sucked the cream off. Then she stood, quick as a viper, and flung a fistful of roast beetroot back at Cinn. Magenta burst across his linen shirt, vegetable falling in chunks to the table.

The scrape of Cinn's chair as he climbed atop the table, snarling viciously, spurred Eaon into action.

"Don't," Eaon said as he grabbed Cinn around the waist and hauled him back across the table. "She's baiting you to make a point."

{Rogue bitch.}

Eaon didn't bother interpreting. "Go home. I'll deal with her."

{I hate her.}

"I know."

There was something fragile about the way Cinn suddenly stopped fighting. Wiping his nose on the back of his hand, he let Eaon help him down properly before storming off without another word. Clearing their throats, both William and Sarah went after him, the latter carrying two plates of food with her.

"That was cruel and unnecessary," Siobhan said once they were out of hearing range.

Kaelean only stared at Eaon as she took a napkin and wiped her face clean.

"You didn't have to do that to make your point," he said through clenched teeth.

"What point?" Siobhan glowered, looking between the two of them.

Kaelean didn't answer, continuing to hold Eaon's stare.

The point was Eaon's hypocrisy. How many times had he scolded Kaelean for making decisions on Cinn's behalf without asking what he actually wanted? At least a dozen. And now here he was, willing to declare war against the most powerful coven in Nir without even asking Cinn what he wanted to do about the whole situation. And as for wanting to protect Eavha . . . as true as that was, they both knew Eaon would not be able to control himself. He would explode and take the city with him.

"It's not up to me," Eaon admitted. "But it's not up to you, either. If Cinn asks, I'll go to war for him and there is nothing you can do to stop me."

Kaelean scoffed. "You have no idea what you'd be signing up for, witchling. None."

Eaon was done arguing about this. "Do you need help getting back, Siobhan?"

"No, I'm fine."

"Well then, goodnight," he said curtly, wiping his hands on his own napkin before leaving the pavilion.

Eaon found Cinn laying fully dressed in the empty bathtub with his eyes closed, the cat curled up on his chest. The plates of food Sarah had taken were cold on the kitchen table, the humans not long gone.

Placing a candle on the floor, Eaon sat on the edge of the tub and sighed deeply.

"You alright?"

Cinn shook his head. {I understand if you want to go south, but I can't go back there.}

"I would never ask you to."

He sniffed, opening his eyes to scratch Puddles under the chin. Eaon waited patiently, and after a few minutes petting the purring cat, Cinn took a deep breath and sat up.

{Even if you kill her, how do we know who else she told about me? How will we know it's ever safe for Sarah and William to go home? It's a mess and it's my fault and I don't know how to fix it.}

Carefully, Eaon slid his legs over the edge of the tub and lowered himself in. There wasn't really room for the both of them, and the cat opened one eye to give Eaon an annoyed look as his pants grazed its tail.

"If you weren't a kinner anymore, it would be safe."

It was what Cinn had wanted for as long as Eaon had known him. A way to take the mark off his neck—to remove the spell that kept him immortal. There was such longing, almost pleading, in Cinn's face as Eaon said it.

"I can start looking into it. I have absolutely no idea where to start, so I don't know how long it will take, but—"

Cinn shook his head. {Thank you, but . . . What if it's not enough?

I've been thinking about it the last few days, and I think it's time for me to go north.}

To Ahrenhale. To Moyra.

Eaon sat back and took that in for a moment. "You think the answers Yomra was talking about Moyra having are how to remove the mark?"

{I don't know, but I also don't know what else to do. I've ruined Sarah's and William's lives. Siobhan's, too. Her friends, Owen and Nora . . . I can't keep waiting around, letting other people get hurt trying to protect me. If there's a chance this Moyra person can help me, I have to try.}

Eaon stuck his knuckle between his teeth as he considered everything involved in what Cinn was suggesting. "There's a lot of land between here and Qiri." A lot of ways for Cinn to end up in a world of trouble.

Cinn nodded solemnly, tightening his grip on the cat.

A sudden weightlessness made Eaon close his eyes, dizzy and nauseous. When he opened them again, the candlelight seemed to flicker, colors brightening impossibly in the now dark night. The sensation was familiar. Soon, his mood would turn. He would start hallucinating. How long had it been since he last took a stabilizing tonic?

Cinn noticed the sudden shift in Eaon's attention, a deep frown growing on his brow.

"I'm okay," Eaon assured him. "And, if you want, I'll get you to Qiri."

Cinn's eyes widened with hope, his brow furrowing with guilt. {What about Eavha?}

As hard as the decision was, Cinn needed him more.

"Dearmead is with her."

The oily churning in his gut every time Eaon thought of his old friend had faded the past few weeks. If there was one thing he could trust, it was that Dearmead would not break another promise to him. He would keep Eavha safe.

CHAPTER TEN

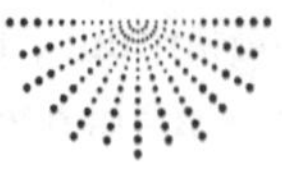

AISLING

FROM THE BALCONY OF HER TOWER, AISLING WATCHED THE HORSE-drawn carriages arrive through the palace gates. She'd sent her finest to collect the Wyldeden delegation as soon as they crossed the singular bridge over the Dividing River into Oford.

"This will work," said Davina from where she perched on the railing.

Aisling took her gaze away from the halting carriages only for a moment, giving Davina a sidelong grimace. "I thought your visions ceased after you passed."

"They have. Doesn't mean I don't know a good idea when I hear one. The tattoos were always a backup plan."

"Quite the sacrifice for a backup plan," Aisling muttered, clenching her fists. A sacrifice she had not been consulted on before Davina had made it.

"Speaking of the tattoos, when are you going to start practicing with them?"

A shudder ran down Aisling's spine and she released her fists to flex her fingers. There was enough to do without wasting her energy practicing something that she wouldn't need for another six months.

Ignoring Davina, she returned her attention to the delegation in the courtyard.

From the first carriage stepped four guardians dressed in supple brown leather, bare footed and carrying long spears. With them, their Morvish prisoner.

The prophet's wrists were bound in thick ropes, the scales coating her arms glistening in the dim afternoon light. If the direness of her situation had occurred to her, she wasn't showing it; chin raised, a haughty smirk plastered in her pointy face, Aadya was the epitome of Morvish arrogance.

The similarities between Aadya and Davina were limited to their golden hair and constellation tattoos, the former harsh and cold in every way Davina had been bright and lively. The rogue's icy gaze to Davina's lime eyes, her sickly pallor to Davina's unblemished brownness; Aadya could have been anybody, save for whatever mutation had been done to her, but Davina was the culmination of the most interesting family history Aisling had ever learned. She was from everywhere, and it was unfortunate that the reputation forged by Morvish witches like Aadya meant that Davina's arrival in Kerveda half a dozen years ago had been utterly unwelcome.

Two of Aisling's palace guards came forward in their pristine crimson and gold uniforms, taking Aadya by the arms. Two Wyldeden guardians followed them toward the exterior dungeon access while the other guardians stalked to the second carriage. From within, Aadya's coven were pulled out, wrists bound and sacks covering their heads. More of Aisling's guards jogged over to assist in detaining them.

Finally, from the last carriage, three more witches emerged. The male and one of the females wore guardian leathers, but the second female was dressed in common pants and a loose cotton blouse. No high priestess or any other form of authority.

Bristling, Aisling began to pace. To consider how best to greet the delegation since there was no clear figurehead. Should she demand the high priestess join her? Or settle for the motley crew downstairs?

Davina stood from the railing, taking a step forward. "Think about it."

Aisling stopped and tilted her head at where Davina watched her, those calculating eyes almost sparkling. Though that might have been the glistening of the sun behind her.

"If I were traveling to a strange place, to the palace of a rival coven," Aisling realized, "I would not announce myself as the prime target for a possible attack before Imsa was enacted."

"Whoever Kaelean sent is in disguise. Do not be hasty to dismiss them," Davina warned. "You need them on your side."

"No, what I need is a miracle."

Davina sighed, turning back to the sun that she could not feel. "Anything is possible."

The throne room was warm thanks to its large glass wall, the sunset diffusing red and purple light over the black stone floor. But warm by Oford standards wasn't saying much; compared to the heat Aisling had grown up with in Dusarn, summer in the south was brisk at best. The bronze sconces along the wall were lit to keep her and her advisors comfortable, but the usual heavy fabrics the important lords and ladies from Oford wore—who had gathered to await the formal initiation of Imsa—had been exchanged for lighter, brighter cottons. Lace sleeves and décolletages alongside bare-armed tunics with dapper vests had the humans and demi-kin waiting in lines along the walls fanning themselves.

Sitting on her throne, Aisling wore a stiff, plum gown that covered her from the top of her neck to her wrists, skirts dragging on the floor when she walked. A golden silk cape and matching gloves complimented the gaudy crown perched atop her tightly bound hair. A second throne had been placed beside hers, currently vacant.

Finally, trumpets announced the delegations' arrival. She had given the Wyldeden representatives a few hours to freshen up after their journey before sending messengers. The rite was ready.

First, the Southern Mountain Clan.

The snow had been cleaned off their knee-high calfskin boots, the thick animal-hide coats they had worn upon arrival replaced by ceremonial robes of icy white. Yellowing fangs pierced the witches' ears and hung from chains around their necks and wrists. The number of fangs and the placement of them meant something to the clan, but Aisling had never learned their customs.

Unlike other clans, the southern mountaineers didn't train guardians. With the permafrost of the frozen wastes to the west, they'd built their homes in the toughest terrain in all of Nir, and though they worked as a community for the most part, it was the responsibility of every witch to keep themselves alive.

From among the delegation, one male stepped forward.

"Introducing Sar Vin, High Priest of the Southern Mountain Clan," the herald announced.

Aisling had met Sar Vin numerous times during negotiations for winter supplies and safe passage through the mountains to reach Bernt. All the clan witches had dry skin, lips chapped from the cold, as well as full beards matching the thick mass of hair framing their faces. In the mountains, the witch who lived the longest was named high priest, and Sar Vin's white hair, crested with a silver circlet, was the only sign of his true age.

Blue eyes like glaciers beheld Aisling as he dipped his chin. "A pleasure to see you again, Princess."

"And you, Sar Vin."

The trumpets sounded again, and the Southern Mountain Clan moved aside to make room for the Wyldeden delegation.

The guardians had remained in their leathers, bare foot and carrying spears, while the female who'd worn plain clothes had changed into a formal tunic. They walked through the doors warily, fanning out to secure the female who followed.

A priestess, and the only one of them worth noticing.

She wore a spectacular skirt of emerald gauze with layers cut like butterfly wings, sitting so low on her sun-browned hips it was almost indecent. A matching chest binding with golden thread embroidered into patterns of leaves and flowers glistened in the sun pouring through the colored glass wall. While she didn't wear a circlet or tiara, there were peonies and baby's breath braided over the crown of her head, mousy curls flowing loosely down to her waist. White lace fingerless gloves adorned her dainty hands, her honey-brown eyes aglow with wonder.

"Introducing Eavha Nemuse, Heir Apparent of Wyldeden." The herald bowed.

Heir Apparent. Aisling had always thought the succession of power in the Wyldeden clan was odd. Not based on blood or trial, but on display of magic.

"A pleasure," Aisling said as she lowered her chin.

Eavha kept hers raised.

"Your Highness, my name is Milnova," the other female said, stepping up beside Eavha and bowing deeply. "I will translate. Eavha's appointment to heir is recent and her Nirnish is rudimentary, though she understands more than she speaks."

"Of course. I have some skill in Terranian, if it is preferable," Aisling offered.

"Then the pleasure is mine, princess." Eavha's voice was like a song as she smiled, dipping into a shallow curtsey.

The delegation moved aside, joining the rest of the gathered crowd in awaiting the final arrival. Aisling had invited the sea witches from the south, but they had declined the invitation, as had the river clans. Follow-up messages asking for reasons had exposed that, while Aisling herself had proven amicable enough, the sea and river witches had no intention of ever sitting in the same room with other members of her coven.

Running a finger beneath the tight collar of her gown, Aisling was sweating.

"You look lovely," Edwina whispered beside her.

Forcing a smile, Aisling glanced at her maiden briefly before straightening in her seat once more. Since Nora had been gone, Edwina had been her closest confidant. It wasn't the same, and every minute of every day since Nora had boarded the ship bound for Pirevia, Aisling had missed her Second. She had made every decision since then based on the singular logic of whether Nora would approve.

An earsplitting crack of thunder inside the throne room jerked Aisling from her thoughts. Every guard in the room somehow found a way to stand straighter, while to her left, Clayton tightened his grip on his sword. Edwina backed away, almost hiding behind the throne as the air before them tore apart. Beyond the shimmering edges of the tear in their world was a blinding whiteness through which a large delegation of golden-clad guards marched through.

Sucking in a steadying breath, Aisling held perfectly still as the last witch through the portal presented himself. The air closed with a vacuous whoosh, leaving the room still and silent once again.

"May I present King Phineas Aurnia of Dusarn," the herald announced with a grand bow.

The lords and ladies of Oford knelt, as did the guards. While the other witches stayed standing, they did lower their heads in a show of respect.

Aisling stood from her throne and stepped down from the dais. Bowing her head, she curtseyed deeply.

"Father. Thank you for honoring us with your presence today."

"Thank you for hosting, daughter. You are as lovely as always."

In hindsight, she would have preferred the sea and river witches to have come to Imsa, but she could hardly disinvite the king, whom she had summoned in the spring when plans to assassinate her mother had been at play.

From another room, servants carried in a brass cauldron the size of a barrel and placed it in the center of the room.

"Here stands the witness of promises to be made," the herald said solemnly before slinking back into the crowd.

Clayton had come down from the dais to stand beside Aisling. Until they had all sworn in, Imsa had not officially begun and thus the window for this gathering to turn into a battlefield was still open.

In a show of hospitality, Aisling stepped up to the cauldron first. The sole servant remaining held a silver tray, and from it Aisling took a bone knife carved with spellmarks. Piercing the flesh of her palm, she squeezed a few drops of blood into the cauldron.

"I, Aisling Aurnia of the Sparrow Coven, hereby offer my life forfeit should I break any of the three promises of Imsa. To those who offer their blood to the cauldron, I shall cause no harm. To those who speak the truth to me, I shall offer only truth in return. And to those who bring grievances before me, I shall strive to make peace. In the names of Mother and Death, for the sake of the Creator and the Lover and their Balance, I pledge myself before your witness."

Magic lay heavy in the air as she pled the forfeit, sending a few weaker members of the delegation to their knees. Stepping back, Aisling watched as Sar Vin came forward.

Word for word, he recited the forfeit as well. Then Eavha.

Finally, the king stepped up to the cauldron. "I, Phineas Aurnia of the Sparrow Coven, hereby offer my life forfeit should I break any of the three promises of Imsa. To those who offer their blood to the cauldron, I shall cause no harm. To those who speak the truth to me, I shall offer only truth in return. To those who bring grievance before me, I shall strive to make peace. In the names of Mother and Death, for the sake of the Creator and the Lover and their Balance, I pledge thyself before your witness."

The four witches bowed deeply to the cauldron before making way for the others. Every member of the delegations and every Hyrschan courtier stepped forward to add their blood to the cauldron until it was brimming with thick, dark fluid.

With a grunt of effort, Milnova and the other Keepers from each of the four courts took the cauldron on their shoulders. With the help of a few servants, they would take the blood and pour it around the palace walls, locking the spell in place. Their oaths would be binding.

As soon as it was done, a sigh of relief befell the room.

Aisling waited for King Phineas to mount the dais, choosing whichever seat he preferred, before standing in front of her throne again.

"Thank you all for coming," she said, smiling tightly. "Tomorrow I wish to begin discussions regarding a matter that will affect all of us, but tonight, let us celebrate the peace we have promised during this Imsa. Drink, eat, and be merry."

Applause preceded the swell of music coming from the small orchestra in the corner, and the party began.

Aisling watched the revelry but did not join in. Neither did her father, but for very different reasons. While he peered haughtily down on the lords and ladies of Oford, Aisling surveyed the interactions between them and the foreign clans. A ghostly figure wandered between them, eavesdropping on the crowd and occasionally returning to the dais to report on gossip, keeping Aisling ahead of any nasty rumors sprouting.

After all, there were so many conflicting roles the princess had to play.

The king's loyal but wayward daughter clashed with her advocacy for the demi-kin, many of whom were already whispering warily about why the king, who outside Hyrsch's walls would have them back in collars, had been invited. Her father's capacity and proclivity to undermine her also put at risk the authoritative persona she had previously adorned during her dealings with the Southern Mountain Clan, jeopardizing her reputation with them. And then, of course, there was Eavha.

Aisling had never met a witch from Wyldeden before, and she didn't know how much stock she could place in stories. It was unlikely that the Anfar Forest Clan knew much of her, either, so her options were open regarding what role to play for the heir—what version of herself would garner the results she needed.

Eavha captured the attention of everyone in the room, smiling and laughing as she twirled and danced freely. Most of the Hyrschans watched in utter disbelief, her wildness at odds with the stiffness of court etiquette, while the mountaineers watched with a sneer, laughter laced with mockery.

If Eavha noticed, she didn't seem to care. Grabbing the hand of one of her accompanying guardians, she pulled him into a dance that nobody Aisling had ever known would dare to do in public.

"I know we do not see eye to eye on everything," the king said mildly, drawing her attention away. "But I am proud of you all the same. The Anfar Forest Clan are wildly notorious for being difficult to reason with. Getting them to agree to Imsa is a feat in and of itself."

"Yes," Aisling agreed. She had taken excruciating measures to get a representative here today.

"Even if they agree with me in the matter of this supposed invasion, you should take the opportunity to form an alliance."

"Of course. It would be wasteful not to."

Aisling gave him a pretty smile, despite the way her skin crawled.

Lovely words she had heard many times before, masking an insidious agenda. Her father had been lusting after Anfar land for at least as long as Aisling had been breathing, but any alliance she formed with Wyldeden would not be in favor of the Sparrows.

"Just be careful," he continued. "She may look like a lamb in a lion's den, but Wyldeden witches should not be underestimated."

Aisling turned from her father, whose greedy, hostile eyes were locked on Eavha's twirling form. Phineas and Tallula had fought the Third War against the Anfar Forest Clan; a sure victory, they had thought. All the might of the Sparrow Coven and their armies of Lover-blessed Returned, against a disorganized band of tree-loving savages. Watching Eavha laugh and spin and dance, it was easy to see why the Sparrows had thought taking Anfar would be simple.

It had not been.

The Sparrows had eventually agreed to form a truce with Kaelean Caesarea, writing the Anfar Treaty and raising wards between the great forest and the colonized lands surrounding it. Aside from Qiri, it was the only Nirnish land not under the reign of the Coven. Out of greed or spite, she didn't know, but it had been King Phineas's mission ever since to rectify that.

Aisling narrowed her eyes, signaling with the jut of her chin for her guards to keep a closer eye on the black-and-gold armored Sparrows. In planning for Imsa, she had spent endless nights lying awake, thinking on ways to protect the demi-kin from the visiting Sparrows; only human servants would tend to the king and his delegation, the demi-kin courtiers assigned personal guards. The visiting clans would bring guardians, she'd known, but it was an oversight on her behalf that they might need Hyrschan protection as well.

"When we begin discussions tomorrow, will you at least let me explain before you share your opinions?" Aisling asked quietly.

"Of course," King Phineas said scornfully, as if her request was offensively unnecessary. "And when they realize you've wasted their time, panicking over superstition, I will ensure they do not hold it against you."

Aisling remained impassive, even as her teeth ground together. "If you still harbor such disbelief you could have simply not come."

"An invitation to spend time with my daughter is not something to be disregarded."

"And, of course, you couldn't risk the others actually believing me. Believing the warnings of an esteemed Morvish prophet."

"A lying Morvish prophet with an agenda," the king hissed.

Aisling's upper lip curled, sharp nails biting into the armrests of her throne.

Swallowing his temper with a sigh, the king placed a cold hand on her arm. "Sorry, my little visionary. Let's leave the talk until tomorrow, shall we?"

There was no comfort to be found in the gesture. Her parents humored her, tolerating her "visionary" behavior these past years out of pity and telling anybody who'd listen that she was out of her mind with grief.

Edwina chose that moment to approach the dais, carrying a glass of wine. Aisling tried not to sag with relief as she took the drink, exchanging a knowing look with the timid maiden. Sipping the sweet red liquid, Aisling watched as her throne room devolved into a dance hall, the Wyldeden delegation somehow convincing a great majority of the courtiers to join in.

Eavha was still dancing, a grin on her face as she spoke in her guardian's ear. Then she looked up, and Aisling wondered how many times the beautiful creature had looked to her that night. Often enough that she was jolted by Aisling's returning stare. Face slackening, a flash of hostility blazed in her eyes before being dampened with a polite smile.

Aisling dipped her chin but continued to watch as the heir turned into another spin.

Indeed, Eavha Nemuse was not to be underestimated.

CHAPTER ELEVEN

EAON

Arriving at the Sanctuary, one of Kaelean's personal guardians escorted Eaon up the winding staircase to the high priestess's rooms. It didn't seem to matter that Eaon already knew the way—not so long ago, the suite had been Lorelei's and he had been snooping for a book on deadly curses. And a level below had been Aadya's.

Placing a hand against the ragged scar on his sternum, Eaon avoided looking at the closed door. No matter who it had been reassigned to, it would always be the place where Aadya had killed him. Where he had died his second death. Where Dearmead had said words Eaon didn't know he still hoped to hear until it was too late.

At the top of the stairs, Eaon knocked on the large engraved door before poking his head in. "Kaelean?"

"Eaon." Kaelean's voice went high with surprise as she rose from an arrangement of crystals and dried herbs on the floor. "You're not who I was expecting."

Eaon took a steadying breath. "You promised me Eavha was safe."

"I would not have sent her if I believed otherwise," she assured him.

It was what had already been said, but he needed to hear it one more time.

"Alright. Then I was wondering who has been brewing my tonics since Eavha left. Cinn and I will be leaving for Qiri soon and I need to pack." Traveling was different to living on the farm, after all. Nobody would be able to bring him regular doses, so he had to be prepared.

Kaelean stilled, eyes widening. "You're going to Qiri?"

"That's what I said." Eaon crossed his arms, staff tucked under his bicep. "Cinn wants to go, and it's not like he'd get there in one piece on his own. So, yeah. I guess you're getting your wish. Hyrsch is off the cards."

Kaelean grimaced, leaning on her work bench. "I would take him myself, but I cannot afford to leave the clan right now."

"It's fine. We'll figure it out."

"Go west around the Heart Lake—"

"I know."

"And make sure you carry a pocketful of rowanberries—"

"I know, Kaelean. I've been traveling for seven years."

Kaelean bristled, jaw muscles twitching. He wasn't sure what he'd said to anger her, and he didn't care to ask.

"Regardless," she continued. "I want you to send a whispering leaf if you have any trouble. And I'm sending a guardian with you."

"That won't be necessary."

"I wasn't asking your opinion on the matter. Don't leave before seeing me again, either. I'll have things for you to take. The brewer's name is Cleo, and she works out of an apothecary near the deep fall."

Eaon frowned. He hadn't expected someone who didn't work at the clinic to be brewing for him. The deep fall was a waterfall that plunged into a valley, the pool beneath the deepest in all of Wyldeden. It wasn't a heavily populated part of the city, rather a place where witches went looking for something a little taboo.

Kaelean watched him carefully, an assessing gleam in her beady black eyes.

"I'll go there now. And I'll bring Cinn to say goodbye before we go," Eaon agreed, turning for the door.

Kaelean hissed, muttering under her breath, "Oh, goody, he'll love that."

Eaon held back his smirk.

Even on the hills by the deep fall, Eaon was given a wide berth. Witches watched him warily as they shopped for extracts of mandrake and jimsonweed, henbane and belladonna that—thanks to the studying Eaon had helped Eavha with for her healer's exams—he knew could be brewed to make hallucinogenics. Other stalls bragged a variety of yew apparatuses that made Eaon smirk. Since the discovery that yew enhanced the effects of hallucinogens, the wood had gone from being a sacred symbol of resurrection to evidence of a witch's proclivity to indulge in debauchery. Most homes had switched out their yew broomsticks in favor of walnut to avoid the stigma, but the change had other advantages. Walnut was a much stronger wood, meaning the broomsticks didn't need to be replaced so often when they were inevitably snapped over somebody's back.

Barely a minute's walk from the deep fall itself, a small riverside cottage with belladonna and tear-drop daffodils growing in yellow windowsill planter boxes came into view, matching the description Kaelean had given him for the brewer's workshop. There was no glimmer of recognition as the bald-headed witch behind the stall raised her gaze, yet she greeted him with a twitch of her nose and a dry cough.

"You must be Eaon."

Raising his eyebrows, he answered, "Did Kaelean warn you I was coming?"

"No, but Death's blessing has a very particular smell." The brewer wiped her hands on her apron and narrowed her eyes. "Did your last order not arrive?"

"It did, but I'm traveling soon and need extra supply. Do you have stock on hand?"

"Won't take long to make some. Couple of hours. Three months enough?" she asked, already collecting ingredients from the open jars on her table.

"Should be. Thank you." A couple of hours. There was no point walking all the way back to Kaelean's guest house just to turn around and come right back. "I might mention though . . . I keep getting these headaches every time I take a tonic."

Cleo raised her eyebrows as she took out jars of lavender infusion and purified water from beneath her work bench. "Really? You never sent word."

Eaon grimaced. "I thought Eavha was brewing them, and it had never been a problem before so I didn't think the two were related."

"I see. But because it's me, and I couldn't possibly be as talented as the incredible Eavha Nemuse, it must be my fault."

Eaon didn't imagine the excessive force the brewer used as she began grinding salt. He knew how it felt to be treated as lesser. He should have thought it through before saying anything.

"I'm sorry, I just meant—"

"Save it," Cleo muttered. "Go somewhere else while I work."

Biting the inside of his cheek, Eaon apologized again before leaving. Spending a couple of hours with his feet in the river wouldn't be a bad way to waste the rest of the morning anyway.

By the time he returned to the guest house with his supply of tonics, both the Copelands and Siobhan had gathered at the table for lunch. Cinn was slightly less despondent than he had been last night and was in the middle of explaining their plans to go to Qiri.

"It sounds dangerous," William said, shaking his head. "Things are very different in the north, and I don't know anybody who has ever gone to Qiri. How do you know it's safe there?"

"This place, Wyldeden, isn't so bad," Sarah added. "We could get used to being here if you wanted to stay."

{You shouldn't have to get used to it,} Cinn signed to her, then turned to William. {And I don't know it's safe, but it's a risk I'll take. It's the least I can do for you both. And Eaon will be with me.}

He looked up to where Eaon lingered in the doorway and managed a smile.

"I'll keep him safe," Eaon promised.

Siobhan grimaced. "Don't take this the wrong way, but that didn't really work out back in Belden."

{That wasn't Eaon's fault.} Cinn's motions bordered on aggressive.

Sarah placed a gentle hand on his shoulder and gave a reassuring smile to Eaon that did nothing to soothe the pang in his heart.

"I didn't say it was, I just said it didn't work." Siobhan crossed her arms over her stomach. "Besides, the rebels have been trying to contact Qiri for decades, looking for a safe place for the demi-kin to go. None of our messages ever got through, so how exactly do you expect to do it?"

Eaon had actually thought of that.

"I have contacts in the Northern Mountains. They share a border and are right by the wards. If anyone knows how to get in touch with Qiri, they will."

It would make a good place to rest and restock at the very least. Sitting down at the table, Eaon helped himself to a large plate of food. He wasn't particularly hungry, but they would be living on traveler's rations and wild produce for the next month, so he indulged while he could.

"We can't talk you out of it, can we?" Sarah asked, eyes reddening.

{I'm sorry but I need to do this.}

"Don't apologize. We just want you to be safe. And happy," William added, reaching for Sarah's hand. "Just come back in one piece. And we'll keep Puddles safe until you get home."

"Both of you." Sarah pushed another bread roll to Eaon. "We'll stay here and wait for you to get back."

Eaon was glad he had his mouth full so he didn't have to find something to say. He returned Sarah's smile and nodded, grateful for the genuine affection in her words.

When he could speak, he warned Cinn, "Kaelean wants to see us before we go."

Fists clenching on the table, Cinn took a long, calming breath.

"I can't decide if I like her or not," Siobhan said as Sarah put a comforting arm over Cinn's shoulders.

William took a sip from his cup of tea and muttered so quietly that Eaon wasn't sure anyone else heard him. "Not. Definitely not."

As Eaon and Cinn reached the top floor of the sanctuary, Selina's usually quiet voice brought them to a standstill. The words were unintelligible, but her tone was sharper than Eaon would have thought her capable of. A hand on Cinn's chest to keep him back, Eaon crept closer to the door to eavesdrop.

"If you want to see your boyfriend, invite him here," Kaelean snapped.

"It's not about that."

"Your senior said no, your elder said no. That you even have the gall to come to me with this—"

Eaon didn't like hearing Selina talked down to like that. Didn't like it at all. Letting go of Cinn, he knocked loudly on the door and waltzed in without waiting for an invitation.

Selina was bright red, head ducked low as Kaelean turned to Eaon.

"You're leaving already?" she asked.

"Don't see any reason to linger." He looked to Selina, a crease growing between his brows at the heat blaring across her cheeks. "What are you doing here, Sel?"

"I heard you were leaving again," she answered as Kaelean went to collect a sack from her desk. "And I know why. I'm coming, too."

Eaon froze.

"I've told you, no," Kaelean snarled as she spun back around. "Disobey me and—"

"Brach knows things about Qiri," Selina interrupted, trying to ignore the black fury brewing in Kaelean's eyes. "He knows a place where Qiri witches come through the wards. I don't know where it is, and he won't tell you, but I can convince him."

Eaon had started signing for Cinn since Selina spoke little Nirnish, but it was becoming increasingly difficult to make his hands do what he wanted them to. His brain tingled, the colors of the room growing too bright. Cinn grabbed his elbow as Eaon swayed.

Both Kaelean and Selina stopped talking as they waited for him to pull one of the tonics from his satchel, the high priestess stepping forward with tense lines stretching around her mouth.

"I'm fine," he said before sipping from the vial, cutting off Kaelean's worry. It took him a moment to steady himself, his next words clear as ringing bells, so persistent that there was no other option than to let them pass. "Of course you can come. The more the merrier."

"When has that ever been true when traveling?" Kaelean argued.

Eaon shrugged, a smirk playing in his lips. "We'll need someone to leave behind for the wolves if they give chase. Give the rest of us a chance."

Selina gaped at him, stepping back.

Before Eaon could promise he was only joking, he caught the coy crinkling of her nose.

"Wow," she deadpanned, dragging the word out. "I'd heard you had a poor sense of humor."

A smile crept over Eaon's face. One that fell as Kaelean slammed a fist on her workbench, rattling the crystals. "No. Traveling is not like leaving the Boab for trade festivals. I will not send an untrained witch into Nir, and that is the end of it."

On that, Eaon agreed. It would be a risk taking Selina, who had only occasionally ventured a few miles away from the Boab for festivals, but he couldn't shake the feeling that she was meant to come with them.

Pissing off Kaelean was an added bonus. Especially with Cinn standing stoically behind him, glaring fiercely at her.

"Go and pack only what you absolutely need," he told Selina. "I'll talk to her."

Breaking into a grin, Selina hurried from the office.

Kaelean leveled the full heat of her glare at Eaon. "How dare you."

"You are the high priestess of Wyldeden. You are in charge, I know. But we need her."

"No, you don't. I will send a whispering leaf to the high priest in the north requesting Brach share what he knows. I have also written you formal acknowledgments of clan-bound status to negate the brands on your hands, as well as declarations of peace to counter the stigma against your blessing. There are multiple copies for when you get to Qiri. As long as you have them, you will be protected. To cross you is to cross the Anfar Forest Clan and incite war."

Eaon stilled. A declaration of peace was standard for travelers, but they were usually signed by the elder, not the high priestess. And they definitely didn't usually carry threats of war.

"Of course, that's assuming you're not still planning to go rogue on me."

Kaelean smirked at Eaon's flinch. He had threatened to renounce his affiliation with the clan last night; threatened to renounce his last name as well. And he had meant it, even though he knew that by doing so he would be considered unbound. Only with Kaelean's permission could he leave and be considered "wild."

But she hadn't called him unbound. She'd said "rogue." After all those months of her snapping at them for using the term, she was now using it against him. And it hurt.

{I'm going to rip your tongue out and make you eat it.}

Eaon grabbed Cinn's arm and stepped in front of him.

"Thank you for the declarations, Kaelean. And for getting Cleo to keep up with my tonics. And for all the sacrifices you have made to protect us." As he had been taught to do, Eaon bowed deeply until he had to bend a knee to stop from falling on his face. "I am indebted to you, and am so further still with my formal request for Selina's presence on my travels. I understand the concerns you have expressed, but I believe she will be invaluable to our success."

Was it manipulative? Yes. Did it make him feel slimy and shameful? Very.

Did it work?

"Oh, stand up, you intolerable brat," Kaelean hissed, tossing the sack of papers at him. "If she dies, it's on your head."

"Noted," Eaon said, catching the sack as he stood.

"And you will send word when you arrive safely."

"I'll send word of our safety as often as you like."

Kaelean scowled at him once more before turning to Cinn, calming her features. "I will take care of your family."

{You'd better.}

Kaelean scoffed and threw up her hands. "Ungrateful worms. Both of you. Go, before I change my mind. My guardian, Vira, will meet you at the Boab."

The words were bitter, but Eaon didn't miss the small smile gracing her lips as she turned away.

Still holding onto Cinn, Eaon made it all the way back down the spiraling staircase and outside the Sanctuary before the weight of responsibility settled on him. His shoulders fell, and he had to take a number of deep, aching breaths to keep his head from growing too heavy.

Cinn noticed, removing Eaon's hand from his wrist and keeping him steady.

{Last chance. I can go on my own. You can go to Eavha.}

Eaon squeezed Cinn's shoulder. "I'm with you on this, okay? Eavha will be fine without me."

The words didn't taste like a lie. Eavha would be absolutely fine. Dearmead was with her.

CHAPTER TWELVE

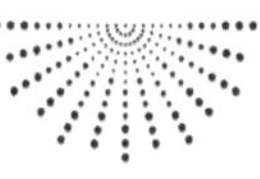

AISLING

The halls of the palace had never been so crowded, nor so full of chatter. The Hyrschan courtiers milled around, gossiping as they made their way from one meeting to the next, the capacity of the palace's many council rooms pushed to their limits. With Imsa in place, the guards were relaxed. Magic did half their job for them as long as the ring of blood around the palace gates was intact. It was simply a matter of controlling who was and was not permitted to leave the grounds.

The only guards still fully alert were Aisling's as they cleared the way to her main council room. Clayton snapped at a few of the Hyrschan doormen to straighten up as they passed. It was part of why she had chosen him to be hers; not a single day passed by that Clayton was not high strung. She needed that, because there were more than a few that went by where Aisling was less than functional.

Not today though. It was standard practice to meet with visiting parties individually before hosting the main event of Imsa, usually to get formal introductions out of the way as well as smooth over any differences so that the main issue could be discussed without impingement. Aisling was glad to have a moment alone with the Wyldeden delegation. She needed to ensure that the history of their two peoples was not going to be a barrier during discussions to come.

"

But it made her nervous knowing her father was in another room, taking the opportunity to have a one-to-one conference with the leader of the Southern Mountain Clan.

"They are on their way," Edwina told her quietly as Aisling took her seat at the head of the table, leaving the kerfuffle of the halls behind her.

Giving her handmaiden an assessing appraisal, Aisling frowned. Hair untidy, and still wearing the same dress from yesterday, it was uncharacteristic for her to be in such disarray. Edwina noticed Aisling's attention and blushed.

"Pardon me, Your Highness."

"Have you not rested?"

"I . . ."

"Find Larissa and send her to help me today," Aisling said quietly before turning to the opening door.

"Larissa is not aware of—"

"Go," Aisling hissed.

With a start, Edwina lowered her head and rushed for the servant's entry.

The young demi-kin had been chosen out of all the palace servants to be Aisling's maiden partly because of her work ethic, but also because she had proven loyal. It took courage to come to Aisling's rooms in the middle of the night to warn her that rebels dressed as servants in the kitchens were planning to poison her. To choose a Sparrow witch over her own kind.

Of course, Clayton and Nora had still thoroughly vetted her, but Aisling couldn't imagine how she would manage in this place without Edwina shadowing her, anticipating her needs.

But that devotion was also her flaw, and Aisling didn't always remember to check when the demi-kin had last taken a break. Larissa was an adept substitute, but unlike Edwina, she could not be trusted with the inner workings of what went on in the palace.

Regardless, as Edwina left, Clayton stepped closer to Aisling's seat, his hand resting casually on the hilt of his knife. In an effort to appear approachable, Aisling had not wanted any other guards present for the Wyldeden meeting, but it appeared that Eavha had not felt the same.

She entered in a simple sage shift, hair braided loosely over one shoulder with fresh flowers woven into the twists, five guardians and her Keeper by her side.

To add to the insult, or because Anfar witches have no concept of formal arrangements, Eavha took the seat directly to the right of Aisling instead of at the other end of the slab of marble. The guardian Eavha had danced with the night before took the seat beside her while Milnova took the one beside him. The other guardians stood against the wall, eyeing Aisling's own guard warily. If things weren't quite so urgent, Aisling would have been curious to see Clayton skirmish with the Anfar guardians.

"Refreshments?" Aisling offered.

Eavha shook her head. "I couldn't possibly. The breakfast feast was plenty."

Larissa hurried in from the servant's door, clean and fresh, immediately bringing Aisling a glass of wine. Milnova also accepted a glass, but as none of the other witches indulged, Aisling thought the gesture was meant to stave off any further offense.

"I know our people have a hostile history," Aisling acknowledged. "So I wanted to see if a clean slate was possible, at least between you and I. My ancestors made choices I would not have made."

It was Milnova who answered, Eavha's wide doe-eyes blinking heavily. If the heir's appointment was as recent as Milnova suggested, perhaps Eavha did not have the authority yet to speak on behalf of the clan on such matters.

"We took time to learn more about your work with the demi-kin in this city. It would seem you are not much like your ancestors at all. A clean slate between our clan and *you* does seem possible."

There was nothing that delighted Aisling further than being considered separate from the Coven.

"Thank you. How was your journey?" she asked as she sipped her wine.

Eavha picked up the end of her braid and twirled a curl around her finger. "Much more pleasant than the last time I left Wyldeden. Your city is nicer than Pirevia."

Aisling sat stunned, then covered her hesitation with another sip of wine. Eavha was very forthcoming. Too forthcoming. Naive. Perhaps her presence instead of the high priestess's was a blessing in disguise.

"You've been to my brother's disgraceful city, then?"

"Yes. This past spring, he captured my brother and I, as well as our friend Cinn, the kinner," Eavha stated calmly.

There was no hiding the surprise that jolted Aisling this time as her head snapped up. She remembered the report of Nevan capturing the kinner, and the later escape. Reports had trickled in that the other prisoners he had captured had been witches: a Returned responsible for the surge that left Nevan's city in mourning, and the necromancer attributed with raising such a power from the void. If Eavha was telling the truth, it meant she was one of them. More than that, she knew about the kinner. Had called him a friend. The number of Wyldeden witches in the council room had been a mere insult a moment ago, but now they set her pulse racing.

"Ah. I was very pleased to hear of your escape and the damage it caused Pirevia."

"I was not pleased to hear of your treatment of my friend."

Not naive at all, just playing a different kind of game. The sort Aisling thought only she knew how to play. The dress, the skin, the innocence wafting off her—a façade. A disarming distraction.

"I have many regrets," Aisling said slowly. Carefully. "And that is the biggest of them. I received the message to leave him be, and I have done so. Should I ever cross paths with him again I would only wish to make amends."

"On our travels, we heard that a band of Sparrows had tried to abduct him from his home in Belden. They almost killed my brother."

Aisling's shoulders stiffened. She had spies in Belden to keep tabs on things, yet she had not heard of an attack.

"If that is true, I can offer assistance in tracking the culprits down so they can be punished."

"Of course it's true." Eavha frowned. "I don't know how you do things in these cities, but where I am from we don't waste time with lies and tricks. We brought the Morvish witch and are willing to share what information can be gleaned from her. In return, we await the counsel you offered Kaelean regarding some political business. But I am worried how much we can trust you after what happened in Belden."

Aisling sat back in her seat, unsure again what game Eavha was playing.

"Belden was not my doing. I didn't even know that was where he was," she lied. About the second part, anyway. "And for the record, the people who live inside these walls cannot entirely be trusted. If I were you, I would be more careful with the things you say. You give away too much too freely."

Eavha blinked twice, and Aisling thought her initial assumption might have been correct after all. Eavha had absolutely no idea what she was doing.

"I understand the Morvish witch is a criminal," Aisling continued.

"Yes," Eavha said, refraining from further explanation.

"I will be sure to interrogate her thoroughly. As for the counsel I offered, I would first ask if you know much about the First War?"

Eavha looked to Milnova, who grimaced.

"It is a creation legend, unfounded by evidence."

Aisling couldn't help but roll her eyes. It was the same disbelief she'd heard from the Sparrow Coven. The disbelief her father was intentionally stoking. Davina's visions had not been enough to persuade anyone all those years ago, but it was still her only proof. She needed them to trust it. Or at the very least, fear the possibility enough to act.

"I can assure you, it happened. I'm not a good storyteller, but our theater performs a wonderful ballet that explains things well. Would you join me, tomorrow perhaps? Then my warnings will make sense."

"Ballet?" Eavha tilted her head, frowning.

"Theatrical storytelling through dance and music," Milnova explained. "It's a recreational activity among humans and those who dwell with them."

Aisling raised her eyebrows. She knew Wyldeden witches were recluse, but she hadn't thought a ballet would need explaining.

"Is it the most efficient way?" Eavha asked.

"Efficient? No. Effective, yes," Aisling explained. "I understand you don't want to be here longer than you have to. I am also pressed by time. But this is too important to explain wrong, and the theater is the best way."

"Then I would like to go and see the ballet." Eavha nodded, turning to her guardian. "Dearmead, will you join Milnova and I? The others should stay and keep their eye on Aadya."

The male with the long black braid nodded once.

"Then it is settled. I will send a servant in the morning with details of our departure."

Aisling stood, and the witches followed suit. Finishing her wine and passing the empty glass to Larissa, she left the delegation to attend her next meeting. Eavha knowing the kinner had been an unpleasant surprise, but an alliance was not out of the question yet.

CHAPTER THIRTEEN

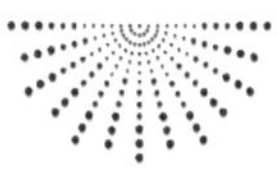

EAVHA

THE WYLDEDEN WITCHES DIDN'T DARE SPEAK IN THE HALLS OF THE palace as they once again returned to the suites assigned to them. Not after Aisling's warning.

Being within spitting distance of Princess Aisling had left Eavha breathing too hard, pulse battering her ears. Despite whether Aisling had gone after Cinn at the farm or not, she was responsible for hurting him in the first place. Not to mention it was still her coven that had killed Eaon this time. Holding her tongue was becoming increasingly difficult since simply being in Aisling's presence left Eavha seething.

Another whispering leaf was waiting on the windowsill as Eavha, Dearmead and Milnova closed the door to their suite, as if Kaelean knew that anything short of twice daily updates on her brother would send them all batty.

She held the scalloped leaf to her ear and plucked a curling strand free from her braid.

"He's up and about, causing trouble with Cinn, as per usual," Eavha told the others, tossing the leaf onto the table with the rest.

The foyer of their suite was fitted as a sitting room, a circular table and four armchairs displayed in the center of the room. A large window opened onto a balcony made of the same dark polished stone as the interior. It was a cheerless space, but the rugs and tapestries added enough color to keep it from resembling a dungeon.

Dearmead sunk into one of the armchairs and covered his face. News of the attack and Eaon's condition had been hard on him, too. When the first whispering leaf arrived, he had argued with Eavha long into the night about whether they should turn back and go home. But there was nothing either of them could have done to help and they had only been half way to Hyrsch, so Dearmead let her win.

"Did you believe Aisling when she said she wasn't responsible?" he asked, sliding his hands down the armrests of the chair until he held the ornate ends. As if only by doing so could he keep himself here in the palace.

"I don't know. She confuses me," Eavha sighed, turning to Milnova. "You did not seem impressed with her."

"Quite the opposite." Milnova went to the window and gazed upon the city. The shawl the old witch wore over her coily hair hid her face as she mused. "Aisling has accomplished much for someone so young, and she has not done so by being superstitious and rash. I'm very curious to what prompted such a relentless campaign to have us attend this Imsa."

Sitting down, Eavha took her Blessing Charm from the pocket of her dress and muttered a prayer, wrapping the plucked hair from her braid around the stem. It had only been a few weeks since she had wandered the fields in Wyldeden, trying to choose a new base for her charm. Daisies were no longer appropriate, and her ma had once warned her that choosing a base just because you liked it was unwise. It had to feel right. After searching for hours, the peonies had called to her. They had always been her favorite, but she had not been ready for one back when she was eight years old and frightened.

"Her asking about the First War was strange," Dearmead added, scratching mindlessly at the luxurious dusky fabric of the chair.

"Do you know much about it?" Eavha asked.

"Eaon knows more."

Milnova and Eavha shared a look. Any opportunity to bring up her brother, Dearmead took it.

"It's one of those stories told amongst the fae that somehow ended up in the books of witches," Milnova explained. "Anyone scholarly minded knows there is little stock to be put in it."

"But all our major wars are numbered based on that being the first," Eavha pointed out. "How can it not be believed?"

"Do we not bury our baby teeth when they fall out so the fae don't assume it is an offering, even though there have been no faeries in Anfar in nine-hundred years? Of course. Because of superstition and tradition, and the fear of a few who ask 'what if.' Not to mention that not everyone believes in the Second or Third wars, either."

"Kaelean literally fought the Third War." Dearmead gave her a pointed look.

"I didn't say *I* didn't believe in them. Your kinner friend is proof that the Second War was even possible, while Kaelean is proof of the Third. But no such evidence exists for the First. It is just a story."

Eavha plucked out another hair, yawning as she began to weave the magic around the stem. She was pushing herself, but she had a lot of work to catch up on if she wanted to regain the power she once had.

"Aisling obviously believes it, so it's worth finding out what we can." Eavha turned to Dearmead. "What did Eaon say about it?"

"That it was the birth of Balance. Of the Spirits and magic as we know it. Parts of Nir were formed during it, like the Womb. It created the Kinner."

Eavha raised her eyebrows. "Well, there's a great big red flag. The princess certainly seems preoccupied by the Kinner race, doesn't she."

"Surprisingly so, considering her coven's dedication to eradicating evidence of the Kinner's existence at all," Dearmead added.

"Supposedly," muttered Milnova.

Both Eavha and Dearmead rolled their eyes. "You literally just said—"

"I said the Second War *might* have happened since we can now be sure that Kinner exist, but it is hard to imagine an entire race of Kinners losing a war to the Sparrow Coven. They deal in death, which the Kinner are immune to. And if what is said about the First War is to be believed then the two conflicts contradict each other."

"What is said about it?" Eavha asked.

Dearmead sighed. "Supposedly, the Kinner were created to end the

First War. After they did that, they ruled Nir for a millennium until a fight broke out between them and the Sparrows. Over what, nobody knows. The Sparrows obliterated them, then spent centuries making sure people forgot the Kinner existed."

Milnova nodded. "Supposedly."

"Then the Third, with the Sparrows against Anfar." Eavha tapped her fingers on her lips. "So, for the sake of argument, let's say it all happened. Aisling seems to think it did. What does it have to do with Cinn, and with this Imsa? Do you think she's going to tell everyone about him and try to make us surrender him?"

The three of them sat in silence while considering the implications, until Milnova stepped away from the window.

"It is wasted time to hypothesize all possible motivations of a witch we do not know. Get some rest, and I will see what information I can get from my meeting with the Sparrow advisors in an hour," Milnova suggested.

Eavha nodded.

"It is not wasted time," Dearmead muttered under his breath, standing abruptly and storming down the hall toward his room.

Eavha waited until his door slammed closed before sinking deeper into her seat. She needed to talk to him. Ever since hearing about the attack at the Copeland farm, Dearmead had been temperamental and distracted, neither of which they could afford while deep in an enemy stronghold.

But first, before she grew too tired, she needed to do her daily prayers.

Learning to be a priestess had mostly been about discovering her soul—how to locate it inside her body, how to detect it in others, and how to use it to commune with the spirit realms. As someone who had spent her entire life dedicated to the body, with a few intensive years learning to understand the mind, Eavha had found connecting with her soul challenging.

Wishing Milnova luck with the advisors, she pattered back to the bedroom she'd slept in last night. The grand canopy bed had fresh silk sheets, the towels she'd spread over the floor to dry after her morning bath replaced with fresh ones folded neatly beside the tub. Her empty breakfast tray was gone, tea and cakes waiting for her on a silver cart. Once, such service would have gone unnoticed, but as she pressed a finger against a perfectly square slice of sponge cake, her eyes watered. If she had the choice between such luxury and sitting at the little kitchen table with Eaon and another of his inedible meals, she knew where she would prefer to be.

Wrapping her Blessing Charm in a protective cloth, Eavha placed it by the window to sun. She had set up a temporary altar just beneath it, small bowls of burnt herbs and bird bones to represent Terra and Balance alongside an array of candles and incense ready for burning. Kneeling on the cold stone floor, Eavha lit a rosemary-infused candle and dipped her fingers in the burnt herbs, drawing Marks of Concentration on her face.

Closing her eyes and taking cleansing breaths, the Terra-blessing she had often put aside in favor of her Sanni-blessing began to swell somewhere deep in her belly. Kaelean had been trying to teach her how to relax her mind enough to connect with her soul, and though it took a few minutes, the world eventually began to pull away.

The spirit realm was everywhere, but being so far from the forest made it difficult to sense it in any tangible way. Distantly aware of her body, she reached for a bouquet of flowers she had brought from Wyldeden and pressed them against her forehead.

Since joining the priestesses, only once had Eavha been able to sense Terra, and that had been while praying at the temple in Wyldeden, already inside a pocket of the spirit's realm. Trying to find her way there now . . .

Sighing, Eavha tossed the flowers back beside the altar and rose to her feet. She was too tired and too unpracticed, but she had tried. At least Kaelean could not reprimand her later.

Her next task was to speak with Dearmead, but as she made to leave there was a sharp tug in her gut. Looking back to the window, her scalp itched from all the hair pulling and she knew she needed to brew herself an ointment for hair loss soon. But now, the compulsion to add one more hair to her charm was undeniable.

Unwrapping the peony, Eavha twirled another curling strand around her finger and pulled it out.

Praying silently, her fingers crept back to the balding patch behind her ear and found another.

Just one more.

One more.

———

Knocking gently, Eavha waited for Dearmead's grunt before cracking the door to his room. Identical to her own, including a somewhat cruder altar by the window, she found Dearmead kneeling by a lit candle with his eyes closed, lips moving in a silent prayer. In his open hands sat the first whispering leaf Kaelean had sent informing them of what had happened to Eaon.

Sitting on the bed, Eavha crossed her ankles and patiently waited for him to finish.

Wrapping it with sage, Dearmead held the leaf over the flame until the message was nothing but smoke on the wind. Then he stood up, sat beside her on the bed and put his head in his hands. His braid was undone, the sheet of black a curtain between them.

Eavha gave him a moment, but when he didn't speak, she did.

"I won't blame you for going back, if you want."

Rubbing a hand over the scruff on his chin, Dearmead looked toward the window and shook his head. She had never seen such longing before. How had she missed it? All those years, how had she thought he was looking at her like that?

Sighing deeply, she flopped back on the bed and put her arms behind her head. "Out with it."

"What?" he asked, as if he genuinely didn't know what she was asking for.

"You need to talk about it, Dea. You literally talk about him every five minutes. So, out with it."

Frowning, he turned to look down at her. "I don't talk about him that much."

Eavha raised an eyebrow and his frown crumpled into a grimace.

"Fine, maybe I do. But you're the last person I should talk to about it."

"Because I had a crush on you?" Eavha asked. "I'm over it."

It was Dearmead's turn to raise an eyebrow.

"To be honest, Dea," Eavha sighed. "It was Ma's suggestion to pursue you in the first place. For breeding purposes. It would have been a good match but it's hard to tell whether I really liked you that way, or if I was just trying to convince myself to like you. Considering how quickly I got over it, I'm leaning toward the latter."

It was honest of her, and when she turned to gauge his reaction he was surprisingly stony.

"You didn't really like me, but you didn't speak to Eaon for weeks when you found out about us. Did you even care what that did to him?"

"I was mad he lied to me." Eavha sat up, chin stiffening. "And I had a right to be."

"It was my idea to lie."

It didn't make a difference whose idea it had been. The deception had made her feel foolish.

"Yes, well, in case you didn't notice, I avoided you as well."

"Oh, I noticed."

Eavha scowled at his tone. "In the scheme of everything, does that petty little spat really still bother you? Eaon and I made our peace."

She didn't understand where this was coming from. There had been months between Eaon's departure and now for him to bring up these issues. So why now, when they were in the middle of negotiating with the enemy?

Dearmead sighed and turned his face up to the ceiling. "No."

He didn't elaborate.

"Dea."

He didn't look at her.

"Dea. Talk."

"I'm not over it," he said. "I don't mean the drama, but . . . him. You got over your crush, but I . . ."

Scooting closer, Eavha placed a gentle hand on Dearmead's firm, leather-clad shoulder. "It's more than a crush for you, Dea, and we've all been through a lot lately. He needs time to process it all. Give him some time."

"Then there's the fact that we can never touch each other again." Dearmead looked at her hand before running his own over the crown of his head, sending the silky strands of his hair rippling. "He wants me to move on. I need to. It would be better for him to be with Cinn."

"I don't think they're like that."

"You didn't think he and I were like that, either."

"Um, ouch." Eavha chuckled, picking at invisible lint on her dress.

He was right though. Dearmead had always been around, and he and Eaon were always off doing stuff, and never once had it crossed her mind that there might be more to it than friendship.

"Tell me," she asked. "Tell me about it. You and him."

Dearmead wrinkled his nose.

"It will help. With this grief for what you two had."

Collapsing back on the bed, he put an arm over his face and sighed. Eavha thought he might actually talk, but after a painfully long silence Dearmead only managed yet another sigh.

"Seriously?" Eavha hissed. "You mention him every time you open your mouth, but now that I want to hear about it, you clam up?"

"I'm not good at talking. Eaon always gives me shit about it."

Eavha smirked, shaking her head at the irony. "Pick something. Anything. Just to start."

Dearmead removed the arm from over his face and stared at the ceiling. "I can't."

"Why?" she asked gently.

"Eaon always says his thoughts are either moving too fast or too slow, but mine are just . . . I'm not even convinced they're words. It's just a big . . . I don't know. It's like watching Eaon sign with Cinn. You can figure the gist of it, but I have no idea what they're actually saying."

Eavha watched him talk, the frustration creasing his brow and darkening his eyes.

"You didn't just say it because he was going to die, did you?" Eavha prompted. "You really do love him."

A shudder ran down his spine as he closed his eyes. "I wish I'd gotten the words out sooner."

"He knew," she offered.

But Dearmead shook his head. "For the rest of my life, I'm going to regret that day you two were excommunicated. Regret everything that happened from the moment Apaete died. I was frozen. I was weak. I promised him . . . but I just stood there. I dream of it all the time. The branding. I wake up sick to my stomach."

She wasn't sure how his mind had gotten there from what she had said, but it was progress. It was a tangible thought.

"I can make you a tonic for that."

Dearmead nodded, but no more words came out.

"I'm always here," she told him. "Any time, any day. If you find the words, Dearmead, let them out. In any shape or form they take, just let them out. It will help."

A small smile graced his ridiculously handsome face and he reached over to squeeze her arm.

"I appreciate that. Thank you."

Eavha smiled back before looking out the window where the smoke from the leaf Dearmead had burned lingered in the still night.

CHAPTER FOURTEEN

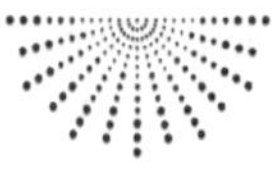

EAVHA

ON THE THIRD DAY OF IMSA, THE THREE WYLDEDEN WITCHES MET Aisling and her entourage in front of the palace. Two of the strange boxes on wheels that Milnova had explained were called "carriages" were latched to the same horses that had carried her through the city upon arrival. Hitching up her long green skirt, Eavha hurried to the mares, heart fluttering. Before arriving in Hyrsch she had only ever seen pictures of horses in storybooks, and they were even more beautiful in real life.

The servants checking the bridles watched her warily, but the chestnut mares happily let her stroke their velvety necks, as pleased as she was by the reunion.

"You look lovely," Aisling said, hands clasped in front of her as she stood by the first carriage, a prudish gown of white and gold fit to her rigid frame.

Eavha spared the princess a glance. "Thank you."

Once again, she was taken aback by the strange, ghostly elegance of the princess. The image she had concocted in her mind of the evil Sparrow witch who'd tortured her friend into muteness was vastly different.

Turning away sharply, Eavha whispered a blessing of good health to the horses before approaching the carriage. "I'm excited to see the theater."

Aisling's eyes widened as Eavha ignored the helping hands of servants, climbing the frame and swinging herself inside. Blinking, the princess looked from Eavha to the other carriage behind them, and it dawned on Eavha that this might not have been the one she was supposed to ride in.

"We will take the other," Edwina said quietly, indicating to Milnova and Clayton.

Dearmead leaped into the carriage and took a seat beside Eavha, shifting his spear around in the cramped space.

A little uncertainly, Aisling followed, letting her servants help her with her volumous skirts.

"Did I make an error?" Eavha asked, cheeks pinking.

"No." Aisling's lip twitched in an echo of a smile. "There are customs that matter and ones that do not. I am glad to have this opportunity to talk."

"Oh?" Eavha raised her brow, holding onto the seat as the horses jolted forward. "What about?"

"The Southern Mountain Clan and I have a history. We've had to work together many times before. And of course I know the king well, for obvious reasons. But you and I have not been as lucky. What you know of me is what you have heard, and I'm afraid what you have heard is not of my kindest angle."

"I see." Eavha straightened her back as she once again made herself look away from the princess and out the small, curtained window. They were approaching the palace's wrought-iron gates, the pointed spires on top gleaming with fresh polish. "So going to the theater is not just an effective way to learn about the First War, but also an opportunity to woo me?"

Rather than shame, Aisling's painted face cracked with a coy smile. "It would not be the worst consequence of this outing if you are wooed. Though all I meant was that I wish for you to know I am not only a monster."

She did not deny her appalling behavior, and Eavha supposed a scrap of respect was owed for that.

"Where I come from," Aisling continued, "things are done a certain way. I wanted to be kinder. I thought I *was*. But my Second, Nora, made me realize I am not as I hoped. But I am trying. As I said yesterday, I wish things with your kinner friend had been different."

"I thought her name was Edwina," Dearmead said with a frown, interrupting before Eavha could say something she probably shouldn't.

"Edwina is my maiden. Nora is . . . securing valuable real estate elsewhere. She would have made a much better first impression than I have."

"Ah." Eavha didn't particularly care but Dearmead's ears had perked up, so she kept Aisling talking. "Is it a secret, this real estate?"

"For now, but I assure you it's irrelevant to Imsa," Aisling said, lifting her chin. "My brother and I have a score to settle, that is all."

"Yes, your delightful brother." Eavha wrinkled her nose, breath catching at the thought of the prince in Pirevia.

Aisling stiffened at her reaction, noting Dearmead's much more hostile one. Softly, she said, "Rest easy knowing he will get what he deserves."

"You have no affection for him?" Eavha raised her eyebrows, wiping her now sweaty hands on her skirt.

"None."

"I couldn't imagine that. Even when I hated him, I loved Eaon."

Aisling waved her hand dismissively. "Such things are of little consequence in Dusarn."

"What, family?" Eavha frowned. The Sparrow Coven's whole power system was built on blood.

"Love." Aisling clarified, lips pursing as if the word left a bitter taste in her mouth.

"Oh." Eavha turned away again, not sure why the princess's statement made her so uncomfortable. "Well, having no love for Nevan is at least one mark in your favor."

Aisling smiled, this time genuinely, "Ah, the wooing is working."

Eavha bit her lip as she tried to hold back a smile of her own.

<hr>

The part of the city Aisling's carriage took them to was different from what they had seen coming in. The streets were smoother, posts erected along the road supporting gilded oil lamps, while shop fronts lining the street had fancily lettered plaques. The people who stopped to bow at the carriage as it passed wore flashy dresses and brightly colored shirts, their hair coiffed in strange arrangements beneath their hats.

All of it paled beside the towering structure Aisling explained was the theater. Whoever had built it must have been to Wyldeden at some point, because the marble columns surrounding the building were laced with carved quartz and amethyst vines. The detail was far too reminiscent to be coincidence.

"I thought you might like this particular theater," Aisling said, watching Eavha stare.

"Those stones . . ."

"An Anfar witch had a hand in the design of this city back when the Kinner built it."

Eavha turned from the enormous domed structure to stare at Aisling. "The Kinner built this city?"

"They built all the cities. All the villages, towns and ports . . . all with and for the humans after the First War. Before my coven came and took everything."

Unsure what to say, Eavha hummed in interest before standing. The carriage had come to a stop.

"Let me," Dearmead said gruffly, opening the door and stepping out first. Clayton was already waiting outside, hand on the hilt of his weapon.

Until that moment, Eavha had not considered that leaving the palace would be dangerous. The blood poured around the inner walls of the palace would not protect them out here, where none of the visitors were bound to their promises. While she did not fear Aisling, the Southern Mountain Clan was a different matter. Let alone the danger the king posed.

For a fleeting moment, she was frozen. Even Aisling had brought only one of her guards. Edwina was there to help Aisling down, fixing the skirts of her dress as she placed her strange shoes on the footpath.

She caught Dearmead's gaze and he gave her an encouraging nod.

"Everything will be fine," she whispered to herself, taking a measured breath before climbing down from the carriage.

The people walking by gawked but gave them a wide berth. Especially when Dearmead sidled up beside her, spear strapped once more across his back, a hand at the small of her own. His towering frame and warmth was a familiar comfort.

"The theater is ready for you, Your Highness," Edwina announced.

Aisling managed a sincere smile for her maiden, then led the way toward the heavy double doors waiting open for them.

Stepping inside, Eavha gasped at the softness of the carpet beneath her feet. Dearmead, too, wiggled his calloused toes on the thick red pile. The glass dome ceiling flooded the reception room with light, slowly fading as they walked down a long hall ending in a set of ornamental double doors. Beyond them, Aisling led Eavha up a winding staircase that opened onto a balcony, high above a room full of civilians already seated and waiting for the show. The handful of chairs on the balcony were upholstered in black velvet, the booth enclosed in purple drapery.

"That is the stage," Milnova explained quietly as she sat in one of the plush chairs. "The curtain will rise when the dance is ready to start."

Eavha nodded, taking a seat beside Aisling.

"Refreshments?" Edwina asked in Nirnish.

"Yes, please," Aisling asked.

"Lady Eavha?"

Eavha blinked at the title given to her. "Um, yes. I will try it."

The maiden smiled warmly before leaving the booth. With only seconds to spare before the lamps in the room dampened, she returned with two glasses of sparkling wine. Eavha took a tentative sip as, below the stage, an orchestra played the show's opening notes.

The curtains rose to blackness.

Ever so slowly, a ball of light grew in the center of the stage before exploding in a flash of white, leaving four figures standing there. Dancers, Eavha realized, as two of them slunk into the background, leaving a female and male in the spotlight.

She had never seen anything like it as the two of them began to move, and yet she understood exactly what the dance was about. A courtship. A male, infatuated, and a female, doting. As she spun, the swathes of silk that made up her dress blew open, scattering vibrant petals over the stage, butterflies taking flight into the audience.

"Mother," Aisling whispered to her, but Eavha had already figured that out.

The female portrayed the Mother, but the male . . . she did not know who he was meant to be.

A hand against her chest, Eavha watched in awe as the music swelled. The courting dance was reaching its climax, and from the sides, more dancers leaped onto stage wearing costumes of beasts, fae, and naked humans. The song turned chaotic, magic filling the theater as the dancers threw up their arms, hazy images of forests and oceans and deserts flashing by like a dream.

Below, the beast dancers chased the humans. Pounced and tore and consumed.

Slowly, Mother stopped dancing, stopped her creating to watch the pain of the humans writhing on the floor.

Stop, she mouthed, reaching for them.

The beasts did not listen, and the leading male just laughed as he spun her around, ignoring the tears now streaming down her wailing face.

Mother wasn't the only one who saw the human's suffering and resented it. A few of the fae slowed as the music darkened, turning to the beasts and entering combative dances with them. Others dragged the injured humans away, soothing their crying and kissing their faces.

The lead male stopped dancing to scold the fae, but Mother blocked him.

The music stopped. The dancers froze.

And from the shadows, another of the original four who'd blared to life at the start of the ballet stepped forward.

Clad entirely in black, the entity moved with ethereal grace until they stood beside Mother.

It's okay, they mouthed. *See*.

The dancers on the stage disappeared and the stage took on a new aesthetic. Darkness again, but a sweet-smelling smoke floated along the floor, stars shooting across the theater in arcs of color. Lounging, sleeping, were the ravaged humans from before.

Death—because that was who this new figure was—smoothed back Mother's hair.

And Mother smiled.

Together, they began a new dance. Not one of passion, but one where they mirrored each other. Each sensual movement was so synchronized that Eavha forgot they were actors.

This was the story she knew. As Death became the Lover, Balance was born.

From the sidelines, the male from before crept back on stage, rage contorting his features. He tried to take Mother's hand, but she snatched it away.

Once again, the stage went black. The music stopped.

One beat. Two. Eavha's heart was pounding so fast she had to place a hand against her chest to make sure it stayed there.

A thunderous swell of music announced the sudden bright lights that flooded the stage. The Lover's realm was gone, replaced with too much movement, too much sound, too much of everything.

War.

The male and his favorite beasts on one side, Death and Mother, alongside the fae, on the other. And everywhere, humans lay dead.

A warm, gloved hand covered hers.

Peeling her eyes away from the ballet, Eavha met Aisling's soft gray stare.

They did not speak, but Aisling's thumb rubbed soothing circles on the back of her hand until Eavha no longer felt the rising bile in her throat. The princess must think her pathetic to be so affected by a theatrical display, but there was nothing but understanding in her sharp, beautiful face.

By the time Eavha turned back, the male had somehow been convinced to retreat. Balance reigned. The play concluded with another beautiful, symmetrical dance between Mother and her Lover until the curtains finally closed.

The crowd stood, applauding loudly. The black velvet parted once more, the stage now bare, the dancers lined up to take a bow.

"He is called Chaos," Aisling explained, remaining seated as the rest of the audience threw flowers and coins on the stage. "And he is returning."

PART II

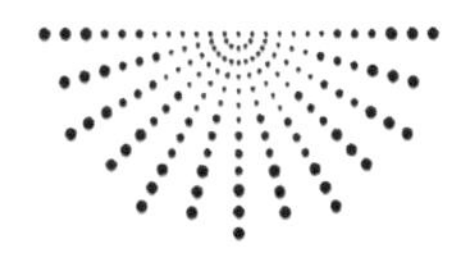

DAWN OF EMBERS

CHAPTER FIFTEEN

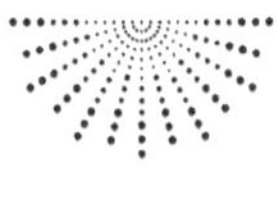

EAVHA

"Well, that was certainly entertaining." Milnova scratched her chin as she sat in one of the plush chairs back in their suite. None of them had spoken since leaving the theater, but as Eavha looked from the keeper to Dearmead it was blatantly clear the effect the ballet had on them. Milnova had not been convinced, but Dearmead looked as lost in thought as Eavha.

"It is worth considering the possibility that Chaos is real," she said softly.

Milnova lifted her chin as she countered, "If there was a fourth High Spirit, it would be known."

Mother and her Lover had taken their places at the top of the spirit hierarchy, and despite the mystery surrounding her, Morvia was still known. None of the books Eavha had ever read suggested there was a fourth.

"Would it?" Dearmead countered. "There seems to be a lot of things that used to be mere legend becoming reality lately. Kinners are real. And Old Ones."

"Yes, this swamp hag near Pirevia you spoke of. Its status as an Old One is yet to be corroborated." Milnova disregarded him with a wave of her hand.

Dearmead clenched his eyes and fists, taking a long breath as if trying to contain a remark he knew was better kept to himself. As Eavha's personal guardian, Dearmead had a new authority he was still getting used to, but she wasn't sure either of them outranked an elder still.

"It has been a long morning," Eavha said soothingly as she rested a hand on Dearmead's forearm. Even with the leather of his vambraces between them, she could feel the hard muscle tensing underneath. "Why don't we all take a few hours to rest before lunch and talk about this later?"

"I've been meaning to speak with the palace chef about the state of their vegetables anyway. It simply will not do." Milnova rose and straightened her tunic.

"Good idea. Dearmead and I have been doing some therapy, so we'll stay here," Eavha said with a smile, ignoring Dearmead's frown of confusion.

"Very well." Milnova nodded to them both. "I'll see you at lunch."

Eavha kept her hand on Dearmead's arm until the door to their suites closed behind Milnova with a soft click.

"What are you doing?" Dearmead muttered with a frown. "I'm not doing therapy."

"Not right now," she said with a raised brow. "Though you're in desperate need of some if you ever figure out how to talk about your feelings."

Dearmead scoffed.

"But, I think you and I should go for a walk," she continued. "Milnova will argue about theology until the final dawn, and I have no intention of boring myself to death listening to her. I'm going to get answers. I figured you would want to come with me."

Sighing loudly, Dearmead lay his head back against the chair he sat in. "Like I have a choice."

"Exactly." Eavha beamed, pulling Dearmead by the arm as she rose.

"Do you have a plan?" he grumbled.

"Yes. Come. Let's walk."

It didn't take long for the two of them to find their way back to the palace grounds. Carriages lay waiting in rows for anyone who wished to explore the city, but Eavha led Dearmead along the gravel paths leading away from the front gates. Her feet had grown used to rough surfaces since first being excommunicated from Wyldeden, and Dearmead didn't seem bothered by the small, sharp stones pressing into the soles of their bare feet.

The grounds were mostly empty, only a few stray courtiers roaming the paths or making use of the strange squares of grass Dearmead told her were called "lawns" used for "sports"—a pastime nobody in Wyldeden ever bothered with. And by the time they passed the lawns and reached the gardens, they were alone. The grounds stretched on, begging to be explored, but Eavha kept to the winding paths through manicured gardens of dry shrubs and flowers not ready to bloom, ponds with little orange fish hiding from the summer sun beneath lily pads scattered throughout.

"See up there?" Eavha finally said as she looked up to one of the spiring towers of the palace. "All the way at the top? The window with herbs hanging in the window?"

Dearmead followed her gaze and nodded. "A prayer room."

"Aisling's prayer room," Eavha corrected. "I've watched her go to the stairs that lead up that tower, and there are always guards. Nobody else except her servants and her personal guard go up there."

"You want to get in there, don't you?" Dearmead shook his head. "Don't you think that's pushing the laws of Imsa?"

"Not at all. I have no ill intentions. I just want to know what's going on," Eavha explained.

"What makes you think her prayer room is going to help with that?" Dearmead asked, scanning the grounds.

A woman was meandering through the gardens with a book in her hands, and though Eavha doubted she would understand Terranian, she lowered her voice regardless. "Because that's where Aadya kept her secrets. It's worth a look."

Dearmead's eyes darkened, his shoulders stiffening at the Morvish beast-witch's name. Whatever pressure had been released since they'd handed her over to the Hyrschan guards settled back in.

"Alright," he agreed. "But even so, that's a goal, not a plan."

"Semantics."

"We'll never get past the guards."

"I know. That's why I brought us outside."

Eavha watched as realization slowly dawned on Dearmead's face.

"Lover take me." He glanced again to the woman growing near, shifting himself slightly to stand between her and Eavha, a hand open and waiting to reach for his spear if he needed to. "That's insane, Eavha. It's the middle of the day, and there are guards on the palace walls, too. They'll see us."

"I was hoping you might have cataloged their movements. Know if there's a window of opportunity where they aren't watching this wall." She looked up at him, batting her eyelashes.

Dearmead scowled down at her. "Of course I've been cataloging their movements. We haven't been here long enough for me to know yet, but even if there was, this is still a terrible idea."

The woman stopped as she reached them and Dearmead reached for his weapon.

"Eavha Nemuse?" the woman asked, butchering the name with her thick Hyrschan accent and utterly unperturbed by Dearmead's roiling aggression.

Eavha blinked at her, still and silent.

"I thought I saw a fox before," the woman continued, her gaze unbreaking as she held Eavha's stare, a slight pucker growing between her brows.

"Who are you?" Dearmead snapped, the Nirnish words slippery on his tongue.

"A friend of a friend," she answered, closing the book and holding it against her chest. The cover was engraved with a seven-pointed star. "Thought you might like to know about the fox in the large tree."

Eavha still had no idea what she was talking about, but Dearmead let go of his weapon.

"I would like to know," he confirmed with a nod.

The woman smiled and glanced around as if taking in the scenery. Her eyes went up to the tower, lines framing her mouth as she pursed her lips.

"There are shiftier creatures in these gardens than the fox," she finally said. "Those who dwell here tend to band together. Protect each other." Her fingers traced the seven-pointed star as she spoke.

"That is wise," Dearmead answered, watching her.

Eavha narrowed her eyes. She needed to study more Nirnish when she had a chance. Clearly Dearmead was picking it up faster than she was.

"Oh, and guess what I saw." The woman smiled, but it was a tight expression that didn't meet her eyes. "The fox had some friends. I think they will join the gardens soon. In case one of those wily creatures I mentioned shows up."

Nodding slowly, Dearmead returned her smile. "Safety in numbers."

"Yes," she agreed, then bowed deeply. "It was lovely to speak, but I must finish my walk."

"Enjoy the sun," Dearmead said in farewell.

As the woman moved on, Dearmead looped Eavha's arm over his and began to walk away as well. She resisted the pull, looking back to the tower before giving in and hurrying her steps to keep up with him.

"What was that about?" she huffed.

"She was a rebel," Dearmead answered. "The elder guardian debriefed us before we left Wyldeden about how to spot them. She was talking about Kaelean. Our high priestess doesn't trust Aisling and is sending more guardians. Plus, if something goes wrong during Imsa, we have the rebels' support."

Eavha's eyes widened. "You got all that from that strange conversation about foxes?"

Chuckling, Dearmead finally slowed their pace. "When you grow up with Calla Bayfield as your ma, you learn how to hear what's not being said."

Eavha wrinkled her nose at the sound of Calla's name. She didn't want to think about her single interaction with the female and that awful dinner all those months ago.

Looking back to the tower, Eavha let go of Dearmead's arm. "I still want to get into the prayer room."

Sighing deeply, Dearmead looked along the palace walls where guards stood stoically in intervals of a dozen meters, alternating their watches from within to outside the line of Imsa. Then he turned to the old gray stone that formed the palace, counting the windows between Aisling's prayer room and their own suite.

"It might be doable."

"Yes!" Eavha gave a little skip.

Shaking his head, he took Eavha's arm once more and led her back the way they came. "If we're quick, we can catch up with the rebel."

"Why?" she asked, her body shivering with the sudden excitement of what they were about to do.

"We're going to need a distraction."

***

The balcony from Eavha's room was not large, but the stone was coarse and the exterior walls of the palace would be easy to navigate. Drying her sweaty palms on the gray leggings and tunic she'd changed into, Eavha removed the twine from around her wrist and tied back her hair.

Dearmead stood by the window, watching the guards. Waiting.

Waiting and waiting.

"Now," Dearmead said, hurrying out onto the balcony.

Sure enough, the guards on the wall had all turned to look outward, shouting down at the disturbance the rebels were causing on the other side.

It was perfect climbing weather—not windy, nor too hot. The stone didn't scald her scarred hands as she pulled herself up, becoming a limpet on the wall, the muscles in her back and arms taut.

"Tell me, how many high priestesses do you know who'd scale the outside of an enemy castle in the middle of the day?" Eavha grinned, glancing up to where Dearmead was striding ahead, feet finding easy purchase on the ridges and bulges of the building's facade.

"First of all, you're not high priestess yet. Secondly, Kaelean definitely would. She'd do it in those weird pointy shoes the humans wear while juggling knives and breathing fire."

Eavha snorted. "True."

They avoided windows as they made their way up the palace, fingers and toes aching as they shimmied under other balconies, but otherwise without much trouble. Dearmead was keeping an eye on the perimeter wall but whatever was going on outside was keeping the guards thoroughly distracted. Chuckling to herself, giddy with the brashness of what they were doing, it almost felt like being a teenager again, sneaking into parties she and Apaete weren't old enough to attend or stalking males in the forests after school to see if they would talk about them.

As they edged up beneath the window at the very top of the tower, Dearmead swore.

"It doesn't open."

"What?"

"The window doesn't open," he repeated through gritted teeth. "We need to get back down. Abort mission."

"Abort mission?" Eavha huffed as she climbed up beside him, seeing that the window was indeed a built-in pane of glass and not one that could be opened. "You've been reading too many of Eaon's human spy novels."

"So have you if you know what I'm talking about," Dearmead snapped back.

Limbs trembling as a cramp spasmed her biceps, Eavha closed her eyes to think. "There has to be another window."

"Eavha, no. We can try again another time, but the guards aren't going to stay distracted forever."

He was already starting to descend, but Eavha didn't follow. Instead, she reached to her left and began creeping along the curve of the tower. It was wide enough to look flat, meaning it was wide enough to have a second window.

"Eavha!" Dearmead hissed up at her.

"Dearmead!" she mimicked his condescending tone back at him.

"Lover take me, Eaon was right. You are so fucking annoying."

Bristling, she had to resist the urge to kick him as he began clambering up after her again. "I'm getting answers, Dearmead, and I'm getting them now. I refuse to be sucked into some witch's scheme because I don't have all the information again."

He had nothing to say to that because he knew she was right.

On two counts.

Whimpering with relief as a balcony finally came into view, Eavha managed to keep it together long enough to clamber onto it.

Dearmead wasn't far behind her, shaking his hands and breathing hard as the two of them lay on the concrete for a moment. Or half a moment, Dearmead rolling onto his belly and pushing up, eyes wide as he looked through the enormous glass windows behind them.

Aisling's suite. It had to be.

Staying utterly still, Eavha waited as Dearmead watched for signs of movement.

"I think . . . I think we're clear."

Eavha's legs were shaking as she climbed to her feet, but the ache in her body didn't stop the smile from curving her lips. "Then let's go."

CHAPTER SIXTEEN

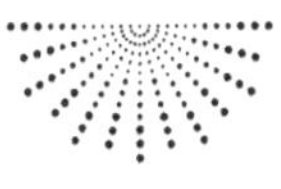

AISLING

Standing in front of her aged brass mirror, Aisling took the pins out of her hair, cleaned the blood from her lips and the kohl from her eyes. The bone crown she wore upon her head went back on the mantel, along with the gold-trimmed gloves and collar from her dress.

For a moment, she let herself be. The stiff angle of her shoulders dropped and her jaw unclenched, sending a wave of pain to her temples. Rubbing a moisturizer into her décolletage, she took deep breaths to release the lingering negative energy her façade left in her body. Then she grabbed a wine bottle, removed the cork and drank from the neck. It was time for Aisling to put her next costume on.

Braiding back her hair, she coiled it into a tight bun at the nape of her neck, before pulling a pair of crimson trousers from the drawer as well as a tunic that covered her wrists and throat. She matched them with black leather gloves, boots and a mask that covered her mouth and nose, patches of mint sewn inside that would barely cover the smells of waste where she was headed.

Finally, she draped an old servant's cloak over her shoulders and pulled up the hood. Stepping outside her suite, Clayton straightened.

He knew what this costume meant.

The two made their way through the halls of the palace, Clayton keeping several dozen feet ahead, meandering as if off duty. The courtiers Aisling passed stepped aside, oblivious, but she was encouraged by the number of guards alerted by the presence of a strange, hooded figure stalking the halls. Clayton quickly distracted them with orders and demands, sending them away before they could look too closely.

In the empty throne room, she unlocked the door to a small holding room for prisoners and a staircase that would take her deep into the bowels of the palace. She waited for Clayton to catch up before descending, unlocking two more doors before stepping into another dark hall. Sparsely lit with torches that could not keep the mildew at bay, she led him to the final door that opened into the dungeon.

When Aisling had first come to Hyrsch, these dungeons had been overflowing with rotting demi-kin. It had been one of the first things she had ordered after declaring the demi-kin a free people; clean up the prisons, both this one and the others across the city for those serving long sentences. Not even the criminals in her city were to be kept in such poor conditions.

In the weeks since sending the rebels to Pirevia, her dungeon had been empty. Now, only the rogue coven the Wyldeden delegation had brought sat on the floor of their barren cells, watching her hatefully. None of them shouted or spat at her, like the rebels before them had, which she hoped was a sign that they did not recognize her and not an omen for how these interrogations were about to go.

At the end of a long row was a vacant cell with a broken door, nothing inside but old hay and a few rats that she kicked aside as she approached the back wall. Removing one of her gloves exposed the tattoo on her left palm: The Key Mark for Those Unbound. Having it on her body meant she could not be bound either physically or magically, though the cost of bearing it permanently was a heavy one to pay. As she pressed her palm against a particular stone in the wall, focusing the dormant Celeste-blessing in her blood and praying quietly for permission to use it, a pulse of magic pushed the mark's power from her skin into the stone.

A click echoed through the dungeon as a hidden door swung open, revealing another stairwell.

Once, there had been two guards she trusted to accompany her down this final hall. Patterick had alternated shifts with Clayton until he had confessed to showing the door to another guard he'd been trying to impress. A guard who, as it turned out, had only joined the ranks to spy for the rebels. A rumor about a kinner being kept in a secret dungeon had spread, and they had come to find him.

To this day, it was still a mystery as to where that rumor had originated but since discovering how deeply her inner circle had been infested with traitors and liars, she realized it didn't matter. None of them could truly be trusted.

Down they went.

A single chamber opened at the bottom of the stairs. They were so deep underground that the summer sun could burn for a thousand days and never reach them. Without any torches, the dark was absolute. Navigating her way through the room by memory, Aisling found a lamp and a match to light it. Soft light warmed the room. A wooden table with leather straps was the central feature, surrounded by cabinets full of herbs in jars and razor-sharp tools. In the corner of the floor was a hatch with three small holes drilled into it. She let her steps thud heavily on the stone floor, eliciting a muffled whine from below.

Shedding the cloak and putting her glove back on, Aisling crouched beside the hatch, listening to the ragged breathing from underneath.

"Sorry it took so long for me to come and see you, Aadya. I hope you've been comfortable."

Rabid, muffled screaming was her response.

She had never enjoyed keeping the kinner here. Never enjoyed the taunting and torturing. Sometimes when she slept, she could still hear him screaming and would wake covered in her own vomit.

But this . . . this she would enjoy. Just a little.

"My name is Aisling Aurnia. Do you know who I am?"

Silence. Aisling could taste the fear in the air.

"Grunt once for yes. Twice for no. If you cooperate, I'll open the hatch for two minutes. I might even give you some water. Would you like that?"

A moment of silence, followed by a single grunt.

"Do you really think continuing to kill them, to torture them down in your dungeons, is going to work? It hasn't worked for you yet, and it never will."

The memory of Nora's scolding dried out her mouth.

"How many times will you say you're not like the rest of the Sparrow Coven in Dusarn, and yet walk in their footsteps anyway? Walk it, because you're too much of a coward to forge your own."

She had been right. Nothing Aisling had done to the kinner had convinced him to talk, but she didn't know a different path to get what she wanted, and Nora wasn't here to help her anymore. The reinstated high priestess of Wyldeden, who had lived as a rogue for seven-hundred years, who had pretended to serve her brother in Pirevia, had not been able to glean any information from the Morvish prisoner. What other hope did she have?

Nodding to Clayton, who rested a hand on his dagger, Aisling drew back the bolt on the hatch and pulled it open, letting it bang on the hard stone floor. The witch inside immediately began thrashing, screaming madly against the muzzle over her mouth. The pit was cramped and putrid from her waste, the stone walls marred with bloodied scratches. Not from the new prisoner, whose wrists and ankles were shackled to the ground, but from its previous occupant.

"Please! I don't know anything! I don't know!"

After a while, he'd become too weak to fight, and so she had stopped having Clayton put the restraints on him. But as hunger and thirst drove him mad, his lack of energy hadn't stopped him from trying to claw his way through the stone.

Aisling would have to remember that the Morvish witch would not survive what she had put the kinner through. Not that it had worked, anyway.

The witch glared up at her hatefully, yanking at her chains. The scales over most of her body may have protected her skin from the cuffs' chafing, but the silver coating them kept her from breaking the links.

Carefully, Aisling lowered herself into the pit. Breathing through her mouth, tasting the peppermint on the back of her throat, she unbuckled the muzzle over the witch's mouth. The contraption fell away and Aadya bared her teeth, lips too dry and chapped to spit.

"Swear a vow to work with me, and I will let you out." Aisling tried.

"You promised me water." Her voice croaked painfully.

"I did. I'll offer you even more if you take a vow."

"I will never serve Death," Aadya spat. "Why you do is bewildering. Why you allow yourself to be relegated to a gift for a deity who relishes in taking Mother's gift. My master is a giver. Swear a vow to *me* and I will make sure you are rewarded beyond your wildest dreams."

Fanatical. Seductive. Aisling kept her voice level as she asked, "This master you speak of. It is Chaos, the fourth High Spirit, correct?"

Aadya's eyes widened, the cracks in her lips beginning to bleed as a wild grin broke her face. "You've heard of him."

"He is more well-known here in the city than in the wild, though many think he is mere fantasy. He is painted the villain in our stories."

That made her scowl. "He is no villain. He is the victim of Death's deceit! He is Mother's true love, and he will free her from that leech!"

"Does he not still delight in watching his beasts devour us?"

"Aid his cause and he will make sure you are one of the predators, not the prey."

"His cause. To reunite himself with Mother and dispose of Death?"

Aadya's eyes flashed, but whether Aisling was correct or not she would not say. Not until she got her vow. Or until Aisling convinced her to speak anyway.

Climbing out of the pit, Aisling paused, Nora's scolding ricocheting in her brain.

"Your Morvish gift is prophecy, yes?" Aisling asked, wandering to the cabinet of tools and looking them over. Her stomach turned as the lamplight gleamed off the steel.

"I can answer any question you ask about the future with nothing but free hands and a quill. Is that what you want? I will give you any prophecy you like if you join us."

Us.

"You and your coven of rogues?" Aisling asked, a snort of derision in her voice. "I have an entire city and the most powerful coven of all history behind me. What makes you think you and your band of miscreants appeals to me?"

Aadya only snorted. "You know nothing of power."

Aisling left the tools untouched and returned to the hatch, giving Aadya a condescending smile.

"I know a great deal. I know your army of beasts will arrive from the south. I know Chaos will make a move on the Womb. And I know how he will be defeated."

The surprise in Aadya's face could not be hidden.

"You are not the only Morvish witch to leave the sanctity of Qiri, and I can assure you that the one I keep company with has greater powers of prophecy than you could ever hope to achieve. So," Aisling continued. "Tell me something I don't know and, like I promised, I will get you some water. Agree to take a vow, and I can make you very comfortable. Because I can assure you, Chaos will not win this war."

She could do no such thing, but the bluff was working. Aadya lowered her head and stared at the wall of her cell, fists clenching.

"The twenty witches I took with me to cull anyone that might stand against Chaos are a mere drop in the pool of our forces. Our coven is thrice the size of the one you think supports you, though we both know that it is a lie you can't keep a straight face telling."

The blow cut deeper than she expected it to, but Aisling remained impassive as Aadya raised her head again, arrogant grin splitting her face in two.

"I can see the lies in your eyes, so I know you tell the truth about what the Morvish witch in your pocket has told you. But I also hear the lies beneath that truth. The Morvish vagueness around these prophecies. You may know about the beasts in the south, but you do not know how to stop them or you would have already taken care of it. You may know that Chaos moves toward the Womb and that he can be defeated, but there is not a thing in the world that cannot be defeated, including the gods themselves. Just because he can be, does not mean he will be."

Finally, Aadya stopped talking. So many words, and yet she said so little. It was not a complete waste, at least. She had confirmed what Aisling already knew, and now she knew the size of the force against them. That Aadya was not Chaos's sole agent.

Standing, Aisling kept her promise.

Collecting a jug of water from the top of a tray, she returned to look down at the beast-witch hybrid. Then she dumped the jug's contents over her head. The water soaked Aadya, mixing with the filth beneath her.

Aadya's initial gasp turned into a scream of frustration.

"Liar!"

"Am not."

"How can I drink this?!"

"I never said I'd let you drink it. But if you're desperate, there's nothing stopping you. The chains have enough slack."

Ignoring the screams of frustration that quickly became screams of terror, Aisling closed the hatch and locked it. Then she blew out the lamp.

In the hall outside the room, Aisling leaned against the wall. Clayton watched her warily, glancing between the princess and her prisoner.

"She will not survive much longer without a drink."

"I know. I have to meet with the Southern Mountain Clan this afternoon, then with the rebel representative. She'll last till morning."

Clayton grimaced but nodded. "As you say."

The expression was reminiscent of her Second, and Aisling had to push away the ghost of Nora's voice in her ear.

"Aadya might not be ready to talk, but the rest might. Can you handle that for me?"

"Sar Vin . . ."

"I'll find Gogh to guard me during the meetings."

Shadows falling over his eyes, Clayton nodded once again.

CHAPTER SEVENTEEN

AISLING

After five minutes of looking at Sar Vin's smug face, Aisling was picturing him in her dungeon, too. But she kept her face empty and her words vapid as she asked how they had fared over winter, if the supplies Hyrsch had traded them were sufficient, and thanked their favored Spirits that most of their clan had survived the freezing months.

"It was a surprise," Sar Vin continued, "to receive another summons to Hyrsch so soon. Even more of a surprise to hear Imsa was being invoked. When will you tell us what this is all about, Princess?"

"I'm going to be upfront with you," Aisling said, smiling at Edwina as she brought her another glass of wine. Was it early in the day to be drinking so much? Yes. But the day had already been long and her head was still beneath the palace with Clayton. With the kinner. "I would like to move a portion of my armies into your territory."

The request clearly took Sar Vin off guard. He sat back and raised his thick eyebrows, scratching the hair on his chin.

The arrangement with the Southern Mountain Clan was a complicated one. Technically, the Sparrow's claim encompassed the entirety of the mountain range known as the spine, as well as the branch across Vertlyn. Everything in Nir, aside from Anfar and Qiri, was theirs. However, it had always been in the Sparrow Coven's interests to let the elemental witch clans and nomadic covens roam freely. Let them stake out little territories on Coven land as long as when the Sparrows called on them, they came, and when requested, they yielded.

"Of all the things I thought you would ask of us, I did not expect that," Sar Vin narrowed his eyes. "For what purpose do you require passage?"

"I have information that a large gathering of beasts plan to attack Oford from the frozen wastes. Your clan is between them and us. Consider this a warning to prepare your own warriors as well, or move on from the area."

A frown slowly deepened his brow, wary glances passing between the others. "A gathering of beasts? Unusual for them to be so organized. And if this is true, why have the Sparrows allowed it to form? You do control Bernt, do you not?"

The jab should have bothered her, except she had been asking herself the same question. Raising her chin and sipping her wine, she moved on with the point.

"It is a complicated story. Do you know much about the First War?"

The mountain clan's keeper waved a dismissive hand. "Yes, of course."

She may imagine Sar Vin in her dungeon, but his keeper belonged spiked on the city gates. The weedy little male looked like he shouldn't have survived the winter, sitting beside the hulking mass of Sar Vin and the other mountain clan witches along the feather-shaped table. Unlike Eavha, they had taken their proper seats at the other end, by the door.

"While there has been no official report of a gathering in Bernt, a Morvish witch has prophesized the return of the King of Beasts. I can assure you that they are coming, and we will all be better off if we ally ourselves now."

She had expected more surprise from him. More questions. More attention. But he merely leaned back and snapped his fingers at Edwina. Aisling clenched her teeth but dipped her head at the maiden, who quietly poured him another glass of wine.

"Or," he said, pausing to take a sip. "This is all nonsense, and you wish to trick us into helping you overthrow the king and queen."

Aisling narrowed her eyes. "I have no interest in being queen."

"So you say."

"The Morvish—"

"Yes, where is this Morvish witch you say has prophesized the return of Chaos incarnate, the King of Beasts?"

The gleam in his eye told Aisling he knew exactly what had happened to Davina. Knew she was dead, and that there was only Aisling's word that these prophecies had happened at all, let alone attest to their accuracy. How he had learned such things was even clearer.

"You have already spoken with the king."

"You are a very compelling female, princess. But without any evidence—"

"Even if Davina was alive"—Aisling's voice went cold as she leveled a glare at Sar Vin, dropping her mask entirely—"you would not believe her. Not if the king has gotten in your ear."

"The Morvish witch you refer to was a known liar."

"Not about this."

"The king was very persuasive."

The shift in Aisling's posture, her attitude, had no effect on Sar Vin. As if he knew she was a liar too.

"I see. What did he promise you in exchange for opposing me?"

A knowing smile. "Land rights."

Aisling blinked. She knew her father did not believe her, did not want her wasting resources on a war he did not think was coming, but . . .

"He promised you the mountains surrounding the pass?"

"He promised us the entire southern spine, as well as the wastes."

Stone. She was stone.

Swallowing her anger, she made her face passive again. The façade was ruined, but there was no need to give away just how deeply this had wounded her.

"I see that I will need to be more convincing. Let us reconvene another time."

"Let's," Sar Vin agreed. He stood, his delegation readying to leave the council rooms as well.

Aisling stayed in her seat, running her finger over the lip of her glass.

"Sar Vin," she called out, just as he reached the door. "Should we not reach an agreement before you leave, know that when your people are being massacred, I will hold no grudge should you come running back to me for aid."

He sneered, but his footsteps were heavier as he stormed from the room.

"Well, that went splendidly," Davina sighed from the windowsill.

Aisling drained her glass.

"If we can't get the Southern Mountain Clan to unite with us, we should reach out again to the sea witches along the coast," Davina continued. "If the king is promising the mountaineers land, riling the rivalry between them and the sea witches could work to our advantage."

Aisling nodded, stretching her neck before holding out her glass for Edwina to refill.

"You're angry at your father," Davina pressed as Aisling still didn't speak.

"But not surprised," she answered, though that wasn't entirely true. The wastes west of the spine were uninhabitable, the southern mountains inhospitable, but even so. "Nora's plan in the north may be our best chance of allies after all."

"I still think it's optimistic to think any allies will come from Pirevia." Davina snorted, but her tone softened as Aisling continued to sit quietly. "Has there been any news?"

"Nothing." It was still early, she supposed, though to have received word that Nora and Owen were at least safe would be a load off her shoulders. "But they will come through. Nora will not fail. And when they are ready, there is a shipment of soldiers waiting off the coast to help them take the city."

"Has there been any word from them, either?" Davina asked, a note of concern in her voice.

Shaking her head, Aisling drank again. There hadn't been news from the north at all, but she wasn't too concerned. Unnecessary messages were a risk. When her knight made her move, when her pawns moved into position, she would hear about it.

CHAPTER EIGHTEEN

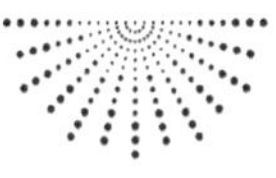

AISLING

Climbing the stairwell back to her rooms, Aisling tried to organize all the new pieces on her mental chessboard. There was nothing she could do about the situation in Pirevia, so she put it to the back of her mind. She had anticipated Aadya giving her problems, but she would have to think on whether it was worth trying to maintain a relationship with the Southern Mountain Clan or find a way to rid herself of them entirely. Then there was her father, whose commitment to undermining her had reached new levels. The question was, why? Not wanting to waste money on a war he didn't believe in was one thing, but to give away half the spine was absurd.

Later. She would figure it all out later. For now, she had yet another costume to adorn.

At the top of the stairs, Aisling came to a sudden halt.

The heir apparent of Wyldeden was picking the lock to her prayer room, about to ease open the wooden door.

"What are you doing?"

Eavha squeaked and spun around, back against the wall and hand searching for something at her side that wasn't there. Her mouth opened, as if she was trying to speak but nothing came out. The rules of Imsa wouldn't let her lie.

Aisling looked between Eavha and her prayer room, raising a single brow.

"If you wanted a tour, you only needed to ask."

"I . . . I'm sorry," Eavha dipped her chin. The first show of respect the heir had shown her. "A tour would be lovely."

"I'll have Edwina schedule something. Perhaps tomorrow."

A blush crept across Eavha's cheeks as she glanced between Aisling and the prayer room, easing the door closed again. "I'm sorry."

The two females stood in the hall, silence thick between them. Had it really been just that morning they'd attended the ballet? Had sat in the dark, Eavha's heart beating too loud, the quick rise and fall of her chest beneath her revealing dress thoroughly distracting? With everything Aisling had to worry about, she didn't want to be paranoid about Eavha too.

As if she could read her mind, Eavha took a sharp breath and added, "I was snooping for information about what you really want from us this Imsa."

"Ah." Aisling nodded. "Well, I did plan to discuss that with you in the morning before tomorrow's grand meeting, but I can make time this afternoon if you cannot wait."

Eavha nodded, darting a glance to the door of Aisling's suite. "Are you retiring for the day?"

"I still have another meeting."

"Oh? With who?" Eavha seemed almost panicked as she asked. "Your king?"

"No. My father and I do not need to speak." Aisling wasn't sure if she could do so without losing her temper at him anyway. "The meeting is not for Imsa, actually. It's a Hyrschan matter, but I must change."

Her tone carried a clear dismissal, yet the priestess lingered.

"Have you had a chance to speak with . . . Aadya, yet?" The waver in her voice gave away her fear.

Aisling gave a terse nod. "She is yet to be as forthcoming as I hoped, but I have learned a little. We can discuss it later as well, if you like."

Eavha nodded. "She can't get out though, can she?"

Aisling frowned, tilting her head. "I'm not sure if I should be offended that you think my security so lacking."

"No!" Eavha startled. "I just . . . there's history, between she and I. She killed my entire family. My brother twice."

The message Kaelean Caesarea had sent regarding the rogue coven had outlined what had occurred the past fifty years, and what she had done to try and convince the rogue coven to talk. Aisling knew Eavha had been the one to capture the beast-hybrid now rotting in her dungeon. Looking at her, listening to the crack in her voice, it was hard to picture.

"She will not escape. And she is getting what she deserves."

She had meant it as a comfort, but Eavha stilled. Her eyes narrowed, shoulders stiffening.

"We might have to agree to disagree on what suffering people do and do not deserve. Good luck with your meeting," she snapped, then shoved past Aisling to stalk down the stairs on eerily silent feet.

Swallowing the lump that had formed in her throat, Aisling turned to her suite and went inside. Everything was just as she left it. If Eavha had been in here, there was no physical sign.

Taking a deep sniff of the air, there were strange scents lingering. She couldn't find it in herself to care that Eavha had been in them; there was nothing she had to hide in her rooms anyway.

Actually, that wasn't true. She did care. Aisling's heart fluttered as she pictured the priestess's dainty feet hurrying around the room looking for secrets. The way her hair would swing, her strange skirt billowing behind her.

"Pull yourself together," Aisling snapped at herself, pinching her own earlobe as she stalked to the dressing room to find her next costume.

She decided to meet the rebel representative in the parlor rather than the stiff council room or the grand throne room, hoping to make them feel at ease. She'd done her best to humanize her appearance, too, leaving her hair in a loose half up-do, her face bare of cosmetics, and wearing a simple but still elegant dress of lavender and rose silk. The dress still covered her throat and wrists, her hands concealed in lace gloves. A heavy pendant hung around her neck and a small tiara balanced on her head; approachable, but still royal. A false softness with an air of authority.

She stood waiting in the sunlit cream-and-gold parlor, the hearth glowing lowly, a platter of tea and nibbles on the table between an assortment of sofas and chairs. Clayton was with her again, wearing noticeably cleaner armor than he had been earlier. Edwina waited nearby as well, but Nora's comforting presence was a poignant absence.

Thoughts of her Second had her stomach clenching.

A knock on the door scattered them and Aisling clasped her sweating hands in front of her skirts as a guard stepped through the opening door.

"Mister Radley Lightman and his company, Mister Philip Turner."

The two males, or one male and one man, entered the room. Neither bowed for her, their faces laden with barely concealed hostility.

Radley was the representative for the demi-kin rebels; Aisling could tell because he had the kinner symbol stitched onto his vest like a crest or badge of honor. Though he was broad shouldered and ruggedly handsome, there was still a leanness about him. As if even after five years free of servitude he still hadn't quite recovered the body of the male he ought to be. There was soot under his nails and in his cuticles, a bleakness to his face that made him look older than she thought he really was. He carried no weapons, but his piercing navy eyes seemed poisonous as they stared her down. The brassiness of his hair did nothing to soften him.

Aisling didn't curtsey for him but held a hand toward a sofa long enough for Radley and Philip—a bulky human man with mousy hair tied in a ponytail at the base of his neck and a silver seven-pointed star pinned to his doublet—to sit.

"Princess Aisling Aurnia, her guard Sir Clayton Grint, and her handmaiden, Edwina," the guard from the door introduced them before sealing the room.

Edwina came forward to pour three cups of tea, her hands trembling slightly.

Aisling waited for Radley to move first. After watching the handmaiden closely, he finally took a seat, Philip beside him. Aisling went to the chair she had chosen earlier, two daggers hidden in the upholstery.

"Thank you for meeting me," Aisling started, holding back a polite smile. "Is there anything we can do to make you more comfortable?"

"You can tell me where the kinner is."

Radley's tone cut through the room like a clap of thunder, rage billowing beneath his hard gaze. Aisling paused as she went to collect her teacup.

"He is no longer here," she answered truthfully.

"We know that. And we heard about the attempted abduction of him in Belden, but there has been no word of him since."

Again, she wondered how he knew these things. "That was not me."

"Maybe. But I'd bet you know where he is."

"Is that what it will take for your resistance to cease?" she tried to get the topic back on track. "Information about your ancestors?"

Aisling brought her cup to her lips and took a sip, demonstrating that it was not poisoned. Nobody else seemed interested in refreshments.

"It would be a start. Along with your resignation from Hyrsch and the removal of all witch interference in this city."

Aisling raised her eyebrows. "There would be anarchy."

"Because we are such savages that we cannot rule ourselves?"

"Oford belongs to the Sparrow Coven."

"The Sparrow Coven stole it from the Kinner. The land is ours."

Aisling blinked, placing her tea back on the table. As true as it was, she had never heard the rhetoric spoken by the demi-kin before.

"Do you think I have the kind of power it would take to return it to you?" Aisling tilted her head. "This city is the lowest prize among the Coven. Believe me, my position here is as much a punishment for me as it is a burden to you. If I leave, the Sparrow Coven will simply lay siege. Does your little guerrilla force have the capacity to defend this city from an army of Lover-blessed witches?"

Radley's shoulders dropped for a moment before he caught his composure, tone hardening even further.

"Where is the kinner?" he repeated.

"I will tell you everything you want to know about the kinner, and everything I know about the rest of his kind, and more. If . . ." Aisling reached her tea again. "And only if, you and the rest of the rebels take an oath of forfeit and join my army."

"That will never happen," Philip dismissed.

Aisling ignored the man and locked eyes with Radley, waiting for his response. She could see that he would deny her, so she cradled her teacup in her hands and leaned forward, letting her sheet of gray hair fall around her face.

"Let me make something very clear," she said lowly. It was a gamble, but time was running out. "This petty squabble over cities and territories will mean nothing if we cannot find a way to work together. I helped your people the best way that I could. Help me, and when everything is over, the city is yours."

"You just said you don't have that power."

"Not now. But by winter, there most likely won't be a Sparrow Coven. If we don't play our pieces right, by winter there won't be a Hyrsch, or an Oford, or a Nir, either."

Radley's eyes narrowed.

"Lies. She's Sparrow. She'll say anything," Philip spat.

Red burst in Aisling's vision as she whipped her head to glare at Philip. "Do not presume to tell me what I would and wouldn't do. Do not think you know what I will sacrifice. I have given more than you know, and I will give everything before this is over."

With her attention elsewhere, Radley lunged forward and grabbed a fistful of Aisling's hair. Pulling her head back, he slipped a tiny blade from somewhere in his vest, the point of it pinching the flesh over her jugular. Undiluted rage battered her from Radley's twisted face.

Clayton was conspicuously silent as Aisling's teacup slid from her hands to shatter on the rug beneath them. From the corner of her eye, she saw Edwina holding onto his sword hand, a blade of her own at Clayton's throat.

"Where. Is. The. Kinner, witch," Radley hissed in her face. "Where is my brother?"

Aisling stopped breathing, hardly daring to answer.

"Free."

His grip tightened in her hair as he pressed in closer, blood welling beneath the blade.

"I will not ask you again."

"Rad," Philip warned. "She can't tell us if she's dead."

"Free," a soft, feminine voice called from the door.

Radley glanced over.

At his distraction, Aisling hooked a foot around Radley's ankle and shoved him back, pulled her daggers from the upholstery and lunged for the demi-kin's throat. Philip tackled her around the waist and sent them both crashing into the shattered tea set on the table, but as they landed Aisling twisted and slashed.

Screaming, Philip rolled away, holding the wound on his face closed as blood gushed down his front.

Eavha hissed from the doorway. She must have followed Aisling, slipping past the guards outside somehow. Running, Eavha skidded to her knees and took the man's face in her hands. Magic pulsed through the room, filling it with skin-crawling energy. Even Aisling stopped and stared in wonder as the bleeding stopped, the skin pulling closed.

Movement to her left.

Aisling crouched into a defensive stance as Radley got to his feet and snarled at her.

"Sit down!" Eavha snapped at them, her words thick with the Anfar accent. "Now! Cinn is free. I know this."

"What are you talking about? Who are you?" Radley snapped without taking his gaze off Aisling.

"She speaks little Nirnish," Aisling explained. "She is Eavha Nemuse, Heir of Wyldeden. She traveled with the kinner this past spring and received word he is safe with her people in Wyldeden less than a week ago."

"You healed my face," Philip said in awe, touching his now scarred cheek. "She healed my face."

"Stop the games," Eavha demanded, looking to both of them as she pointed at the seats. "I hear you say Nir is in danger. Who told you this?"

"Alright," Aisling said, but refused to move until Radley did. He seemed inclined to do the same. "A Morvish witch—not Aadya—had a prophecy many years ago. I will explain everything, I promise, because I cannot do this alone. We must be united. All of us."

Radley moved, and Aisling was too busy blocking his knife hand to notice the second blade that shot up from a device around his knee until it sunk into her gut.

Gasping, black spots danced across her vision.

"That is for what you did to Ryson," Radley spat.

Then the blade was gone, her body collapsing to the carpet as Radley, Philip and Edwina fled the parlor. She could hear guards shouting in the halls, but she couldn't focus on them. Couldn't focus on anything beyond the pain, the blood spilling from the wound in her gut, staining her dress.

"Lie down, lie down," Eavha said in Terranian as she scrambled across the floor. Lowering Aisling onto her back, Eavha ripped open the fabric of her dress to expose the wound. "You! Guard! Apply pressure!"

Clayton was instantly beside them, face crumpled in guilt and panic as he pushed down on her stomach. Aisling screamed.

"I'm sorry, Your Highness. I'm so sorry."

Eavha muttered a prayer, dipped her fingers in Aisling's blood and drew spellmarks on her face. Then she pushed Clayton's hands aside and laid her own softer ones on the wound. The itching that spread through her body had Aisling gritting her teeth to bear it without screaming again.

"No . . . scars . . ." she managed to pant between breaths.

Her tattoos. As the pain eased, it was all she could think about. Her tattoos could not be marred.

"I'm doing my best," Eavha panted.

"No scars!"

Eavha's eyes widened, but she nodded and closed her eyes as a sickening wave of magic beat through the air. Aisling thought she might faint. She hadn't felt magic like this since Davina had tattooed her in the first place.

When it was over, Aisling's hand fluttered to the bare skin on her abdomen and felt nothing but smoothness. Eavha leaned against the couch, eyes closed as her nose began bleeding.

"Clayton," Aisling wheezed. "Get her some help."

Her guard was halfway out the door calling for a medic before she finished talking. Dragging herself upright, Aisling felt the blood rush from her face as she noticed how limp Eavha had gone.

"Eavha?" Her voice cracked as she reached for Eavha's paling face.

Nothing.

"Eavha, wake up."

"Davina, wake up."

Aisling begged, shaking the witch's limp body. The last of her tattoos were complete, her body burning with the weight of the magic in her skin, but Aisling couldn't see past the blood leaking down Davina's face. Her nose, her mouth, her eyes and ears. Everything was bleeding. "Stay with me. You promised I wouldn't be alone. You promised."

"I'm here."

Aisling raised her head, searching Davina's face for signs of life, but she was just a corpse now. Her soul was gone. She could feel it.

"I'm here."

Shaking, Aisling turned to look behind her. A misty aura stood by the window and Aisling finally understood what the mirages she'd been seeing these past months were. How her Lover-blessing had finally manifested. Celeste, Spirit of the sky, and the Lover had combined their blessings to show her the souls lingering in the darkest realm.

"You said you'd stay with me," she sobbed.

Davina's chin wobbled as she smiled. "Always."

CHAPTER NINETEEN

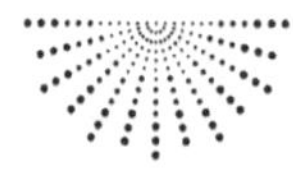

DEARMEAD

Eavha had distracted Aisling in the hall while Dearmead snuck back out the princess's window, scaling the outside of the palace once more. He'd listened first, realizing that Aisling believed Eavha on her own posed no threat, but if she found him here as well her mood might change. Taking a risk with the guards outside was the safer option.

By the time he'd reached their own rooms, gotten to the staircase leading up Aisling's tower, caught Eavha's scent, and followed it through the crowded halls, he knew he was too late to stop her from doing something stupid. He spied her mere seconds before she slipped silently into the parlor, invisible to the guards too deep in their own conversation to notice.

Dearmead simply sighed.

Unable to follow, he lingered around the corner and tried not to look suspicious. When a few of the mountain clan witches eyed him warily and started whispering, he moved on, pretending he had a purpose among this crowd of strange, foreign people. He barely understood anything they said, their curious and judging glances disconcerting.

It was enough to make him miss home.

Then the screaming and shouting started. Quick and heavy

footsteps pounded through the halls, and he knew—just *knew*— Eavha was involved.

When Eaon had asked him to take care of his sister, he hadn't imagined it being such a demanding job.

Following the palace guards, Dearmead picked up on the gossip already running through the halls.

Rebels.

Princess is wounded.

Anfar witch healed her.

Proper panic quickened his pace as he passed the demi-kin guards, following the clamor across the grand foyer toward the infirmary.

"Idiots! Move!" a female voice screeched, echoing down the halls. It wasn't Eavha. "Get out of the way!"

Shoving through the crowded doorway, Dearmead skidded to a halt as he watched Clayton lay Eavha's unconscious form down on a cot. Human healers rushed around, but none of them seemed to know what to do.

"What happened?" Dearmead demanded.

The princess either didn't hear him or outright ignored him, shoving Clayton away from Eavha as soon as he'd placed her down. Baring her teeth, Aisling snarled in the most feral display of rage Dearmead had ever seen. Which, considering the family he grew up in, was a considerable feat.

"Get out, you useless rogues! All of you! Just get out!" Aisling screamed at them as she crouched over Eavha, fists clenched.

He might have been stupid about a lot of things, but sensing danger was not one of them. This was not a fight he would win. Not even a fight worth having. He knew what a dead body looked like, smelled like, and Eavha was not even close. Her chest rose and fell, even if there was blood drying in rivulets from her ears and nose. She had no doubt pushed her magic again. Some rest and she would be alright. Plus, Imsa was still in effect—nobody could harm her.

Knowing Eavha would be safe with the princess didn't stop him from clenching his jaw as he backed out of the infirmary. In the hall, he didn't protest as Herbe and one of the palace guards opted to stand by the door in case there was trouble. Clayton opened his mouth to argue, then touched the small cut on his neck. The way his shoulders dropped, the pull at the edges of his mouth . . . Dearmead knew what shame looked like too.

"Come," he said, nodding to another door.

Clayton stared at him, brow puckering, but followed Dearmead into a second infirmary. He was no healer but he knew basic first aid from training with the guardians. Rifling through the contents of the drawers by the wall, he found some cleaning alcohol and a bandage.

"This is unnecessary. The cut is minor and I am demi-kin," Clayton explained, voice gruffer than Dearmead had expected from the shorter, usually silent male. "It will heal within the hour."

"Ah." Dearmead sighed, putting the bandages away.

Clayton didn't move to leave, staring at the door. His breath was growing shallower, faster, sweat beading on his creased forehead.

"I don't know what we would have done had Lady Eavha not been here."

Dearmead closed his eyes against the swell of terror clawing at his chest. Those moments—carrying Eaon into the clinic, Eavha fighting with everything she had to save his life and failing—haunted his every sleeping moment. What would he have done if Eavha had been an iota less powerful? Less willing to destroy herself to bring him back? He couldn't bear imagining life without ever again seeing the wrinkle of Eaon's nose when he was trying not to laugh. The way he chewed his lip when he read. The molten gold of his eyes when they were alone.

"What happened?" Dearmead asked again.

This time, he got an answer.

"As soon as the rebel representative moved, I moved. But Edwina . . . I did not see it coming. I did not know she even knew how to hold a dagger. I've known her so long. We were close. But I knew she would kill me if I so much a flinched. I could taste her hatred in the air."

He, too, had underestimated the servant girl. A mistake that could have cost Eavha her life.

"You could not have seen Edwina's betrayal coming," Dearmead tried to comfort the guard, his Nirnish uncertain on his tongue.

"I should have. It's my job. I . . . I failed." Bewildered, Clayton looked down at his hands. "How . . . I should have . . ."

Dearmead grimaced.

"You will think about this. You will obsess. Look at every detail leading up to it for what you could have done. Believe me, I know. People will tell you it is a waste of time, but . . . you won't be so easily tricked again."

What Clayton was feeling was too similar to the failure Dearmead had ruminated on for weeks.

A wet thud. Dearmead spun. The floor collapsed from under him as he saw the spear sticking out of Eaon's chest. Not again. Eaon was so afraid. In pain. There was nothing Dearmead could do. He should have guarded the door.

"I love you."

Eaon had never said it back. Dearmead didn't know if he could bear it if he did. He didn't know anything anymore.

The demi-kin's face had darkened, his brow low over his eyes. "You're right. I will not be fooled again."

Standing, hand on the hilt of his sword, Clayton stormed toward the door. As he reached the threshold, he turned back to give Dearmead an evaluating glance.

"I'm going to hunt them down. Are you a good tracker? I could use assistance."

Dearmead raised his brow. He was a good tracker. Good enough to have been offered the choice by his teachers between guardian and scout.

Eaon had asked him to take care of his little sister, and now she was lying unconscious in the medical wing of the enemy's city.

He could not sit idle.

"Do you have something of hers I could scent?"

Clayton raised his chin and nodded. Dearmead got up, checking the straps keeping his spear across his back and tapping each stone knife strapped to his chest, his thighs.

"Then let's go hunting."

As Dearmead explored the servant woman's quarters, saturating his senses with her apricot scent, he contemplated exactly what he was going to do if he and Clayton did find her and the other rebels. In all his years, he had not outgrown his distaste for violence, nor his desire to avoid conflict. Just like Eaon had never outgrown his lack of self-worth and compulsive tendency to put his own needs last.

What would Eaon do, if he were here? The old Eaon, not the new one that probably wouldn't have been able to control his magic, obliterating the entire city.

That magic scared him in a way Dearmead had never been scared before, and the shame of that fear, of what it had made him do, forced him to steel his nerves.

"I should be able to pick up her scent when we cross it," Dearmead said, putting down a hairbrush on the vanity.

"Good. I know a place to start to start looking." Clayton nodded, leading the way out of the servant quarters.

Hyrsch was a different city to Pirevia, from what he'd seen. There was no reek of rotting bodies, no sticky blood-soaked road. Clayton had not bothered trying to disguise himself, so Dearmead didn't either, following silently on bare feet, sweating under the thick brown leather.

The human artisans selling goods from stalls and storefronts looked at him strangely as he followed Clayton down the busy roads, but they did not move to attack. A few stepped back, throwing a protective arm out around their loved ones as the males passed. Even fewer leveled glares of utter hatred, fists curling in promised violence. Not directed at Dearmead, but at the demi-kin guard who moved like a bull beside him.

Clayton had training, and he glared right back at the humans without a shred of fear, but the old instinct to interfere with the promise of violence swelled up anyway. Ironic, considering what he was following Clayton to do.

"Here." The guard stopped outside a shop and looked up to the windows on the second story. "When she isn't staying at the palace, this is where she lives."

"I doubt she will be here."

"So do I. But it is a starting place."

Dearmead nodded, once again following the guard down the alley beside the shop. A rickety staircase had been built along the side, leading to a door far above them. Dearmead crouched by the base, sniffing deeply, trying to push aside the smell of stale wine and rotting fruit that littered the alley. The wood of the stairs was worn, small dents from shoe heels dotting the softest parts. He could tell which ones were older and which were new, and he didn't think she had walked the steps recently.

Nobody had trained him to notice these kinds of things, but he had always felt in tune with the details of Terra's domain. If the stairs had been made of stone or steel he would not have been able to tell so much, but made of wood, their secrets were open to him. It was the kind of intuitiveness born of blessing and would have made him a good scout if he'd been allowed to choose his own path.

Silently, Dearmead crept up the staircase to the landing. The lock on the door was rusted and rattled loosely when he tested the knob.

"I should be able to use an unlocking spell—" he started, but flinched back as Clayton rammed his meaty shoulder into the door and sent it flying open. "But that is also effective."

He wasn't sure what he thought he would find in the royal servant's personal apartment, but the mess was an honest surprise. There was a small moth-eaten couch in front of an empty fireplace, threadbare blankets and pillows strewn over it. A similar pile covered the floor between the couch and the hearth, along with varying types and sizes of boots, belts, scabbards and cloaks. A sink and a coal-burning oven sat beneath the only window, a small table with three chairs nearby, while through the only door in the apartment sat a tub, plumbed the way the tub in Kaelean's Pirevian apartment had been, but only large enough to stand in. In the corner was a refuse bucket, identifiable by the smell that no amount of cleaning could truly remove.

Clayton stood in as much surprise as Dearmead.

"She is paid well. I don't understand why she would live like this."

On the table was a pile of papers. While Dearmead may have learned to speak enough Nirnish to pass in the human cities, he had not bothered to learn to read it.

"Any clues?" he asked Clayton, who immediately began to rifle through it.

As he did, Dearmead went to the window and gazed out at the alley below. There were not many places he could think of that would be drearier to live.

Despite the mess, the place was clean. There were no crumbs left out for rats around the oven, nor any dust on the windowsill. What was there, however, were three little bundles of yarn. Only as large as his thumb, the yarn had been twisted and looped until it loosely resembled a body, with two arms and legs and an oversized head. Gently, Dearmead picked one up. The yarn felt musty and left a dark stain on his fingertips. From the smell, he would guess old soot.

"This is interesting," Clayton said, bringing over a scrap of parchment. When he saw what Dearmead was replacing on the window, he grimaced.

"I worried they might be hexed, but there is no magic attached to them," Dearmead explained. He had seen one of his sisters become vindictive enough against one of their cousins to hex them, using a doll to transfer physical pain to the victim.

"No. In the beforetimes, we would make what toys we could for the demi-kin children to play with. These were common."

"The servant has children?" Dearmead asked.

"No," Clayton said again. For the first time since Aisling's injury, Clayton seemed to doubt what they were doing. "She'd mentioned having two brothers, but . . . I checked her family history before choosing her for Aisling. There was no connection to . . ."

"People lie," Dearmead said flatly, taking the paper from Clayton. "What does it say?"

Pinching the bridge of his nose, Clayton let out a breath and refocused. "It's just scrambled letters and numbers, but I recognize the pattern. The demi-kin created a code during the beforetimes, and I think it's a variation. Meaning it's probably rebellion related. Give me a few minutes, I should be able to decode it."

Taking the slip back, Clayton sat down at the table and grabbed an almost-empty ink bottle and a quill.

Frowning, Dearmead looked around.

He had said he didn't think Edwina would return here, but . . . she had left the dolls. From what Clayton said, she had been prepared for the meeting to go awry. Had known she may likely have to flee today and thus would have made preparations.

She would have taken the dolls.

Returning to the door, Dearmead closed it and took up a vigil. Clayton looked up with a frown.

"What are you doing?"

"I think she will return."

"Edwina is not that stupid."

"She knows that we expect her not to be so stupid. She's betting on us assuming she will not return, and so this is exactly where she will come."

"I—" Clayton began to argue, but then turned back to the window, as if he too had made the connection.

Dearmead closed his eyes and let his mind focus on the sounds coming from outside the door. The moment someone stepped on that staircase, he would know.

It was dark before Dearmead opened his eyes, the creak of the timber frame outside alerting him to the arrival of two people, one heavier than the other, both trying and failing to move carefully.

Clayton had a hand on his sword, but Dearmead had not removed his spear from his back. Holding up two fingers to Clayton, who nodded sternly, Dearmead found his balance and readied himself.

The door creaked open. The male came in first.

In three seconds, Dearmead had pulled him into the room, thrown him on the floor and pinned him, letting his full weight rest on the male's back and arms.

"Eddy, run!" the male shouted, but Clayton was already chasing her down the stairs. "Get off me, you fucking oaf!"

Dearmead didn't know what an oaf was, so he just snarled in response. "I'm not the oaf who came back home after trying to kill the princess."

The male thrashed and fought beneath Dearmead, but it was too easy to keep him down. There was no satisfaction in proving his strength. Unlike his sisters and brothers, who had been painfully smug when dominating the training ring, Dearmead only used what was necessary to keep the male restrained.

Clayton dragged a thrashing, spitting Edwina back up the stairs and threw her roughly on the ground.

"Traitorous bitch!"

The male beneath Dearmead roared with rage and a pang of something feral almost had Dearmead letting him go. Too much about this was unsettling. Too much of this was reminding him of another brother and sister he knew too well, being treated cruelly for committing crimes that should not have been considered so.

"Clayton," Dearmead warned him. "That is unnecessary. What is your procedure for arrests?"

There was a bloodthirstiness wafting from the demi-kin guard, a hatred unfettered. Perhaps Dearmead had made a mistake coming with Clayton. Or perhaps he hadn't. Perhaps it was good he was here to keep the male in line.

Through gritted teeth, Clayton said to the both of them, "On behalf of the Royal Guard, I hereby place you both under arrest for conspiring and attempting to kill the princess of Hyrsch."

"Attempting? Meaning the bitch didn't die?" the male beneath Dearmead hissed. Dearmead noted the slightly breathless quality to his words and eased off slightly.

"You'd better shut your mouth before I remove the need to take you to prison at all," Clayton threatened.

"Enough," Dearmead warned him, but the male beneath him was thrashing again, trying to turn enough to look at the guard.

"Do it. I dare you."

"Radley, stop it," Edwina said softly. "We give them nothing. For Ryson."

The words deflated Radley so thoroughly Dearmead nearly lost his balance.

Letting his forehead bang against the floor, Radley surrendered. "For Ryson."

CHAPTER TWENTY

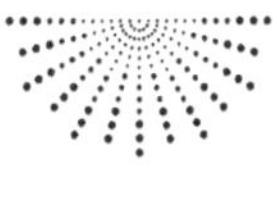

EAVHA

Eavha could count on one hand how many times she had passed out from using magic. Peeling her heavy eyelids open, she flinched back at Aisling's stern face hovering over her. Those silver eyes were rimmed red, her narrow brows pinched tightly. The princess loosed a shuddering breath and stepped back to give Eavha space.

There didn't seem to be anyone else in the room; a healer's clinic, she realized, as the smell of cleaning alcohols and burnt herbs tickled the back of her nose. It was simple compared to the clinic in Wyldeden, perhaps only large enough to manage three or four patients at a time, but it would be enough for the palace, she supposed. By the bed was a bowl of pink water and a cloth stained with blood. Her blood. Had the princess cleaned her face?

Fatigue made her bones ache as Eavha tried to sit up.

"What do you need? Water? Pain relief?" Aisling asked, darting off the bedside stool so fast it tipped over. She still wore her blood-soaked gown, the middle torn open to reveal the perfect flesh beneath. Perfect, bar the stark black spellmarks intricately tattooed all over her stomach. Eavha recoiled, sucking in a sharp breath as she realized some of them were not just spellmarks—there were witchmarks etched on the princess, too.

Returning with peppermint leaves and a glass of water, Aisling helped Eavha sit up, either oblivious or pointedly ignoring her shock.

"I've been trying to think of how to apologize for making you use so much magic without saying it wasn't necessary, but I can't. It was necessary and I am grateful, but I am sorry it hurt you. I'm sorry I wasn't quick enough to avoid needing your assistance."

A muscle in Aisling's jaw twitched as Eavha drank greedily from the glass.

"The peppermint won't help. Is there any ginseng?"

"Should be." She went back to an apothecary table against the far wall and rummaged through the drawers in search of ginseng instead, clearly unfamiliar with her own infirmary.

"It shouldn't have been so difficult," Eavha explained, laying back down. "I wasn't carrying my Blessing Charm."

Aisling returned with a long piece of root and helped Eavha sit up again. She would have preferred it ground, or boiled in a tea, but she would take what she could get. Only once Eavha was chewing the root, breathing slowly through the tightness of her ribs, did Aisling seem to calm.

"You use a Blessing Charm?"

"Yes. I used to think . . . everyone believed I was the most powerful healer in Wyldeden, but it turned out not to be true. I am a powerful charmer, which is something I am learning not to be ashamed of."

It was one of those moments Aisling probably thought Eavha was oversharing, but she felt the need to even the field after Aisling's tattoos had been exposed. Her gaze slipped down to Aisling's bare stomach again, somehow both hard and soft at the same time.

Instead of explaining, Aisling pulled a necklace from under the high collar of the ruined dress. Tied to the end was a thick wad of tangled hair.

"Me too."

Eavha smiled. "What did you use for a base?"

"A feather. Sparrow, of course. My original blessing was from Celeste, before I became Returned. The opportunity to honor both my blessings could not be overlooked."

"Ah," Eavha nodded, but she knew her bewilderment was clear on her face. Not much of what Aisling was talking about made any sense to her.

Aisling smiled, too, the expression softening all the sharp angles of her face.

"I can explain the process of becoming Sparrow another time, if you are curious. It is not a secret. Rest for now."

The princess moved toward the door, but Eavha reached for her wrist. "Where is Dearmead?"

Aisling frowned. "Which one is that?"

"The guardian with the long braid."

"Ah. I sent him away. I sent them all away."

Eavha frowned. "Why?"

Color stained Aisling's pale cheeks as she looked away from Eavha's prone frame. "Because . . . I thought you needed to rest."

"That is not true." Eavha frowned. "I thought we could not to lie to each other."

Swallowing, Aisling looked at the end of the bed, the wall, her shoes. "Alright. I panicked."

"Was I that ill?"

"No."

Eavha waited. After blinking a few times, Aisling straightened her shoulders and seemed to realize she was still in her torn and bloody gown. Holding the edges together in one hand, she cleared her throat.

"I will explain that later, too. Please excuse me. I am indecent."

"Oh, please. I show more skin that that on a daily basis and nobody has ever accused me of such a thing."

Even more color blossomed across Aisling's face, dark lashes fluttering so quickly Eavha worried she was having a seizure.

"Regardless. I will fetch your Dearmead for you and return later."

Quickly, the princess hurried for the door.

"Will you tell me about the tattoos later, as well?" Eavha called after her, struck down with a sudden dizziness as she tried to rise. She did need rest.

Aisling did not answer as she stalked from the room.

Dearmead never came, but another of the Wyldeden guardians stayed by her bedside until she was well enough to stand. Without hesitation, she sought out Aisling. The palace guards escorted her to the stairwell she already knew would take her to the top of the tallest tower.

Aisling's rooms were not as grand as she had imagined them. When she and Dearmead had rifled through what little belongings the princess kept, Eavha had almost convinced herself they were in the wrong suite. Now, as she reached the top of the staircase and pushed open the gilded door to her right, she was struck again by the emptiness of it. A large reception room greeted her with nothing but a deep purple chaise and a full drinks cart facing the open balcony where a small table and two chairs awaited in the summer light. Aisling leaned against the wall beside the cart, filling a crystal goblet with dark red wine, not remotely surprised by Eavha's entrance.

"That didn't take long."

"You promised me answers." Eavha crossed her arms under her chest.

Aisling's glanced at the movement, then quickly away again. "I did. Sit. Wine?"

"No, thank you," Eavha refused, taking a seat on the chaise. A light breeze dulled summer's edge, blowing the stray curls that wouldn't stay in her topknot across her face.

Aisling downed the entire contents of her goblet before refilling it to the brim. There was no servant to do it for her anymore. Again, Aisling's heavy-lidded gaze swept over Eavha with an expression close to anger.

"I thought I had hardened against your kind of connivance, but it seems I am still frustratingly vulnerable."

Eavha frowned deeply. "What?"

"Don't pretend you don't know."

"I'm not a very good liar, even outside of Imsa. And I'm certainly not . . . conniving. What exactly do you think I'm doing?"

Aisling turned to the door, leaving her back exposed as she drank deeply from her glass. Her ruined dress had been replaced by another, grey silk from her throat to her wrists to her ankles, black gloves encasing her hands. Not an inch of skin below her face was on display.

"What question would you like answered first?"

"The one I just asked you."

"Just a poor translation. Next?"

"How can you keep lying, Aisling?"

The princess stiffened at Eavha's casual address, but she did not excuse herself. Instead, Eavha leveled the same glare she gave patients when they tried to lie about how they received an injury. Doing so only hurt them further and prevented her from helping appropriately.

It was strange to think that she did in fact wish to help Aisling. She had come to Hyrsch with half a mind to exact revenge on Cinn's behalf, but now . . . something heavy sat between them. A horrible truth that felt more important than vengeance, no matter how justified.

"If I admit that all I meant was that I find your beauty disarming, would you move on to other topics?"

The words were unexpected and full of bite. Eavha's surprise only lasted a moment before she was smiling, tucking another stray curl behind her ear. "Thank you."

Aisling only raised her glass again, keeping her back to Eavha.

"The Sparrow Coven, as the name suggests, is a coven of devoted Lover enthusiasts," Aisling went on, as if the previous exchange had not occurred. "While all sorts of witches congregate in Dusarn, you only become a Sparrow by taking a vow or enduring the Passing. I was born Celeste-blessed, but took the Passing rite when I came of age in order to become Returned. Only by doing so could I enact my blood-right to the throne my parents hold, and only by doing so could I prevent my brother from being the sole heir."

"After having met your brother, I can honestly say I am grateful for your sacrifice," Eavha admitted.

Aisling snorted. "I'm not sure if the pun was intentional."

Eavha smiled. It did not take a genius to figure out that the Passing rite involved a self-sacrifice. To become Returned, one first had to die and she doubted Aisling was the kind of person to allow herself to be murdered.

"It was an opportunity that could not be ignored."

Aisling turned around, suppressing a smile as she sipped at her wine. "Again, I am sorry you had to endure Nevan."

"I was not the main target of his attention." Eavha shrugged, preferring not to dwell on those memories. "Can anybody take the Passing?"

"No. The council must approve your request. They keep the Coven elite, giving preference to blood-relatives of members but making exceptions for witches who show great potential. They also take vows from strong healers they recruit from all over Nir, as well as from Returned witches who have evolved through whatever means, looking for a place to belong. Had you not been hidden so well in Wyldeden, the council may very well have tried to recruit you. If they get wind of your brother, I imagine they would be very interested in offering him a place amongst their ranks."

"Eaon doesn't think very highly of the Sparrow Coven," Eavha admitted, though something about the statement didn't sit well. Her brother hadn't held strong views toward the Sparrow Coven until he met Cinn, and it had become painfully obvious over the past decade how much he resented being born in Wyldeden where nobody ever made him feel like he belonged. Perhaps he would have been attracted to a coven like the Sparrows if it weren't for Cinn's history with them.

"I can understand why he would feel that way. To be upfront with you, Eavha, I am not a huge fan of them myself."

That made Eavha sit up and pay attention.

"Really?"

Aisling drained her glass once more and refilled it before wandering slowly onto the balcony. When the princess took a seat on one of the wrought-iron chairs, Eavha got up to follow her.

On the matching table was a glass square tile with a pattern of smaller squares etched into it. An arrangement of glass tokens had been blown into strange shapes, sitting in no pattern that Eavha could decipher. The only one that looked like anything Eavha recognized was a horse's head.

Warily, Eavha took the seat across from Aisling, turning her attention from the odd decoration to the bustling city beneath them. It was ugly, as far as cities went. At least in her limited experience.

"The other question I left unanswered relates to why I panicked," Aisling continued, though her voice had become quieter. Softer. There was an edge of pain in the words as she went on. "Many years ago, I had a lover. Her name was Davina. She was Morvish and foresaw a terrible conflict. The return of Chaos, King of Beasts.

"When she tried to warn the Coven, they did not believe her. They said Morvish premonitions were too often misinterpreted for them to move on her information, not to mention that Davina . . . she had not always been truthful to my parents. They called her a liar and threw her out of Dusarn. It was absolute lunacy.

"So, she and I made our own preparations. We made a plan, and she died of a magic-burnout in the process. Died, making these tattoos on my skin. It was why I panicked when I thought a scar may break their power. Why I panicked when you passed out, bleeding from your face after almost burning yourself out."

Eavha's hand fluttered to her throat.

"I'm so sorry."

"Don't be. I've scolded her frequently enough that my grief has become bearable."

Eavha frowned, making Aisling smile. Leaning forward, she whispered, "My Lover-blessing. Because I was Celestian before I passed, my Lover-blessing manifested in the ability to see the ghosts of the dead who have not yet accepted the Lover's embrace. Davina lingers, insisting on seeing the plan through with me."

Eavha's chest ached horribly, but she couldn't stop the frown pulling deeper on her face. "I am confused. My brother has passed twice now, and he said there is only dark and cold in the Lover's realm. How could Davina linger here with us?"

Aisling glanced down at the glass thing on the table and placed a pinkie finger on one of the tokens, taking a long time to answer.

"She doesn't linger here," she finally said. "She lingers in that dark and cold. But she and I are tied together, and since my ability allows me to peer through the veil that separates the Lover's and Mother's realms, she is able to peer back. It helps that she is disgustingly stubborn, and far too clever for her own good."

Aisling picked up the token she was toying with and moved it to a different square. Eavha watched, glancing between the board and the princess. Aisling caught her staring.

"Have you ever played chess?"

"I've never heard of it."

"It's a strategy game. This board lets me continue to play with Davina."

"Ah." Eavha smiled. "It is nice that you two have been able to stay together, even through death. Though I am surprised she was not revived by one of your healers. Necromancers, I mean."

Aisling's entire being seemed to brim with sudden rage.

"Like I said. I am not particularly fond of my coven anymore."

Lips parting in a silent *oh*, Eavha didn't know what could possibly be said about that. She thought she knew what it was like to have family turn their backs on someone they should have been first in line to help, but despite their calloused behaviour at home, the Nemuses had always been willing to heal anyone and everyone in need.

Questions brimmed and cooled in her mouth as she forced herself to leave the matter alone. Instead, Eavha watched the pieces on the glass board and, after a moment, one of the horse-head tokens moved on its own.

A grin so wide it hurt broke across Eavha's face. "That is amazing. Hello, Davina."

Aisling calmed as quickly as she had angered, looking fondly at Eavha.

"Davina says she loves your hair. And your dress. And literally everything else about you. She's very jealous that I get to exist in the same realm as you."

Eavha laughed, almost falling from the seat at the twisting mixture of amusement and pride at the compliment. She didn't acknowledge the way Aisling's face slackened, her eyes blinking madly as she stared unabashedly.

"I would like to learn," she said instead. "About chess. About strategy. Would you teach me?"

"I would be honored."

CHAPTER TWENTY-ONE

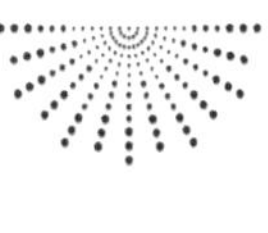

EAON

THE VEIN WAS EVEN WORSE THAN THE DIVIDING RIVER IN TERMS of what lived beneath the crystalline surface, so as Eaon had always done with his da when traveling, they went west to circumvent the Heart Lake. Even from a few miles away, as they crested a hill and stepped into Vertlyn, the glistening surface of the Heart Lake was utterly blinding. The water itself was nothing special, but beneath lay a city of diamond.

Since the first time he'd seen it, Kailevi had warned Eaon to never be tempted. Yes, the stones in the lake were worth more than anything anyone could mine from the land—purer, cleaner, and imbued with a magic unlike anything a land witch could imagine—but to step foot in the water was calling for an excruciating death.

The beasts that lived in the Heart Lake and used the Vein as a throughway to the ocean were vicious and territorial, while the faeries that lived among the diamond delighted in their own cruelty to the land folk. Legend had it only one witch had ever touched the diamond city and returned to the land to brag, but even he would never attempt such a thing again.

Thus, two bridges had been built. One near Pirevia while the other lay between the lake and the mountains. The clans that lived in the upper half of the Spine and the North Mountains had built the latter so they could come to Anfar for trading festivals and Imsas.

As the four travelers began to descend the hill, the grass becoming drier and interspersed with pebbles and sharp stones, Selina's heavy panting turned into a whine.

"You alright?" Eaon called back.

"I think I have a blister."

Vira, whom Eaon had not taken a liking to in the weeks they had been traveling, snorted. Cinn wrinkled his nose at the guardian, stopping when Eaon did to stretch his calves.

"I know, I know," she sighed, lowering her pack to the ground with a wince. "You tried to tell me."

"It's not a shortcoming," Eaon told her, pulling the first-aid kit from his own pack. "The pace is faster, the packs heavier. I had bruised feet and blisters for months when I started traveling and I complained much more than you do. So, complain away."

He narrowed his eyes at Vira as he said it, but the guardian was too busy watching the bushland warily. Cinn, too, had frozen, eyes locked on a patch of small cabbage trees.

As quick as he could, Eaon placed a scrap of moleskin over the blister forming between two toes on Selina's left foot and bandaged it tightly with straps of leather. Selina had noticed the shift in his posture and kept quiet, pulling her pack closer as Eaon tied the strap. If Selina was tired, she didn't show it as she got to her feet, braced to run.

Eaon tightened his grip on his staff.

"Easy, friends!" a voice called from the shrubbery.

None of them relaxed as five witches emerged from various hiding places nearby. The foliage was thin and spread out, but the clans native to the north had learned to hide well despite it. Their skin painted in lines of white and green to camouflage among the ghostly trees, some shimmied down from trunks while others with branches sticking out of their clothes and hair came scuttling out from the bushes. They all carried sharp spears, leather whips coiled at their waists.

As Eaon looked the group over, he smirked.

"Nice try, Killian."

One of the witches painted in ghostly camouflage grinned. The contrast between his dark brown skin and the streaks of paint made him almost impossible to see among the shrubbery.

"Your new friends were the ones who caught me. Not you."

"Semantics." Eaon shrugged.

Killian strode forward, large arms spread wide. Eaon took two steps back.

"Keep your distance."

Killian jolted to a stop, frowning. They had known each other since Eaon's first visit to the Northern Mountains, and never once had he refused a hug.

With the tension growing, Vira stepped forward, her face pinched in annoyance. "Care to introduce us?"

"Killian, this is Vira and Selina, from Wyldeden. And this is Cinn, a demi-kin friend of mine. Killian's a scout from the Northern Mountain Clan. Though what he's doing this far from home is a wonder." Eaon signed as he spoke, but Cinn was barely watching him. His hard gaze was focused on the newcomers.

"We're hunting. A number of our scouts have gone missing and we tracked a lupanis to the area. Probably lucky we found you first," Killian smiled, but it was strained. "Where's Kailevi?"

"Passed," Eaon explained.

The flash of pain in Killian's gaze was unexpected, drawing Eaon's attention to the poignant numbness in his own chest at the sound of his da's name. Kaelean had instructed him to grieve, but there weren't any books on how exactly he was meant to do that.

"And lucky for who?" Vira smirked. "Any beast would find us difficult prey."

Killian turned to take in all six and a half feet of Vira, narrowing his eyes. "You think our scouts were easy?"

"That's not what she meant." Eaon raised his free hand to placate him. Which is when the Northern Mountain witches noticed his leather gloves. The staff in his hand that was not an ordinary staff. Taking a deep breath, the first test had arrived earlier than he'd hoped. "A lot has happened. I'm Returned now."

Killian's eyes widened as his scouting party raised their spears. Vira raised her own. Cinn wouldn't have been able to follow the conversation, but he drew his dagger anyway.

"Please. I'm not Sparrow. I still come from Wyldeden. I have a letter from our high priestess to prove it."

Selina rummaged through the outer pocket of his pack to retrieve the parchment Kaelean had prepared in case this happened. It explained everything, and the Wyldeden seal proved it was official.

Without even reading the note, seeing the green wax on the outside calmed the mountain witches.

"I think you have some stories to tell, Eaon."

At the familiar kindness in Killian's face, Eaon let go of the breath he'd been holding.

Killian nodded to the rest of the party, who strapped their spears to their backs. "Naani, take point. If the trail crosses into Spine territory though, just return home. I'll escort Eaon to the clan. I assume that's where you were heading?"

"Um . . . yes." Eaon raised his eyebrows, glancing between Killian and the other scouts. The last time he had been to the North Mountains, Killian was a junior scout. Seeing him in charge of an entire team both drove home how long it had been and filled him with a bubbling pride. "But as much as the offer is appreciated, we will be fine if you're busy."

A wild lupanis would not be fun to run into but, as Vira said, their group would not make for easy prey.

"Never too busy for a friend." Killian smiled.

That word made Eaon frown.

A female with leaves braided into her hair nodded, scuttling back into the shrubbery. The other three also retreated to the bush, quickly becoming invisible. Such was the skill of a good scout. Their magic encouraged the land to hide them, to take them into its fold and let them become a part of it. Dearmead had been given the option to train as a scout or a guardian, and while Eaon had thought his temperament was better suited to the first, Calla Bayfield had not given him the grace to make his own choice.

Shaking thoughts of Dearmead away, Eaon held still while Selina put the parchment back in his pack. Then he fell into step alongside

Killian while Cinn and Selina kept close behind. Vira brought up the rear, even more alert with the confirmation that at least one dangerous beast could be roaming nearby.

"So, what's been going on, you big senior scout chief," Eaon teased.

"You noticed that, huh?"

"Yeah, I noticed. I could have been asleep and noticed."

"I promise, me getting promoted is not as interesting a story as yours."

Eaon sighed and glanced back. Selina was still walking tenderly, but Cinn had let her put an arm over his shoulder. As if sensing Eaon's gaze, the kinner glanced up and gave him a reassuring nod.

"Yeah," he said. "It's definitely interesting."

Stopping by the waterway leading into the Heart Lake wasn't something Eaon would normally have recommended, but Selina was exhausted, and night would fall in an hour or so away anyway.

After setting up a campsite, all five of them went to the riverbed to fill their canteens and a few extra waterskins so they wouldn't have to return to the water when it was dark. Selina sat in the sand and gently washed her feet. Cinn was less delicate, stripping down to his undershorts and wading into the river.

"Careful," Eaon and Killian called out at the same time.

Cinn just raised an eyebrow at them and sunk down into his neck. Vira was removing her weapons, preparing to go in after him. It was hot, and the odor of Eaon's sweaty clothes revolted even himself. Unlike the others, he couldn't risk exposing too much skin until he was alone. The chances of accidentally brushing against someone were too high.

"There's enough of us that the fae will probably leave them alone," Killian said, drinking deeply. "At least while the sun is up."

"Probably." Eaon grimaced.

"None of them have traveled before?"

"Cinn has been around, but Selina and Vira are new at this."

"I understand Vira's presence, but why did Selina come?"

Eaon hesitated. He didn't know Selina's boyfriend, or how this Brach guy knew about a gap in the wards. Such information would be enough to put a price on his head. But Eaon trusted Killian. He and Kailevi had stayed with Killian's family during their visits, and while a lot of the mountain clan witches could be rough and brutal, Killian had never given Eaon a reason not to trust him.

"Do you know a witch named Brach?" he asked.

"I know at least five different Brachs. You'd have to be more specific."

"Ah. I don't know his last name. But Selina and he have started some kind of relationship during the trading festivals."

"That makes sense. She must really like him," Killian said as he watched her pick splinters out of the soles of her feet.

"I think so. But it's more than that." Eaon took a drink from his canteen, keeping an eye on the water in the river. "Cinn and I need to get into Qiri and apparently this Brach knows a place where the wards are weak enough to let us through. She's going to convince him to help us."

A stunned silence sat between them until Killian softly said, "Eaon, that's insane. Nobody goes to Qiri."

"I know."

"If there was a weak spot in the wards . . ."

"There must be. I've met two Morvish witches who've come from Qiri to pass on or fulfill some kind of prophecy in the last few months alone."

The borders of the northern-most territory had always been tightly held. Unlike the rest of Nir, it had never been invaded by Sparrows. Nobody would dare to try. And likewise, very few of Qiri's occupants ever ventured south of the mountains. Recluse was the kindest word Eaon had heard used to describe the way the Morvish had cut themselves off from the rest of Nir. Elitist, would be one of the more common. So few Morvish witches ever bothered to converse with lowly elemental witches that hardly anything was known about the High Spirit that blessed them. Nothing at all was known about their culture. Kailevi had said he'd never even seen a Morvish witch, and yet Eaon had met two now. Aadya and Yomra.

"Don't . . . don't tell anybody what you're really doing in the mountains." Killian continued to keep his voice down. "Tensions are already high. The last thing we need is to be dealing with Qiri issues."

Eaon nodded.

Then stiffened. A shadow was moving beneath the surface of the river.

Killian let out a low whistle at the same time Eaon shouted for the others to get out of the water. They scrambled away from the riverbed quickly, watching silently as the shadow moved downstream toward the Heart Lake. It didn't pay them any mind.

It wasn't fair, but as evening crept in Eaon became increasingly agitated. His patience for Selina dwindled quickly, as did his ability not to snap at every word out of Vira's mouth. He didn't want to be sitting at a campfire, eating rations and listening to Killian's ghost stories. He wanted to be moving.

Just out of the firelight's range, Eaon stripped off and washed himself with water from his canteen and a scrap of cloth. His skin was irritated—oversensitive and too thin. He could almost feel the night's breeze brushing against his veins. The skittering sounds of animals in the bushes, of bats flapping invisibly overhead, filled his ears.

Cinn kept shooting him worried glances.

{You okay?}

Eaon nodded once, dressing in clean-ish clothes. {I'll take a tonic.}

One of the vials wrapped carefully in his pack was labeled *Calm* and smelled strongly of lavender and turmeric. Just like at the farm, the tonics didn't seem to be working as well as they used to, and he regretted not standing his ground with Cleo. Still, he took it. It was better than nothing.

Then he sat as far as he could from the group and buried his nose in a book.

Some hours later, the chatter went quiet. Sleep had taken Vira and Cinn, who both deserved a break from keeping watch. Selina was trying to get comfortable, tossing and turning on her sleeping mat.

Eaon didn't look up from his book as Killian sat beside him, drinking from his waterskin.

"What are you reading?" Killian asked.

Eaon turned up the cover so Killian could read it, not taking his eyes from the pages.

"*History of the Sparrow*. Thinking about converting after all?"

"Definitely. Anything to differentiate myself from you feral elemental witches," Eaon said flatly, finally glancing over with a little smirk.

Killian was grinning. "Ah, yes, us lowly elemental witches are so inferior compared to the elegance of the Sparrow Coven."

"Disgusting, really."

"Revolting. How could we possibly think well of ourselves living amongst the land as we do, instead of the boxy cage-like castles of the almighty Coven? A disgrace, really."

Eaon chuckled. Knowing the Sparrow Coven thought the rest of them were as savage and uncivilized as the faerie folk had always been a point of mockery. They thought they were so much better than everybody else because they were blessed by the Lover. The upside was that, for the most part, the Sparrows didn't particularly care what the other clans did. As long as the elemental witches acknowledged the land they lived on belonged to the Sparrows, they let them roam Nir, living in their communities, with very little interference. The Anfar Forest Clan was the exception because they had not surrendered their land for colonization.

"It's a pompous read," Eaon admitted, closing the book, the starlight not enough to read by anymore. "But understanding the bond between Mother and the Lover helps me understand this new magic I have. I'm hoping that if I can understand it, I might have better luck controlling it."

Killian nodded. "I'm not sure I said before, but I'm sorry about what happened to you. I'm glad your sister could bring you back."

"Me too," Eaon sighed. The rational part of him knew that rehashing everything for Killian during their walk was a part of why he felt so raw. "And I'm sorry about the missing scouts from your clan. Did you know any of them?"

Killian nodded, gazing out into the darkness.

"I'm sorry," Eaon repeated quietly.

"We'll find them. And if something has taken them, we'll make sure the beasts of the north remember why they shouldn't fuck with us."

"Are you sure it was a beast? There's a heavy fae population here too."

"It was only recently that we had to remind the fae why they shouldn't fuck with us, either." Killian smirked.

"Revenge?"

"We checked with them first and they denied knowing anything about it. It could be a different faerie creature, but there isn't really anything strong enough around here to have disappeared so many well-trained scouts."

"Any faerie rings in the area?"

"None that we've found."

Eaon grimaced. Being held captive by faeries would at least mean the scouts were still alive. "Perhaps there is one you haven't found yet. Perhaps it isn't a lupanis that got them."

"Perhaps," Killian echoed, but there was little hope in his tone. "You're being strangely optimistic. Where's all the bitter logic and barely concealed pessimism we all came to know and love?"

Eaon rolled his eyes and leaned back against a tree trunk. "Pardon me for trying to be nice. I won't do it again."

Killian chuckled. "That's better."

"How's your ma and da, anyway?"

"Same as always. Worse, now that Miika is getting married."

"Really? Married?" Eaon raised his eyebrows.

Killian's older brother was an elder among the Northern Mountain Clan and took himself far too seriously. It was a big deal when elders married, as the witchlings were usually heavily blessed.

"It gets worse," Killian wrinkled his nose. "He's marrying the Alpha of a sky coven."

Eaon's mouth fell open in shock.

"Yeah. So you're arriving just in time for possibly the biggest union in our clan's entire history. We're adopting a sky coven. Terra shield us."

"*How?*" Eaon's voice cracked. "How did Miika even meet her?"

"Trading festival. The coven stopped by looking for leather for new saddles. Miika happened to be at the tanner's stall, investigating claims that the owner was . . . I don't know, doing something illegal." Killian shrugged. "But ever since the engagement, Ma has been on my case. 'When are you going to get a girlfriend, Killian,' 'why don't you and Reigan get married, Killian,' 'I'm going to die before I get grandchildren from you, Killian.' 'Why would you break my heart like this, Killian.'"

Eaon laughed. "Why *don't* you and Reigan get married?"

Killian was the first witch aside from Dearmead who had treated Eaon like he wasn't lesser. He hadn't been embarrassed to take him to meet his friends—Tomaii and Reigan—who had been excited to show him Igni culture.

Tomaii. Eaon banished thoughts of the male from his head.

"Don't you start, too," Killian grumbled. "Where's your partner, then, smart ass? Weren't you and . . . what's his name, the friend you had in Wyldeden. Weren't you two becoming a thing?"

The last time Eaon had seen Killian, he and Dearmead had just started being more than friends. Now, he banished thoughts of that male from his head as well.

"It got complicated."

"Because you died?"

Eaon looked down to the brands on his palms. "Yeah."

From the campfire, Selina cleared her throat loudly, rolling onto her back and shooting them a glare.

"As if it wasn't hard enough to sleep in these conditions, now I've got to hear you two gasbagging all night?"

"Sorry Selina." Eaon grimaced. After so many difficult weeks, the lack of quality sleep was starting to taint even Selina's patience. "A few more days and you'll have a bed."

She flung an arm over her eyes.

"You should get some sleep," Killian said, reaching for Eaon's book.

He flinched away, hissing, "You have to be more careful than that."

Killian grimaced. "Sorry. I forgot."

Eaon put the book away and pulled his gloves back on. Even

though the leather should protect the others, he still didn't trust it. Wouldn't touch anyone on purpose if he could help it.

"You probably haven't slept in a while. I can keep watch," Eaon offered.

Killian didn't bother to argue, but he didn't go to lie down either. Sitting in silence, the two of them kept an eye on the camp. A few more days and they would reach the mountains. Maybe then they could both get some sleep.

CHAPTER TWENTY-TWO

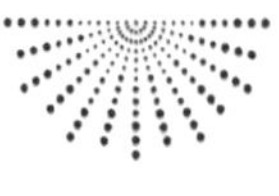

EAON

As they reached the peak of the small mountain they'd been climbing, Eaon watched Cinn's face go slack at what lay on the other side. There was a sheer cliff instead of a slope back down, and between one peak and the next lay a mile-wide gorge, stretching in both directions farther than the eye could see.

At first, the gorge appeared as any other. It wasn't even impressive when compared to the pit in the center of Nir fondly referred to as the Womb. Only those who knew where to look could see the trodden paths leading down the cliff face, or the ashwood and rowanberry talismans dangling in tree branches to warn away the fae, or the shrewd eyes of camouflaged guardians peering out from crevices and shrubs.

Eaon remembered the first time he'd come to the Long Gorge vividly. Wyldeden had layers upon layers of protection against invasion—the wards around Anfar, Terra's shadowy guardians, Wyldeden guardians, the witchmark on the Great Boab itself—but the Long Gorge was, comparatively, open to attack.

The entire time he and Kailevi had stayed during their travels, Eaon had been on edge. It hadn't made sense to him why their high priest would leave the settlement so exposed, but he understood now—not every clan had a witch like Kaelean Caesarea to protect them.

Carefully, the group followed Killian down one of the steep paths of the gorge. Every now and again they passed a wide crack in the cliff's side, the inside lined in mosaicked stone.

Eaon signed to Cinn, {Much of the North Mountain Clan lives inside the mountain itself. There is a network of caves and tunnels that, if you know the way, can take you safely all the way to Ignatius's temple at the base of the bleeding mountain.}

{Bleeding mountain?} Cinn asked, eyes darting between Eaon's hands and the careful placement of his feet on the path. Falling might not cause Cinn any permanent damage but it would still be unpleasant to splatter against the bottom of the gorge.

"Volcano," Eaon whispered, showing Cinn the sign for the word. {It is the dividing point between Vertlyn, Kerveda, and Qiri. The Ignatius-blessed have a legend that it is from within that mountain that the Spirit of Flame was created. The wound still 'bleeds' occasionally, and the Ignatius-blessed will often make sacrifices into it to return the 'blood' to the earth.}

Cinn's eyes widened. {Like, people sacrifices?}

{Very rarely someone might sacrifice themselves, but nobody's thrown in against their will. Animals, on the other hand . . .} Eaon pursed his lips, letting the explanation dangle as he returned to concentrating on his footwork.

They were far enough down the cliff that the shadows cooled the sweat on Eaon's neck when Killian stopped by a narrow crack in the stone. Far below them, tiny lights flickered like stars in a night sky in an upside-down world. The famous phosphorescent flower farms were one of the largest trade items to come out of the Northern Mountains, and up close, they were utterly beautiful. The flickering was from the farmers as they moved through the fields, cleaning and cutting the blooms ready for preservation.

"We go in here," Killian said, urging the travelers inside. Since Eaon knew where he was going, he led the way.

The passage only stayed narrow for a short time, widening as torches of everlight began to appear on the wall. A fancy bit of magic, the everlight. Fire that needed no fuel, and never burned out; a secret that the creators wouldn't share with anyone else, no matter what they were offered in return. Eaon supposed it was no different from how the Sanni-blessed in Wyldeden refused to migrate to other clans. It gave them an edge of power over others.

Jealousy and resentment bred too easily among the clans, wanting the secret to everlight, to union with Sanni-blessed healers, access to the few safe passages through the spine, or even to claim parts of Anfar, thus living outside of the watching eye of the Sparrow Coven. The politics of it all were complicated, and coexistence through trade festivals and traveler relations was the only thing stopping war from breaking out between Anfar and every other clan who wanted a piece of free land. Eaon often thought that if the clans were so inclined—could put their pettiness aside and band together—they would be a force to be reckoned with against the Sparrow Coven. They could all have free land.

Eventually the tunnel opened up to a large cavern that the residents called "the warren." More tunnels branched in every direction, both along the ground and higher up the walls, where rope ladders strung throughout made the latter accessible. Everlight held in colored glass lanterns dangled from the ceiling in macramé pendants, while carved alcoves in the walls served as little homes for a number of fire sprites the mountain clan permitted to live alongside them. The glow from their bodies glittered off the lanterns, dancing shadows illuminating the warren in perpetual motion.

The cavern itself was a thoroughfare, witches clambering the rope ladders to and from the different tunnels, as well as a central meeting space with a dais built under a glass chandelier. Eaon had seen both formal ceremonies and debauch revels take place under that chandelier, and the memories of them sent his heart aflutter.

"It's beautiful," Selina gasped, holding a hand to her throat.

Eaon gave her a smile and adjusted his pack.

"Come," Killian called, taking the lead toward a tunnel on the far left. "Let's get you all settled. Then we'll see the elder traveler to let her know you're here. Then you can find Brach."

"Thank you."

The mountain clan used the same terminology for clan roles, but their system was very different. It had taken Eaon a long time to wrap his head around the idea that a witch's clan role was not the epitome of their purpose in life. It was not a definition of their worth. When he realized how much easier life could be had he been born into the mountain clan instead of Wyldeden, he had begged Kailevi to let him stay.

If only it was that simple, Kailevi had told him, a pitying look on his face.

As he followed Killian through familiar tunnels, memories of his da became loud and demanding in his head.

Cinn grabbed hold of Eaon, removed his glove and squeezed his hand. Only then did he realize how cold his skin had gotten, the wary look Vira was giving him as her breath fogged in the otherwise clammy tunnel. Taking a slow breath, Eaon focused on getting himself under control.

Especially when Killian reached a carved doorway with a red and orange tapestry draped across it. Privacy was not something the mountain clan really did.

"Ma! Da! I'm back!" Killian announced as he pushed back the tapestry.

Like in Wyldeden, Killian's family lived together in a large dwelling. The first room as Eaon stepped beyond the doorway was an open space, stuffed bags and tall cushions strewn about that witches used to lounge on. More yellow-and-orange colored lanterns as well as strings of phosphorescent flowers dangling from the ceiling gave everything a soft hue. Being the middle of the day, the living room was empty, but Eaon knew by the end of the work shift it would be full of rowdy, hungry witches.

"And I brought you a present!"

From behind another tapestry limped an older female, wiping her hands on a greasy apron around her waist. Her eyes widened as she took in the sight of him.

"Eaon Nemuse," Killian's ma beamed. She had the same thick, black hair as her son, but while Killian was tall and dark like his da, Kerinna was small and fair. "Last time I saw you and your da, you were running from the warren with your tail tucked between your legs."

"It was that or lose something else that hangs between my legs." Eaon returned her grin. "How have you been, Kerinna?"

"Same as always; popping out fiendish miniatures every other year." Just like her son had, Kerinna strode forward with her arms open.

Killian stepped in front of her. "Wait, ma."

With a frown, Kerinna sniffed at Eaon. "Why do you smell like that?"

"It's been a long journey," Eaon joked, the longing he felt to hug her weighing heavily on his shoulders.

"I don't mean the stink of your unwashed body," she chastised. "Why do you smell like death?"

Eaon sighed as Selina began to retrieve the parchments from his pack again.

"These explain everything," she said, bowing lowly as she handed them to Kerinna.

"These are Eaon's friends," Killian introduced as Kerinna unrolled the parchment. "Selina and Vira are from Wyldeden, and Cinn is a demi-kin."

Interrupting Eaon's pending explanation about Cinn, Killian's sister Pippa came running around the bend of a hall. At the sight of Eaon, she skidded to a halt.

"Oh, stake and burn me, not you again."

"Pippa!" Killian scolded her.

Eaon only smiled. "Nice to see you, too."

Pippa rolled her eyes. "Ma, I'm going to the markets. Need anything?"

"No, no. You go," Kerinna said distractedly, rolling up the parchment and handing it back to Selina.

She waited until her daughter had gone before saying, "I'm very sorry to hear about your troubles, Eaon. Please know, you are not any less welcome here."

Eaon sagged, blowing out a sigh of relief. "Thank you."

"Get them settled." Kerinna rose onto her toes to give her son a kiss on the cheek. "Then come to the kitchen for food. I want to hear about your hunt."

"Not much to tell," Killian told her. "And I should take Eaon to see the elder traveler."

"You never sit and eat with me anymore, Killian," Kerinna pouted. "It breaks my heart."

Eaon drew his lips in to hide his amusement.

"Next time, Ma," Killian promised. Then to Eaon, desperate pleading in his eyes, "Come on. I'll take you to the spare rooms."

"We will catch up over tea soon, Kerinna," Eaon promised as he passed, bowing deeply. Selina and Vira also bowed for the matriarch.

Down the hall and around two bends, Killian showed Selina and Vira where they would be sleeping before taking Eaon and Cinn to another doorway across the hall.

The colored lantern theme continued, glittering off the pebbled floor in a rainbow of soft lilac and peach. Piles of clean furs, blankets and pillows adorned a large hammock made of tightly woven ropes, while in the corner waited a steaming hot spring carved into the natural stone. Water trickled out of a crack in the wall, filling a basin large enough for a single person to lie down in. Unlike the crystalline water of the Heart Lake, the liquid pooling in the room was cloudy with sediment; not suitable for drinking but great for bathing, the mineral traces more cleansing than any soap.

"Thank you," Eaon said again.

Killian went to pat Eaon on the shoulder, remembering only as Eaon flinched away that he shouldn't.

"Take your time," he said with an apologetic smile. "I'll go placate Ma. We'll eat, then go find the elder. Nice to meet you, Cinn."

Eaon translated, and Cinn gave the witch a tight nod in return.

Clean and stuffed full of spinach and goat's cheese pastries, Eaon could have curled up in the hammock in his and Cinn's room and napped for hours. The humidity underground didn't help, but no doubt the feeling would be gone by the time night actually came around. As it was, he didn't have the luxury of sleeping yet.

Killian led Cinn and Eaon back through the tunnels toward the warren while Selina and Vira went to find Brach. Eaon took the opportunity to send a whispering leaf to Kaelean, letting her know they had arrived safely in the Northern Mountains.

They had barely made it back to the large cavern when Eaon heard a familiar delighted crow.

Killian sighed. "I was hoping he hadn't heard yet."

But there was affection on Killian's face as he said it. Affection mirrored behind the grimace Eaon put on his face as he looked across the cavern to where a male and female witch were making a beeline toward them.

"It's fine, but you're going to have to stop him from—"

Killian stepped forward before Eaon had even finished the sentence, grabbing Tomaii out of the air mid-leap.

"Hey!" Tomaii cursed, shoving off Killian.

"Slow down. You can't hug him."

Tomaii turned to Eaon, a familiar gleam of mischief behind his burning hazel eyes. "You're not still mad at me, are you?"

"I was almost banished from ever returning here because of you," Eaon reminded him. But he couldn't help the way his chest swelled with fondness and excitement at the sight of the male. The memories he had tried to tuck away were playing at double speed through his mind as he remembered all the trouble he and Tomaii had gotten into over the years.

"And yet here you are."

"I had hoped to avoid seeing your ugly mug," Eaon teased.

The lie felt blasphemous on his lips. Tomaii was the farthest thing from ugly Eaon had ever seen. Brassy golden curls cut just above ears that were decorated with a dozen different jewels. Full lips and deep dimples, a jawline that could cut glass; Eaon had to force himself not to let his eyes stray any lower than Tomaii's face. To the broad shoulders and chiseled chest that not even the fittest of Wyldeden guardians would ever be able to mimic. To the long, powerful legs that Eaon knew could outrace a fleeing buck. Legs he didn't want to remember the feel of. Taste of.

Especially not when such thoughts led to images of a much darker, slightly shorter male with a long black braid.

Tomaii put a hand to his stomach as he laughed loudly, unbothered by the other witches staring as they walked past. Beside him, Reigan crossed her arms.

"Why the fuck do you smell like Pirevia?"

Her words had always been as sharp as the rest of her. All pointed angles that somehow managed to find the most tender places to jab.

"Why do you know what Pirevia smells like?" Eaon raised an eyebrow at her, defensiveness sharpening his tone.

"You never could just answer a fucking question, could you?" She smirked, dimples matching those of her cousin. "Guess we'll just have to get the papaver out and loosen you up a little."

"Ah." This. This was exactly why he had gotten into so much trouble last time. "Because things went so well the last time we smoked."

"Who's your friend?" Tomaii asked, giving Cinn a once over.

Compared to the mountain witch, Cinn looked like a literal child with his lanky limbs and wide blueish eyes.

"This is Cinn," Eaon explained, remembering to sign as he went. "Cinn, this is Tomaii and Reigan. They're cousins, and we've known each other for a long time. Cinn is a demi-kin friend of mine. He only understands Nirnish and doesn't speak."

"Oh. My Nirnish is still really bad." Tomaii grimaced.

"You stopped studying after I left." Eaon rolled his eyes, not even remotely surprised. "It's okay. He's used to me translating."

{Hello,} Cinn signed.

"We don't take demi-kin runaways here," Reigan reminded him, refusing to acknowledge Cinn's presence.

Choosing not to translate, Eaon mimicked her pose.

"I'm aware of that," he said coldly.

"Seriously though," Tomaii jumped from foot to foot. "What's going on, Eaon? You show up unannounced, reeking like a royal piece of shit with a demi-kin in tow . . ."

"It's a long story. A really long story. And I promise to explain everything, because I'm going to need a favor."

Killian had said not to tell anyone else about what they were doing here, but Tomaii and Reigan didn't count. The three of them were thick as thieves and had been for as long as Eaon had known them. He trusted them.

"You know we don't do favors here," said Reigan.

"Yes, I know." His impatience was rearing its ugly head again.

"Let's walk," Killian raised his chin to the exit tunnel. "Eaon needs to report in with the elder traveler anyway. He can explain as we go."

Even though Cinn knew the story, Eaon signed as they walked. The way the kinner's eyes darted around, the distance he kept from the others, told Eaon enough about how on edge he already was. The last thing he needed was to feel even more alienated.

He let Cinn take the parchment from Eaon's satchel and hand it to Reigan to read while he went on to explain about the crack in the wards to Qiri.

"Stake and burn me," Reigan muttered, shoving the wispy bits of dark blond hair away from her face as they exited the tunnel into the gorge once more. "It's never dull when you're around."

"Oh, I am *so* coming with you," Tomaii chuckled. "I heard they have some next level smoking herbs in Qiri."

Killian smacked Tomaii up the back of his head.

Scowling, Tomaii hissed at him. "That was rude."

Killian only huffed. "I'll take your thanks whenever you're ready, by the way."

"Why would I thank you for giving me a concussion?"

"If I hadn't stopped you from jumping on Eaon, you'd be dead right now."

The idea made Eaon nauseous.

"Oh, puh-lease. I'd just give the Lover a little"—Tomaii waggled his eyebrows—"and they'd send me right back. Not even the High Spirits can resist this face."

"The Lover would hurl you back into the Mother's realm just so they didn't have to listen to your bullshit," Reigan muttered.

Eaon tried to smile, but he couldn't fight past the panic of the idea of Tomaii facing the Lover. Of being lost in that dark, cold void.

Cinn took his hand again and squeezed tightly.

"Yeah, well, the Lover would toss you back just so—"

"Where are we going, anyway?" Eaon interrupted, not wanting to talk about death anymore.

"The Elders are all at the flat. The sky coven I mentioned? Ma said they arrive today. Soon, actually."

"Your timing is impeccable. There's going to be some wild parties the next few days." Tomaii grinned and crowed into the gorge once more.

Killian hit him up the back of the head again.

"Quit being so obnoxious."

"Quit smacking me like a little bitch."

"Both of you quit speaking before I shove you off the edge of the cliff," Reigan warned them.

Tomaii was right though. Their timing was impeccable. The chances of showing up on the cusp of the biggest union the Northern Mountain Clan had ever held were tiny, let alone arriving exactly in time to see the sky coven land. Eaon frowned, shaking away the discomfort of such a coincidence. Ever since Yomra had foretold prophecy to the three of them—*Go to Ahrenhale. You are exactly who you need to be. Power corrupts*—Eaon had been paranoid of coincidence.

He didn't understand Morvish magic. It wasn't something he could read about in a book. How would he know when his prophecy had come to pass? *Stop fighting it*, Yomra had told him. He thought he had done that in the courtyard in Pirevia, but that couldn't have been what she meant. She wouldn't have brought him to that prison just to give him the answer to escaping it.

Reaching the flat, the tug on Eaon's hand pulled him out of his head. Cinn was looking at the gathering of witches standing around in the only flat plane near the Long Gorge.

"Killian?" one of them called out, separating from the crowd to approach. Miika, Killian's older brother and the elder scout of the Northern Mountain Clan, was frowning deeply. "What's wrong?"

"Nothing," Killian assured him. "Eaon and a few others arrived and we need to report to the elder."

"It couldn't wait? Yasmin is about to arrive."

Killian just shrugged, stiffening his jaw.

Really, it could have waited. Interrupting the arrival of the sky coven seemed like a bad idea, now that Eaon was thinking about it. Tilting his head, he looked closer at Killian's posture. The stiff back and crossed arms, feet set wide apart. Defensive.

Turning to Reigan, his suspicion was confirmed by the slight puckering of her eyes as she glared at Miika. There was something bigger going on.

Now wasn't the time for Miika and Killian to get into it. A sharp whistle alerted the gathering, and Eaon joined in as everyone looked up to the periwinkle sky.

From above the wispy clouds, a swarm descended. No, not a swarm; a flock of winged creatures twice as long as a man is high, their wingspans double that again. Paper-thin wings translucent against the sun, colors varied as nature itself etched in beautiful patterns along the undersides of the creature's bodies.

{Are those . . . moths?} Cinn asked, mouth hanging open.

"Cunea. They're beautiful, both harmless and carnivorous," Eaon said a little breathily, awe widening his eyes. He had only ever seen pictures of them drawn in books.

"Yasmin's coven call themselves beast tamers," Killian explained, rolling his eyes. "I'm not sure giant moths really qualify as beasts, though."

Miika hissed at him, stalking toward the other gathered witches.

Atop the enormous beasts, figures in saddles rode with their faces low to the cunea's furred backs. It was difficult to see from the ground, but as the moths banked the riders became clearer; wrapped in fleece, their heads were covered in veils that turned stiff and transparent over their faces with some magic that protected them from the wind.

Eaon had never met a sky witch either. Seen them in passing, studied their sky Spirit, Celeste, and read about the various cultures of the covens, but never truly met one. His heart was beating so hard from the nauseating mixture of nerves and excitement he had to place a hand over his chest to make sure it didn't fall out.

From the mountains, an earsplitting screech pierced the air.

Shouts and pointing from the guardians on the flat showed Eaon where to look as another beast shot into the air. Smaller than the moths but significantly more vicious, the harpy had wings like a hawk and a serpentine neck, but the legs and face of a human. The product of ancient times when beasts roamed unchecked, taking humans as both food and playthings. This one's wings boomed as it rose higher and higher, its underbelly stained with dark blood.

"Shoot it down!" one of the elders shouted.

Guardians prepared their arrows.

"No! I won't risk the coven!" Miika waved his arms, pulling the weapon from one of the witches' grasp.

The approaching coven noticed the harpy and split into two, fanning out in a practiced maneuver to surround the beast.

"Damn it! I told you to kill that thing before they arrived!" the elder guardian, identifiable by the black leather cladding her body, shouted at someone.

The sky witches flew in a spherical formation around the harpy, who screeched in frustration as it tried to dart between them, only to be struck by pulses of unnatural air pressure, sending it bouncing back and forward inside the living cage.

One of them missed. The harpy caught a clawed foot on the soft wing of a moth, instantly shredding it. Its rider screamed as they began to plummet—not in fear, but in grief. As the rider detached from the saddle, a second witch broke formation to chase after them in a mad spiral.

With the formation broken, the harpy dashed through the ranks to shoot skyward before turning and taking aim. The sky witches, still on their mounts, drew wands and bows, readying arrows. Arrows that, if they didn't find their target, would rain down on the mountain clan below.

Cinn tugged Eaon's arm to warn him, but Eaon was already shucking off his gloves. With his eyes fixated on the predator above, he took a slow steadying breath and aimed his staff.

As he rallied his magic, the others began to notice.

"I command you to stop!" Miika shouted, storming back in Eaon's direction.

Killian looked between his brother and Eaon, eyes widening in panic.

Calm, Eaon released a ravenous spear of death from his staff. He felt it hit, and the harpy faltered, its wings in spasm as the feathers began to shed en masse. With a terrifying screech, the beast began to fall.

It did not crash to the mountain below. It was nothing but red mist long before it had a chance.

Cinn took a hold of Eaon's arm as he swayed, a rush of violent ecstasy crashing through his veins.

More.

"I've got it," he assured Cinn, panting hard through gritted teeth as he denied his magic. His staff hummed painfully in his hand, absorbing the excess pouring from his skin.

"You stupid fool!" Miika hissed, but turned his back quickly as the delegation of sky witches landed their mounts. One of them was weeping.

{You okay?} Cinn asked, watching Eaon warily.

Looking around the clearing, half the witches were staring at him and only about half of *those* looked like they wanted to put an arrow in his head.

Swallowing against the bile in his throat, Eaon nodded.

"That"—Tomaii's eyes were wider than Eaon had ever seen them as he turned to face the male—"was so cool."

Scoffing, Killian hit him up the back of his head again.

CHAPTER TWENTY-THREE

EAON

Tomaii meant well, but Eaon still cringed at the title.

The warren was full of witches celebrating the arrival of the sky coven, barrels of aged whiskey and cider lining the walls. Pipes stuffed with papaver were being passed around, but Eaon refused to take one. Partly from fear of somehow hurting someone during the transfer, but also because he was determined to keep his head. They were here to get into Qiri, not fall into endless days of debauchery.

Cinn was laughing at the drunk witches stumbling over themselves, but there was a tension in his shoulders that hadn't left since they'd arrived at the mountain. No, since the moment those Sparrow witches had shown up at the farm.

Killian refilled Eaon's empty tankard that he had left atop a barrel of whiskey and held it out to him. The group had gathered by the edges of the warren, partly for quick access to the alcohol, but also because Eaon was trying to avoid any more attention. All things considered, meeting with the elder traveler and the high priest after his little demonstration had gone as well as it could have, but he needed to be on his best behavior for the rest of their visit.

It wasn't easy.

{You okay?} Cinn asked him again, just like he had every half-hour or so since using his magic.

"Yes," Eaon assured him.

He had his magic under control. It had settled at the back of his lungs, purring softly, but the lingering taste of the harpy's essence on the back of his tongue had not helped the spike in his mood this past month. He wanted to drink. To smoke and dance and crow alongside Tomaii. He wanted to run and scream and fight and fuck until the whole world fell away. He wanted it so badly his hands and feet kept twitching in anticipation of movement, leaving dark splashes of whiskey at his feet. Any other day, under any other circumstances, he would have given in. Only that his hands were gloved, the scars on his palms echoing with the healing itch, kept him standing beside Cinn. Too much drink, and he could kill every witch in the warren without meaning to.

{Do you need a tonic?} Cinn asked.

"They're fucking useless," Eaon snapped, snatching his tankard from Killian and taking a long drink.

"What are you talking about?" Killian asked, leaning against the wall, watching Tomaii dance to the fiddles being played upon the dais.

"My tonics," Eaon explained.

"You're still taking those?" Killian raised his brows, taking a pipe from Reigan and drawing deeply.

"Yeah, but the new brewer whose making them for me must be messing it up. They're weak, and I keep getting these headaches." He could feel one coming on now.

"I thought the healers in Wyldeden were meant to be some of the best," Reigan sniped.

Careful, Eaon reminded himself. These people were kind to him, but he wasn't so tipsy that he had forgotten he was there as a traveler. Wyldeden's reputation was on his shoulders, and he was required to be diplomatic.

"Now, now, Reigan. None of that," Eaon tutted, keeping his tone light.

He didn't miss the way Killian shifted his weight, letting his hip slide against Reigan's.

"You don't share your anti-burn recipe," he reminded her. "You can't expect Wyldeden to share all their secrets, either."

"Yes, fine," Reigan sighed, taking the pipe back from Killian. "I know my jealousy is old news."

"You're probably a better brewer than the one Kaelean sent me to," Eaon admitted.

"Why don't you bring some of your tonic by my stall tomorrow at the markets? I'll see what's wrong with it."

Eaon turned to raise his eyebrows at her. "Really? I don't have anything to trade."

Reigan gave him a filthy look. "Don't insult me."

"Actually," Killian drawled, "Tomaii had an idea earlier, since you're so paranoid about your magic. Remind me to tell him in the morning to meet you down there."

"Tomaii had an idea?" Reigan snorted. "How bizarre."

Eaon chuckled, sipping from his drink as he looked over to where Tomaii was dancing with one of the sky witches, arms interlocked as they spun each other around. The fiddlers played loudly, trying to be heard over the thunder rolling over the mountains outside. Summer storms weren't uncommon in the north, but the way the sky witches whispered to each other with deep frowns on their brows as they drank deeply from their tankards was suspicious.

One of them caught his eye and lifted her chin.

"Excuse me a moment," Eaon said in Terranian before patting Cinn on the shoulder, repeating in Nirnish.

The rainwater dribbling through the tunnels made tiny rivers Eaon had to step over as he crossed the warren, images of himself as a god traipsing over a tiny Wyldeden threatening to pull his mouth into a smile. Which would be inappropriate judging from the somber expression on the sky witch's face.

He recognized her—sheer veil now soft over her face, hair wrapped in a white shawl.

"I'm sorry for your loss," he said in greeting. "I'm Eaon."

"Iniz. And thank you," she said with a nod, her heavy-lidded eyes puffy and bloodshot. "Thank you for saving the rest of them."

Her accent was thick enough that Eaon asked, "What language are you most comfortable with?"

"Celish. Do you know it?"

"Enough," Eaon answered. "Do you need a drink? Somewhere quiet to rest?"

Wise enough not to touch him, she placed a hand over her own heart and smiled sadly. "You know."

"Sorry?" Eaon frowned.

"What it is like. I am sorry for you, too." Her statement still didn't make sense to him, but she continued on regardless. "You are Terranian, yes? Killing is not your way. It mustn't be easy bearing the power you do."

Eaon grimaced. "I'll pray for forgiveness later."

"While Yasmin is at the ritual, the rest of us will go outside and pray to Celeste, to comfort her." Iniz waved a hand toward the tunnel where the rain poured in, thunder breaking overhead. "She mourns too. If you like company when you pray you are welcome to join us."

Eaon smiled. "I would appreciate that, thank you."

"I will find you later, then. I do need to sit for a few minutes and your friend is trying to get your attention." Iniz pointed back to where Cinn was rising onto his toes, trying to catch Eaon's eyes.

"Over there is Pippa. She will take you somewhere quiet if you ask," Eaon said as he pointed out Killian's shrewd sister.

Iniz thanked him again before weaving through the crowd toward Pippa, so Eaon returned back to the others waiting for him by the whiskey barrels.

"Everything okay?" Killian asked.

"Yeah, here?" he asked, turning to Cinn.

{There's Selina,} he signed, pointing toward the fiddlers.

Selina and a male Eaon didn't know were about five seconds away from ripping their clothes off right in the middle of the warren. Not that anyone would have cared. A number of others were similarly distracted.

"Might not bother her about Brach until morning," Eaon said.

"Speaking of lovesick idiots, where's your brother?" Reigan asked Killian.

"He and Yasmin went to take the moth that was killed to the bleeding mountain. They had to make a sacrifice before the union anyway, so it made sense." Killian shrugged.

"What's going on with you two?" Eaon asked as he pushed off the wall. His cup was empty again, but as he tried to walk over to the barrel, he found himself unsteady on his feet.

"Between . . . between who?" Killian asked, unexpectedly flustered.

"You and Miika. Who else would I mean?"

"No one, I don't know. Fuck, this smoke's gone to my head. Miika's just been extra haughty since the engagement. That's all."

"Really? Because you look like you wish he'd throw himself into the bleeding mountain instead."

Reigan spat out her drink as she began laughing.

"You heard the way he talked to you out on the flat. He's like that all the time. Thinks he's something special. It's fucking annoying."

Eaon frowned. Miika was an elder, and Eaon was a traveler; he hadn't given a second thought to what Miika had said on the flat but clearly Killian was mad about it. His fists had clenched. Reigan passed him the pipe.

"Chill out," she told him.

"One of these days I'm going to remind him he's not better than anyone else, just because he's an elder. Just because he's marrying an Alpha sky witch," Killian huffed.

Eaon rolled his eyes. "Have I ever told you to never visit Wyldeden? You'd burst a vein."

"Yeah, I think you have, actually."

"Another round for Eaon!" Tomaii crowed to the crowd from where he had climbed halfway up a rope ladder, dangling precariously. "Fuck harpies!"

"Fuck harpies!" the witches around him chanted back, raising their cups into the air.

Eaon shook his head. "Someone should get him down from there before he breaks his neck."

"Not it," Killian said, grabbing his nose. Reigan had gone to grab hers too, but was just a fraction slower.

"Well obviously I can't do it," Eaon shrugged.

"Lover damn the both of you," she hissed, then strode off to coax her cousin down off the warren wall.

Many hours of drinking and dancing later, as well as a solid hour in the rain praying with Iniz and the sky coven, Eaon and Cinn collapsed against the wall in their cave with grins across their faces. Barely capable of sitting upright, Cinn struggled to get his boots off while Eaon ran a hand through his drenched and tangled curls. They were getting too long again.

"I didn't know kinners could even get as drunk as you are," he chuckled, holding Cinn by the elbow as he yanked a boot off, nearly falling to the side.

Cinn wrinkled his nose as he peeled a wet sock off too. {It won't last. But if we never go further than this mountain I would not complain.}

Eaon grinned wider. "It's not the worst place in Nir. And the company isn't awful."

{Flirt.}

The word shouldn't have made his heart stutter as hard as it did. Shouldn't have fixated his attention on the curve of Cinn's lip as his long fingers brushed against them while making the sign. Shouldn't have conjured the sudden need to know what those lips and fingers would feel like against him.

"I was talking about the two red-haired females following you around all night, or did you not notice?" Eaon poked his tongue out, dragging himself to his feet again before Cinn could notice the way his face had heated.

{Did you notice Tomaii?}

Eaon sighed, pulling off his gloves and stripping out of his wet shirt. Ringing the excess water from it, he hung it to dry over one of the ropes suspending the hammock. Between the dampness lingering on his skin, the steam rising from the hot spring and the humidity of the cave, Eaon could pretend he wasn't sweating at the idea of being undressed in the same room as Cinn. Something that had happened often enough the last few months, and yet had never elicited such a full-bodied tightening.

Clearing his throat, he eyed the hot spring. "Even if it were possible, Tomaii is dreaming if he thinks I'd bother with him again."

Cinn raised his eyebrows, laying down on the ground and propping his head on his hands, as if waiting for a story.

Eaon shook his head at him. "You're a terrible busybody, you know that?"

Cinn smiled innocently, making Eaon laugh.

{Last time I was in the Long Gorge,} Eaon signed, not wanting anyone wandering past to hear. {I spent a lot of quality time with Tomaii. While my da was doing business with the elders, I lost myself in this place. It was fun for a while, but I wouldn't do it again.}

{Why not?} Cinn asked.

Keeping his back turned, Eaon got rid of the rest of his clothes and sunk into the hot spring in the corner of their cave, the lanterns casting long shadows across the stone. The water was warm enough to melt away the ache of the past month of traveling.

"Go try it for yourself and see. One of us might as well enjoy ourselves."

Cinn grimaced and folded down his arms, resting his head on them.

"Don't tell me those two red-headed witches aren't your type," Eaon teased, heart pounding loud enough to rival the thunder. "You're welcome to find Tomaii if you'd prefer."

Cinn didn't take the bait, continuing to stare vacantly at the wall. Eaon could almost see the heavy darkness hovering over him.

"Cinn."

Nothing.

"Hey, what's the matter? Did I say something?" Eaon sat up, frowning.

Cinn blinked a few times, shook his head, faked a smile and rolled onto his other side. Usually Eaon could take a hint but tonight he didn't want to play this game with Cinn. Getting out of the hot pool, ignoring the water dripping from him as he crossed the floor, he sat down on the warm rock beside Cinn. The kinner looked over his shoulder, frowned, and threw a nearby cushion at him.

Eaon rolled his eyes, putting the pillow over himself. "What's wrong?"

Cinn sighed, rolling onto his back and tucking his hands under his arms. His official I-don't-want-to-talk-about-it pose.

"Come on. No sulking."

Cinn glared at him, releasing his hands. {I'm not sulking.}

"That's the sulkiest sulking face I have ever seen." Eaon pouted and poked Cinn's nose.

Batting Eaon's hand away, Cinn sighed again. {You're an annoying drunk.}

"Correct. But talk to me."

It took a moment, but Cinn raised his hands and slowly signed, {I think something is wrong with me.}

Eaon frowned and blinked a few times trying to clear his head. Cinn slowing down meant he didn't know if he had all the words he needed, so Eaon tried to concentrate as he continued.

{You are so sad that you can't . . . touch. You talk like I should want to, but I don't.}

Sitting with the words for a moment while Eaon tried to read between them, Cinn began to fidget with the hem of his shirt. Trying to ease his nerves, Eaon held out both hands and helped Cinn sit up.

"After what you've been through, I mean, I don't know what you've been through, but I can imagine it's normal to not . . . feel certain things again yet. It's not like life has been easy since you've been free, either. Don't worry about it. You've got forever. Sex isn't going out of fashion."

Cinn shuffled and crossed his ankles. {It's not that.}

Eaon frowned. "What do you mean?"

{What do you mean by *feel certain things*? What am I supposed to feel?}

That was not what Eaon had been expecting Cinn to say and it took a moment for it to dawn on him what Cinn was getting at. "Before everything that . . . happened, was there ever someone you were interested in? Did you ever see someone and just feel the need to touch them? Be touched by them."

Cinn frowned as he thought about it but eventually shook his head.

{Am I broken?}

"No," Eaon snapped, running his tongue over his teeth. "There's nothing wrong with you."

Cinn's shoulders began to cave, so Eaon softened his tone.

"Even if you never feel like having sex for the rest of your life, there's nothing wrong with you. There's no one way to be."

{It just seems like I'm missing something. Maybe if I tried it, I would understand why you're so obsessed.}

At the tiny smirk on Cinn's face, Eaon scoffed and elbowed him.

"Just do me a favor. If you're going to experiment with someone, be careful. People can be absolute pieces of shit and you don't need that. If you're not sure, ask me."

Cinn tilted his head, brows pulling together. Whatever serious thing he'd thought about saying was discarded as his expression became quizzical. {Even the mouth thing?}

"Mouth thing? Do you mean kissing?" Eaon balked. "Lover take me, we really need to have a talk, don't we?"

Eaon dragged his hands down his face. If they had to have this conversation, at least he was drunk. Cinn slapped Eaon in the chest.

"Ow!"

{I know what it is, I didn't know how to sign!}

"Well, thank all the Spirits for that. Sorry. I didn't realize there were things we hadn't covered." Eaon made himself more comfortable and showed Cinn the sign he needed. "So, you've kissed then."

{No. Not me. But my . . . my brother used to talk about it.}

Eaon stilled. It was only recently Cinn had even shared that he had a family in Hyrsch; opening up about anything from before was such a rarity that Eaon caught himself holding his breath.

{There was this one time he was . . . hurt? Hit? Beat. For kissing the master's daughter. And after, he kept doing it! I asked him if putting mouths together was worth it. He just did this.} Cinn imitated a wry smile, waggling his eyebrows.

Eaon laughed, even as his chest ached. "Not going to lie, it sounds like your brother and I would understand each other on an intense level."

Shaking his head, Cinn said, {I miss them.}

"You said you had a sister too, right? What were their names?"

Cinn signed them, letter by letter.

"Rad and Eddy?"

Cinn nodded, smiling fondly. {I would like to see them again one day.}

"I'd like that for you too."

{Anyway. My point is that I have never understood the appealing.}

Eaon corrected his sign before placing his hands on Cinn's knees. "Some people just aren't that way inclined. And that's okay."

The two of them sat in silence, listening to the halls beyond their door slowly quiet as witches went to sleep. Tomorrow would be another big day.

{I'm sorry,} Cinn signed, not able to look Eaon in the eye as he did.

"What for?"

{For being the one person in the world who could give you what you want, but being the way I am.}

Eaon grimaced. He'd be lying if he said he wasn't disappointed. The empty possibility left a gaping abyss inside him that nothing and nobody would ever be able to fill. The whiskey had gone to his head and a burning started behind his eyes as Eaon shook his head.

"That's ridiculous."

After a moment, Cinn grabbed Eaon's hand and pulled him to his feet, leading him to the hammock. Climbing in, Cinn patted the space beside him. Eaon frowned until Cinn grabbed his wrist and yanked, sending the whole thing rocking. Scrambling to keep Cinn from falling out, Eaon half fell half climbed into the hammock, staring as Cinn curled up against him, skin to skin. Like the first time under the willow, the touch broke the spell dragging him into the dark parts of his mind.

Maybe it wasn't what he wanted, but he'd take it. Resting his chin on top of Cinn's forehead, the warmth of their bodies lulled Eaon into the first true sleep he'd had for a long time.

CHAPTER TWENTY-FOUR

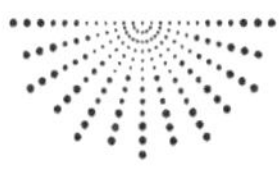

EAON

The markets in the Long Gorge were anarchy compared to the lanes in Wyldeden. Along winding paths deep enough in the canyon that shadow concealed them, colorful stalls embellished with embers of everlight and glowing flowers housed vendors boasting their wares as people passed by. Richly spiced meats infused the air with their mouth-watering aroma, but Eaon was not tempted the way he had been during his first visit to the clan. Cinn, on the other hand, happily took samples from everyone who offered them as well as the different curries and alcohols passed out in little ceramic bowls.

"Careful. If you get too drunk and slip off the edge of the mountain I'm not coming down after you."

Cinn rolled his eyes but was wary of how much he drank as they continued through the markets. Especially since, aside from the food and drink, the everlight dancers twirling batons of white fire alongside bright cloths and shiny jewels were a dangerous distraction for Cinn-the-magpie, who made Eaon stop at yet another stall to look at something that had caught his eye.

"Take it," the vendor said, noticing Cinn stroking a fossilized claw of some kind.

"We're not carrying anything to trade," Eaon explained.

"You're Eaon Nemuse, right? Everybody's talking about how you saved the sky witches from the harpy. Consider the fossil a gift of thanks."

The witch's joyful smile as he picked up the claw from the display and placed it in Cinn's hands was contagious. Eyes widening, Cinn looked from the vendor to Eaon with such a boyishly hopeful expression that Eaon couldn't help grinning.

"Thank you," Eaon said, interpreting the rapid gesturing from Cinn. "You've made his whole week."

The vendor waved as the two of them moved on, Eaon putting a hand on Cinn's back to keep him moving in the right direction, his attention wholly fixated on the fossil in his hands.

Eventually, they reached Reigan's workshop down a quiet crevice in the mountainside. Shielded by a white sail, two wooden benches displaying jars of peculiar substances and a variety of neatly arranged tools ran alongside a wall of caged critters, some sleeping, some drinking from little bowls of water, while others chewed futilely on the bars. Reigan stood with her back to the path, hands and face covered in protective gear as she milked a six-legged salamander.

Not wanting to distract her, Eaon signed to Cinn.

{The milk is toxic, but it also puts out flame. With water being so scarce in this area, the Ignatius-blessed use it when training witchlings. They also use it against natural bushfires, which can happen around here.}

{They're going to need a lot more lizards to put out a fire.} Cinn frowned, watching as Reigan corked a vial of pearlescent milk and put it to one side. Wiping down its scales, she cleaned up the critter before returning it to a cage.

{That one is barely matured. Adult ones can get up to four-feet long and produce much more milk. Reigan uses the young milk for antivenom.}

"I hope you're not gossiping about me," Reigan said as she pulled off the protective face covering, wiping the sweat off her forehead.

"Just about your milk," Eaon chuckled, lifting his chin toward the salamander. "I didn't want to distract you."

"Appreciate it. Did you bring it?"

From his satchel, Eaon took out one of the tonics Cleo had given him. It was meant to slow down his brain when things got too out of control, but like the ones that were meant to help him sleep or keep away his darkest thoughts, it barely worked anymore. Despite what he'd said while drinking his weight in whiskey last night, assuming Cleo wasn't a good brewer was unfair. It was just as possible that his condition was worsening and he simply needed a stronger dose.

Popping the cork, Reigan took a whiff of the tonic and raised her brows, nodding slightly. "Smells legit. Let me take a sample."

While they waited, Cinn wandered down the crevice to look at other stalls. Eaon watched him go with a flutter beating his stomach, the disappointment of last night easing like butter in a hot pan. Whatever this feeling was, this settling, this knowing that what lay between the two of them was all there would ever be . . . he could live with it.

What was not as simple was the way a part of him still balked at seeing the salamanders being caged and used like this.

"Don't even think about it," Reigan warned, shooting him a sidelong glance.

Putting a hand to his chest, Eaon promised, "I wasn't thinking about anything."

"I see right through you, Nemuse. Fool me once—"

"Tomaii and I were very drunk. Pranks always seem like a good idea when you're drunk, but I swear, I'm not going to let your critters loose again. Even if they do look very sad in their cages."

Clicking her tongue, she turned away to focus on extracting a portion of Eaon's tonic, placing it in a different vial.

Corking the sample, Reigan shook it as she began muttering a spell under her breath. A piece of parchment was spread on the counter, the corners weighted with carved gemstones, and as she finished casting the spell over the tonic she pulled the cork and let it splash out onto the page. Eaon had no idea what Reigan saw in the stains, but the frown on Reigan's forehead grew deeper.

"Odd."

"What?" Eaon asked, stepping closer.

"I've never seen this combination before. And . . . the ingredients are not blessed," she said, glancing over to Eaon. "It might as well have been brewed by a human for all the benefit you'll get out of it. Your headaches are likely withdrawal symptoms."

Eaon blinked. "But the high priestess recommended her."

Cinn had wandered back, concern pulling at his brow at the frustration in Eaon's voice.

Reigan shrugged. "Well, she either forgot to bless it or chose not to."

He had offended Cleo that day he went to gather supplies for traveling, but the headaches had begun weeks prior. Did Cleo just not like him? That would make sense.

"Well, thank you for looking into it. I don't suppose you know a good brewer that could make something for me?" he asked, putting the useless vial back in his pocket.

"I do know a few who could do it, but with the union tomorrow they might be low on supplies. Here." She tore a piece of parchment from her recipe book and wrote down a few names. "You'll find them farther down. If they can't help I could try to whip something up, but it's not my specialty. Oh, and if you see Jiminika could you pick up some more papaver for me? I promise to share later."

"No, thanks." Eaon rolled his eyes, pocketing the parchment and the pouch of buck teeth Reigan handed him to trade for the opiate. "But I'll let you know if I have any luck."

Reigan nodded before turning back to the cages, selecting another salamander to milk.

As they walked, Eaon explained to Cinn what they had found out.

{Will you tell Kaelean?} he asked.

"I don't want to get Cleo in trouble. I'll just get a new batch."

{You've been really unwell, Eaon.}

"I know. I'm sorry it's been such a burden on you."

{No, shithead, I meant that it's not right to let her get away with giving you a useless tonic just because she doesn't like you for some reason. It's unprofessional.}

Eaon shrugged. "Maybe, but it's just how things are for witches like me. There's a reason Eavha was brewing for me even though it was well below her station to do so; I couldn't contribute to the clan, so why should anyone do anything for me?"

Cinn scoffed in disgust, fists clenching at his sides for a moment before signing viciously, {That's unfair. You don't still think that, do you?}

Eaon didn't know how to answer that. The shame of his uselessness had always been so heavy, he'd never had room to think about whether he believed he deserved it. Whether it was *unfair*. Going to the mountains or the human cities had been a wonderful reprieve, but that's all it was. A reprieve. It had never felt like something that could be normal for him.

Pressure gathered at the base of his skull, his thoughts becoming thick and syrupy, quieting to near silence as they walked through the market. Thinking about things like that was too hard.

Cinn put a hand on Eaon's elbow, the anger having left his face.

{Sorry. I didn't mean to make you . . .} He didn't have the sign to express himself, so he dragged a finger down in a spiral.

It seemed accurate enough, though even Eaon didn't know how to describe what was happening in his head right then. Forcing a smile, he gave Cinn's hand a quick squeeze and the next time they passed a wine vendor offering free samples, Eaon took a cup.

One of the healers Reigan recommended had enough ingredients to brew a small batch of calming tonic but the rest would have to wait a couple of weeks until the new crop of valerian was ready.

He'd manage. He had to.

"There you two are!" Tomaii's voice boomed through the crowd as he weaved between groups of people, almost knocking someone off the ledge. He grabbed a hold of them quickly, pulling them back as he apologized profusely.

Eaon just shook his head while Cinn smirked coyly.

{Not a word out of you,} Eaon warned him.

Cinn raised his brow, eyes shining with amusement. {Obviously.}

"In all my life, I have never met anyone as graceless as you, Tomaii," Eaon commented as he came to a stop before them.

"Thanks! Come on, I want to show you something." Without waiting, Tomaii immediately speared back into the growing crowd.

"Lover take me," Eaon muttered, grabbing Cinn's hand so he didn't lose him.

They followed Tomaii, careful of the edge of the path. Vendors saw them coming and pulled their wares back, trying to stay out of Tomaii's way as he rushed through the crowd.

"Slow down, you oaf!" someone shouted at him, but Tomaii just laughed and waved.

"Save some pies for me!"

"Only if you pay me this time!" the vendor called back.

Tomaii blew them a kiss, looking back to make sure Eaon was still following before heading down another crevice.

He had forgotten how easy Tomaii was. How fun. All the trouble he had gotten in while chasing Tomaii through the markets, intoxicated on rum and papaver, stealing food from vendors who shook their heads at them in weary amusement . . . the *freedom* he had felt here. Leaving it behind to return to Wyldeden had been too difficult to let himself think about it often.

Tomaii finally stopped outside a tanner's stall; boots, armor, scabbards, reins and whips hanging on display. The woman smiled at Tomaii, the scar trailing from her ear to her mouth making it difficult to tell how genuine it was.

"Got those gloves for you," she said, reaching under the counter to pull out a package.

"Ah, thanks," Tomaii mumbled, blushing a little as he looked to Eaon. "Come here. This is my . . . distant relative of sorts. She's great. Bevv, this is Eaon and Cinn. I was hoping you could help us with something."

"I can try. What are you lads after?" she asked, giving Eaon and Cinn a once over.

Eaon looked to Tomaii expectantly. "That's a great question."

"I was thinking about those marks Kil said you were talking about. The ones that repel your magic. If they can be put on a collar and cage, then maybe we could make something for you so you wouldn't have to worry about surging."

Unsure when Killian had found the time to fill Tomaii in on the details Eaon had shared during their travels, he raised his eyebrows, looking over the leather wares again. "I can't always be walking around in full leathers. I'll sweat to death."

"No, obviously. But what about a collar?"

Eaon wrinkled his nose. "I'm not wearing a fucking collar."

There was nothing he'd rather wear less. Not after having a metal one clamped around his neck, nearly strangling him to death. Not after listening to Cinn's stories back on the farm, when he would wake in the middle of the night from a nightmare and tell Eaon how the Sparrows used to keep the demi-kin in similar collars.

"Alright, keep your knickers on. What about a pair of cuffs?" Tomaii asked, holding up his own wrist to show off the strap of leather wrapped around it.

Being the way he was, Tomaii struggled doing the same job for too long, so the clan let him jump from role to role. One of the more dangerous tasks he did was maintenance on the sprites' little houses. Sometimes, the faeries got a little cheeky and would bite his hands. Too many witches had nearly bled out from a bite on the wrist, hence the cuffs.

Eaon sighed. "Better than a collar, I guess."

"They'll be great. This is a good idea, right?" Tomaii asked, picking out a couple of new cuffs with brass buckles.

It was a good idea. He'd sleep a lot easier knowing his surges would be contained at least.

"I appreciate it, Tomaii," Eaon told him truthfully. "But I'm not sure how to make it work. Drawing them on a doorway is one thing, but this . . ."

He hadn't been able to mark his own skin. No matter how he'd pushed himself, he couldn't get past the pain of it.

"I can do it, that's easy." Bevv waved off the concerns.

"It's . . . it's Sparrow magic. Death magic," Eaon reminded her.

Bevv just smiled at him. "I know. I can do it."

It took longer than expected for Eaon to understand what she was saying.

"You're Lover-blessed?"

"I defected from the Sparrow Coven many, many centuries ago." She nodded, grabbing a piece of charcoal to start outlining the marks along the interior of the cuffs.

Eaon stood there, slack-jawed for so long that Tomaii had time to put his new gloves on, walk over to him and close it. Flinching back, Eaon glared at him.

"Don't touch me."

"Why do you think I got the gloves?" he asked with a mischievous grin.

"That's not the point," Eaon muttered, looking past him back to Bevv. "Could I ask you some questions? I'd love to hear your story."

"Come to our cave for dinner sometime after the wedding," Bevv agreed. "We'll talk."

Eaon wanted to talk *now*, but that wasn't fair. "What are the cuffs worth? I don't have anything on me, but I can get—"

"A gift," Tomaii interrupted. "From me. A late quarter-century gift."

Clearing his throat, Eaon shifted his weight. "That's unnecessary."

"Oh shut up," Tomaii teased, either oblivious or ignoring Eaon's discomfort. Then to Bevv, "You know which marks they are?"

"Yes. I know very well which spell you're talking about. Give me a few days. With everything going on . . ."

"Thank you. Very much," Eaon told her, bowing deeply.

"None of that," she said, waving them away. "Go cause trouble elsewhere."

"Naw, Unt, I promised Ma and Da I would be on my best behavior today. And Eaon's too stuck-up to get in trouble anymore," Tomaii teased.

With another sigh, Eaon turned to Cinn and signed, {Let's go before I push him into the gorge.}

Cinn grinned. {I want to know everything you two just said.}

{Don't be annoying.}

{Me? Annoying?} Cinn blinked at him innocently, a hand at his chest.

"I'll see you later, Tomaii!" Eaon called back over his shoulder as he led Cinn back to the markets.

"Definitely!"

He was so busy waving back at Eaon that Tomaii knocked a basket of pineapples out of a vendor's hands, a few of them flying over the cliffside.

Cinn chuckled, but Eaon just shook his head again.

"Lover take me."

CHAPTER TWENTY-FIVE

EAON

The ceremony began at sundown.

The clearing went dark as every torch was put out, leaving only the stars to illuminate the whispering crowd. A drum sounded, blue sparks shooting from where the stick made contact with the canvas. Another, then another, blue and orange, magenta and violet embers bursting into the night with every impact like a display of fireworks in perfect harmony with the steady beat now filling the clearing. Witches were starting to move, their feet stomping along to the rhythm, hands beating chests, heads thrown back as they vocalized in unison a melody that filled Eaon with anticipation. It pulled at something deep in his bones, his body trembling with the need to join them.

The great bonfire in the center began to smolder. Witches from the sky coven leaped and twisted in a fluid dance around the pyre, flames fanning every time they raised their arms, the tendrils of smoke writhing in a perfect funnel toward the sky.

Eaon was aware of Cinn watching him, noticing the rapid rise and fall of his chest, the clenched fists as sparks flickered to life in his eyes. When the witches beside them began to move, Cinn nudged him.

{Go.}

Eaon blinked and looked away guiltily. He couldn't very well leave

Cinn standing alone, even if the drums had taken a hold of him, sweat gliding down his neck from the effort of keeping still.

Cinn shoved him. {Go.}

Whatever tether held Eaon's sensibility in place snapped. Grabbing Cinn's face, he grinned gratefully before slipping into the masses.

At one with the mountain witches, primal joy empowered every stomp, every turn and twist and leap. Bone horns began to play, their deep rumble like soft hands over his spine as the dance became wilder. With the drums and horns, the vocalization and the impossible gracefulness of the sky-witch dancers, with the bonfire and the sparks flying from the pounding drums . . . There was so much to look at. So much to see and feel and taste and hear.

Tomaii found him, grinning with contagious feral mischief that Eaon mimicked. Mirroring each other's movements perfectly, they danced to the carnal rhythm, their movements sure and powerful. There was freedom in it, life and energy and joy, as they spun and leaped as if they'd practiced the dance for years. All these witches were so different—Terranian, Igni and Celestian—and yet in this moment they were one people.

When he could, Eaon spared a glance to Cinn. He had a tankard of whiskey in one hand and held the hand of a red-haired witch in his other as she danced. Moving awkwardly, as if he had never danced in his life, an honest smile half glowing in golden light from the flames broke across his face.

In all of Nir, Eaon had never seen anything so beautiful.

The dancing lasted all night, the heat of the bonfire growing until most of the gathering had abandoned their clothes. Only when the first hint of color warmed the sky did the drums finally stop, the mountain clan's high priest entering the meadow. The firelight glistened off the male's sweaty skin, a pattern of swirls and sharp lines painted in soot on his bare chest.

Eaon jogged back to Cinn, pushing back his thick damp hair, eyes sparkling with their own little bonfires.

"They're about to start the Omen Ceremony," he explained breathily. "We should stay back. It can be dangerous sometimes."

{What's going to happen?} Cinn was just as drenched with sweat, having abandoned his shirt and boots. He envied Cinn's ability to strip down, boiling beneath the long linen sleeves and pants clinging to him. But short of wearing a sign, he couldn't always stop people from trying to touch him. Not that the linen would be enough to protect them, but it was better than nothing, and a few accidental brushes during the dancing hadn't amounted to anything.

"Don't know. Sometimes a union's omen is just a color change of the fire, meaning it will be a simple coupling. Sometimes a phoenix arises from the flames, meaning great change for the clan. Once, the Heads of three different Houses spontaneously combusted, meaning those families would suffer greatly because of the union."

{Shit.}

"Yeah," Eaon snickered, wiping his forehead on the back of his sleeve.

The two of them watched as Miika and Yasmin stepped forward to join the high priest at the bonfire. A bone knife in one hand, Yasmin split open her palm to drip blood into a bowl held by the high priest, who then passed the knife to Miika, who did the same. Passing the bowl to them to hold, another witch brought forward a sparrow struggling to spread its wings and escape.

Eaon grimaced, explaining to Cinn, "A fresh sacrifice."

{Poor thing.}

"A sparrow was the first gift from the Mother to the Lover. They represent Balance. Many are bred for these kind of sacrifices here in the north."

The high priest snapped the bird's neck and placed the body in the bowl before praying over it. Magic rolled through the crowd, turning the heat suffocating. Cinn held Eaon's elbow to keep him steady, his head getting hazy. The bonfire crackled loudly in anticipation.

Once the prayer was finished, Miika and Yasmin threw the bowl into the flames.

The entire gathering stepped back and held their breath as they waited for the omen.

Slowly, the coals and embers of the bonfire began to stir. Twisting and churning, they gelled together and began to take shape.

"Oh, fuck," Eaon gasped, pulling Cinn back.

Witches screamed and ran from the flames as a beast rose up, roaring with all the rage of the world. Eaon had never seen a dragon, let alone one whose flesh was made of ash, its wings and frills wreathed in fire. Its enormous head swiveled and glowing eyes of coal locked directly onto him.

"Oh, *fuck*," Eaon repeated.

Before panic could truly set in, Miika and Yasmin drew hasty spellmarks on their faces from the ash and began chanting loudly. The dragon whipped its head around, screeching loudly as Yasmin twisted herself into a spin at the same time Miika stomped his foot on the ground. As if commanded, the beast spread its impossible wings, the few trees on the crest of the meadow catching fire as it did, and took two great flaps to heave its mass into the sky before disintegrating.

Ash and ember began to rain down on the clan. Cinn pushed Eaon down, covering him with his own body. Magic burst all around them as witches pushed the air away from the crowd, sending the spiraling flames up and away.

A sole spark fell on Eaon's shirt, scalding him, but Cinn quickly patted it out.

The high priest raised his arms and declared the ceremony over as Eaon pushed himself up, frowning deeply at the burns already healing on Cinn's bare back.

{What does it mean?} Cinn asked, scratching the raw skin.

Eaon swallowed and shook his head. "I don't know."

CHAPTER TWENTY-SIX

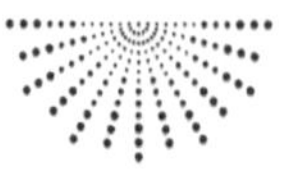

EAON

EXHAUSTED AND RATTLED, EAON AND CINN MADE THEIR WAY BACK to Killian's family cave. A cacophony of panicked conversation met them as dozens upon dozens of witches stood around discussing the omen, theorizing about what it meant. Most of them ignored Eaon and Cinn, the latter carrying his boots in one arm while holding Eaon's hand in the other as they skirted around the gathering, trying to get back to their room.

As they turned down the hall, Eaon stilled at the sight of Brach and Selina waiting outside their door.

"I just got the heads up. We have to go," said the male they still hadn't had a chance to meet properly.

"Now?" Eaon sagged, eyes itching from the lingering smoke. He had hoped to soak in the hot spring for a few hours before trying to get some sleep.

"It's now, or not for another month," Brach said as he crossed his arms. "And if you're not quick about it, we'll miss our window."

Sighing, Eaon turned to Cinn and translated.

{I'm so tired,} Cinn complained, rubbing his face. {But we can't wait another month.}

"No, we can't. Let's get our bags. Do we have time to say goodbye?" Eaon asked.

Brach grimaced. "Very, very quickly."

With a nod, the two of them hurried to gather their things before stepping into the hall.

"Vira!" Eaon called out. "We're going."

"Finally," she called back, pushing back the tapestry over her doorway, dark bags under her eyes. "After some sleep I'm going back to Wyldeden. A few travelers want to go and see Kaelean. Set up new relations and such."

Eaon nodded. "Safe travels."

"You too."

Then she was gone. Eaon and Cinn hiked their packs onto their backs.

"What about you?" Eaon asked Selina.

Taking Brach's hand, she said, "I've been invited to stay. Do you think Kaelean will mind?"

"If she gives you any shit, send me a leaf. I'll talk to her."

She deserved to be happy, and he'd fight Kaelean until he was blue in the face to make sure Selina could stay with her lover.

"Thank you."

She reached for his gloved hand, and Eaon made sure his magic was well and truly locked down as he let her squeeze it.

In the main room, Killian was nowhere to be found but his ma was putting out platters of hot breads and hummus, ushering people to eat. There would be days of celebrating in the warren after this, and people were fueling up.

"Eat. Drink. There's plenty more where that came from," she said before looking up. Seeing the packs on their backs, her face fell. "You're leaving."

"It's time, apparently." Eaon nodded. "We can't linger but—"

Nodding, Kerinna placed a hand over her heart. "I'll tell them you said goodbye."

"Thank you. And thank you for having us."

"You are always welcome here, Eaon. Always."

He smiled at her and bowed deeply. Brach was snapping his fingers at them from the front doorway, already edging down the hall.

"Alright." Eaon turned to Cinn. "Let's do this. Let's go to Qiri."

The Igni temple at the base of the bleeding mountain should have been the strongest point of the wards, but the opposite turned out to be true. The mountain marked the meeting of Qiri, Vertlyn and Kerveda, but with the temple right beneath it and the volcano so regularly sacrificed to, as well as it being active if not explosive, the wards must have grown tired.

The fire spirit's place of worship was not a novelty to Eaon, but Cinn was wide-eyed as he took in the towering pillars framing the cave entrance, carved from stone and inset with glittering jewels. Guardians crouched casually against the pillars playing a game of dice, barely lifting their heads to greet the approaching group.

"We're going inside?" Eaon asked, raising his eyebrows as they neared the cave. "How has nobody else noticed the gap?"

"You'll see," Brach grunted.

The basalt floor had been smoothed and polished, the walls decorated with tapestries and colored glass sconces. No sprites lived here, the lanterns filled instead with simple candles as they walked the hundred paces it took to reach a cavern. An impressive limestone altar laden with candles of mixed shapes, sizes and colors was spread along the farthest wall, but in the center sat a brazier large enough for three people to have lounged inside, burning brightly as it had been for thousands of years. A priestess was tending to it as they came in, sparing them a quick smile before stoking the flames.

No suspicion. No questions. Eaon looked to Brach once more, but he was too busy whispering to Selina before promptly leading the way to the three archways lining the eastern wall.

Quick footsteps echoed loudly in the cavern as Cinn rushed to catch up to Eaon, slipping a hand in his.

"You okay?" he whispered.

Cinn took a deep breath and pulled his lips inside his mouth, his hand sweaty against Eaon's glove.

"Nervous?"

Cinn tilted his head from side to side, unable to look at Eaon properly as he used his free hand to sign. {Ugly thoughts.}

Eaon squeezed his hand tighter before letting go so he could wrap an arm around Cinn's shoulders, mussing his hair slightly. One of these days he would see to it that Cinn's thoughts only knew beauty.

Beyond one of the stone archways awaited an intricately carved wooden door with a large brass handle. The images carved in the door depicted a firebird on the brink of crashing into the peak of a mountain. Whichever artist had been commissioned the work was talented, somehow able to portray rage and pain on the bird's beaked face.

"The story goes," Selina started as Brach pulled open the door and began descending the stairs that lay beyond, "that Ignatius was so angry at Terra that he transformed into a firebird and broke apart the mountain, turning the earth molten. Some of the lore states that every time the two of them fight, the mountain begins to bleed again."

{Why was he angry?} Cinn asked after Eaon translated, content to stay at his side as they stepped into the dark.

"Who knows," Selina shrugged, feet padding down the rocky steps. "I suspect the same reason they bless some witches in abundance while others get mere drops; they are simply capricious beings."

Eaon snorted, a familiar pinch twisting his face. He knew all about how capricious the Spirits could be. As if he knew where Eaon's thoughts had gone, Cinn's arm slipped around his waist, squeezing tightly. That Cinn even had the mental space to worry about Eaon when he was distressed left a knot in Eaon's throat. Before he could stop himself, he turned to kiss Cinn's temple. Only as his lips brushed the warm skin of his face did he realize what he was doing.

Pulling back quickly, he was glad it was too dark in the stairwell to see Cinn's face. A line had been drawn, and Eaon thought he might have just crossed it. But Cinn's arm stayed around Eaon's waist, neither tightening or loosening, as if he hadn't even noticed.

Good. That was good.

Before long, they reached the bottom of the stairs. And for the first time in a long time, Eaon didn't know what he was looking at. Torches were lit along the walls, held in brass sconces, sending shadows flickering over rows and rows of stone cubes. No higher than his knee, Eaon couldn't even begin to count how many there were, dizzy from the odd symmetry of the lines.

"Brach, what is this place?" Selina asked, as confused as Eaon.

"The catacomb," Brach said, as if that explained anything. "It is one of the highest honors of our people to have our ashes stored here after our souls pass to the after realm. That"—Brach pointed to a raised platform near the center of the room where a much larger rectangular shaped stone sat, unadorned bar the carvings along the side—"is where we keep Ignatius's bones."

Eaon and Selina exchanged a look.

"What are you talking about?" Eaon asked. "The Spirits don't have bones. They're spirits."

"They had bodies once. How else could he have transformed into a firebird to create the bleeding mountain?" Brach said, not hiding the condescension in his tone.

"Well, that's just lore. There's no evidence to suggest that's—"

"You Wyldeden witches think you know everything, don't you?"

"Brach!" Selina hissed at him. "Enough. We are allowed to believe different things. It's beside the point anyway. Let's find this smuggler before people start asking questions about where we've gone."

Brach nodded once, leading the way once again through the rows of cubes.

"Real charmer you have there," Eaon muttered to Selina.

"Oh, shut up," she hissed. "You were goading him."

"Was not."

"Were too."

They didn't have time to argue long. At the farthest end of the catacomb, a narrow crack in the wall only wide enough for a person to shuffle through had formed in the stone.

"Through there?" Eaon raised his eyebrows.

"She'll be here any minute," Brach assured them, leaning against the wall.

Quietly, they waited. Cinn and Eaon separated, the kinner unable to stop shifting his weight or the pack on his back. But when his shuffling wasn't the only sound in the otherwise silent catacomb, he went still.

From within the crack, a face appeared. At the sight of the gathering waiting for them, her eyes narrowed, lips pursing.

"What is this?" she asked in Terranian, her high voice heavily accented, vowels almost silent between the elongated s's.

"I help you, you help me," Brach said, raising his chin as the short and gangly witch eased out, two other witches emerging from the wall behind her. Packs held tightly to their chests, their dusty clothes were worn and unnaturally colored. "Where do these two want to go?"

"Kerveda. What do you want from me?" the short one snapped.

Brach pointed at Eaon and Cinn. "Take these two back with you."

"No. Absolutely not."

Eaon stepped forward, raising his hands as the witch flinched back. "My name is Eaon. This is Cinn. A Morvish witch named Yomra instructed us to get to Qiri. To find someone named Moyra Thorne."

The witch narrowed her eyes even further. "I don't know any Moyra, but Yomra, yes." Stepping closer, she sniffed deeply at the both of them. "Okay. He can come," she pointed at Cinn, then to Eaon. "You cannot."

"What?" Eaon blinked.

"You stink of death. I will not take you."

"It's just my blessing. I have it under control," Eaon explained, but the small witch had turned into a pillar of steel as she glared.

"You are not welcome. The wards will not let you pass. Should you try to cross them without me, you will die."

While that hardly felt like a threat anymore, Eaon wasn't sure what would become of him if he was struck down wedged in the crook of a mountain. Who would find his body? Who would restore it so he could be returned?

"There has to be a way," Eaon pleaded, reaching for Cinn's hand again. "He doesn't speak, and he doesn't understand anything but Nirnish. I've taught him to communicate through sign, but he needs me to translate for him."

"This is not my problem. And I don't have time for these shenanigans. If this human-ish thing wants to come, then he comes. If he wants to stay with you, I don't care. But you, soul-eater, are not stepping foot in Qiri."

The words hit him like a kick to the face. Soul-eater.

Cinn tugged on his hand. {What's happening?}

{I'm not allowed to go,} Eaon explained silently.

Instantly, Cinn's breathing turned sharp and shallow. His hand tightened in Eaon's to the point of being painful, eyes widening as he glanced between the new witch and Eaon desperately.

{But I need you.}

Eaon's chest ached. His head felt heavy, spots dancing across his vision. Color glittered in the air. Blinking rapidly, Eaon turned his face up and took a few deep breaths. Now was not the time for this nonsense.

"I'm leaving. Now," the Qiri witch stated, turning for the crack.

"Wait," Eaon called for her. "Please, just wait a minute."

He turned to face Cinn, letting go of his hand so he could sign properly. {You need to go.}

{I don't want to go if you're not coming with me.}

{I know. I want to come but I can't. So you have to go. For Sarah and William. So you can go home. I will wait here for you to come back.}

Cinn crouched down and pushed his clenched fists into eyes. Eaon gave the Qiri witch one last pleading look, but she held firm. When Cinn managed to stand again, there was bleak steel in his reddening eyes.

Reaching for the twine around his neck, Eaon untied his necklace. He took the button Cinn had given him off and tucked it in his pocket before tying the willow tree amulet around Cinn's neck.

{What are you doing? Eaon, no. Eavha gave that to you.}

{And I'm giving it to you. Keep it safe and bring it back.}

Cinn clutched the amulet and, after a moment's hesitation, finally nodded.

Eaon smiled sadly, laying a hand over Cinn's. That willow tree meant something between he and Eavha, but it meant something between he and Cinn, too.

"That's where we met, you know," he whispered.

Cinn managed a smile too, looking down at the carving in his hand.

The Qiri witch was getting impatient, but there was one more thing he needed to do.

"Just a moment, please," Eaon begged, putting down his pack and pulling out the parchment Kaelean had given him. Tearing off the edge where there was no writing, Eaon took out his quill and quickly scrawled a note for Cinn to take with him.

My name is Cinn. I cannot speak and I only understand Nirnish. I am looking for Moyra Thorne. A witch named Yomra sent me. The witches of Wyldeden support me if you require trade.

Blowing on the ink to dry it faster, he folded it and tucked it into Cinn's pack.

{Thank you.}

"You can do this," Eaon told him in earnest.

{You'll be here when I get back?}

"I promise."

Cinn blew out a shaky breath as he pulled Eaon close for a hug, resting his chin on his shoulder.

It dawned on Eaon that this would be the last hug he would get until Cinn came back. The last touch that would not ride him with anxiety. Digging his fingers into Cinn's back, he held him tighter, longer than was really appropriate, but Cinn didn't pull away. He only held him back.

They might have stayed like that forever had the Qiri witch not cleared her throat.

Cinn pressed his lips ever so gently against Eaon's cheek as he stepped back, quickly turning away to follow the Qiri witch into the crack in the wall before Eaon had a chance to respond. Before he had a chance to change his mind.

Eaon waited until he couldn't hear the shuffling of bodies against stone before picking up his pack and turning around. Brach was leading the two runaway witches toward the stairwell, but Selina was waiting for him.

"I'm sorry," she said, wiping her face on the back of her hand.

Eaon grimaced. "Probably for the best. I don't think I'm feeling very well."

"Come on, then."

Selina walked beside Eaon as they left the catacombs. Every step, he fought the urge to turn around. To see if Cinn had come back, wanting to find some other miracle solution rather than be apart from him.

But he wouldn't. The answers were in Qiri, and Eaon knew he wouldn't ever matter to someone enough to make them stay.

CHAPTER TWENTY-SEVEN

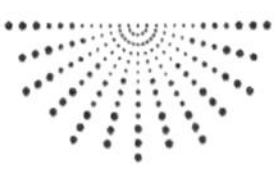

AISLING

SHE WAS YET TO CONVINCE THE SOUTHERN MOUNTAIN CLAN TO assist her or find a way to make them believe Davina's visions. Her father had declined an invitation for a private meeting prior to the grand meeting of Imsa. No reason had been given, and now that the evening had begun, he was late. Aisling knew in her bones that he was planning something, and to say she was nervous was an understatement.

Then there was Eavha. She wasn't even sure the witch was on her side. The Wyldeden delegation were more open-minded and the two of them had shared a nice moment together, but Aisling knew she was not forgiven for what happened with the kinner and Eavha was yet to comment on what Aisling had told her about Chaos.

Edwina was gone. Clayton was missing.

The advisors standing behind her on the dais were likely brimming with glee at the humiliation Aisling was likely about to endure.

"You're not alone," Davina reminded her. A ghostly hand hovered beside Aisling's, nails digging into the throne's arm as she dipped her chin in acknowledgment.

The king's throne was still beside hers on the dais, but two platforms had been erected on either side to give the clan leaders the respect they were owed. On Aisling's left, Sar Vin sat on a high-backed seat, legs spread wide as he drank from a tankard and watched the rest of his delegation mill around, whispering impatiently as they ate and drank. On her right, Eavha perched on an equally lovely chair, once more in the butterfly-wing skirt. The guardian she preferred was also missing, but others stood stoically around her platform with their spears upright beside them.

Finally, the heavy door to the throne room creaked loudly.

But it was Larissa, her other maiden, fists wringing her skirt and head ducked low, burning red as she hurried across the throne room. At the look on her face, a thousand possibilities ran through Aisling's mind: she had been too slow and the beasts were already here—though that made no sense as snow had not yet fallen on Hyrsch again—or perhaps the rebels had done something. Or Clayton had betrayed her, too. Worse, what if Nevan had discovered the insurgence building in his city?

"Your Highness," Larissa panted, falling to her knees before Aisling. "You should run."

Before Aisling could ask what Larissa was on about, the doors opened wider and the entire delegation that had come with the king came storming in. Stepping down, Aisling grabbed Larissa's arm and hid her behind the throne, whispers turning to cries as King Phineas came barreling through. In his gold and black armor-clad arms, a body lay gray and limp. One of the stable boys, judging by his attire.

"Nobody leaves." The king's voice boomed through the throne room, magic amplifying his voice above the growing cacophony.

Aisling remained standing on the dais as her father approached. Said nothing as he dumped the boy's body on the floor at her feet.

Face like stone, he demanded, "Explain."

Throat slashed, eyes still wide with the fear that chased him into death, the boy was demi-kin and barely grown. The throne room quieted as Aisling swallowed, a familiar sickening ache in her belly. She had been afraid this would happen. Had been afraid that someone from Dusarn would find a way around Imsa's laws.

"Where was he found?" she asked icily.

"Do you think I would be so furious if it had occurred outside of

Imsa's so-called protection?" the king barked. "The safety of everyone here was your responsibility, Aisling."

Meeting her father's eyes, she narrowed her own. Now that he'd said it, it was rather out of character for Phineas to be so disturbed by a demi-kin's death regardless of where or when it happened. She knew his views.

Knew more than that. She had spent her life listening and watching her father scheme and manipulate. His performances.

How convenient that a dead body would appear on palace grounds the moment the grand Imsa meeting was about to take place.

Aware of their audience, of the game she was being roped into playing, Aisling crouched down beside the body. "I shall see who is responsible."

Phineas grabbed her arm and pulled her back to her feet.

Nobody moved. Nobody even breathed as the king held his daughter in a vice grip. Not the advisors watching stoically from the back of the dais, not her guards, whose only response was to tighten their grips on their hilts.

Flaming heat burned her face as Aisling met her father's glare. For a long moment, she was only aware of the two of them. Of the silent battle passing between them. The spark behind his eyes gave away how much he was enjoying this. Humiliating her. But he would never do this for the simple thrill of it. He had refused to meet with her, had already undermined her with the mountaineers, and now this. Despite his promises, she realized he never had any intention of letting this Imsa happen. Why he had allowed it to go on so long already was a mystery, but it was clear that this was an attempt to ruin her plans. That his days of humoring her were over.

"You will not lay your hands on him again, daughter."

"Do not accuse me in my own home," she warned him. "You'll note that the only threats to the demi-kin at present are the ones you brought with you."

"Liar," he hissed. Though the sound was soft, it echoed through the room like a war-cry.

So did the scrape of her throne on the marble dais as Phineas shoved Aisling back into it.

Gasps rang through the room, while both Sar Vin and Eavha sprang to their feet. Phineas stalked forward, radiating such a pure anger she almost believed it was real.

"You thought you could hide this from me?" he spat down at her as he grabbed her arm, ripping off her glove. "The Key Mark for Those Unbound? Tattooed on your very skin?"

"So what?" Aisling hissed, pulling back her hand.

But she knew she had paled. Knew the gathering could see the marks. Her secret was out, and as the cacophony began to build once more, speculation turned to accusations.

"This spellmark, like all marks, can be manipulated depending on the intention and power of she who cast it," King Phineas was preaching now, tossing Aisling's arm aside and turning his back to her. "For instance, it could be used to negate the bindings of Imsa's laws! She has us all bound, while she is free to lie and scheme and kill!"

The usual steady rhythm of her heart faltered, then began to fly. The threats being hurled at her became nonsense in her ears, but her guards finally grew the spine to step forward. To form a line between the dais and the delegations, drawing their weapons. The king's men drew theirs, too, forcing the hands of the Southern Mountain Clan and Wyldeden.

Everything was falling apart. Why had she not expected something like this? Planned for it? Stupid. Because now, she didn't know what to do.

"Aisling, breathe." Davina's ghost knelt beside her.

People were blurring together, but even though her hands were trembling, Aisling pulled her glove back on.

"This Imsa has been a circus from the very beginning!" Sar Vin shouted. "The Southern Mountain Clan will never support Hyrsch!"

As if they were ever going to.

"Enough!" Eavha had climbed up on her chair to see over the heads of the dozens of guards preparing to kill each other should anyone make a mildly threatening move. "Have calm! We will find the truth about this mark, and you will look as fools for this behaviour!"

"Anyone willing to trust a word that comes out of the mouth of a witch who cannot even take a simple truth vow, who has taken measures to ensure she is always free to lie, is the fool." King Phineas sneered as he looked to Eavha. "And Sar Vin is right. As soon as Anfar sent a child to represent them, this Imsa became a joke."

As Aisling managed to take a proper breath, she had enough clarity to wonder how he had done it. Killing someone outside the walls of the palace and bringing them back inside would not have been too difficult, but to stand here and lie about who was responsible . . .

But he hadn't. He hadn't outright accused her. Hadn't even answered her question about where he had been found. She was not bound by the law, but he still was. They all were.

"I may be able to lie, but you cannot," she said, finding some steel for her voice as she forced herself to stand from the throne. "Say it. Say you did not plan this. That you are not trying to frame me and destroy my Imsa."

Phineas ignored her.

"The laws of Imsa have been broken, and I will convene with the Coven to discuss what punishment is fitting for someone who defiles the sacred oath—"

"Say it!" Aisling interrupted, fists shaking with rage as she screamed at the back of her father's head.

"—whom her advisors have told me is often ill with drink, and has likely organized this whole farce in a state of inebriation—"

"You bastard," she hissed at him.

"—I beg of the Southern Mountain Clan and of Wyldeden to forgive my daughter for wasting all of our times and permit this Imsa to be called to a close."

Aisling's hand fell inside the split in her skirt to wrap around the handle of her dagger. There had been times as a witchling she had wished her father dead. Long days after he had denied Davina the Passing rite where she had lay awake at night imagining the way she would kill him. But never before had she been so close to doing it.

"Easy," Davina whispered beside her. "We lost this game. And that's okay."

Slowly blowing out the murderous urge between her teeth, Aisling sunk back into her throne. Sar Vin and the Southern Mountain Clan were already departing. Eavha was being helped down from her chair, her Keeper whispering in her ear as the guardians kept their spears in hand.

By the time King Phineas aimed his arrogant smirk in her direction, Aisling had pulled on a mask of indifference.

"You are angry with me now, but I did this for your own good," he said softly.

Aisling ignored him. She didn't care what last taunts he had before departing. Didn't care about how or why he had done this. Didn't care about anything except finding a bottle of wine.

<hr>

The body had been moved to the infirmary, covered with a white sheet. The healers in her employ stood against the wall, their heads bowed, hands clasped in front of them as Aisling stalked into the room and approached the corpse laid out on the bed. She pulled back the edge of the sheet to expose the demi-kin boy's frozen, terrified stare once again. Carefully, she lowered his lids. It was time to rest. The Lover had him now.

And though she already suspected, and though there was nothing she could do to bring the perpetrator to justice, she needed to know the truth.

Gloves off, she placed her palms on either side of his face, closed her eyes and muttered the spell she had practiced since the very same day of her Passing, waiting for the death to play itself out in her mind's eye.

There was only emptiness.

Brow furrowing, she let a little of the power wrapped around her bones flare, repeating the spell again and again, but it was as if the body between her hands had never lived. There was no death to be seen.

That's when she saw it.

Pushing back the thick hair across the boy's forehead, Aisling cursed at the spellmark scratched onto his forehead. It was one her father had taught her when she had become Returned in case there was ever a death she didn't want looked into. No matter how deep she dug, she would find no answers. His mind had been erased.

A knock on the door forced her to cork the rising questions. Turning slowly, she glared at whoever had dared to interrupt her.

Clayton blanched at the look on her face.

"I'm sorry, Your Highness."

"Where have you been? What could possibly be so important that you felt it appropriate to miss Imsa?" she hissed.

Clayton's throat bobbed as he looked from Aisling's face to the body on the table, paling further.

"I shouldn't have interrupted—"

"Yet you have, so spit it out!"

Stepping back, he made space for Dearmead, who came through the door with a chained Edwina and Radley. Both of them had murderous looks on their faces, but while Radley was practically rabid, fighting Dearmead with every ounce of strength, Edwina kept her savage glare calmly leveled right at Aisling.

Never, not once, had Edwina been anything but meek and mild mannered, standing quietly in the background ready to tend to whatever Aisling needed. It made her ill to think of what information might have been leaked. And to whom.

Aisling narrowed her eyes. Her decree had been not to imprison demi-kin anymore, but that had only been so she could send a guerrilla force to overtake Pirevia from underneath. Besides, she was getting a new idea of what to do with these two.

"Put them in the dungeon for now. I'll deal with them later."

CHAPTER TWENTY-EIGHT

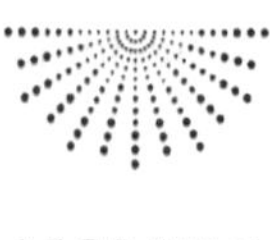

AISLING

There was only one person in this palace Aisling was in the right mood to speak to.

Back in her dressing room, she shed her dress. She had not worn a corseted dress since Edwina had betrayed her as she could not tie it on her own, so she unbuckled the belt around her waist and slipped out of the long yards of fabric she'd been wearing all day.

Then she donned the garb of the worst part of her, the part the king and queen had manifested, the one she hated most, and headed for the dungeon.

She didn't care who saw her striding the halls, unmasked and undisguised. Her soldiers and guards were escorting the visitors of Imsa out of the palace and either didn't notice or didn't care that their princess walked alone among them.

In the bowels of her palace, Aisling ignored the rogue coven members still wasting away in her dungeons, some in better shape than others. She didn't even bother looking at Edwina and Radley, huddling together in one of the better-kept cells. She went right to the one at the end of the hall and pressed her bare palm against the stone, pushing the Mark from her skin.

The Morvish bitch would talk today.

As she lit the lantern, soft whimpering seeped from under the hatch. Aisling crouched by it, not bothering to mask the tangled emotion in her voice.

"Eavha Nemuse has become a friend of mine. She told me about what you did to her family. Her brother. The only thing she didn't tell me was why, because she does not know. I have some interesting theories, though. Shall we discuss them?"

The whimpering quieted.

"You told me you could tell things about the future with nothing but a free hand and a quill. Offer me that, swear a vow to help me —*only* me—and I will let you out."

Aisling waited, listening to the labored breaths of the witch beneath the hatch. After giving her time to consider, Aisling slid back the lock and pulled it open.

Aadya flinched, squinting against the light. The witch had in fact become desperate for drink, her face stained with filth from the bottom of the cell, but her hatred had also intensified. Just as it had with the kinner. She thought he would eventually break, but resentment had only strengthened him.

This witch was not kinner though.

"You want out?"

"I will die down here before I do anything for you."

"Fine then," Aisling hissed.

Rolling up her sleeve, she let Aadya see the tattoos inked down her arms. Let her see the one on the back of her wrist shimmer, sinking into her skin like the void. Gritting her teeth, rallying the Celeste-blessing lying in wait, Aisling sucked the air right out of Aadya's body.

Mouth gaping, hollow cheeks drawn tight, the witch yanked pitifully at the chains around her wrists, trying to claw at her chest that was no doubt in spasms with the sudden loss of air.

Aisling released her magic, the air whistling as Aadya sucked in a deep lungful.

Then she took it away again.

Let it go, just to take it again.

Every time, Aadya's fight against her chains weakened a little more. Her eyes bulged and rolled back in her head, her chest barely rising before the air was snatched away once more.

Shaking her hand, the witchmark burning deeply, Aisling gave her air back and let Aadya take a few deep lungfuls.

"Just . . . kill me . . ." Aadya begged.

"That's what I'm doing. I don't owe you an easy death."

Celeste wouldn't let the magic flow so easily if she didn't agree to this, Aisling told herself. At least the Spirits believed she was doing the right thing.

From behind her, a soft voice said, "Her tattoo."

Aisling turned slightly, raising an eyebrow at where Davina had appeared by the workbench, fists clenched, lime-green eyes staring up to the ceiling.

"What about it?" Aisling asked.

"Threaten to carve it off. She'll break." Davina's voice trembled, a finger tracing the pattern tattooed across her own forehead. "Just hurry up. I hate being down here."

Aisling stood and went to the workbench. "You don't have to be down here."

"Something has to give," Davina said. "I know my power doesn't work anymore, but . . . something is off."

Aisling nodded, then grabbed one of the small silver knives. The blade was so thin and sharp it wasn't good for much else bar peeling off flesh.

She took it back to the hatch and let Aadya see her with it. Then she got down into the filth. Without her mask to lessen the stench, her stomach revolted against the proximity to the source of it. But she didn't care.

Grabbing a fistful of Aadya's limp, oily blond hair, she twisted it in her fist and pulled tight until the Morvish witch couldn't move. There was still defiance in her eyes, right up to the moment Aisling placed the blade against her forehead.

"Wait."

Aisling paused, tilting her head.

"Wait. Just wait."

"I'm waiting," Aisling said smoothly.

Blood trickled down Aadya's face.

"If you cut my constellation, I can't access my magic. I can't help you."

"You weren't going to anyway."

Aadya swallowed, lashes fluttering as she realized there would be no mercy from Aisling.

"I'll tell you more about Chaos," she said breathily.

Inching closer, Aisling tightened her fist until she was sure Aadya's scalp was tearing. "I don't want to hear more about Chaos, unless it's how to defeat him."

"Nemuse," Aadya whimpered. "A Nemuse can do it."

"How?"

"I don't know."

Aisling slid the knife beneath Aadya's skin.

"I don't know! I don't know!" Aadya cried. "I only asked who, so I could get rid of them. I didn't ask how. I didn't ask. I can ask now! Just please. Please."

Aisling stopped cutting.

"Swear a vow to me."

Aadya began sobbing.

"I can't."

Aisling dug the knife in deeper until Aadya loosed an agonized wail of despair, the tether between the Morvish witch and her magic straining bleakly.

Pausing, Aisling asked calmly, "Why not?"

"I swore one to someone else."

"Who?"

"Another of Chaos's disciples. Our leader."

"What is their name?"

Aadya's lip trembled. "I can't say."

"Can't or won't?"

"Can't! I swear, I can't."

If she couldn't tell her the leader's name, couldn't take a vow, couldn't tell her how to defeat Chaos, then she wasn't really of any use.

Then there was what Aadya had done to Eavha. As she watched the witch struggle and cry, the memory of Eavha shaking as she spoke about what had become of her family flashed through Aisling's mind.

For that, if nothing else, the bitch deserved to suffer.

Aisling clicked her tongue, then sliced the flesh off Aadya's forehead. The tether snapped and a scream of horror tore from Aadya's bleeding lips. Aisling used the opportunity to shove the flesh down Aadya's throat, holding her mouth closed as she tried to vomit it back out. Blood ran in a dark mulberry torrent down her face, tainted with globs of white like curdled milk from whatever mutation had been done to her.

Finally letting go, Aisling climbed out of the pit and slammed the hatch closed. Davina was gone, but Clayton stood by the door. He stepped aside to let Aisling pass. After slamming the door behind her, she leaned against the moldy wood and closed her eyes.

"I doubt she will tell you any more than she already has."

Aisling took a deep breath, stomach churning.

"I know."

Clayton was right. Nora was right. Taking that witch out of the cell, putting her on the blood-soaked table in the middle of the room, would achieve nothing.

"None of the others are talking?" she asked quietly.

"No."

Pushing off the door, Aisling grabbed the handle again. "Then I have to at least try."

"Your Highness—"

"Leave me."

"I don't think you should be alone right now."

Halting, Aisling's nostrils flared as she turned her acidic glare to her guard.

"I don't need your supervision, Clayton. I don't need those stupid rebels you wasted time hunting down. What I need is a way to defeat an army of beasts, as well as a coven of disciples three times the size of the Sparrows, and a literal god. So I'm going back in that room and I'm going to patch her up. Make sure she lives. Because I am not done with her. What I need from you is to go upstairs and find Eavha Nemuse. Stop her from leaving."

She had never put it in so many words before. The weight of what they truly faced was starting to dawn on Clayton, his mouth falling open, hand slackening on his hilt.

"What, exactly, do you think a forest witch is going to do against . . . all of that?"

Aisling clenched her jaw as she pulled the door to the cell back open.

"She's going to help me find the Kinner."

PART III

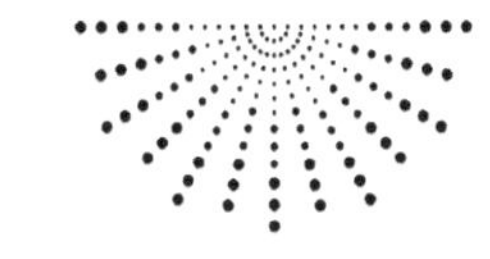

ENEMY OF MY ENEMY

CHAPTER TWENTY-NINE

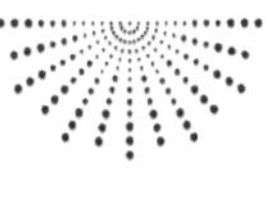

AISLING

It wasn't often that Aisling bothered to wander the palace gardens, but that was where the guard said Eavha was waiting. The hydrangeas were in full bloom, bursts of blue and white in an otherwise barren maze of greenery. Beneath one of the many lanterns lining the winding pathways, the heir of Wyldeden stood, feeling the dry leaves of a rose bush that was struggling in the humid southern climate.

Either ignoring or ignorant to the princess's approach, Eavha closed her eyes and rubbed her thumb over the coarse shrubbery. Aisling was close enough to feel the tingle of magic in the air, but knowing something was about to happen didn't lessen the surprise as the rose bush began to brighten, buds forming moments before blooming in delicate displays of peach and pink.

The ache that burned in Aisling's chest was unexpected.

Stepping forward, her boots crunching on the gravel so loudly that Eavha had to know she approached, Aisling slid the stem of a new rose between two fingers until the large flower rested in her palm.

"It's beautiful," she said, the heady scent filling her lungs.

"I was curious to what colors you had planted," Eavha admitted. "I was expecting red."

"I didn't plant them," Aisling admitted. She had never cared much for the garden or anything to do with the palace. The rugs, the furniture, the paintings—none of it.

"Ah."

Aisling pinched the stem she was holding, her sharp nails slicing right through it. Lifting the rose, she tucked it into Eavha's braid.

The priestess didn't move, watching Aisling with a surprisingly soft expression. "I'm not sure why you wanted me to stay. What happened was horrible, and if it were me, I would want to be alone."

"You're not as angry as I thought you'd be."

"Angry?" Eavha frowned. "Why would I be angry?"

"The marks. The lies. We promised each other honesty," Aisling started, straightening her shoulders. "If it were me who'd been duped, I would not have waited."

Considering it, looking to the ink etched onto Aisling's bare hands, Eavha twirled a loose curl by her ear. "I already knew about the marks, remember. That I didn't take the time to look into which ones you wore is my own fault. Using The Key Mark for Those Unbound like that was clever. I'd never thought of using it to be free from spell bindings."

Stunned, Aisling could only stare. There was definitely annoyance in Eavha's tone, but it took a back seat to true appreciation.

"I wish I could take the credit, but I didn't tattoo myself."

"Who did?"

"Davina."

King Phineas might be the bane of her existence, but he had been right about Eavha. She was clever, not to be underestimated. The widening of her brown eyes softened her face even further as she put it together.

"That's a lot of magic in your skin. It burned her out, didn't it?"

Swallowing, turning over her palms to expose the marks there, Aisling nodded. The warmth of Eavha's hand as it rested over Aisling's was enough of a surprise to make her flinch.

"Did it hurt? Do they still hurt?"

"They were an ordeal to have done, and their presence is a constant heaviness. I try not to use them unnecessarily because they are very taxing. But when Chaos comes, I will bear it."

Eavha watched Aisling's face for a while, frowning as the words she wasn't saying became clearer.

"You plan to face him. You think it will kill you."

"Most likely. Davina was concerned about it."

Tilting her head, Eavha stepped closer to the princess, brushing the satin of the princess's dress. "It's still painful to think of her, even though she's here in a way."

Aisling pursed her lips. This is why she didn't enjoy spending any length of time around healers. The priestess was too perceptive. "Sometimes."

It wasn't pity as Eavha squeezed her hand. It was knowing.

"Why did you ask me to stay?" she asked, letting the matter go. "What do you need?"

Dropping her hands and taking a deep breath, she doubted Eavha was going to respond well to this request. "The interrogation of Aadya has not been as fruitful as I hoped, but she insinuated that you would be a threat to her master's cause in some capacity. It's the Kinner, Eavha. They're the key to all of this, but I need help. I cannot find them alone."

As expected, hostility flashed behind Eavha's pretty eyes. "Don't you dare ask me about Cinn."

Aisling swallowed the lump his new name left in her throat, ears ringing with the echo of his screaming.

"Nir is at stake. Possibly the entire world, if Chaos doesn't already rule it."

The Sparrow Coven, in all their centuries, had never managed to successfully communicate with peoples outside of Nir. Messages disappeared into the wind, travelers never returning from their trek beyond Kerveda's western border, entire ships disappearing once they left Nirnish waters. The Sparrow philosophers preached it was because there was nothing out there, but Aisling was convinced it was because Chaos still reigned, his defeat during the First War limited to the borders of Nir. But she couldn't know for sure. Not without speaking to someone who had been there.

The Kinner knew what happened during the War. Knew how to defeat him. They would be invaluable in the coming war and she would trade her embrace by the Lover and exist in the void for eternity for the chance to merely ask their help.

It wouldn't be so bad, the void, with Davina beside her.

"He does not know where they are."

"I don't believe that."

"He is second generation, Aisling. He was not there during the First War."

"His parents must have told him what happened. Where their people are being kept."

"He was only seven when he arrived in Hyrsch. What kind of parents would tell a tale like that to a seven-year-old? And besides, it's *your* people who are keeping them somewhere. Why don't you try interrogating one of *them*?"

"I did."

Eavha stilled.

"My people's hatred for the Kinner race is so deep they have tried to erase knowledge of them from the history of our nation. Few are still living who even know they are real, fewer with any kind of details on their existence. But those I found, I asked. Very impolitely. And learned nothing. I have appealed to the Lover themself for information, but they will not deign to speak with me. Nor will Celeste. I have scoured the libraries of Kerveda and Bernt and found nothing but rumors. Rumors I investigated anyway, with no results. I have scried, I have begged for Morvish support and heard nothing back; not even Davina is able to find anything. Your friend is my only lead, and I am begging you to just ask him."

Eavha lifted her chin. "No."

Aisling didn't mean to let her teeth snap, but Eavha heard it, stiffening her jaw even further.

"He already said to us that he doesn't know, and I believe him. Even if you don't." Eavha plucked the rose from her hair and lowered her gaze to inspect it. "But I will make you a deal."

"What deal?" Aisling bit out, immediately chastising herself.

Eavha ignored the flare of temper. "Leave Cinn out of it, and I will help you find the rest of them."

Sighing, Aisling rubbed her temples. "There is nothing you could do that I haven't tried."

"Perhaps." Eavha tilted her head, lazily brushing her chewed fingernails over the delicate blush petals. "But I had a thought when you said you tried scrying. The Kinner mark is a witchmark, and it undoubtedly has something to do with healing. Guess who happens to be Sanni-blessed? Guess who might have more luck scrying than someone who is Lover-blessed, the complete opposite of what the Kinner mark is?"

Again, Aisling stared at Eavha in surprise. "I've had a necromancer try to scry, too."

"Necromancers are in bed with the Lover. Despite having revived Eaon once, I am not. In fact, the Lover and I are about as far from being on good terms as one can comfortably be without risk of being struck down. If the Kinner are connected to Sanni, she will help me."

She was reluctant to let go of the lead she had. This friend of Eavha's. *The kinner.* Admitting she had handled the situation poorly was one thing, but abandoning it all together left her squeamish. But it made too much sense.

"It cannot hurt to try," Aisling admitted.

***

The palace halls seemed empty after the bustle of Imsa. Courtiers either confined themselves to their rooms or had left the palace entirely, retreating to their own homes outside the palace gates. Servants kept out of the way, averting their eyes and bowing deeply as the princess passed, leading Eavha back toward her tower.

She nodded to them as she always did, but paranoia kept her actual respect fettered. That any of them could be rebels or spies was a persistent suspicion since Edwina's betrayal. Same with the guards. Her soldiers.

As for her advisors, whom she already knew were all two-faced, they were keeping themselves busy and far away from Aisling.

At the top of the stairs, she unlocked the door to her prayer room. Eavha blushed behind her.

"I'm still sorry about trying to sneak in here."

"I would have done the same in your situation. There really isn't anything interesting in here anyway." Aisling shrugged.

Judging by the way Eavha's mouth fell open, she must have never seen the prayer room of a Lover-blessed witch before. She didn't balk at the obsidian altar, nor at the bones of the assassins Nevan frequently sent to kill her, splayed in particular arrangements among the candles and jars of blood. No, there was no disgust or fear in the heir to Wyldeden's eyes. Only awe.

Aisling joined Eavha where she wandered to the wall across from the tiny slit of a window. Bolted there was a painted map of Nir, as high as a horse, the leather stretched taut like a scroll between two gilded posts. The four territories of the Coven—Kerveda, Bernt, Oford and Vertlyn—were colored in gold, black sparrows marking where the main cities were. Anfar and Ornh were dusted in shimmering green to show they were treaty lands—not owned by anyone, exactly, but fought for and kept free of Sparrow control by Kaelean Caesarea and the Anfar Forest Clan. The Great Boab had been carefully depicted, along with landmarks of other notable covens that lived among the whispering forest. At the very top-right corner of the map was Qiri. The Morvish lands. Shaded in purple, there was no insignia, no markers for the cities in the scrap of land above the mountains. Unlike Anfar and Ornh, it was not treaty land. It was not a place any witch besides those born there were permitted, nor did any dare to encroach. The wards around Anfar were spiderwebs compared to those around that untouchable northern-most territory.

Davina had promised to take her one day. But that was before everything went to shit.

Aisling waited as Eavha took it in.

"I never really understood how big it is."

It didn't feel big to Aisling, but she had seen most of it. Eavha had not.

Placing one of her long nails on the leather, Aisling traced a line from the southern crater in Bernt, through the mountain and toward her city. "Davina saw an army of beasts entering Oford from the frozen wastes, here. That's where I want to focus the army."

Eavha's eyes flickered from the black sparrow painted in place of Hyrsch and the enormous tree she called home. There was not a lot between them. The river and wards would not slow the coming army for long.

"I will have Dearmead send word to Kaelean. Perhaps we have some guardians to spare."

"That would be appreciated."

Swallowing the fear nestled in her throat, Eavha turned from the map and squared her petite shoulders. "See, we can compromise."

Aisling grimaced, still not convinced.

"Anyway, as I said, an army of beasts will come across the frozen wastes. It will be the depths of winter before Chaos presents himself. And when he comes . . . she saw me. Facing him. Alone."

She didn't want to think about the way Davina had sobbed, had been unable to speak for hours before finally telling Aisling what she had seen. That vision had changed something in Davina. The Morvish witch had become obsessed with finding a way to protect her.

"But if that is my fate," Aisling continued, "then I plan to take Chaos with me."

She didn't care if Eavha laughed at the arrogance of such a statement. Too much had been lost already, and Aisling would make Davina's sacrifice worth it.

"I don't think you'll be alone." Eavha was using that petal-soft voice again as she watched Aisling too closely.

"Davina's visions are never wrong."

"But are they complete?" Eavha asked. "I was given a prophecy once, and I thought I knew what it meant at the time, but now I'm not so sure. Kaelean says Morvish witches are notoriously vague and unhelpful, but I think it's because they can't say for certain what their own visions even mean."

"It doesn't matter. We must be prepared."

Pulling a smaller version of the map from one of the sketching desks, Aisling lay it across the benchtop and collected her scrying pendant.

"Well, in the name of preparedness," Eavha sighed, taking the pendant from Aisling. "When I speak to Kaelean should I tell her that Bernt is already lost?"

A mostly unoccupied land, barren and overrun with fae, Bernt was still an important place. Silver soaked the earth, or it had before the non-beast occupants of Nir had mined it for weapons. Whatever spell Kaelean had cast to keep beasts out of Anfar was a secret she seemed intent on taking to her grave, and so the rest of Nir still had to defend themselves the old-fashioned way. Aside from that, veins of every variety of crystal grew in caves beneath the surface, which were valuable for an entirely different reason.

"My scouts say the borders have not been breached, but they will come. Davina's visions are never wrong."

"So you keep saying," Eavha muttered.

Clasping the Blessing Charm dangling freely from her neck in her other hand, the Wyldeden witch closed her eyes and held the scrying crystal over the map. Once more, the air began to prickle with warm magic.

Unlike the Terra-blessing that allowed her to bloom roses, Eavha's Sanni-blessing was potent enough to make Aisling step back. Dizziness, as if she'd already had an entire bottle of wine, blurred her vision. But exposure to strong magic was not a new experience for her, so she clutched the edge of the desk and focused on staying upright.

Eavha's hands began to shake, the soft muttering of an incantation on her lips giving the magic an edge, but the crystal that hung from the end of the silver chain did not move. After a few minutes, she dropped it with an exasperated sigh.

"Sorry. I thought that would work."

"Perhaps if I left," Aisling suggested.

"Sanni knows I'm searching on your behalf. She does not want to help."

Aisling pursed her lips. "I don't understand why not. The Spirits have to know what is coming. They ought to be doing everything they can to prevent Chaos's return."

"Why?" Eavha asked. "If the First War was about Chaos and Mother, Death becoming the Lover, and their Balance, what does any of it have to do with the rest of them?"

Aisling raised an eyebrow. "Because of the slaughter, mostly. We are nothing but sacks of blood and meat for Chaos's favorite beasts. Whatever he wants, it will not be good for us. After seeing the ballet, what it was like back then, you can't honestly believe otherwise."

"I still don't know why the Spirits should care."

Aisling scoffed. "I didn't realize you had such a calloused side to you, Lady Eavha."

The heir just grimaced.

"But I suppose you have a point. Perhaps they don't care the way I think they should. I don't know as much about the seven elemental Spirits as I do the four High Spirits. Or three, anyway. Who really knows anything about Morvia."

"Davina," Eavha pointed out.

Speaking of Davina, she was notably absent. Aisling made sure she hadn't accidentally risen her mental shield against the souls of the in-between, but it was as open as it always was. Davina just wasn't here.

"Morvia doesn't matter right now, anyway." Aisling carefully packed away the small map and placed her crystals in a glass bowl of water sitting directly in the sunlight piercing through the window. "What matters is that we don't lose this city when the beasts come. Wyldeden's help would be a boon, but it will not be enough. So will you ask the kinner now?"

"No! Lover take me, Aisling, how many times do I have to say it?" Eavha snapped. "I will not involve Cinn. You have to let go of this obsession with him. Why are you so convinced we need the Kinner anyway? There are plenty of beasts in Nir already and we manage them just fine."

"Unorganized beasts, but I am talking about an army, Eavha. I am talking about tens of thousands of deadly, vicious and hungry fiends descending upon us. There has been nothing like it since the First War, and what little documentation there is about it says that the Kinner and the Old Ones as a united front are a part of the reason the First War ended. It would be beyond audacious to think that we could do without them the second time around."

Eavha shook her head, frowning deeply. "I just don't understand it. If the Kinner were heroes, then why did your coven get rid of them?"

"I have asked the same question more times than I can count. And it's because power corrupts, Eavha. The Kinner *were* heroes, and then they weren't. They were left in charge of the humans once the war was over. The Old Ones went back to their ways. Fae and human breeding continued, birthing the Fair Folk. Then, as the fae blood of the Fair Folk became diluted, it took intervention from the Spirits to draw out their fae magic, and we began to be called witches. A term meant to make us separate from the superiority of the Fair Folk of old, yet also separate from the humans who began to resent us. Resent all creatures with magic.

"This was the Second War: the war between magic and humanity. No more pure Fair Folk were being born, such was the human anger at being used and abused by magic wielders. Witches were lumped in with the fae, which we thought was unfair since we were more human than fae by that point. So we appealed to the Kinner that ruled over the humans and their cities to let us stay. Us, descendants of those who had made them what they were, had given them not only immortality but invulnerability—we called on them to defend our rights to exist beside humans. And they denied us.

"So the Sparrow Coven was formed. The High Spirit of Death had long resented that there were creatures that could not be claimed, and so they bestowed blessings upon the witches who called for help. Legend says that the Coven turned the gift their ancestors had given the Kinner into a punishment, took everything and claimed it for themselves. That is why the Sparrows now rule the humans, both to spite the Kinner and to spite the humans who had wanted witches gone. That is why the half-breed offspring of humans and Kinner were enslaved. Punishment and hatred for the mark on their neck that proved they had the traitorous blood of Kinner running through them, no matter how many generations diluted it was.

"Before you say anything, I do not believe the dribble they spout in Dusarn. I do not believe that slavery was ever an acceptable punishment for an entire race of people who have done nothing wrong. I do not even harbor ill-feelings toward your friend—"

"Cinn." Eavha's voice was barely a whisper.

"What?"

"His name is Cinn."

Heat flushed through Aisling's body, her skin beginning to sweat beneath the layers of her dress. "That is what he calls himself now, I know. But you're missing the point—"

"Then say it."

Aisling paused, her heart hammering wildly as she looked at Eavha. Her jaw locked up, an invisible fist tightening around her throat. His boyish face flashed through her mind. She didn't want to see it.

"Say his name, Aisling."

"Why?" Aisling asked, choking on the word. "You want me to admit I'm a monster for doing what I did? I know that. I have already told you that I know that. He is pure-blooded, but he is a new generation. He was innocent, and I tortured him. I am the culmination of every terrible thing my coven is known for, and I should be grievously punished for what I did."

"Then say his name."

She couldn't.

After a moment, Aisling turned away from the window and moved toward the bookshelves crammed in the shadowy corner. Picking up a large tome with yellowed pages and a worn leather jacket, Aisling dumped it on the table before Eavha and strode for the stairs.

"Everything I know about the Kinner is in that book. Get up to speed, then come and find me. I will likely be drinking in my rooms."

Alone.

CHAPTER THIRTY

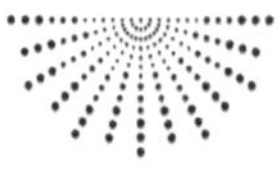

EAVHA

Sitting cross-legged on the floor with the heavy book Aisling had thrown at her, Eavha managed to read by the light of the moon and a single candle perched precariously on the balcony ledge overhead. Most of it was incomprehensible, but she had borrowed the Nirnish translating dictionary Milnova had brought and planned on persisting into the night.

It was just another thing that made her feel dumb. She was not picking up as much Nirnish as she really wanted, and she felt like a scolded schoolgirl for not knowing the extensive Nirnish history that Aisling did. That Eaon probably knew. He should be here instead of her. Or with her. He would know what to do about all this. He would figure it all out and have them home before the end of the week.

All Eavha knew was what she couldn't do. Not ever. No matter how Aisling begged, she would not involve Cinn.

Her door creaked open and Dearmead peered through the gap. At the sight of her on the floor, he flinched.

"What?" she asked, looking around.

"Nothing. You just . . . reminded me of your brother."

Eavha smiled. She supposed it was very Eaon-like of her to be up in the middle of the night, translating books. She had teased him mercilessly growing up, and no doubt if he saw her now, he would have a few choice things to say.

"Don't tell him you caught me studying," she said, closing the book to talk to Dearmead. "You haven't been around much since the incident with the rebels."

"Sorry. Did you need me?"

"No, I just noticed. Where were you?"

"Making sure Edwina and Radley are being taken care of properly. I don't get a good vibe from a lot of the guards here, and I know they're Cinn's family, so . . ."

Eavha smiled. "Thank you. That's kind. Come in. Help me with this."

Dearmead closed the door behind him and limped over, easing onto the floor.

"You're hurt?"

"I didn't want to bother you, but Radley caught me by surprise."

Eavha put the book aside and held out a hand expectantly. Embarrassed and a little reluctant, Dearmead lifted one of his bare feet and put it on her lap. The dark skin was discolored, and as she probed the injury with her magic she felt the fractured metatarsal bones beneath.

"Don't push yourself if you're tired. It will heal on its own," he warned her, but Eavha was already readying her blessing, offering it to Sanni. The Spirit accepted her intentions quickly—the Spirit had always liked Dearmead—and the magic spilled into his body in an unfettered torrent, making him hiss.

"Sorry," Eavha grimaced, reining it in. "It's been a while."

"It's fine. What are you reading, anyway?"

He reached for the candle balancing on the balcony ledge and brought it down closer, opening the book to the pages Eavha had left a leaf between. Realizing it was in Nirnish, he wrinkled his nose and pushed it away.

"A book Aisling gave me about the Kinner," she explained. "She wants me to help her find them. I tried to scry but it didn't work, so she wants me to ask Cinn."

Dearmead grimaced. "Eaon said that he said he doesn't know where they are."

"I know. I think deep down, Aisling knows too. But if she admits it then she has to admit that what she did to him was for nothing. And I don't think she's ready to face that."

"Almost sounds like you care."

"It's my nature to care," Eavha reminded him, letting go of his foot. "The healing is not perfect, but you should be able to walk without pain."

"Thank you, that's all I need."

"How are you going with everything else?" she asked.

Dearmead shrugged. "I still miss him."

"You've been friends for thirteen years. You're allowed to miss him."

"Yeah."

"Have you thought about moving on?" she probed, making Dearmead do this weird thing with his jaw until it clicked loudly, eyes looking over the cityscape below.

Eavha grinned. "Is it Clayton?"

"I'm going to bed," he said, getting up and testing his foot tenderly.

"Coward."

"Goodnight, Eavha."

He shook his head, but there was a smirk on his face as he left the room. Eavha smiled, then sighed. She would much rather deal with Dearmead's broken heart than try to read this book any longer. She didn't know how Eaon could focus for so long, literally sitting in the same spot for hours and hours. Even days at times.

Actually, yes she did.

Worrying her lip, she hoped he was okay without her brewing for him. It was arrogant of her to assume that nobody else could brew his tonics the way she could, but her ma had always made such a big deal about making sure it was done just right. They were old family recipes, and while Eaon was not the first witch in Wyldeden to suffer from such extreme mood changes, treating matters of the mind was very different from treating matters of the body. The Nemuse family was the best. Used to be the best.

They should have known better than to do to someone what they had done to Eaon. They should have known the effects their treatment of him would have on his health. They did know. They just hadn't cared.

She had said to Dearmead that it was her nature to care, but really, how true could that be? She was a Nemuse. She hadn't cared enough about her own brother to try and ease his burden any more than instructed to by their parents. Not until he was all she had left.

Shame burned her eyes. And as the thickness of her throat became difficult to manage, she realized why she found herself almost caring about what Aisling was going through. Why it was so easy to see past the coldness, the masks the princess wore, through to the part of her that was in pain.

In too many ways, it felt like looking into a mirror.

***

The next morning, Aisling was not in her rooms. One of the guards who stood at the base of the stairwell to the princess's tower pointed them in the direction of her personal training grounds, so Eavha and Dearmead found their way to the underground ring and snuck inside. In a poorly lit room filled with equipment Eavha wouldn't have the slightest clue what to do with, the princess of Hyrsch was fighting her guard.

The clacking of wooden weapons was familiar enough to send a pang of nostalgia through Eavha; nothing else in this city was like home, but that sound had rung in the valley every day as long as she had been alive. Dearmead became very serious at the sound of it, eyes darkening, body tense as they stepped onto the landing.

Down the stairs, in the center of a chalk circle, Clayton swung a long wooden sword toward Aisling's head. Huffing, cheeks red as beetroot, Aisling blocked.

"Were you drinking last night?" Clayton was stern, as if only here and now did he have any kind of authority. "You're sloppy."

"I'm tired," Aisling panted back.

Eavha watched as the princess, an entire head and a half shorter than the demi-kin guard, shoved his weapon away with the short-handled wooden battle-axe in her hands—bare again now that the secret was out anyway, the black ink of her tattoos stark against her pale skin.

Aisling's braid snapped the air as she spun, attempting to land a blow on Clayton, who easily disarmed her.

"Should we switch to steel? Would that wake you up a bit?" Clayton asked, ruthlessly whirling his wooden blade over his head to attack her from the other side.

Aisling ducked and rolled, picking up her weapon before blocking yet another attack, the force sending her crashing back.

Eavha covered the gasp she couldn't contain with her hand.

Both Aisling and Clayton turned to stare.

"Sorry," Eavha said. "I didn't mean to interrupt. The other guards said we could find you here."

"You're not interrupting," Clayton began, but stopped when he caught sight of Aisling's face.

Something had shifted since noticing Eavha's arrival. Back on her feet, the sweat-dampened patch of the gray turtleneck that clung to Aisling's spine revealed the supernatural stillness that only a witch could achieve.

"Shit," Clayton cussed, readying himself.

Eavha and Dearmead watched, transfixed by the deadly dance suddenly taking place in the training ring. Clayton stepped and Aisling mimicked it, smooth like a snake in the sand. Where Clayton was raw power and ferocity, Aisling was a scorpion, quick and deadly. Then, as Clayton adjusted to her newfound focus, she exploded in a furious torrent of attacks—gone was the scorpion; here was the bull.

She was relentless. Even as her legs trembled and the sweat dampened her shirt to black, Aisling attacked with a speed Clayton couldn't hope to match. Knocking his blade out of his hands, she didn't stop. Not until Clayton raised his hands and shouted, "Conceded!"

Unable to stop her momentum, Aisling released her axe and let it fly through the room to slam into a rack of javelins, knocking them all to the ground. Her breathing was harsh and ragged as she bent over her knees.

"Could she beat you?" Eavha asked Dearmead quietly, eyes glittering at his appreciative expression.

"Focused like that? Hard to tell."

"Do you think I could ever fight like her?"

Dearmead twisted his mouth and raised a brow. "Would you even want to?"

Normally, no. But if war was truly coming she could not tolerate being shielded by others again. Dearmead must have read the worry in her face because he sighed and squeezed her shoulder.

"Not by winter. But five months of training is better than none. That's all Cinn said he'd had when he fought with us, right? Even without his healing, he did well. You can too."

Eavha nodded.

After letting Aisling and Clayton drink a pitcher of water each, Eavha and Dearmead joined them in the ring.

"Has something happened?" Aisling asked, pointedly talking only to Dearmead.

"I read the book you gave me," Eavha answered anyway. "And I had an idea."

Stiffening her spine, Aisling turned. "Oh?"

"Yes."

Hungover or not, Eavha didn't like this version of Aisling being directed at her. So she waited, refusing to back down as gray eyes like the point of a dagger held her stare.

"Do you plan on telling me, or am I meant to read your mind?"

Clayton and Dearmead seemed to sense at the same time that the two needed a moment. Taking one of the wooden staffs leaning on the stands along the wall, Dearmead took up a defensive stance, facing off against the other male, who grinned.

"I asked Milnova last night, no, this morning, to look into it further for me, but I have a suspicion I know who made the mark on the Kinner. And if I'm right, I think I know where we might be able to find more information about it."

Aisling waited, stiff as a board.

"What if we don't need to find the Kinner?" Eavha went on. "What if we could make our own?"

"I tried to figure out how, but—"

"But you didn't have me." Eavha flicked her hair over her shoulder. "My family were some of the best healers in all of Nir. I have studied healing magic my entire life. I performed necromancy without any training whatsoever, and Eaon came back alright. I can do it. I can cast the mark."

Aisling's staring had taken on a new edge. Something almost hopeful glimmered in her eyes. "How?"

"A few months ago, I broke into the sacred library beneath the Sanctuary in Wyldeden. We were looking for information on a death curse at the time, but I saw a lot of books on Sanni there too. If what you said is true, and witches were not around during the First War, then who could have cast a spellmark like that? Fae don't use that kind of magic, but a Spirit might."

"Sanni cast the mark." Aisling came to the same conclusion Eavha had. "Sanni made the Kinner. Why did I never think of that?"

"It's okay to have flaws, you know," Eavha teased, pulling forward a curl to wrap around her finger. "And Sanni might not want to tell us where the Kinner are, but I think she will help me make more."

"Okay. So we break into Wyldeden," Aisling said, blowing out a breath while pushing back her hair.

Eavha scowled. "Don't be ridiculous. I'll just ask Kaelean."

"Your high priestess won't simply give out information like that."

"Sure she will. She loves me. I already sent her a whispering leaf."

Aisling's eyes widened. Eavha stepped closer, reaching for one of Aisling's bare hands. Her skin was cool to touch, sending a shiver up Eavha's spine in the most pleasant way.

"You are not alone in this. I will help you. But I need you to help me, too."

"What do you need?" she asked, a little breathless.

Eavha glanced around the room, then over at Dearmead and Clayton, who were busy trying to kill each other.

"I want to learn how to fight."

Eavha went back to her room to change into the guardian leathers and boots she had been given as a disguise when she'd left Wyldeden, her hair braided in two ropes over her shoulders. She hadn't expected to begin training right this instant, but Aisling had canceled the meeting with her advisors for the morning and insisted on getting started.

"Have you held a weapon before?" Aisling asked her.

"A dagger," Eavha nodded, fingers hovering over the empty space at her hip where she had worn Cinn's knife.

"We'll start with that then." She nodded, collecting a couple of heavy wooden daggers from the racks.

Taking one from her, Eavha held it the way Cinn had shown her. Aisling nodded in approval.

"Set your feet a little wider. And shift your balance more evenly. Use your toes."

"Do you like fighting?" Eavha asked as she moved her feet.

Aisling stepped closer, her surprisingly calloused hands moving Eavha's hips and shoulders into place.

"I like other people knowing I am dangerous," Aisling answered carefully. "In Dusarn, power is not decided by magic. Not decided by anything besides who is willing to take it. As a princess, my family's power is coveted. Making people afraid to challenge their power is one of many tactics used to hold onto it."

Eavha nodded. Such a society isn't somewhere she wanted to live, and if that was what Kaelean and the old clan had fought against, she was grateful Anfar remained independent.

Aisling's hands settled on Eavha's hips.

"Now, with your frame, any male you encounter will have the advantage of height and strength. Many female warriors will have the benefit of experience and speed. With what little time we have, the best thing you can learn is how to catch them off guard. To strike fast and true where it counts."

"I have studied anatomy. I know how to hurt people."

Aisling smiled. "Good."

After an hour of sparring and losing badly to Aisling, Eavha conceded and sat down, wiping her hot, sweaty face on the heel of her palm. "This is awful."

"I'm aware," Aisling chuckled, collecting a jug of water and sitting across from her.

"I'm not getting any better."

"You're less hesitant to hit me, which is a start."

Eavha grinned. After the first time Aisling had knocked Eavha down, she had been fueled by a burning desire to pay it back. Drinking deeply, she watched the males as they exchanged techniques. Clayton was putting a steel weapon in Dearmead's hand for the first time, the weight of it clearly bothering him.

His words from last night came back. About Cinn's family.

"What are you going to do about Edwina and Radley?"

Aisling loosed a breath. "I have a plan."

"Do you intend to share it with me, or am I supposed to read your mind?"

Aisling raised her eyebrows, but grinned. "Not only do I plan on sharing it with you, but I may need your help."

Eavha looked away, unsure exactly what Aisling was about to ask her to do. They had just mended the rift their spat yesterday had made; she was not eager to tear a new one.

"It's nothing sinister," Aisling said flatly, the smile gone. "I have learned my lesson."

Yet she openly admitted to interrogating Aadya, so really, how much of a lesson had she learned?

Aisling drank again, eyes on her guard as she asked, "Do I inspire so little faith?"

"I know what it's like to hurt people," Eavha answered. "Not . . . Not like you have, but in my own way. I have heavy regrets and a lot of shame for what my actions, or inactions, of the past have done. The pain it caused. As children, we mimic what we see. We believe what we are told. But we are not children anymore, Aisling."

"I know that," she hissed, the cold wall going up again.

"I don't mean to be condescending."

"Well, you are failing."

Eavha tucked a few loose curls back into her braids and straightened her back, lifted her chin.

"As are you."

Aisling bared her teeth. "Did you have a point, or was your plan to see how long I will allow you to insult me?"

"My point, which you so clearly missed, was that I am still struggling to overcome my weaknesses, and I accept that. I let people call me out on that. You need to do the same if you ever want to overcome yours. So, yes, when you said you needed my help, I judged you. I had every right to. Accept that and keep proving me wrong. Trust is earned over time, not given after a few apologies."

Aisling's flushed cheeks were still heating as she glared at Eavha, but she didn't back down. This princess was no more intimidating than any of the Nemuse unts or unks she had faced in her childhood.

Through gritted teeth, Aisling managed, "I need you to occupy my advisors while I discuss matters with the rebels. As soon as I leave this room, they will be watching my every move, hounding me about the king and Imsa again. If they know what I plan, they will try to stop me."

"And what is this plan?" Though if her awful advisors would disapprove, surely it wasn't something terrible.

It was Aisling's turn to straighten her spine, shoulders back, chin raised.

"Forgiveness."

CHAPTER THIRTY-ONE

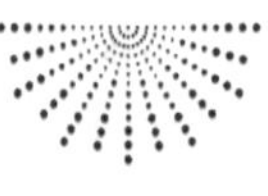

AISLING

ONCE MORE, AISLING SAT UPON HER THRONE, GLAD TO SEE NO SIGNS of the failed Imsa lingering. From the side door, Clayton and Dearmead brought in the rebels, stopping a fair distance from the dais. The sight of Edwina standing proudly in her dirty dress sent a shiver crawling down her spine, while Dearmead gave Clayton a pitying look as he struggled to keep a hold of Radley.

"Stop it, or I'll cut your throat," Clayton warned.

"Do it then, traitorous pig," Radley spat at him.

"Enough." Aisling stood, the dress she had changed into cascading in pools of silk down the steps. Not the best attire if this turned into another fight, but between the costume and the crown she had braided onto her head, she looked the part of the ruler she was supposed to be. Which is why she didn't have time for their antics. She didn't know how long Eavha could keep her advisors distracted. "I offered you peaceful negotiations and you stabbed me."

Radley opened his mouth, no doubt with poison on his tongue, but it was Edwina's hard voice that cut through the stifling glass room.

"And what will you do about it?" she asked, lip curling in a hateful sneer. "Send us to Pirevia to be re-enslaved and butchered? That threat may frighten some, but it was never going to deter us from burning you and your court to the ground. I had to watch you wake up vomiting from nightmares of what you did to our brother. I had to scrub his blood from your clothes. I spent every waking minute I wasn't shackled to your side scouring this palace for where you were keeping him, and never found a trace. Do you have any idea how that killed me inside? Knowing he was so close, but I couldn't help him? So punish us for hating you, if you're so inclined, but don't think for a second that we regret any of our choices. I would stab you in the eye right now if I could. I fantasized about it every night while you slept, or when you were so drunk you could barely walk. You will get what is coming to you, *princess*. I will haunt you for the rest of your life and make sure it is agony."

Dearmead had a deep frown on his face as he took in the female he kept restrained. Unlike Clayton, the Wyldeden guardian was moved by her passion. By the furious tears lining her eyes.

Aisling took a steadying breath. What she was about to do might be the riskiest move she made in this dangerous game she was playing, but if it worked . . .

"I'm not going to punish you, Edwina. Nor you, Radley. I understand your hatred and respect the spine it took to attack me in my own palace. I know my apology will not even scrape the edge off the pain I have caused your family, but regardless, I am extremely sorry. If I could go back and make different choices, I would."

"I don't care how——" Radley started but Aisling raised her voice to speak over him.

"I'm going to give you back the city."

The wind was sucked out of the room as all four of them stared at her, blindsided. Inside her gloves, Aisling's hands were sweating.

"Edwina," she continued. "If you are willing, I would like to offer you a promotion. With Nora gone, the position of my Second remains open and you are by far the most qualified person for the job. Advise me. Scheme with me. And when I am disposed, which will be soon, rule in my stead."

"What?" Clayton shook his head, looking between her and Edwina, who had gone utterly still. "What do you mean you will be disposed soon?"

Aisling let the question hang in the air. "By winter, Hyrsch will belong to the demi-kin."

"You said by winter there wouldn't be a Nir," Radley narrowed his eyes. "What is going on, exactly?"

"You would know if you'd managed to check your temper," Aisling pointed out as she raised her brow.

The doors at the end of the throne room pushed open with a heavy groan and the advisor named Orla came storming through, four others and Eavha on her tail. An apology pulled a frown on her features, but Aisling had not expected her to keep them away forever.

"What is the meaning of this?" Orla demanded, striding up the dais as if Aisling were nothing but a little girl playing at royalty. "You were warned by the king, girl, not to do anything without heeding our advice. That includes sentencing the rebels."

Aisling ignored her, not taking her eyes away from Edwina. It was impossible to read her face as the shock wore off, giving way to something steady.

"I accept."

Aisling smiled.

"Accept what? Whatever arrangement has come to pass is not sanctioned—"

Turning to her advisor, Aisling let how badly she wanted to strangle the old hag flash across her face. Orla stuttered, glancing to the other advisors for help.

"Get off my dais and kneel before Lady Edwina, your new Second in Command."

The sound Orla made was half-scoff, half-screech of outrage. "Absolutely not! How dare—"

Aisling didn't hesitate. Reaching into the hidden pocket of her skirts, she drew a long knife. She didn't have the deadly blessings of her brother or parents, and none compared to the power Eavha's brother had, but all that meant was she had learned to be dangerous in an entirely different way.

Slashing the blade across Orla's mouth, then the back of her knee, Aisling shoved the screaming advisor off the dais and glared down at her with a viciousness she knew ricocheted through the room.

"I said, kneel."

The other advisors didn't hesitate to drop to their knees, all of them avoiding the growing pool of blood. After a nod from Aisling, Clayton released the still twisting Radley and also dropped to his knee, keeping a tight fist over the hilt of his own dagger. Dearmead and Eavha were not under her command, but they too bowed their heads in a show of respect.

Finally, after sharing a silent moment with his sister, Radley lowered himself too.

Sliding the dirty blade back into her dress, Aisling stepped down from the dais to stand in front of Edwina. Part of her was waiting for another betrayal. Another knife in her gut. But as she took Edwina's freckled and calloused hands, the throne room was utterly still.

"Do you know the words?" she asked.

"No," Edwina whispered.

Clayton rose to his feet to stand behind Edwina, whispering in her ear.

"I, Edwina Maiden—" she began.

"Choose a new surname," Aisling interrupted.

Before she had come, the demi-kin had no last names. A tactic used by the Coven to strip any kind of lineage from them. When the collars had come off and they had been allowed a surname, some chose the human names of those who were kind to them but many used the jobs they found as inspiration. Lightman. Turner. Smith. Clothier. Baker. Maiden.

Edwina looked back to her brother, who was watching Clayton closely, that rage still burning in his eyes.

With a small smile on her face, she decided. "Red. I, Edwina Red, hereby declare my allegiance to the city of Hyrsch. I pledge myself—mind, body and soul—to the aiding of you, Princess Aisling Aurnia of the Sparrow Coven, in any and all means that you require as you strive to better our land. Will you accept my pledge?"

Aisling raised Edwina's hands and bowed, resting her forehead upon her knuckles.

"I, Princess Aisling Aurnia of the Sparrow Coven, gladly accept your pledge and hereby announce you Second in Command of the city of Hyrsch. May our witnesses see this contract as valid and binding."

"We do," came a chorus of reluctant voices.

Raising her head, Aisling met Edwina's gaze, a most serious expression on her face. "I'm counting on you to keep me in line. Be honest with me when no one else will. And lead when I cannot."

Edwina bowed deeply.

Letting go of her hands, Aisling turned to her advisors. "Now, if you don't mind, I have private business to discuss with my Second. You are not required."

"But—"

"You. Are. Not. Required." She would not say it again. Looking down at Orla, Aisling sneered. "Take this wench to the infirmary and find someone to clean up her mess. Hopefully the next time she's capable of opening her mouth, it will be full of apologies for her poor behavior."

With that, she stormed from the throne room. By the sound of the feet that followed her, she knew Edwina and Radley, Clayton, Dearmead and Eavha followed.

***

The first order of business was to summon the kitchen staff to bring Edwina and Radley a hearty meal. Seated in the council room, Aisling poured them both a glass of some of the best wine she had, placing it before them herself.

"I watched you run this city for years," Edwina said, managing to cut into her lunch with a politeness not expected of someone who'd been kept in the dungeons. "What game are you playing now? Don't bother to deny that one is in motion."

Aisling couldn't help the slight upturn of her mouth as she settled into her seat. "You were always so quiet that I often forgot you were there. Yes, a game is in play, but I promise you are no pawn. My offer is genuine."

"I would not have accepted if I thought it wasn't."

"I can't stand all this yapping. Get to the point. What's happening in the winter," Radley demanded around a half-chewed mouthful of food.

Edwina scowled, but didn't reprimand him, and rather than explain, Aisling asked Eavha to do her best to tell the story in Nirnish. Partly because Radley was unlikely to absorb much information as long as it came out of Aisling's mouth, but also partly because she needed a minute to put together her next offer.

As Eavha finished, Radley sat back and snorted. "Sounds like a load of horseshit to me."

"We don't believe in the gods," Edwina added. "Or the Spirits. Whatever you call them."

"Be sure to tell them that when Chaos comes to decimate the city and everything else this side of the spine," Clayton snapped.

"Sorry, do you have a muzzle for your dog?" Radley asked, fists clenching on the table.

"Believe in them or don't, it doesn't matter." Aisling ignored them, speaking only to Edwina. "I know what is coming and I have a plan. One that will see me leave this city permanently. As you said, you've seen me run it for years. Nobody else knows what you know about the inner workings of it all. I couldn't find better hands to leave Hyrsch in if I tried. The only thing I ask is, that between now and then, whether you believe it or not, do what I ask of you to help me prepare. And when the attack comes, follow my orders."

"Of course. If an attack comes, no amount of watching you plan for winter snows will have prepared me for a war."

Aisling dipped her chin in gratitude. "Which brings me to the final matter I wish to discuss with you for today. If we are to work together, all of us, there cannot be this much dissention. You are owed for what I took from you."

"There is nothing you could give," Edwina said, that coldness finding its way back to her voice.

"I don't know, your head on the gates would be a good start." Radley drained his glass of wine and slid it back across the table in a silent demand for more.

"When I pass," she said as she obliged, "you may have my body and do with it as you wish."

Radley opened his mouth, but Edwina turned and clamped a hand over his face before he could speak.

"There is *nothing* you could give. You have no concept of what you even took. You have no family, nobody in your life you love. Who loves you. You cannot begin to understand what you did to us. So what we need right now is time. Time to process all this. We need to go home. Sleep in our own beds. And when I am ready, I will return to work beside you. Not a moment earlier."

Of all the things Edwina had said, that anyone had ever said, none had ever cut so deeply. Aisling kept herself very still as she dipped her chin in acknowledgment. Remained still as the two demi-kin rose—Radley snatching the bottle of wine off the table before following his sister from the room. She didn't move, barely breathed, as the door swung closed and the others began to whisper among themselves. Didn't acknowledge Clayton or Dearmead as they silently left the room.

Eavha dragged Aisling's chair away from the table until there was enough room for her to kneel at her feet. She took Aisling's hands and removed the lace gloves, lowering her head to her knuckles.

For a moment, Aisling wasn't sure what the priestess was doing. Didn't hear the near-silent muttering as Eavha prayed. But as she focused on it, she began to understand.

". . . look down upon her and ease the pain in her heart. Take the thorn that poisons her mind, her soul, and set her free. Let her find her most inner truth, and let her kindness shine brighter than any darkness that lurks within."

She didn't know which Spirits Eavha prayed to, but Aisling closed her eyes and let the words wash over her. And when she was done, Aisling began.

"Mother, to you I repent. For what I have done to many of your children. To the kinner. To . . . To Cinn."

Cinn.

She knew him as Ryson.

She had not called him by his name since the moment she put him in that cell, because he could not be *someone* if she was going to do what she thought she had to do to him. He had to be *other*. But he was not other. He was someone. A cadet, training to be in her army. A brother. A son. A child.

For the first time in many years, an actual tear escaped, burning a path down her cheek.

CHAPTER THIRTY-TWO

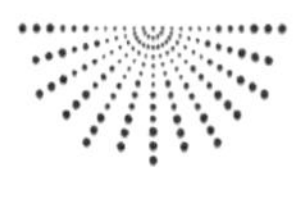

DEARMEAD

There was a tavern in the part of the city called Westgate that Clayton's sources told them the new Second in Command often frequented with her brother. As Dearmead stood outside the dilapidated structure, he didn't understand why. They'd given Edwina the day to adjust before seeking her out, and while he had not seen much of the city—didn't know if the building was poor by human standards or just his own—he had seen literal shitholes more inviting than this quiet tavern.

There were tiles missing from the roof, boards askew on the walls that, during winter, would let the wind and rain right in. Broken glass and puddles of bile lined the entryway, a patron adding to it with a chunky wet splatter.

Dearmead shared a look with Clayton; the guard was just as unimpressed. They waited until the drunk moved on before making their way up the sagging steps and into the ale-soaked tavern. For once, he was glad for the borrowed shoes and understood why such things might have been invented.

Dressed in human attire—brown pants, black boots, and an old tunic of Clayton's—Dearmead had hoped he wouldn't stand out as much as he did walking around in guardian leathers, bare footed with his spear strapped to his back. But as soon as he was inside, every head

"

in the room turned in his direction. Including Edwina's, who's face crumpled into a scowl at the sight of them. Beside her, Radley was seething.

Ignoring the stares, Dearmead and Clayton walked up to the booth the two sat at.

"Interesting establishment for the princess's Second in Command." Clayton raised one of his graying eyebrows as he gave Edwina a reproachful look.

"If I want your opinion on something, kill me, because I have clearly gone demented," Edwina deadpanned, drinking heavily from the tankard in front of her. "Piss off."

"We have worked together for years, Edwina, and we will likely be working together for a time yet. We came here because we thought it best to find a way to put the past behind us." Clayton ignored the hostile words she spat, though Dearmead suspected they rattled him.

Quiet. Meek. Unassuming. That was how Clayton had described the servant. If he had known him longer, Dearmead may have warned Clayton to never trust the well-behaved ones.

"Were you the one who put our brother in a cell?" Radley's voice slurred, a death-promise in his eyes.

Clayton said nothing.

"I met him," Dearmead intervened before another fight could break out. "Your brother. Fought with him. He's a good man."

"He was still a kid the last time I saw him." Radley's upper lip curled, eyes locked on Clayton. But Edwina was paying attention now.

"You fought with him? He's been fighting?"

"This is Ry we're talking about. Of course he's been fighting," Radley muttered, rolling his eyes.

Dearmead looked at the empty seats beside her and Radley. "I will tell you about it, if you want. But excuse my Nirnish. I'm still learning."

The two demi-kin shared a look, then Radley sniffed deeply, rubbing his nose on his sleeve before inclining his chin. "Next round is on you."

Blinking, Dearmead glanced to Clayton; he had no idea what that meant. Clayton just sighed and nodded, taking the seat beside Edwina.

Coward.

Dearmead sat beside Radley, but looked at Edwina as he launched into the story of when he had rescued Eaon, Eavha and Cinn from Pirevia. Then he told them about how Cinn had offered his help to end the curse in Wyldeden. It was impossible not to notice the way both she and Radley clung to his every word, only interrupting to ask more questions about their brother.

"Did he say why he never sent word to us? We would have come to meet him." Edwina shook her head in pained confusion.

"Ah, no. Maybe he might have told Eaon but I don't understand what he says. You know, with his hands."

Edwina frowned. "What do you mean, his hands?"

Glancing between them, Dearmead was uncertain what had been normal for the kinner before his imprisonment and what was not. He glanced at Clayton, but even he looked confused.

"Because . . . he can't speak? Eaon taught him a sign language with his hands, so they could communicate—"

"What do you mean, he doesn't speak?" Radley snapped.

"What do you mean, what do I mean? Am I not making sense?"

"No. Because Ryson was a loud-mouthed little brat when I knew him, so why does he not speak anymore?"

Again, Radley's hateful glare flicked to Clayton, who raised his hands.

"This is the first I am hearing of it."

"What did you do to him?" Radley slammed a hand down on the table.

"I did nothing," Clayton snapped. "I took him to and from his cell for Aisling, and that is it. You want details, you will have to ask her."

Radley talked about Cinn like he was dead, Dearmead realized. Even after listening to Dearmead talk for almost an hour, it still hadn't sunk in for him that his brother was alive. Which was odd, considering he was a kinner and literally couldn't be dead.

"We can help you find him," Dearmead interrupted again, cutting through the violence building in the booth. "Eavha and me. He is with her brother, and she will not stay apart from him forever. When Eaon and Cinn return from Qiri, we can help you see him."

"Is that before or after this supposed war we're meant to fight?" Edwina grimaced, looking across the tavern with a solemn expression. "We came to terms with the idea of never seeing him again a long time ago. We would always keep trying to find him, of course, but as the years went by, he was just . . . gone. He went to train for the cadets one day and never came home. We went to the commander to find out, and he denied even knowing who Ryson was. He'd become a phantom, a myth, like the rest of his people."

Radley drained his tankard and raised it for the barmaid to see. She was immediately bringing over four more drinks. Clayton pulled a pouch from his pocket and handed the woman some coins. The whole exchange was bizarre.

Sniffing at the alcohol, Dearmead took a tentative sip and nearly choked on it. Edwina smiled, drinking deeply. Pushing the tankard aside, he leaned forward on the table to catch her eye.

"He is not a myth. He is a strange kid who, judging by the way he makes Eaon laugh, still has a sense of humor. He would probably love to see you both very much."

Again, she smiled at him, but this time her eyes were glassy. "You sure seem to mention this Eaon character a lot."

Dearmead stilled at the change in topic. "Yes. Sorry."

"You can interrogate Dearmead about his boyfriend later," Radley growled, words slurring to the point of near incomprehensibility as he took another drink. "If you're satisfied we've bonded enough, can you two fuck off now?"

Clayton grimaced while Dearmead tried to hide the heat rising to his cheeks.

"Tell me, Mister Radley," Clayton kept his voice low as he wrapped both hands around his tankard. "Are you this inebriated every night, or only on nights you find yourself joining the ranks of 'traitorous pigs'?"

"Clayton!" Dearmead snapped, holding an arm out to stop Radley from rising from his seat.

"Hit a nerve with that one, didn't I, you Sparrow-tit suckling—"

"Rad!" Edwina slammed a fist on the table, her limp brown hair falling over her ear at the impact. "This is why we have to drink in this piece-of-crap tavern. Put a lid on your temper. You know better."

"We drink in this piece-of-crap tavern because I refuse to pay money to anyone who praises that—"

"Oh, so it has nothing to do with you picking fights with every other barkeep this side of the clock tower—"

"—pinch-faced weasel bitch—"

"—because you just cannot keep your mouth shut. You never could. And that bitch is giving us back this city, so—"

"Oh, don't you dare start defending her. All I've heard these last two years is—"

Dearmead looked between the bickering siblings, stunned into absolute silence. The familiarity brought about a pang of nostalgia that left his chest hollow.

Clayton was watching them too, his face crumpling into exasperation.

"Seriously? *Seriously?*" he shouted over them.

Dearmead looked around the tavern, but there was only one other patron still lingering, and she was so enraptured in some silent song that had her feet slow-dancing across the room that she paid them no mind.

"When Aisling is gone, this is what Hyrsch has to keep the city running?" Clayton waved a hand between them. "Gods save these people."

Silence fell over the table, though if Dearmead was being honest he didn't know how Radley and Edwina would be any different to what he had seen from Aisling: the wine, the mess that was Imsa, and his sureness that every second word out of her mouth was a lie.

Again, Edwina broke the silence.

"She was serious, then. She really does plan on leaving?"

"To save the fucking world," Radley scoffed, draining his drink and calling for another.

But Edwina knew. Dearmead could see it in her eyes that she knew Aisling well enough to know that the princess would not have invested so much of herself into something she did not truly believe. Had worked with her long enough to know there was something bigger going on, even if it was hard for Edwina to believe in the gods.

"On the chance she is right," Dearmead said, his words a little slower as he tried to put together a Nirnish sentence. "You should be ready."

Swallowing deeply, Edwina drained her drink.

The tavern rang their final call bell, but by then Radley was so drunk he could barely stay on his seat. Edwina had watched her brother drink himself under the table with a mixed expression of disgust and pity. Dearmead was just glad the male was no longer capable of putting together a sentence, already tired of the incessant name-calling and bitterness.

"Would you like an escort back to the palace?" Clayton asked, only having drank the one he had been obligated to have.

Dearmead hadn't tried more either. Not only did it taste awful, but it was weak compared to the alcohol made by witches and so wasn't even worth pushing through for.

"I don't think I'm ready to go back yet," Edwina said. "I need to talk to Radley. I need . . . I need some time to wrap my head around everything."

Clayton nodded. Then looked to Dearmead. "We should be off then. Check on Aisling and Eavha before retiring."

"I'm sure they're fine," Dearmead said, though he was sure of no such thing. Looking down at Edwina, he admitted, "I would like to see you home safely, if you don't mind. You might need some help with your brother."

With a glance and a sigh, Edwina nodded. "I might, actually."

Clayton grimaced. "I'll check on Eavha for you, then."

The night had not warmed the guard to Radley at all, which in all honesty was fair. It was hard to imagine the male being friendly toward anyone at all. As they stood, Dearmead practically had to lift Radley to his feet while the male grumbled and slurred nonsensically. Edwina put his other arm over her shoulders, and they went out into the warm night.

Clayton left, and the three of them stumbled along in silence for a while.

"He is still very angry with me," Edwina said.

"Clayton? Yes, he feels betrayed."

"Oh, him too. But Radley. He did not want me to take Aisling's offer. He wanted to go down in a blaze of glory avenging Ryson, like some ridiculous hero from a bedtime story."

Dearmead smiled a little. "He cares for his brother very much."

"We both do."

"It is nice to see. But I would not guess either of you were related to Cinn. Ryson. Sorry, I'm not sure what to call him."

"Me neither. But it makes sense none of us look alike since none of us are actually related," Edwina huffed, focusing on the ground ahead. The dilapidated building Dearmead and Clayton had raided not long ago came into view, and it dawned on him that they would somehow have to climb the stairs. "But we grew up together. We were the only three kids working at Master Ackford's townhouse, so we stuck together. Do you have any brothers or sisters?"

"Many. We are not close."

"That must be difficult."

"It is normal," Dearmead sighed, not sure how to say what he meant to say. Not that it mattered. "It would be more difficult to be a slave."

Edwina's lip pulled up in a mockery of a smile, sad eyes meeting his. "It was normal."

Conversation died as they reached the stairs. Dearmead took Radley's weight, who wasn't as heavy as he should be, and pulled the male onto his back, mostly dragging him as they climbed the stairs.

Finally, they got inside and Dearmead dumped Radley's half-conscious form on the lumpy couch.

Edwina covered him in blankets, fetched a glass of water from the sink to leave beside the couch, then looked up at Dearmead. "Would you stay for a minute? I can make some tea."

Dearmead looked around the stuffy old room. "You sure you don't want to stay at the palace?"

"It's not much, I know," Edwina shook her head. "But this is and always will be my home. Ryson, Radley and I bought this place together when we were first freed. Neither of us could bear to leave after he disappeared."

Dearmead closed the front door and took a tentative seat at the rickety little table he and Clayton had searched. Filling a pot with water and setting it over the stove, Edwina lit the flame beneath it with the last match in a box.

"Don't use your supplies on me," Dearmead said, rising from the chair.

"I could use the tea, too. Will help keep the hangover at bay."

"You didn't drink that much."

"One of us had to be sober enough to remember how to get home," Edwina muttered, looking back across at Radley, who gave a hearty snore in response.

"Seeing Eavha and Eaon, sometimes I would wish for a better . . . bond, with my siblings. Then sometimes I see how bad the fights are, and I'm grateful I'm not." Dearmead wasn't sure what he was trying to say. He had a point, but it eluded him.

Edwina sighed and nodded, adding tea leaves to a strainer as she waited for the water to boil.

"They are both a curse and a blessing. Radley has some issues, and as much as I love him, after Ryson disappeared it can be too much for me to be around all the time. That's the only time I stay at the palace. And when I was on night shift with Aisling." As she spoke, she fiddled with an old piece of yarn tied around her wrist, a single rock tied in an intricate hammock. Edwina noticed him looking and lifted it for him to see better. "Recognize it?"

"No. Should I?"

"It's a witch charm. When Rad and I were young, before Ry came along, a traveling witch made these for us. One for him, one for me. She said it would tie our souls together, so that if one of us was in trouble the other would feel it."

Dearmead raised his eyebrows. "What kind of witch was she? I've never heard of such a charm."

"No idea. But they work. Sometimes I wish Ry had been given one too so we would have known he was in trouble. Maybe we could have helped him the way he helped us."

"He seems to like doing that."

"What?"

"Helping people."

Edwina didn't say anything for a while, but when she did continue, her voice was heavy with an old sadness.

"People used to think Radley had a bad influence on Ryson, but really, it was the other way around. Rad and I were born by breeders. Back before, demi-kin women were sold and kept as breeders so there would always be a supply of us for working or selling. We grew up learning how to be good slaves, fed on stories about how our kind were lesser, slavery our penance for the crimes of our ancestors. But some of the breeders told us different stories. About the legend of the Kinner, and how they saved Nir from the clutches of a great evil. They were warriors, and one day they would return to free us.

"I was nine when I ended up at the Ackford house. Radley had been there a few years, already twelve. And then a year later, Ryson showed up. Nobody knew what he was then, but he wasn't like us. He'd been caught in the wild, and whenever Master Ackford gave us orders Ry would do it with this feral look on his face. Like he was planning how best to kill him."

Dearmead smothered a chuckle. He had seen that expression from Cinn directed at Kaelean, but he wasn't sure if it would be a gift or a wound to tell Edwina that at least that part of her brother was still the same.

"And then, one day, I felt a panic that didn't belong to me," Edwina continued. "It was coming from this charm, so I ran around looking for Radley. I found him in the alley behind the house. He was meant to be taking out trash but some stranger had tried to kidnap him. Demi-kin organs were, and in some places still are, a lucrative black-market trade.

"Ryson had been close enough to hear the one scream Rad managed to get out before they'd shoved a gag in his mouth. Little seven-year-old Ryson had tried to fight off a full-grown man and I got there just in time to see the trafficker break Ry's neck. Just in time to see him get back up and pull his head back straight."

Dearmead had seen the kinner do that, too. Not specifically with his head, but with a wound so deep in his chest the male had literally been holding his lung inside himself. It had been the single most disgusting thing Dearmead had ever seen, terrible and awesome at the same time.

"The man was so stunned . . ." Edwina cleared her throat, pouring the boiling water over the tea leaves into a jar, then the diffusion into two chipped teacups. "The three of us together managed to get the upper hand. I won't tell you what we did to the trafficker. But after that, Rad took it on himself to make sure nobody found out what Ryson was. Because if demi-kin organs were worth trying to kidnap kids off the street over, what would happen to a seven-year-old kinner who could barely defend himself?

"And in return, Ryson gave us hope. He told us the Kinner were really out there. That his parents would be looking for him, and when they arrived we could all run away and live with them. The promise of potential freedom lit some fire in Radley that I had never seen before, and he started rebelling against our master at every opportunity. It was stupid, but it gave him purpose, you know?"

He did. Again, Dearmead was thinking of Eaon. How working with languages and making discoveries in books would light a fire in Eaon like nothing else could. More often than not, it was one of the only things that brought him any joy. Dearmead couldn't count how many hours he had sat and listened to Eaon talk about the books he was reading, or the language he had learned while traveling, the history of it, the nuances of it, his mind soaking up the information the way Eavha's had soaked up medical knowledge. The way Dearmead had soaked up the nuances in scents. He hadn't always been able to follow Eaon's ramblings, but he would have let him talk endlessly for days, watching the joy in his face build and build.

"Ryson's parents never showed up, but we got freedom seven years later anyway. From Aisling. I was seventeen and, unlike my brother, I had a stellar reputation as a good slave, so I was able to apply to work for her. For a wage. I was offered schooling and learned to read and write. Radley was nearly twenty and got a job as a streetlamp lighter pretty quickly, and between the two of us we were able to take care of Ry. He was only fourteen, you know? Aisling had given him the freedom his parents had never come to give him, and so when he was old enough, he wanted to protect her. He joined the cadets, even though Rad and I told him a hundred times it was a bad idea.

"And, yeah. One day he just . . . never came home. I was working in the palace, working closely with Aisling herself. I heard her talking to Nora and Clayton. I heard her admit she had him locked in a cell. That she knew what he was and he was not cooperating. I went and told Radley, and he took me to meet the demi-kin rebellion he was a part of. A group of our kind that didn't trust Aisling and her kindness. We told them she had our brother in her dungeon, but, two years later, we still couldn't find him. Couldn't get him out. And I felt that breaking Radley through the charm. He felt it breaking me."

Edwina had taken the seat across from Dearmead and wiped her damp cheeks, staring at her tea as it began to go cold.

"Sorry. You didn't ask for this story. I don't even remember why I started telling it."

"It's okay," Dearmead assured her, reaching to rest his hand atop of hers. She flinched at first, but didn't remove her hand. "Tell me the rest."

Edwina took a deep breath, wiping her nose on her shoulder before looking across at Radley.

"Then one day there was a rumor. That deep in the dungeons was a secret cell that needed magic to access, and that if we could get there, we would find the kinner. An amulet had been left at our headquarters with a note: *This will get you in. It will expire in twelve hours. Use it wisely.*

"It was likely a trap, but Radley was going to do it anyway. Which would be a disaster. He's not exactly subtle, you know? So the rebellion made a plan. We waited until night. I made sure Aisling was too drunk to go down to her dungeon, Radley and some of the others caused a ruckus with some traditionalists outside the palace walls to distract the guards, and a few of our best snuck in and got Ry out. We knew he couldn't stay in the city, but we hoped that once he was safe he would reach out. When he didn't . . . we thought something had gone wrong. But I heard from being near Aisling in the following months that he had turned up at a farm in Belden, but by that point he was already gone again."

She sniffed and sighed, pulling her hand away to guide her cup to her lips, drinking deeply from her tea. Dearmead sipped at his, too, trying not to wrinkle his nose at the bitterness of it. These human cities wouldn't know what hit them if they tried some of Wyldeden's tea.

"I think I'll be okay if I never get to see him again. Eventually, I mean. As long as I know he's okay. Safe. But Radley . . . I think a part of him still doesn't believe he's really free. Not until he lays eyes on him, you know? I'm not sure he'll ever get that peace."

As much as he did not enjoy Radley's company, not even on the shallowest of levels, that was a pain he would not wish upon anyone.

"As I said," Dearmead said quietly. "I spent some time with Cinn, and the witch he is with now . . . your brother couldn't be in better hands. I have every reason to think they will return, and it will be an honor to make sure you three are reunited."

Edwina smiled sadly, reaching back for Dearmead's hand and giving it a feeble squeeze.

"Wyldeden has been a kindness to this city we did not expect, nor deserve, but are very grateful for."

Dearmead wasn't entirely sure what that meant, but it seemed nice. Finishing his tea, he cleaned the cup at the sink before clasping Edwina's hands in both of his and bowing.

"I will see you at the palace when you're ready, Lady Edwina."

"It might be sooner than I first thought," she replied, stepping in to hug Dearmead in what he thought was meant to be a tight hug. The girl had no strength, and he was sure he was breaking her ribs just by hugging her back.

CHAPTER THIRTY-THREE

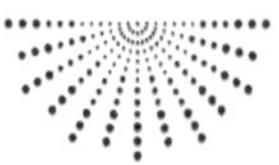

EAVHA

It was the middle of the night when a soft wind blew in a weathered oak leaf. The whisper of magic humming from it was enough to rouse Eavha from a heavy sleep. Grumbling, she slipped from the luxurious sheets and collected the leaf from where it slid to the marble floors, bringing it to her ear. Kaelean's voice, utterly inaudible, whispered in her ear.

"Only you would dare ask to bring a Sparrow to the Boab. I suppose I should be glad you asked at all. Tell that hag she will be swearing fifty different vows before I let her step inside Wyldeden, but as long as she does not leave your sight, she is allowed. And for the Lover's sake, keep her away from Cinn's humans."

It was a better response to her request than Eavha had expected. With a little skip, her bare feet prancing across the bedroom floor, she dressed quickly in a soft pink chest binding and matching floor-length skirt, running her fingers through her flattened curls to bounce some life back into them.

Not bothering to wake Dearmead or Milnova, she hurried from their suite and went straight to the stairwell that would take her up Aisling's tower. The guards at the bottom gave her a once over, but they knew who she was now and waved her past.

There was no servant to announce her anymore, so when she

reached the closed door at the top of the stairs, Eavha knocked. When no answer came, she knocked again. Kept knocking until she heard the creak of another door within and the unartful padding of feet.

Aisling opened the door bleary eyed, unbound hair falling limp and ratty down to her hips. Eavha blinked, not having realized the princess's hair was so long.

"This better be an emergency," Aisling croaked. She smelled of stale wine and sweat.

"I heard back from Kaelean just now. We can go to Wyldeden."

Aisling stared at her, unimpressed.

"I didn't think you would want to waste time. It's a long journey."

Finally, letting go of a sigh, Aisling opened the door fully and walked away, expecting Eavha to follow. The first door to the left was open, and beyond it Eavha could see the tousled sheets of an enormous bed, stuffed with an indecent number of pillows.

Speaking of indecent, Aisling wore only a silk robe that she hadn't bothered to tie closed, a strip of her tattooed body on display for anyone who wasn't shy enough to look away.

Eavha was not shy.

"You weren't kidding that you have them everywhere."

Aisling went to a door on the right and shoved it open. Beyond lay an entire room full of shoes and jewelry kept in orderly assortments, mannequins dressed in some of the stateliest and most ostentatious gowns Eavha could never have been able to imagine, and a display of crowns and necklaces that looked like they weighed more than a small child.

Standing at a dressing table with an aged mirror resting atop it, Aisling roughly brushed out her hair and began to braid it.

"You like my costumes?" she asked wearily, the words laden with disdain.

"Costumes?" Eavha repeated, unsure of the word.

"The clothes. The shoes and jewels. Carefully chosen, you can pretend to be anyone you can imagine. Wear whatever mask will get the job done. When you first arrived, you wore the guardian leathers to fool everyone into thinking you were not important."

"Ah." Eavha nodded, looking around once more. "So which one is the real you?"

Aisling finished braiding her hair, then wound the rope around itself tightly, pinning it to her head in a circlet. Then she turned and looked Eavha over, shaking her head.

"As pretty as you are, this attire will not work."

Eavha looked down at herself. "These are Wyldeden clothes."

"Yes, but they are not flying clothes."

Head snapping up, Eavha practically wheezed. "Flying?"

A smile carved through the marble of Aisling's face, and it was unlike anything Eavha had seen on the princess before. Wide. Mischievous. Feral.

"Yes. It is much faster than traveling by foot. I don't suppose a creature of the soil has ever taken to the skies before."

"No," Eavha breathed.

And there it was again. That smile like a storm. A hurricane incarnate, and yet aimed with unprecedented gentleness.

"Come then. Let me show you."

Out of her usual dresses, Aisling was entirely different. The tight leather pants and white blouse she donned was form-fitting enough that Eavha could see the secret muscle hiding beneath all the layers she wore daily. The tattoos on her throat and hands were exposed, but only for a moment; pulling on short leather gloves and buttoning her blouse as high as she could, Aisling's secret weapon was once more concealed. On top of that, she pulled on a fleece-lined coat that cut off at her waist before finding similar gear for Eavha to pull on.

"Here. I'll loan you some boots, too."

"Boots?" Eavha frowned as she pulled the pants on under her skirt, discarding the gauzy fabric. The shirt and coat she wrapped around her binding, tucking her Blessing Charm underneath.

"For your feet. You won't enjoy flying barefooted."

"I won't enjoy your clunky feet traps, either," Eavha complained as she followed Aisling to the back of her dressing room.

She pointed at a padded seat, so Eavha sat down and watched the princess bring over a pair of supple boots that would tie up to her knees. Kneeling in front of her, Aisling gently took Eavha's foot and braced it against the sole of the boot.

"Might be a little tight."

"Tight will be fine." Eavha shook her head. "I'm less likely to trip over myself if they're tight."

"I can't imagine someone so graceful falling on their face." Aisling smirked as she found some cotton lining to roll over Eavha's feet.

"Make me wear more shoes and you'll see a lot of it," Eavha grumbled. But her mouth had gone dry as she watched Aisling slide her hand up the back of Eavha's calf, guiding her foot into the long boot. It *was* a tight fit, but that hardly mattered as she watched Aisling's nimble fingers pull the laces taut.

Swallowing hard, not entirely sure why she was so nervous, Eavha returned to her unanswered question.

"The flying, this is not a role you play, is it?"

"No," she answered, voice hoarse. "If I had not been born to royalty I would have wanted to join a sky coven. I often dream of the veil I would wear once initiated. But even if I left the Coven tomorrow, I would be hard pressed to find anyone Celeste-blessed who would accept me."

"Why?"

"They would smell my Passing."

"So what?"

Aisling grimaced as she finished tying one boot and moved onto the other, her hands both gentle and firm.

"Celeste-blessed witches tend to enjoy a nomadic lifestyle. By colonizing the land, the Sparrow Coven has made such a thing difficult. None of the other clans enjoy having the Coven keep tabs on them but at least they stay in one place and are, for the most part, left to their own devices. But the covens that move around are harder to track, and thus the Sparrow Coven has a history of . . . making their lives very difficult. Many have started to form unions with settled clans to avoid the continued pressures. Having a 'base' and calling themselves 'travelers' of the clan is a cheeky way around the problem."

"Cheeky? Or clever?" Eavha grinned.

Aisling did too. "Regardless, they will know who I am. They will smell the Lover's blessing on me and not want a bar of me."

"Maybe some, but you can't know the minds of every Celeste-blessed witch in all of Nir."

"It doesn't matter anyway," Aisling said, standing up and offering a hand to Eavha so she could get to her feet and find her balance in the shoes. "It is not my destiny."

"I don't believe in destiny," Eavha declared as Aisling began to braid her hair for her.

Lorelei and Aadya both said it was the Nemuse family's destiny to pass to the Lover, but it wasn't. It was the crazed whim of a Morvish rogue, and she was glad she had spat in destiny's face and saved her brother. Would do it over and over again.

"You haven't spent enough time around the Morvish," Aisling said.

The pull of Eavha's braid exposed the bald spots she'd developed from ripping so much hair out for the Blessing Charm. Aisling didn't mention it, but went to her dresser again to collect a soothing salve for the bare patches.

"There aren't that many Morvish witches outside of Qiri to spend time with," Eavha countered.

"Not cooped up in that tree there isn't." Aisling took hold of Eavha's arm to lead her out of the dressing room. "There's usually at least one in Dusarn at any given point. An emissary, or so they say, to ensure there are no attempts to bring down the warding around their secret state. Only the Mother knows how they get through those brutal wards at all."

"You've seen them?"

"Once. Davina and I went flying together and she wanted to show me where she was from. She had a good laugh when we tried to cross the boundary and the wards hit."

"A prankster." Eavha smiled fondly.

"She's lucky I didn't die," Aisling huffed, but there was joy behind the words. Reminiscence and nostalgia, tinged with just a little sadness. None of the shadows that seemed to haunt the princess's face were present as she spoke about flying.

Eavha looked down to watch her feet as they approached the stairs, and she was glad for a reason to concentrate. Listening to Aisling talk about Davina made her think of Apaete. They had not been lovers the way Aisling and Davina had been, but she was the only friend Eavha had really gotten along with. They had spent a lot of time learning and exploring and practicing magic together, and Eavha missed the calm, steadiness of her friend.

Unlike Eavha, Apaete had been curious about the outside world but never had the chance to see it.

As they reached the bottom of the stairs, Eavha raised her head. She could no longer afford to be afraid of the world. It was a luxury of a life of comfort. She would see it all, face it, no matter what horrors it showed her. Because Apaete never got to.

Aisling was watching her curiously.

Eavha just smiled. "Let's fly."

Aisling led Eavha past the stables and over a manicured lawn to a second, more heavily guarded set. It was bewildering that she was still within the palace walls, and that all this space belonged to the princess. Not even Eavha's family manor had been so extensive.

"Your Highness. Lady Eavha." The demi-kin guards bowed their heads as the two approached.

Aisling dipped her chin in acknowledgment while Eavha smiled, chasing her inside. The stables weren't what she expected. Sure, the floor was covered in fresh hay that tickled the back of her nose, but the wooden structure that appeared so bland on the outside had been painted in great detail to replicate golden dunes and scraggy bushland, the doors to the generous stalls plated in ivory and silver.

This was not a home for an ordinary horse, and when Eavha spotted the creature drinking from a trough, her mouth literally fell open.

"This is Volya," Aisling said as she unlatched the gate. "She's been my mount since I was a witchling. Don't worry, she's very friendly."

Slowly, Eavha took a step forward. Coat the color of pale sand, the creature raised its elegant head to peer at the unfamiliar witch. The intelligence behind its dark brown gaze was not what had Eavha so entranced; it was the thickset shoulders supporting two large feathered wings that had stolen her ability to speak.

Aisling watched, amused as Eavha took very slow steps toward Volya. She raised her hand to gently trail her fingers over the impossibly soft coat stretched across those massive shoulders.

"Winged horses are rare, but my family in Dusarn have been breeding them for the past hundred years. My father is Celeste-blessed as well. We used to ride together sometimes. He refused to hide away that part of him just because he became Returned."

It didn't sit well, the story about the king. Not after seeing him humiliate Aisling in front of her entire court. So she didn't comment, combing her fingers through Volya's mane.

"She's beautiful," Eavha sighed.

"I'll never forget the first time I showed Davina," Aisling chuckled. "She was so confused that we didn't ride broomsticks."

Eavha choked, making Volya rear back.

Laughing as she came all the way into the stall to calm her mount, Aisling assured her, "I did the same thing. I didn't have the heart to explain."

"Why . . . Why did she even think that was a thing?"

"Well, I don't know if you've ever tried riding a broom—"

"No! Absolutely not!" Eavha put a hand to her chest, face blushing madly.

"Well." Aisling grinned wider. "It's rather intoxicating."

"Aisling, I do not need to know that."

"Such a prude," she teased, taking the saddle and bridle off the wall and placing it carefully on Volya's back. "But anyway, Davina said she had heard that elemental witches rode around on broomsticks and assumed it meant flight. I simply explained that it was inaccurate, and that a different definition of 'getting high' was involved. I believe the rumors started from the humans, actually. They must have seen wild witches doing it."

"Well," Eavha huffed, fanning her face.

"I've seen you drink, but herbs are not your thing?"

"I . . . I'm not opposed. It's just that manner of . . . absorbing them." A thought occurred to her, face blushing madly all over again. "Is that why the human stories always describe witches as cackling, too?"

It had always seemed peculiar, the image of witches she'd read about in some of the odd books Eaon left lying around. She'd never put it together until now. But it would make sense that humans didn't know they were watching the scandalous act some of the older witches partook in, hallucinogenic paste applied to yew broomsticks held between their bare legs, which as she knew from her medical studies was where many glands were found, until they were out of their minds.

Aisling was laughing, light and free, but quickly smothered it at the look on Eavha's face. "I'm sorry if I made you uncomfortable."

Taking a steadying breath, she had never been this flustered before. Aisling's vulgar sense of humor came as a surprise; she was usually so proper.

"No." Eavha smiled, pressing her hands against her burning cheeks. "No, it's alright."

With Volya ready, Aisling gave her a hand getting into the saddle.

"Where will you—"

Before Eavha could finish the sentence, Aisling was leading them out of the stall and stables. Then she jumped up onto the creature's back behind her, half standing with her feet in a second pair of stirrups, grabbing hold of the reins and looping them over Eavha.

"Keep your body low," she said, pressing her down until she was laying against the bulky shoulders of the horse. Eavha gripped the pommel at the front of the saddle tightly.

With a click of Aisling's tongue, Volya worked herself into a gallop before those enormous wings unfurled and, with a well-timed jump and flap, they were airborne.

Eavha sucked in a sharp breath, clinging even tighter to the saddle. Higher and higher they rose until, when she peeked past the stream of golden mane, she could see the palace like a doll's house far below.

"Lover spare me," she whimpered, all willpower to be brave in the face of the world's horrors disappearing in a heartbeat.

"You're safe," Aisling assured her. "I won't let you fall."

She had not realized how big the city was from the ground.

She had not told anyone where she had gone.

"Eavha, breathe," Aisling said in her ear, raising her voice against the wind now roaring past them as Volya picked up speed. "Tell me about Wyldeden. What to expect."

She knew what the princess was doing, but she also knew that distraction would help. So Eavha focused on the soft coat of the horse and tried to talk loud enough that Aisling could hear her, relaying Kaelean's warnings. But more than that, she talked about the land. The pocket of spirit realm she had called home her entire life, bountiful and beautiful and safe. Big in the way things could be, yet still have an end. A boundary to keep them safe. Keep them close.

More than ever before, Eavha thought she might understand the Morvish witches and their private bubble up north.

CHAPTER THIRTY-FOUR

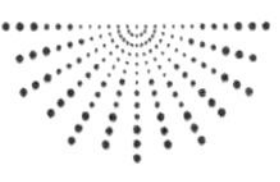

EAVHA

EVEN AS HIGH IN THE SKY AS THEY WERE, THE TINGLE OF ANFAR'S wards brushed over their skin like cobwebs. Volya whinnied as the magic that kept out beasts and fae repelled her, fighting against Aisling's order to keep flying anyway. But Aisling knew how to handle her creature and kept them moving.

The Great Boab stood above the rest of the forest like a teacher in a class of witchlings, its branches splayed out like an open hand. Eavha could almost imagine the canopy acting like a nest for some enormous bird in a world where people were the size of mountains, and she were a mere ant scurrying around beneath them.

Even as Volya began to descend, spearing for the Boab and sending Eavha's stomach into her throat, she managed to chuckle at herself. Her vision sounded like the wild conspiracy theories Eaon would come up with while deep in one of his frenzies. Once, he had woken her in the middle of the night urgently trying to convince her that he wasn't real, the world wasn't real. Everyone was just a dream in some deity's mind, and when he was sleeping was when the dreamer was awake.

It made no sense at the time, and Eavha had told him if he didn't go back to bed immediately, she was going to curse him into an eternal sleep. Which had only sent him on another tangent.

She missed those simpler days.

Aisling landed her mare a few dozen meters from the Boab and dismounted, stroking Volya's nose gently as Eavha slid from the saddle. Breathing deeply, the fresh air of Anfar and the familiar scent of her people nearby was a comfort she didn't know she needed until the humid haze wrapped around her.

Aisling looked around the forest warily, trying to conceal her awe at the size of the trees towering over them. The darkness was thorough, but as dawn peeked over the horizon, the softest gray light filtered through the thick canopy overhead. Gnarled roots blocked their way to the Boab, low-hanging branches creaking in a nonexistent breeze to obscure their line of sight. If Aisling noticed the forest's protest to her presence, she didn't comment on it.

"I thought it would be prettier," Aisling said softly, leading Volya to a nearby root that had buckled and risen over their heads many centuries ago.

"Excuse me?" Eavha raised a disbelieving eyebrow.

"It's gloomy. And kind of spooky."

"Don't tell me the Sparrow witch is scared of the deep dark forest," Eavha teased, ducking beneath the root Aisling was tying Volya's reins to and climbing over another that threaded the surface.

"I'm half waiting for a stryg to come creeping out of nowhere."

Eavha had heard of the blood-sucking beasts, supposedly part wraith with the way they moved through the air, cloaked in darkness. "There are no beasts in Anfar. No fae."

"Yes, but . . . it's one thing to know, and another to actually be here."

Whatever Eavha had planned to respond with evaporated from her mind as she dropped from the root and landed on the soft summer floor.

Eaon had told her how during Anfar's summer months the earth would disappear beneath a ground-cover weed blown in from the North Mountains. No matter how lightly she tread, her footsteps left a slight greenish-blue imprint glowing on the ground. The weed wasn't useful for anything medical, much like the phosphorate flowers Wyldeden imported from the northern clan, so she had never really cared too much. But now, she made an effort to appreciate the beauty of it for its own sake, the way Apaete would have. She grinned, skipping nimbly, trying to defy gravity itself.

Aisling smiled as she watched, her own boots leaving an obvious trail that slowly dissipated as the weed sprang back.

Then she very suddenly wasn't smiling anymore.

"What is that?"

Eavha stopped, looking around anxiously, but she couldn't sense anything. "What? Where?"

Aisling stepped back toward Volya, looking all around at something Eavha couldn't see.

"Can't you hear the whispers?"

"Whispers?" Eavha asked, then gasped. "Oh. That's Terra's guardians."

"Her *what?*" Aisling hissed.

Eavha closed her eyes and took a deep breath. Here in the forest, it was considerably easier to connect with Terra. To feel the other realm sitting alongside their own, spiritually accessible through her soul-form's magic, but not physically unless she passed through the Boab.

Kaelean had taught her about the guardians since joining the priestesses at the Sanctuary. Not even she truly knew what they were, only that they lingered deeper in Terra's realm, beyond the border of Wyldeden that always turned witches back to the settlement. When she and Eaon had broken into Wyldeden back in the spring, they had sensed Terra's guardians because they had been excommunicated. Now that she had been forgiven, she was not approached by them as they neared the Boab.

But Aisling was not of Anfar. Not of Wyldeden.

Struggling to quiet her mind long enough to slip from her body, Eavha continued to breathe until she felt it. The weightlessness that came over her, the sudden intensity of everything. The guardians were not visible, but she could feel their wrath at Aisling, so close to a vulnerable point in Terra's realm.

"She's a friend," Eavha said aloud.

But they did not listen to her.

Not that it mattered.

Strong hands grabbed her by the arms, pulling her sharply

backward. Eavha flung open her eyes as her soul crashed back into her body, gasping and bucking furiously as she was held tightly against a broad chest, a hand clamped over her mouth.

"Hush, Eavha," a familiar voice whispered as they dragged her a few feet away from Aisling. One of Dearmead's brothers.

Other Wyldeden guardians had emerged from the forest, dropping from trees and skulking out of bushes, spears aimed at the Sparrow princess. Aisling's wide eyes looked between them, then to Eavha, who had not stopped trying to get one of the Bayfield males to let her go.

"Release her," Aisling hissed in Terranian, pulling a dagger from her thigh, her axe from her back.

The steel made the guardians pause.

"We are of no threat to our own, leech," one of the others spat back, inching forward.

"I was given permission to be here," Aisling tried, glancing once more to where Eavha was quickly running out of strength.

Eavha sensed it a moment before Aisling did. Screaming into the hand that smothered her face was all the warning she could give before Kaelean dropped from a nearby tree, all muscle and scales, teeth and claws. A deep, thundering growl echoed through the barely waking forest as the lupanis bared its fangs at Aisling.

Blood bleached from Aisling's lips as she took in the high priestess of Wyldeden. Visibly swallowing the nerves in her throat, Aisling slowly slid the axe back into its holster, followed by the dagger.

"I've come—"

Kaelean pounced, claws sinking deep into Aisling's shoulder as she knocked her to the ground.

The scream of pain that tore through the forest, swallowed by the shrubbery as if it hungered for it, left Eavha sobbing.

"It's going to be okay," Dearmead's brother whispered, tightening his grip. "Whatever spell she has cast on you, Kaelean will remove it."

Eavha shook her head wildly.

As the other guardians removed Aisling's weapons, Kaelean retracted her claws and backed off. Uncaring of the wounds now pulsing with toxins from the lupanis claws, the guardians kicked

Aisling in the side, rolling her onto her front before binding her wrists and ankles in ropes.

Kaelean shifted back, naked and covered in ashy spellmarks, black eyes livid as she glared down at the princess.

"Thought you were clever, wheedling an invitation to Wyldeden. Whatever you planned to steal, I will find out. And only after I've removed whatever hex you've placed on Eavha will I bless you with death."

Eavha screamed so hard into the Bayfield's hand she tasted blood. Thrashed until she was sure she was about to dislocate something.

Kaelean only glanced at her with pity, then raised her chin to the guardian closest to Aisling.

"Bring her in. Put her in a cell. See how she likes it."

Bound to a chair in Kaelean's office, Eavha had not stopped cussing at the Bayfield guardian the entire time he stood at the high priestess's door. Did not stop, even as that door opened and Kaelean came in, dressed in a simple green robe.

"How dare you trick me!" Eavha screamed at her, voice growing hoarse. "How dare you have so little faith in me to think I've been hexed!"

Kaelean ignored her as she dusted her hands in burnt herbs before approaching Eavha. Without a scrap of gentleness, she grabbed Eavha's head and dug her fingers into her temples. Magic rumbled through the room until it became suffocating, washing over Eavha slowly and persistently. Searching her. As Kaelean's brow furrowed in confusion, her empty black eyes peering down, Eavha made sure she met only cold fury.

"I am not hexed. Aisling has cast no spell on me."

"Then why in the Lover's void are you helping her?"

"What have you done with her? I need to heal her wounds."

"She will not die. Now answer my question."

"She cannot be scarred, Kaelean! It's imperative—"

"WHY ARE YOU HELPING HER!"

Eavha froze, the blood rushing from her face as her bladder weakened. For the life of her, she could not make her mouth work.

The door opened just an inch and Lorelei's head poked in.

In the time since training as a priestess, Eavha had not gotten used to Lorelei's presence. Had not grown comfortable seeing her waltz around Wyldeden like she still owned it, and was not any less afraid of her now that she was Kaelean's laborer.

"Someone better be dying," Kaelean hissed, turning only slightly.

"I just wanted to suggest trying The Telling Mark of Secrets Unveiled."

Kaelean bristled. "Get out."

Lorelei left, but Eavha was dizzy from sheer terror. She knew that mark. Had healed her brother after their cousin had used that mark on him to force him to tell the truth. Some drama about lost laundry or something. She didn't remember and it didn't matter right then. She did not want it used on her. It was forbidden for being cruel, and her cousin had been punished by the Elder Keeper when Ma found out it had been used on Eaon. Only the high priestess and the elders were allowed to use it, and even then, only under dire circumstances. Even on those occasions it was considered necessary, the mark did not always yield results. Kaelean had used it on Aadya and had learned nothing. The Morvish rogue's will had been too strong.

"Please, Eavha, breathe. I would never do that to you."

Her eyes burned anyway, and she wasn't sure why. There was not enough air in the room, her skin flushing with heat as she pulled at her restraints.

"Eavha. *Eavha*." Kaelean loosened the knots around her wrists and ankles, pulling her head against her chest as Eavha broke into sobs. "I'm sorry I scared you. I'm sorry."

Taking Eavha with her, Kaelean sat on the floor and stroked her hair for the long minutes it took Eavha to calm down. Her breath still hitched painfully, but she let go of Kaelean and righted herself, wiping her face on the back of her trembling hands.

"I know you wouldn't hurt me. I don't know what came over me."

"You have been abused at the hand of a high priestess before. I should not have shouted at you like that."

"I did not expect you to be so angry at me."

"I'm not, Eavha." Kaelean took her face, tucking a loose curl behind her ear, smearing herbs all over her cheek as she did. "I'm angry at the Sparrow, and I don't understand why you would bring her here."

"Did you not receive my messages about helping her investigate Chaos? About the war?"

"I did, and they made me worried for you. For what nonsense the princess was poisoning you with. What lies she was spinning, and why. When you said you wanted to bring her to Wyldeden, it all fell into place. She's playing the game, Eavha. She wanted access to Wyldeden for some reason, and she was using you to get it."

"No." Eavha shook her head.

"You are kindhearted." Kaelean smiled sadly. "I don't blame you for not seeing it."

"No, it's not nonsense. It's the truth."

"What evidence have you seen? What is there besides a ballet and an insane Morvish rogue, spouting garbage?"

Eavha swallowed. There was none. "I believe her."

Kaelean just grimaced. "Aisling is an ambitious female, and—"

"She's not," Eavha interrupted. "She's sad and lonely. And desperate."

Kaelean sighed and stood, helping Eavha to her feet. "Go and get cleaned up. Get some rest. We can—"

"No. I want to see Aisling."

"I need to speak with her first."

"Then I will come with you. Heal her wounds."

Kaelean narrowed her eyes, and Eavha felt another wave of gentle magic brush over her.

"I am not under a spell, Kaelean."

The high priestess merely wrinkled her nose and led the way from the room.

CHAPTER THIRTY-FIVE

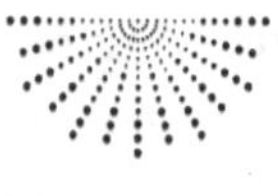

AISLING

COMPARED TO HER OWN DUNGEON, THE WYLDEDEN PRISON WAS cozy. The morning sun shone down on her, her cell's roof open to the brightening sky. The earthen ground beneath her was warm and soft, even as she lay panting through the ravaging pain pulsing from her chest. The lupanis toxins burned with every beat of her heart, dampening her skin with sweat. She tried to meditate through it, but every breath sent fresh blood oozing from the wounds, soaking her shirt. She was lucky the claws hadn't pierced her lungs or heart; as if the high priestess knew exactly where to puncture without delivering a killing blow.

Eavha's kindness had made Aisling soft. Had made her believe she had allies in this war. She had been stupid, falling for this trap. Stupid for believing Kaelean Caesarea would allow her into Wyldeden as a guest.

The door opened and more guardians stepped in, followed by Kaelean in her witch form again. And Eavha.

"Lover be damned," Eavha muttered, dropping to her knees and ripping Aisling's shirt away.

The words made Aisling's head spin. Such a phrase would be a prison sentence in Kerveda, proof that she truly was a very long way from home.

As the painful sizzling of Eavha's healing magic drew the poison from her veins, she hissed through clenched teeth, back arching.

"Don't push yourself," Kaelean said to Eavha, who wholeheartedly ignored her.

"You're going to be fine," she assured Aisling quietly.

The witchmarks inking her skin would be enough, once she was healed, to walk out of this pocket of spirit realm untouched. She could have fought back in Anfar, fought and won, but what would that have achieved except another war she didn't have time for?

Finally, the pain eased, and Aisling took her first easy breath in hours.

Kaelean pulled Eavha away. Not harshly, but the way a mother might pull a child from harm's way. Well, not her own mother, per se, but Aisling had seen such displays of love from the people in her home city.

"What is your business here," Kaelean snapped, fist clenched as if she would pummel Aisling with her bare fist, like some kind of animal.

"It is as Eavha said it is," Aisling said warily, feeling her chest. Yet again, no scars remained, but the magic it took to perform such a feat had not sent Eavha into a burnout. Her peony hung around her neck, the wad of hair tangled around it thicker than the last time Aisling had noticed. Hence the bald spots on the witch's scalp, she supposed.

"You expect me to believe this bullshit about Chaos?" Kaelean sneered, crouching down, thick thighs taut with muscle. Where Eavha was all innocence—flowers and butterflies and songs—Kaelean was a true wild witch. There was something intrinsically feral about her. As removed from humanity as the fae themselves.

"No," Aisling acknowledged, forcing herself to sit up.

This was the witch who, at thirteen, had defeated Aisling's parents and the entire Sparrow Coven in the war for Anfar. To be honest, Aisling had admired Kaelean for a long time, hiding her smiles every time King Phineas went on a rant about his loss to a "barbarian child."

The silence sat between them, brimming with unabashed hostility.

"I will swear a vow—"

"My keeper informed me about Imsa. You cannot be bound," Kaelean sneered, looking at the marks now exposed across her chest.

"Then use The Telling Mark of Secrets Unveiled," Aisling suggested.

"As if it will work on you."

There was such hatred in the words. Nothing Aisling offered would be enough to convince Kaelean she truly had come without an ulterior motive.

"Aisling and I promised not to lie to each other," Eavha chimed in.

That Kaelean did not snort in derision the way Aisling would have if such a statement had been spoken to her cemented the assumption that Kaelean really did care for Eavha.

"A promise is not worth much to her kind."

And those words, "her kind," sparked an idea. It was not ideal, not yet, but if the answers she needed really were here in Wyldeden, she would do it.

"I will renounce my kind, right here, right now—"

"And it will still mean nothing if you cannot be bound!" Kaelean snapped.

Aisling closed her eyes.

"Then ruin the mark."

Silence.

"Cut it, burn it, whatever you want. Take it off me, and cast Secrets Unveiled on me. Have me vow whatever you want. I'll do it willingly. Just, please, believe me."

Her voice had thickened, and when she opened her eyes Davina was back, glaring daggers at her. She had given her life for these marks and now Aisling was giving one of them up.

"Don't you dare," the ghost snarled.

"No," Eavha echoed, a hand at her throat.

But Kaelean grinned. "I don't know why I didn't think of it myself."

She hadn't expected the ceremony, but she didn't fight it as she was dragged through the most whimsical city she had ever seen. The sun glittered off crystal towers that spired into the sky, shining off marble temples surrounding the enormous lake that housed an identical boab to the one in Anfar. Even the platform she was made to kneel on was a stunning slab of stone, rippled with specks of opal.

A crowd had gathered, whispering in a cacophony not unlike the oppressive "guardians" Aisling had sensed in Anfar. Their weight had been smothering, as was the gaze of those who had come to witness the violence about to happen.

Eavha was still pleading with Kaelean not to do this. Davina was screaming at Aisling to fight. But she wouldn't. It was her turn to sacrifice. To bear this humiliation, binding herself in the name of peace to a witch who hated her. She was a princess, but she might as well be a scullery maid for all she mattered to the Coven. Her parents.

As her wrists were unbound, Aisling settled on her knees and raised her palm above her head. The one that bore The Key Mark for Those Unbound. It was one of the first Davina had tattooed on her, and Aisling had complained viciously during the entire procedure.

The high priestess had not changed into anything formal, still wearing the simple shroud of a priestess, her hair a wild mane around her face. But regardless, the clan went quiet as they waited with bated breath.

"Today, an opportunity has brought itself to Wyldeden's doors. Today, a royal member of the Sparrow Coven presents herself, wishing to be bound in a state of honesty with our clan."

Their gasps as the people of Wyldeden realized who was on the platform only strengthened Aisling's spine.

"She bears a mark that prevents her from being held to any vow she speaks, but today we remove that mark."

"No," Eavha said again, falling to her knees beside Aisling. "I won't let you do this."

"Stupid girl," one of the other witches on the podium hissed. Mahogany skin, large black curls, and eyes that turned like a globe, all greens and shifting browns.

Kaelean turned to the witch and leveled a glare that had the first shrinking from the platform. "Be elsewhere. Now."

The entire clan stood silently and watched the dark witch shake with rage before rushing from the clearing.

"As I was saying." Kaelean turned back, looking down to Eavha. "Heir, I need you to trust me right now. This needs to happen."

"You promised to be different," Eavha cried, grabbing Aisling's wrist and pulling it down. "You promised us that if we helped you ascend that you wouldn't be like her."

This was not the time or place for such a private discussion, and yet neither seemed concerned. None of the crowd were bothered.

"The princess is not Wyldeden, and she does not deserve—"

"You don't know her!"

"I know what she did to Cinn!"

"And I don't?!" Eavha screeched back, her eyes red and watering again. "He's my friend too!"

That name made her stomach turn worse than any fear she had about losing a tattoo.

"Eavha," Aisling dared to speak. "Let her do this. I want her to."

"You're a fool!" Davina spat.

"Step aside, or I will have you moved aside." Kaelean's voice lowered dangerously.

Eavha raised her chin and did not move.

When a guardian came, Aisling did nothing to help her. In fact, when Eavha grabbed her arm, she shrugged her off. This needed to happen.

Another witch brought Kaelean an iron poker from one of the braziers burning at the edge of the platform. Aisling raised her palm once more. The branding was entirely unnecessary; the smallest cut through the ink would be enough to break the spell, but she understood the importance of proving one's power in a game like this.

It wasn't the threat of pain that had her breath hitching, it was the pleading that continued from Eavha. From Davina, spiraling into desperate cries for Aisling to *get up and fight this*.

"Announce before all these witnesses that you consent to this branding," Kaelean said, holding the smoldering iron over her.

"I," she began, her voice wavering, "Aisling Aurnia of the Sparrow Coven, hereby consent before all these witnesses to the branding of my palm, destroying The Key Mark for Those Unbound forever. I will afterward vow to tell only the truth to any witch of Wyldeden who asks it of me."

The heat of the branding iron had her sweating as it hovered an inch from her skin. Despite it, she held still, preparing herself.

"I'm impressed, princess," Kaelean said, somehow turning her title into an insult with only her tone. "You truly would let me brand you."

"Of course," Aisling said, frowning. When she looked up, there was the barest scrap of respect on the witch's face. The branding iron had been lowered.

Eavha had stopped begging, her breaths ragged in the otherwise silent crowd.

Aisling was not stupid enough to believe that the high priestess had forgiven her for what she had done to the kinner. But maybe, just maybe, there was enough respect to allow trust to grow.

Heavy footsteps stomped up onto the platform, and Aisling turned in time to see a human man striding toward her, red faced and shaking.

"William," Kaelean said, holding out a hand.

Whether it was because she did not really believe the man would make a move against her, or because a part of her wanted it to happen, Kaelean did not stop the man from snatching the branding iron out of her hand and ramming it into Aisling's face with enough force to crack her cheekbone.

She couldn't even hear her own screaming over the pain that ravaged her face.

Then the poker was gone, William's booming voice cursing viciously. Aisling opened her eyes, not remembering falling onto the platform, just in time to see something utterly impossible.

Nora.

Nora, unblemished and young, with long black hair and a swollen belly, wielding a dagger.

"You deserve so much worse," she said, then sunk to her knees and drove the dagger into Aisling's gut.

Over and over and over.

CHAPTER THIRTY-SIX

KAELEAN

PINCHING THE BRIDGE OF HER NOSE, KAELEAN LEANED AGAINST THE wall of the healer's clinic and waited for Eavha to finish doing her best to heal the princess's wounds. She was just about fed up with the humans. This outburst had her on the verge of throwing the lot of them out on their asses. Only the promise of Cinn's wrath stopped her. That, and the now clearly swelling belly of Siobhan.

Siobhan, who had made herself scarce since being escorted from the elder circle. As had the other humans.

She could have stopped them. She didn't think about why she hadn't.

Eavha stood from Aisling's bedside and wobbled, wiping a stream of blood from her nose. Kaelean reached out to catch her, but Eavha turned and hissed, baring her teeth.

Blinking, Kaelean took in the defensive posture, the feral expression that she had never once seen on Eavha's face.

"I had no intention of actually hurting her," Kaelean promised. "It was a test."

"I don't believe you. I don't believe a word that comes out of your mouth. You stood there and let them try to kill her!"

"That was Cinn's family."

A fraction of the rage in Eavha's face died. She turned away and sat down again on Aisling's bedside, running her fingers over the princess's bare stomach. Her face, cheek red and raw with two lines like a spearhead pointing toward her ear, was still blemished.

"I can't do anymore," Eavha said. "I promised her I wouldn't burn myself out again."

Kaelean passed over a rag for her still-gushing nose, then went to one of the apothecary tables to brew a salve. It wouldn't take the scarring away completely but it would soothe the healing process.

The spiteful part of her wanted to burn the other side of Aisling's face instead, but Eavha was as much hers as Cinn or Eaon, and she would have to be blind to miss the connection between her and Aisling. In a way, the pair reminded Kaelean of herself and Yomra, back when Kaelean had first been thrown from her home.

No matter how many centuries she lived, grief was still a bane, worming into her heart.

She had refused Yomra for so long. Refused to accept that she could not break the curse Nevan had placed on her. Refused to be a part of Yomra's insane plan that would end with her death, so similar to the way Eavha had refused to let Aisling make a sacrifice Kaelean never intended her to actually make.

She could never brand another witch. Never. She had hoped Eavha would know that, would have seen the test for what it was when she had made a spectacle of breaking the spellmark instead of just cutting the princess's palm.

Apparently she still had some ways to go before she could earn even Eavha's trust.

Behind her, a whimper alerted them to Aisling's regaining of conscious. Kaelean turned her head just enough to see Eavha leaning over, placing a palm against her burned cheek once more.

"Don't," Aisling groaned.

"I'm sorry. I'm sorry this happened. I'm sorry I couldn't stop it."

"Don't be."

Kaelean brought the salve over and let Eavha take it, smearing it delicately across the worst of the burns. Then she lifted her chin, crossed her arms, and demanded, "The soldiers that came to the Copeland farm looking for Cinn a few months ago."

"Kaelean!" Eavha hissed.

But Aisling placed a weak hand on Eavha's knee. "It was not me. Do you know what armor they wore?"

"Gold and black."

Aisling sighed and closed her eyes. "Those are my parent's colors. I had to tell my advisors about the . . . about Cinn's existence a few months ago. I thought it strange to not have heard from them about it, especially during my father's visit, but now it makes sense. I should have figured it was them to go after him, but I was . . . overwhelmed."

"If it was really Phineas going after him, I'm surprised the farm is still standing at all," Kaelean muttered to herself.

But King Phineas being on Cinn's tail was a much bigger problem than she wanted to have. Dearmead had been right about their people; they were not ready to live outside the Boab, let alone go to war. Yet it *was* war Kaelean would wage once more against the Sparrows if they were after Cinn.

That her instincts to protect him were already that strong surprised even herself, especially considering he was more inclined to rip her head off at every given opportunity. For some reason, she found it endearing. Which made her want to slap herself.

She took the empty bowl back to the apothecaries' table and began to clean it. Laborers and student healers lingered nearby to do such menial tasks, but she was too restless to stand still.

"While you are here, you are not to approach the humans," she warned.

"While . . . While I am here?"

Kaelean gave the princess a sidelong look. "You wished to explore the libraries, did you not?"

"You're letting her go?" Eavha asked, surprised.

"You meant what you said about renouncing your coven, I could tell. I can smell the hatred when you speak of them. And the enemy of my enemy is my friend. Even if that makes you a friend I would let get stabbed in the gut half a dozen times, and would easily do so again. Do you understand?"

Eavha was bristling, but Aisling nodded in understanding.

"That was Siobhan, wasn't it?"

"It was." Kaelean couldn't help the hand that fluttered to her empty womb as she thought about the human rebel. Yes, stealing a blessing from the Mother had come with a cost, indeed. "And as I said, you will stay away."

"I have no desire to cross ways with her again. None of them."

"Good."

"He . . . Cinn is not here, is he?"

The note of fear in her voice perked Kaelean's ears, even as the instinct to shift, to rip the princess limb from limb at the sound of his name on her lips, almost overwhelmed her.

"No."

Aisling sagged in relief. Kaelean bought her a drink of water and let Eavha feed it to her.

"Good. That is good. I'm sure seeing me again would . . . not be good."

"No," Kaelean agreed, unable to keep the chill from her voice. "In fact, if you want an alliance with this clan, I suggest you stay as far from Cinn as possible."

"Believe me, if I never see him again, I will be glad of it."

Eavha looked to Kaelean, a heavy weight behind her eyes. "Can we talk about what we need from the library?"

"Soon. I have one more thing to ask the princess."

A meaningless title. Unearned and unlikely to result in anything considering who else contended for the Sparrow Throne upon the king and queen's passing. Phineas and Tallula would be fools not to appoint their son as heir given the shared proclivity for senseless cruelty.

"Anything."

"Why do you believe Chaos exists? Why do you believe he is returning?"

Aisling glanced across the room to nothing Kaelean could see. "Because Davina told me he was."

Kaelean frowned, looking to Eavha, who's demeanor became crestfallen.

"Davina is a Morvish witch who was . . . very close to Aisling. She foresaw Chaos's return and worked with her to prepare for it until she passed. It is Aisling's Lover-blessing to see through the veil between our realm and the Lover's, to those who linger, either denied or denying Death's embrace, and openly communicate with them."

Kaelean raised her brow.

The princess's gaze was shrouded in a milky film as she said, "You are as haunted as I am."

Kaelean stiffened. "What?"

"Yomra stands with you."

The hairs on her arms rose as she turned to Eavha. "Did you tell—"

But Eavha's eyes had gone wide as a doe, shaking her head at Kaelean's unfinished question.

Numb, a single question managed to pass Kaelean's frozen lips. "Was she denied?"

"No," Aisling said, a solemn smile curving her lips. "She stayed behind to see you thrive. To see you become all she knew you could be. To see you through to the end."

Kaelean closed her eyes as she felt them burning. She would not cry. She had not cried in a century and she would not do so now.

"And you trust Davina?"

The silence lingered too long, so Kaelean opened her eyes. Aisling was staring at the corner again, listening to someone no one else could not hear. Eavha managed a gentle smile and reached for Kaelean's hand. Squeezed tightly.

"I have and always will put my undying faith in you," Aisling finally said, though the words were not directed at anyone living in the room. "Even when you're mad at me, even when I let you down, I will believe in you."

Then Aisling turned to Kaelean and simply said, "Yes."

Kaelean had put her faith in Yomra, and for her efforts had met three witches and a kinner who made her want to start another coven. Three witches and a kinner she would tear the world apart for if they asked. Three witches and a kinner, she knew, who would change the world.

She saw that faith reflected in Aisling's eyes, and it was enough.

"Then we can talk about what you need from the library."

Aisling looked to Eavha, who took a deep breath.

"The oldest books we have about Sanni and the marks. Please."

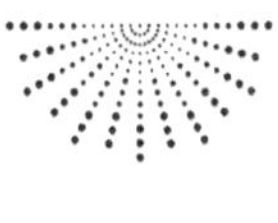

CHAPTER THIRTY-SEVEN

AISLING

She knew she could have been worse off, but damn it, Aisling was in pain. She didn't want to tell Eavha because she knew she had pushed herself just to keep her alive. To keep her tattoos from scarring. But her body ached and her face throbbed as she followed Eavha and Kaelean down a long stairwell underground. Running her tongue across her teeth, she could feel that two of them had broken from the impact of that branding iron hitting her face. Knew her cheek would be permanently marred. Knew she deserved it.

"You deserve so much worse."

She did, and it was coming. Davina had warned her it was coming.

The ghost of her lover trailed her once more, closer than she had been in a long while. Whatever rift had come between them lately seemed to have mended, Davina's concern etched clearly on her face.

Having a second ghost around was an unexpected surprise.

Yomra, so old she actually looked it, smiled as she clung to Kaelean's side.

The Sanctuary's library was much like the libraries Dusarn's high necromancer kept. The smell of old books was distinctive and, just as the books in Dusarn did, Aisling could see a number of tomes sprouting mold and fungus from the spines. She hadn't expected the scale of the collection to be the same, but Wyldeden had an enormity of books shelved in what seemed like endless rows.

"The oldest books are this way," Kaelean said, taking a candle and lighting it before striding down a long passageway. Eavha and Aisling both took one of their own. The lamps became fewer and dimmer the farther they went until only the candlelight illuminated the way.

Perhaps her searching in Dusarn had been fruitless but this seemed promising. Bound in stone and stripped bark, a number of books sung with an ancient magic Aisling was not familiar with.

"Fae magic," Yomra said, as if having read her mind. "Some of these books haven't seen daylight since the First War, two and a half thousand years ago."

"How is that possible if Wyldeden was only made during the Third?" Aisling asked, earning curious glances from Eavha and Kaelean.

Yomra smiled. "Terra loved books, and the fae loved her."

Aisling waited for more, but that was apparently all the information she was going to be given. Typical Morvish witch. Davina smiled as if she knew what Aisling was thinking, too, though that was less likely a Morvish thing and more of a lover thing.

"It is nice to have company," Davina said softly, earning a warm smile from Yomra.

Finally, they reached the end of the passage that opened into a small room with a single table and one chair, both coated in dust. More candles lay waiting, and Eavha went to light them while Kaelean stalked to the nearest shelf.

"Eaon would die knowing there were so many books he hadn't read down here," Eavha said, looking along the row that disappeared once more into the dark.

Kaelean chuckled, then pulled a book the size of her torso from the shelf. Then a second, and a third.

"These are some of the original writings about Sanni. They're the accounts of fae who lived during the First War. I tried to read them once and only remember something about witnessing Sanni's first miracle. They're jinxed so the person who reads them forgets what they read as soon as they close the book. So I don't remember much more than that."

Aisling raised her eyebrow, but it was Eavha who said what she was thinking.

"Well, that's *super* helpful."

"It won't work on the dead," Davina pointed out.

Aisling repeated it, and the three of them opened the books to read aloud to the ghosts in the room who could not forget.

Only when the first candle burned out did Aisling realize how long they had been down in the dark. Her eyes were heavy and weary from reading by candlelight, but they were yet to find the answers they needed. Though there had been plenty of otherwise interesting information.

"The Spirits fought the war," Eavha summarized, rubbing her bleary eyes as she looked to the others. "Not from their realms, but from ours. They had physical bodies and lived beside the fae. That . . . Is that even possible? Can a Spirit take a physical form?"

"*Did* they take form?" Kaelean countered, sliding her own book across the table and running her finger along a line of prose that Aisling's eyes couldn't focus on. The curling script was difficult to decipher, but she supposed she could be grateful it was in a language she understood at all.

"And though blood and blood were both half of the dryads, it was Terra who presented on their behalf. Sanni did little else but scrawl tirelessly on the flesh-born parchment of her enemies," Eavha read aloud before yawning. "Does that make sense to anyone?"

"Blood and blood, as in, they were related?" Davina asked, and so Aisling repeated.

"Half of the dryads. Perhaps the form they took was that of the Fair Folk. Half human, half fae," Eavha muttered, furrowing her brow. "If Eaon were here he would have figured this out already."

Kaelean's lips pursed as she glanced at Eavha, then quickly away. "Your brother is certainly . . . *talented* at spontaneous deduction. But you're on the right path. I was just wondering if perhaps the Spirits didn't take a form, but were born of this realm first."

Aisling blinked, then shook her head. "An interesting theory for another time, perhaps. Your Highness, if you have other matters that require your attention, we can continue to look without you."

Kaelean tilted her head. "Trying to get rid of me?"

"Not at all. I'm just aware of time passing," Aisling stated, indicating the burned-out candle.

"Your concern for my time is kind, but I think my chaperoning here is the best use of it for now."

"We don't need supervising, Kaelean. I know how to take care of books," Eavha said with a frown, yawning deeply once more.

"I know," Kaelean smiled, messing Eavha's hair that she had unbound from its braid some hours ago.

"The flesh-born parchment." Yomra pointed to the book Kaelean had been reading. "Sanni kept a diary."

Aisling's mouth fell open, earning curious stares. "Yomra . . . Yomra just realized that the line you read refers to Sanni keeping a diary of sorts. Perhaps, if we could find it . . ."

Kaelean turned back to the book, re-reading the line.

"Parchment made of flesh. I don't know if we have any books like that here. But, Eavha, you may be able to scry for it. I have a map of the library." Kaelean was already striding toward the farthest wall where a shelf of rolled parchments waited.

"Worth a try," she said, leaning on the table.

"Here, take the chair. Rest," Aisling said, standing up.

"No, you need it more."

"I've been sitting for hours."

"You should still be in bed."

Kaelean came back and laid a crude map of the library over the table, pinning the curled edges with books. Then she rummaged through her pockets, pulling out odd crystals before stuffing them back until she found a chunk of chalcopyrite. Tying it to the end of a piece of twine wrapped around her wrist, Kaelean handed it to Eavha, who dangled it over the map and closed her eyes.

The last time Eavha had tried to scry nothing had happened, but this time as the swell of magic filled the room the crystal began to swing.

"She's listening now," Eavha said softly. "What was the line?"

"Sanni did little else but scrawl tirelessly on the flesh-born parchment of her enemies," Aisling repeated the line as Davina whispered it to her, the words already hazy with the book still open in front of them.

Eavha's lips moved soundlessly as she focused her magic, then she dropped the crystal. It slid across the page before standing upright on a point where a shelf was marked.

"It worked." Aisling's eyes widened. "It actually worked."

Eavha grinned smugly and flicked her hair over her shoulder.

Kaelean sighed. "Should have figured it would be there. Give me a moment, I'll go fetch it."

With a nod, Aisling watched the high priestess disappear once more into the dark halls. Eavha dropped the grin, swaying on her feet, and this time when Aisling stood to give her the chair, she took it.

"You're not well."

"Just tired," she said. "We should have brought snacks. Water."

Aisling had not even realized she was thirsty until Eavha said it.

"We'll get the diary and go back up. Get some rest, then read it."

Eavha nodded, putting her head down on the table and letting her eyes flutter closed. Within a minute, the lightest kitten-snore purred from her parted mouth. Aisling smiled, looking to where both the ghosts also watched her fondly.

"Thank you for coming back," Aisling whispered to Davina as she waited for Kaelean to return. "I'm not sure why you left, but I'm glad to see you again."

Davina lost the smile, narrowing her eyes. "I told you to practice with the marks. You could have obliterated all of them, but aside from The Key, you never use—"

"I will," Aisling interrupted. They'd had this conversation before. "I've been busy, you know. But I will start training with them. It's time."

"It's past time," Davina grumbled.

"Be wary, young ones," Yomra tutted. "Magic is not muscle. Using it often will not strengthen you. Make you more practiced, more sure, yes, but too much too often will leave you weak."

Aisling nodded. It was what she was afraid of. "I don't want to train too hard and burn myself out before Chaos even comes."

"You won't. I saw you there."

"And your sight has never been wrong?" Yomra chuckled.

Davina scowled. "Actually, it hasn't."

"That only means you didn't live long enough to see Morvia's deceit."

Aisling tuned out the bickering, too tired and sore to follow the complexities of Morvish magic. By the sounds of it, neither of them fully understood it either.

Eventually Kaelean's light came back into view, her candle down to a stub. One look at Eavha had the high priestess placing both the remains of the candle and the small, black leather book down as carefully as possible.

"Perhaps we should come back tomorrow," Kaelean whispered.

"I'm awake," Eavha mumbled, rolling her head to the side. "If it's okay, I'll take it home and have a read after some dinner and a nap. We can return it in the morning."

Kaelean hesitated, narrowing her beady eyes at Aisling. "It does not leave Wyldeden."

"I won't even touch it myself if you don't want me to," Aisling promised, baring her palms.

She understood the suspicion. Sanni was as revered in Dusarn as she was in Wyldeden; her blessings were the reason the Returned exist at all. The reason why any of them could even be Lover-blessed. To bring Sanni's diary to the high necromancer's library would make her parents think twice about appointing Nevan as heir over her.

Which is why Kaelean's decision to directly hand her the book left her frozen in surprise.

"If this goes missing, I will kill you. Destiny or not."

Warily, Aisling took it.

"If you're finished being dramatic, I need food," Eavha said, standing and wobbling on her feet, still clad in Aisling's boots.

Kaelean kept her steady while Aisling began to close the other books. Each one that she returned to the nearest shelf muddled her thoughts until she wasn't even sure why she was in the library at all. What had they spent the last few hours even doing?

She went to put the little black book on the shelf, but Davina stopped her.

"Not that one."

"What is it?" Aisling asked, both Eavha and Kaelean looking just as confused.

"Sanni's diary," Davina reminded her.

Aisling looked at the black book in her hands and raised her eyebrows. Right.

"Wow." Eavha shook her head. "I didn't actually expect to forget."

"Fae magic," Kaelean hissed. "Nasty stuff."

To which Yomra howled with laughter. "Five hundred years and she still holds a grudge."

Aisling held Sanni's diary close to her chest as she followed them back toward the staircase up to the sanctuary. She would have liked to hear the story of whatever fae had pissed off Kaelean, but she doubted she was in a position to ask.

<hr>

Outside, Aisling dragged her feet as she followed Eavha along a winding dirt path all the way down a valley until they reached a lichen encrusted manor at the forest's edge, a trickling stream nearby and tufts of dandelions speckling the unkempt lawn. The setting sun gilded the goat and chicken grazing lazily, along with the dozen vegetable gardens overflowing with perfect produce.

"I have a room at the Sanctuary," Eavha had explained, "but I don't really stay there much. I know I should have given the manor to another family by now, but . . . it's my home."

"You live here alone?" Aisling took in the sprawling manor, tucking the ugly book they had taken from the library tighter under her arm.

"I've employed a few laborers and a gardener to manage things, but yes, I live alone."

Eavha opened a side door into a small kitchen, a little table and living space attached. Aisling put the diary down and looked around at what was essentially a fancy farmhouse.

"It's cute."

Eavha smiled, but it was tired and sad. "This was my family's suite. You can sleep in my room. I'll stay in Eaon's. He'll freak out if he finds your scent in there when he gets back. If he comes back."

"Your brother is in danger?" Aisling raised her eyebrows.

"No. Well, he shouldn't be. But he has a wild heart and never liked being here, so he might not want to come back." Eavha shrugged, but there was a melancholy in the way her hands fell limp at her sides. "Dinner? Laela left some soup I can reheat."

"Thank you," Aisling said, sitting at the little table and rolling back her shoulders as Eavha lit the stove. "So, your brother. He is Returned?"

"That's right. Three times now, I suppose, though the second and third passings don't seem to have had much effect on him. Have you ever . . . I mean, do people do that where you're from? Pass more than once?"

"No. It is not something anyone would want to do more than once. But I noticed that Kaelean had an odd expression when she mentioned your brother's cleverness. Her initial communications suggested he was the one who figured out that Aadya was behind your family's curse, right?"

"Yes, that's right. We didn't believe him at first, which was dumb. He was in a frenzy and hallucinating at the time, but he's good at that kind of thing."

"What kind of thing?"

"You know, puzzles. Putting things together. Noticing connections other people don't. He reads a lot, so he knows a lot."

"So he just . . . figured it out. All of a sudden." Aisling frowned. It was awfully convenient.

"That's Eaon for you."

"And you say he is unblessed?"

"Before? Basically. I think he overcompensated by studying himself stupid. Why do you want to know so much about my brother anyway?"

"Well, you know about mine. I thought I should know about yours."

It was true, but he was also the only other living Nemuse. Aadya hadn't specified which Nemuse could bring down Chaos.

"I wouldn't say I know anything about yours," Eavha said as she turned the stove back off, ladling the contents into two clay bowls. "Except that he's horrible."

Aisling snorted. "That's all there is to know."

She was far too exhausted to read anymore, but she flipped the book open anyway. The pages were thick and leather-like, the colors of each varying, a different witchmark scratched one very leaf. Some she knew, some she didn't.

"I didn't understand a word he was saying at the time," Eavha continued, "but later, Eaon translated and . . . Nevan said he taught you how to torture people."

Aisling splayed her fingers across a page, feeling the familiar sensation of cold, dead skin. She did not want to discuss Nevan, but she had asked about Eaon first. It was only fair.

"In a sense."

"Did he hurt you?"

She asked so tenderly, but Aisling only scoffed. "By the Lover, no. He wouldn't dare do anything so brash lest mother and father deem him unworthy of crowning. His attempts to kill me have always been sneaky, dirty little tricks he thinks I am too stupid and weak to counter. Which is to my advantage. It's easier to pull the rug on someone who doesn't think you capable."

Her attempt to derail the conversation didn't work.

"So he instructed you?" Eavha was not letting this go.

"Not so much."

She turned the page and froze.

There it was. The mark that haunted her.

As Eavha brought the two bowls of vegetable soup over, her eyebrows raised at the image drawn in the center of a dark brown page.

"The Kinner mark," she said, collapsing into her seat.

"The Kinner mark," Aisling agreed, eyes brimming with hot tears. "With a list of ingredients and a methodology."

She should feel ecstatic, but she just felt sick.

Eavha reached across the table to take her hand. "You've gone pale."

Aisling retracted her hand and folded them in her lap, looking away from the soup and the book. Away from the simplicity of it.

"Aisling."

"I don't mean to be rude, but I must retire for the night."

As she stood, Eavha grabbed her hand once more, refusing to let Aisling pull away again.

"You will not find any wine in this house, so you might as well try talking to me instead."

Aisling bristled, but she didn't have the energy to maintain it. Looking at the book once more, she sucked in a shaky breath and closed her eyes against the red clouding her vision.

"You don't know what I did trying to learn this information. And it was right here in a book this entire time. Everything . . . What I did . . . It was for nothing."

"You mean Cinn."

"Yes." Again, Aisling pulled her hand away. "If you knew where these hands have been, what has stained them, you would not touch them so willingly."

Eavha said nothing, but Aisling could not bring herself to look at her. Instead, she took in the quaint room, the candles burning on the windowsill, and shook her head.

"Your family taught you how to heal. How to take away pain. Mine taught me how to cause it. In my home, we would not be sitting quietly at a dinner table over soup. Nobody would be asking me why I had gone pale. I hated them, and yet I turned out just as they wanted me to be. Cruel, bloodthirsty, and ugly in all the important ways. You were right to detest me when you arrived in Hyrsch. Your clan is right to distrust me. Those humans are right to hate me. And . . ." She still choked on his name. "And Cinn . . . I can never make it right."

Eavha stood, placed her hand on her shoulders, and guided her back to her seat. Made her sit down. Put the spoon in her hand. She stood there silently until Aisling had taken a bite, not tasting it.

"No, you can't," Eavha said, sitting down again. "Sometimes there is nothing you can do but accept that you will always be the villain in someone else's story."

Aisling sighed, nodding her head. But Eavha wasn't done.

"But their story does not define you. There is so much good in you, Aisling. I can see it, even if you can't. Nobody can deny the bad is there, but we are all capable of being the villain. We have all *been* the villain."

"If you're going to try and tell me that you stepped on a butterfly once, and that makes you comparable to me—"

"No," Eavha said, chuckling sadly. "Though that you think that's the worst I could do is rather flattering."

"I thought it was a bit of a stretch, to be honest." Aisling forced herself to smile, wanting this conversation to be over.

To Aisling's surprise, Eavha didn't return the smile. She ducked her head and tucked her hair, bringing another spoonful of soup to her mouth.

"My point is, what's done is done. Cinn will find a way to live his life, and you must find a way to live yours."

She made it sound so easy. And Aisling supposed when one was as removed from the situation as Eavha was, it was easy to see such a possibility.

Aisling pulled the book toward her again. All she could do was focus on what had to be done now. "Most of these are common enough. Only the unicorn blood will be a pain to get a hold of."

With a sigh, Eavha let the conversation drop. "We are not killing a unicorn."

"No," Aisling agreed. "Finding one at all would take years, but I know where we can get some without resorting to such things."

"You do?" Eavha raised her brows.

"Yes, I do."

PART IV

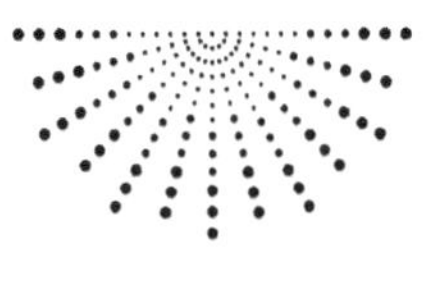

TRIAL BY FIRE

CHAPTER THIRTY-EIGHT

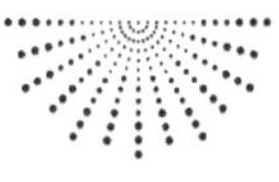

EAON

Cinn had been gone for seven days.

It was the first thought Eaon had upon waking before leaning across the mattress to pick up the half-finished blunt he'd left beside the empty bottle of wine from the night before. Holding it between his lips, he stumbled out of his room toward the kitchen where one of Killian's Igni-blessed cousins was kind enough to light it for him.

"Hitting it a bit early, aren't we?" They smirked as Eaon found a cushion to settle into, gesturing rudely.

He hadn't intended to start smoking again. Hadn't intended to drink much, either. Too many times had he fallen into a spiral here in the mountains, and with his new magic eager to strike as soon as his guard was down, it was too risky.

But Cinn was gone, and Eaon couldn't sleep. His tonics weren't working and all he wanted was to fuck his way to oblivion, but he couldn't do that either.

It wasn't unusual for people to smoke in the mountains, and Eaon had never been shy to partake before. His moodiness was more likely to cause a surge than his smoking was anyway. Or so he told himself.

Killian came out of his room, took one look at Eaon and rolled his eyes.

"Come on, go put a shirt on and come with me."

"Where are we going?"

The others had been doing their best to keep Eaon busy, dragging him to every party they could sniff out, taking him rock climbing and slope skiing and whatever other insane activity Tomaii could come up with.

"The pools."

Eaon had been there before.

"Maybe later."

"No. We're not sulking this morning. Get up before I get Ma's rolling pin."

"You're awful," Eaon said around the blunt, blowing out a plume of smoke. "Can we get more papaver on the way?"

"Absolutely." Killian grinned, carefully pinching the papaver out of Eaon's mouth and taking a drag before passing it back.

Dressed in clothes that covered as much skin as possible, the two of them met up with Tomaii and Reigan in the warren before stopping at a herbologist stall in the markets, where they ran into Selina and Brach.

"Oh, I've never been swimming," Selina said, clinging to Brach's arm and looking up pleadingly.

"I have a shift in two hours," he reminded her.

"So don't come," muttered Eaon, then finished more loudly, "Doesn't mean Selina can't join us."

Brach narrowed his eyes, but Tomaii had taken Selina's other arm and begun skipping toward the tunnels that would lead toward the pools.

The decision was made.

Near the bottom of the gorge was an enormous cavern where the only fresh water in the entire mountain could be found. It bubbled up from cracks at the bottom of large craters, filling until it spilled over the edge and cascaded down a network of slopes and shallower pools. Witches gathered at the base to cleanse sediment from the water, then take barrels full back up the mountain for drinking. It was backbreaking work, the kind Lorelei would have made laborers do if she ruled the mountains the way she had ruled Wyldeden, but that wasn't the way things were done here.

The high priest of the Long Gorge let witches sort out for themselves how water would be collected, and sure enough a roster had been made. Everyone took a turn, for the good of all.

But it wasn't what Tomaii, Killian and Reigan had dragged him to the hot pools to do. Since the water went through cleansing anyway, it was common for those who didn't mind the climb to make their way to the highest levels of the cavern and swim in the spring water.

As Eaon reached the top, steam cloying the air, he could tell they were alone. Tomaii spread his arms wide, threw back his head and crowed into the cavern, the echo of it resounding off the far away walls. Killian was already naked, laughing as he chased Reigan to the edge of the nearest pool and tackled her into the water. Selina laughed, then screamed as Brach picked her up and ran for the pool as well.

"Wait! I can't swim!" she screamed.

"I got you, babe," he said just before leaping into the water.

Wet clothes came flying out, landing on the rock with a heavy *slap*. Tomaii was undressing as well, leaving his clothes in a pile on top of a rocky outcropping.

Eaon leaned against the cavern wall and tucked his hands under his arms. His chest was hollowing quickly as he listened to the laughter and splashing. He had come here to wind down, but for some reason it had slipped his mind that he would have to undress.

Days upon days had been spent lounging in these pools when he was younger. Hours upon hours, hiding away with Tomaii. His gaze flicked over to the male, who had only filled out further in the years between visits, the smooth lines of his shoulders, the hard muscle underneath silky olive skin rippling as he moved.

Tomaii caught him looking and grinned devilishly.

"You're not getting shy on me are you?" he asked.

"I don't think it's a good idea for me to have too much skin exposed," Eaon reminded him, holding up his gloved hands before ducking his head.

"Hey!" Tomaii shouted over the echoing shenanigans going on in the water. "Everybody knows not to touch Eaon, yeah?"

A series of "obviously," "duh," and "I'm not dying today" were the answers.

"See."

"Still."

"I also went and picked up these today, if it helps." Tomaii grabbed his satchel and pulled out two short strips of leather, buckles on the ends. Along the cuffs were rows of carefully carved spellmarks—the ones Eaon had spoken to the tanner about. "Should we find out if they work?"

"You still won't be able to touch me," Eaon warned, but excitement was filling the emptiness in his chest again. At least if these worked, he wouldn't have to spend so much time worrying about surging.

"I know," Tomaii said, hanging one over his shoulder while stretching the other between two hands.

Trembling, Eaon bit his lip as he shrugged off the gloves and placed one wrist over the leather. Very carefully, Tomaii wrapped the cuff around Eaon's tanned skin and secured the buckle on top. Then the other went on and Eaon could feel the spellmarks clamping down over his magic. It railed against the restraints, but there was nowhere for it to go. His bones ached, vision spotting as he waited for it to finish its tantrum.

"You alright," Tomaii asked, concern lacing his voice.

"Yeah," Eaon breathed, leaning back against the wall to keep himself steady. "Just getting used to them."

Slowly, his magic settled. He would have to be very careful when he took the cuffs off that his magic didn't lash out, but when Eaon opened his eyes, he was smiling.

Tomaii grinned. "That's the happiest you've looked this entire visit."

Eaon unbuttoned his shirt and tossed it aside, only briefly self-conscious of the scars peppering his chest and back. Then his pants went, too. Tomaii's pupils widened until the dark brown of the iris was almost swallowed, and a rush went through Eaon at the sight of it.

"Incoming!" Tomaii shouted over his shoulder, racing away and leaping into the water, arms flailing wildly. The *boom* of the water as he landed filled the cavern.

"You imbecile!" Reigan shouted, but quickly dissolved into laughter as Killian picked her up and tossed her into deeper water. Across the pool, Selina and Brach were already making out again.

Eaon eased in carefully, flexing his hands before taking a deep breath and dipping beneath the surface. The water was cloudy, but he could still see the silhouettes of the others as he pushed out deeper. The temperature made him weightless as he dived over the edge of the shallows, spinning slowly.

He had forgotten how much he loved to swim. How often he and Dearmead spent their free time floating down the rivers, climbing beneath waterfalls, or just playing in the small lakes back in Wyldeden. The way Dearmead's long hair would turn into a deadly weapon once wet as he flicked it around. The way rivulets of water would curve around the shape of his body.

Breaching the surface, Eaon took a deep breath and tried to shake the images from his mind. Tomaii surfaced nearby and spat a stream of water, hitting him in the eye. Eaon hissed and splashed back.

Grinning wickedly, Tomaii sunk below the surface again and took a powerful stroke toward him.

Too close.

Paddling backward, Eaon scolded him when Tomaii peeked his head above the surface. "Cut it out."

Tomaii only grinned, continuing to chase after Eaon until his back hit the rocky edge of the cavern.

"Tomaii, cut it out!" Eaon shouted, panicking as he kicked his way closer still. So close that if Eaon moved, they would be touching. Tomaii placed a hand on either side of Eaon's body and rose out of the water, grinning maniacally.

"Back off."

"Chicken."

One wrong kick, one inch in the wrong direction, and Tomaii would be dead. Eaon could barely breathe as Tomaii brought his face within kissing distance.

"You need to relax."

"You will literally die, Tomaii."

"I'm not touching you."

Eaon narrowed his eyes. "This isn't a game."

Dropping the smile, Tomaii tilted his head. Drifted a fraction closer. Eaon's heart squeezed painfully, half out of sheer terror and half out of a sudden rabid longing. The air between them warmed, the breath they shared igniting something that had laid dormant in Eaon for months. His head went silent, and he remembered why he had fallen for Tomaii all those years ago. And again when he'd returned. And again the time after that.

The knot of wanting that left his hands shaking was mirrored in the warm eyes staring back. Longing, desire, and kindness. Tomaii had always made Eaon feel wanted in all the right ways. Had always made the world disappear around them, until there was only pleasure and contentment and joy left.

"Hey, skillet head! The fuck are you doing?" Reigan yelled over at them.

Eaon flinched, and Tomaii moved just enough to avoid contact, as if they were once again dancing, hearts and bodies synchronized in a way that almost seemed like magic.

"Extreme game of keep-away!" Tomaii called back with a grin. Pushing away from the wall, his eyes glinted as if he knew exactly what he'd been doing.

Eaon snarled, splashing water at him again. "You're a fucking prick."

Tomaii just laughed. Winked. "Just admit it felt good."

"What? Having your egg breath in my face?" Eaon spat back, but his heart was still galloping wildly, his skin itching to be touched.

And damn it, it did feel good.

CHAPTER THIRTY-NINE

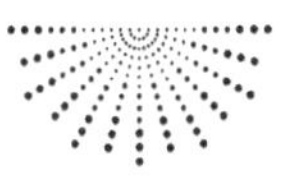

EAON

He still couldn't sleep. In fact, sleeping had become even more elusive than before as Eaon lay awake at night, trying not to think about how close Tomaii had been to him in the hot pools. The way Eaon's entire body had come alive in a way it hadn't done so in months. But no matter how many times he pleasured himself, the need for more would not leave.

And when thoughts of Tomaii gave way to thoughts of Dearmead . . . Eaon started reading instead. Tried to fill his time with things that could distract him from the yearning.

Killian's family had taken it upon themselves to make sure Eaon ate because more often than not he was too busy reading from the large mountain library of adventure stories and folklore to remember that his body required nutrients. They had quickly learned not to ask him what he was reading though, as once Eaon started talking it was almost impossible to make him stop.

But on the days he couldn't sit still any longer, he would get up at the crack of dawn and follow Killian on his scouting duties, walking laps of the gorge with him. Or, when Killian had to go beyond the gorge, he would help Reigan at her stall at the market. When he got too agitated sitting in the hot sun, he wandered the markets to find the tanner who had made his cuffs.

Bevv was happy to talk to Eaon about defecting from the Sparrow Coven, though she did so in hushed whispers, halting conversation altogether when a witch came to inspect her wares. If the buyer was taking too long, Eaon often wandered away again, thus the tanner's story was taking a while to learn. The gist of it was simple enough though; her family was not high status, and when her daughter had undergone the Passing rite to become Returned, the necromancer in charge of reviving her had failed. Hungover, was the excuse. And when Bevv had demanded the necromancer be excommunicated, the king and queen had refused. Why, Eaon was yet to learn.

Eleven days since Cinn had left, and he was considering going for the next installment of Bevv's story, tired of baking under the cloudless sky while Reigan worked. Except Killian came by. The salamanders used for Reigan's salves had grown too large for their cages, so Killian offered to scout new ones. She wanted to go with him, and judging by the way Killian smiled, shifting his weight, Eaon knew it was an activity he should let them do alone.

So he went to Bevv's stall again, but she was swamped with customers. Sighing, he left the markets altogether and made his way to the library to find something new to waste his time on.

Except Tomaii was there, looking for him.

"Ma said I was slowing her down at work," he explained, padding after Eaon as he scoured the shelves for something he hadn't read yet.

A lot of the books were the same as those in Wyldeden, but there were local authors who'd tried their hand at writing fiction shoved at the back of the lowest shelves, so that was where he hunted.

"So I'm free for the rest of the day," Tomaii continued, oblivious to Eaon's distraction. "What do you want to do?"

"I'm tired," he tried.

"Let's get some herbs and go smoke then. Normally puts you out."

"I can't risk smoking with this magic." An absolute lie. He had been smoking plenty and Tomaii knew it.

"Come on," he whined. "You've got the cuffs now and I promise not to play keep-away again."

Eaon grimaced. Knowing that meant he was caving in, Tomaii

started bouncing from foot to foot. "I'll find Reigan. She's hidden the stash from me."

"She and Killian are about to go salamander hunting. You won't catch her."

Instead of looking disappointed, a wildfire broke out behind Tomaii's eyes.

"I haven't been salamander hunting in ages! Let's go!"

"I don't think they want company," Eaon said pointedly.

"Wrong. Who wouldn't want my company?" Tomaii grinned, then raced back toward the markets to find them.

With a sigh, Eaon checked the harness straps keeping his staff on his back and checked his satchel. The flask of whiskey he'd taken from Killian's room was still there, so he plucked a new book from the back of the shelves and followed Tomaii.

⁎

While Reigan and Tomaii hunted for six-legged salamanders, Killian and Eaon lounged on the volcanic rock with the flask, sipping at the bitter alcohol under the blazing sun. This close to the volcano's lip, the heat and smell of sulfur was so intense Eaon was sure the hair on his arms was singeing, but he didn't care. He didn't care that he was sweating through his last clean linen shirt, the long sleeves rolled back past his elbows, gloves abandoned in his satchel. Didn't care that it was barely midday and he was already drunk.

"Would you two get your lazy asses up and help, please?" Reigan shouted at them when she failed to grab a fleeing salamander.

"No," both Eaon and Killian called back at the same time, breaking into hysterics.

"Stake and burn you both, then," she hissed, stomping off.

"Yeesh. Someone needs to chill," Killian muttered, making Eaon laugh again.

"She reminds me of Eavha when she gets all snippy like that," he said, dampening his chuckles so he could take another drink.

"I've been meaning to ask, how is your sister?"

"Living her best life, of course. Heir to Wyldeden, just like she always wanted."

"I bet becoming a rogue and a necromancer was not on the agenda though."

"No," Eaon sighed, rubbing a thumb along the scars on his palms. "Also, they prefer to be called unbound witches."

Killian blinked at him, then nodded slowly. "Dually noted. What about your other friend? The guardian one."

Dearmead.

The longing for his friend to be here on the rocks with him, drinking and laughing, or chasing lizards, was so sudden and intense that Eaon choked. Sitting up, he coughed out the spit that had gone down wrong and took a long drink from his flask.

"That well, huh?" Killian gave Eaon a sad smile. "Well, Tomaii seems like he wants to make you forget about him again."

Eaon had noticed. "Lover spare me."

Killian laughed loudly. "Not keen?"

"Did he ask you to ask me that?"

"Maybe."

"Coward."

"Can you blame him? The last time you were here and he propositioned you, you called him a heathen."

Eaon grimaced. "I was . . . not doing well. But it's a moot point. I'll be alone until the Lover gives me peace now."

And it wasn't regret that he couldn't be with Tomaii again that hurt his heart. It wasn't Cinn's rejection. It was long black hair twisted in his fists and scar-specked skin, dark like the secret cave they'd found behind a waterfall back at home. Strong but gentle hands that knew exactly how to make Eaon forget about how shit the world was, because in those moments there was only love.

"Tomaii is not afraid of you," Killian said gently.

And that hurt for a whole different reason.

"Dearmead is," Eaon said, swallowing the lump in his throat. "And with good reason. I'm not who I was anymore. I've murdered a lot of people, Kil. Some by accident, but not all. Tomaii's an idiot for even considering the logistics of how it might be possible to get together again."

Killian was quiet for a long time, but eventually sat up, turning his face up to the sun.

"We've all done stuff we've had to beg mercy from the Spirits for. Nobody here thinks any less of you for it."

"I do." The people in Wyldeden did.

"Last time you were here, you thought you were unworthy because you had no power. Now you think you're unworthy because you do. I told you before and I'll tell you again, Eaon: you need to stop focusing on that one thing. A witch is so much more than how blessed they are."

"Magic doesn't make a witch. It's your heart, your faith in the Spirits, and as long as you have them you will never need magic a day in your life."

Kailevi's words, so similar to Killian's that a dizzying sense of déjà vu came over him.

"Yeah," Eaon sighed, kicking a loose stone. "I guess—"

Tomaii's guttural scream sapped the alcohol right out of him. Eaon grabbed his staff and leaped from the rock, Killian a step ahead.

"Killian!" Reigan screeched from somewhere down a dip in the mountain face.

Skidding down the slope, running around the bend, both Killian and Eaon came to a sudden stop as they took in the beast slithering out from beneath a narrow outcrop.

Four-feet long, Eaon had told Cinn that grown six-legged salamanders grew to. The one glaring at Reigan and Tomaii had to be at least twelve, its claws as thick as Eaon's wrist. Tomaii was bleeding, still screaming through gritted teeth from the venom now coursing through his veins.

Killian had his knives out, but Eaon dived deep into his magic. Only to be hit with a sickening pain shooting up his neck into his skull.

The cuffs.

Dropping to his knees, Eaon let go of the staff and began tugging at the straps with his teeth. Killian ran forward, tossing one of his knives to Reigan as the two of them tried to protect Tomaii from further injury.

One of the buckles came loose and Eaon tore it off, panting from the pain. The cold rallying beneath his skin was so at odds with the heat from the sun that nausea twisted his gut, but he got the second cuff loose and grabbed a hold of his staff again.

His magic was furious, swelling up and tunneling down the staff before Eaon could even take a deep enough breath to rein it in.

"Move!" he screamed at them just as a blast of power exploded in their direction.

Killian was well trained enough to obey the command without thinking, dropping to the ground and pulling Reigan with him. His warning had alerted the salamander to his presence, and it slipped its body around just in time to miss the force that turned every scrap of foliage in the vicinity to dust.

Gritting his teeth, Eaon clamped down on his magic, hating how close he'd come to hurting the others, but there wasn't time to wallow. The salamander had realized he was the biggest threat.

Salamanders were not predators, they were not meant to be dangerous, but nothing about this one was normal. With the speed of a striking adder, it shot across the ground toward him.

Bracing himself, Eaon reached in for his magic again.

Behave. Just the salamander.

It listened, but it ripped every shred of energy from him as it tunneled through the staff again and speared through the deadly creature. It flinched as if taking a physical hit, scales blackening and peeling off as the rot took hold. Ten seconds, and the lizard had fallen apart into a stinking pile of organs and rotting bone.

Eaon's body sagged and he didn't have the strength to catch himself before falling face first onto the rock. The bitter taste of blood filled his mouth before he blacked out.

Only for a second.

He woke up to Tomaii's suppressed screaming. Turning his head, blinking back the red in his eyes, Eaon saw Reigan wrapping Killian's torn shirt around the wound in Tomaii's arm.

"He's going into toxic shock." Reigan's trembling voice echoed too loudly in Eaon's head. "I've given him all the antivenom I had on me but I wasn't prepared for that monster!"

"It'll take hours to get back to the clan." Killian was panicking, even as he tried to lift Tomaii off the ground.

Eaon opened his mouth, trying to speak, but only ended up spitting blood. Not for the first time, he was glad he had a healer for a sister. Glad he had helped her study for her exams.

"The gum," he choked out, pushing himself up with one arm and trying to roll over. His ribs hurt and he lost the breath to shout again.

But Reigan had heard him. Or at least heard him try to speak. As she ran toward him, Eaon forced his body to take in air.

"Gums," he managed.

"Gums? What gums?"

"Cut out . . . shove in . . ." he wheezed.

It was enough. Racing back to the steaming heap of the salamander, Reigan took one of Killian's knives and scraped what gum was left attached to the rotting teeth.

"Is your magic still on this?" she asked, even as she grabbed a handful of it. "Is it going to hurt him?"

"No," Eaon managed, then closed his eyes against the spinning.

He heard it when Reigan shoved the salamander gum inside Tomaii's wound. He wouldn't be surprised if the clan heard it all the way down the bottom of the volcano. But it would keep Tomaii alive long enough to get back where hopefully someone had some antivenom.

"Don't . . . wait for me," Eaon wheezed. "Go. I'll . . ."

He managed to roll himself over fully, wincing through the ache in his chest.

"I'll stay with him," Reigan said as she crouched beside Eaon. Without a word, Killian ran off down the mountain with Tomaii, who looked close to passing out.

As close as she was, the scent of blood and sweat and fear wafting off Reigan brought his magic crawling back up his spine.

More. More, more, more.

"Go," Eaon wheezed, clenching his eyes closed. The soul of the salamander had already fizzled out, leaving Eaon's body aching with need for *more*. Addled with whiskey and adrenaline and exhaustion, a dark laugh began to bubble in his chest. "You really need to go."

"Hold out your arm," Reigan told him.

She and Tomaii were both blessed by Ignatius. He wondered what that would taste like as their souls passed through him. The human souls he'd eaten were like pearls of bliss, of energy and light and all things pure, bursting inside him, washing everything else away. The beasts, the harpy and the salamander, were a little bitter in comparison. Regular animals barely felt like anything, but a witch? A creature of magic, blessed by the Spirits themselves? He hadn't been conscious for Apaete. He was conscious now.

"Eaon," the mountain witch snapped at him. "Hold. Out. Your. Arm."

The wispy clouds above were spinning, and he felt himself literally starting to drool as he looked at her. At the warm aura emanating from her.

"Eaon Nemuse, don't you dare look at me like that."

She had taken his staff, wielding it like a weapon. In her other hand dangled one of the leather cuffs that would bind him. His magic boiled at the sight of it.

"It's me," she continued, the hostility wavering. "Reigan. Your friend."

Friend.

His friend.

The word was a bucket of cold water dumped over his head. Sucking in a sharp breath, Eaon closed his eyes and clamped down his magic. It thrashed inside him, twisting his bones in a chilling grip until his back arched up off the ground. The sweat on his body had frozen over and he began to tremble, head splitting from the pain of his clenched jaw. Shaking from the effort of not reaching for her, Eaon raised his arm, fist also clenched tight enough his nails were drawing blood.

The first cuff went back on like a boulder on the chest.

The second felt like a noose around his neck.

Unable to surge, Eaon let go of his grip on the power inside him.

With nowhere to go, nothing else to do, it ripped him apart.

By the time he roused back into consciousness, the sun was low on the horizon. He wasn't sure how long ago he'd passed out, unable to bear the fury of the magic inside him any longer. It was getting worse. This magic was getting stronger. Either that, or Eaon was getting weaker.

It was dormant now, curled up in a seething ball at the base of his spine, but Eaon's body had been left ravaged by it. Every bone felt bruised, every muscle strained. He tasted blood in his mouth, fingers stinging from the tiny cuts the gravel beneath him had made as he'd clawed at it.

Beside him, knees pulled up under her chin, Reigan sat staring at the threadbare clouds shifting into a sweet lilac. The last rays of the sun turned her brassy hair into a blushed peach tone, gilding her skin in golds.

Beside her, Selina sat holding her hand. Brach stood nearby, watching the landscape around them, wary of more beasts.

"What happened?" Eaon croaked.

All three of them flinched, and as Reigan turned to stare, he saw the dried tears staining her cheeks.

"Is Tomaii okay?" he asked, forcing himself to move. To roll onto his back so he could sit up. The way his ribs and abdominal muscles screamed stole the breath from his lungs and he quickly laid back down.

"Tomaii will be fine," Selina told him, voice soft. "He lost a lot of blood, so Killian is sitting with him donating. He said you two were still up here, but when you didn't come back, Brach and I came to make sure no more beasts had come slithering out of the volcano."

The male stole a glance toward Eaon, wariness and pity in his eyes.

Eaon closed his own, not wanting to see it. "Sorry. Give me a minute and I'll get up."

"Just . . . take it easy," Selina told him. "I didn't realize your blessing caused you pain."

Eaon ignored that, too.

"It's not normal," Reigan added, the words harsh and clipped. "Nothing about that was normal."

"You mean your magic doesn't hate you for keeping it bottled up?" Eaon snorted, trying to lighten the mood. "I'm jealous."

"Magic isn't *sentient*, Eaon," Reigan snapped at him. "It's not supposed to *feel* anything. It shouldn't be able to fill your eyes with darkness and look at me as if I'm a meal."

It wasn't pity in her voice, Eaon realized. Opening his eyes, gritting his teeth through the ache in his body as he forced himself to sit up, he took in all five and a half feet of Reigan in all her fiery glory. There was so much anger on her face. So much fear.

"I'm sorry. I didn't mean to scare you," he told her.

"I'm not scared *of* you, Eaon. I'm scared *for* you. What in the burning depths of Nir *happened* to you? Because that was not normal magic. Not even normal Sparrow magic."

She was serious. Eaon looked from Reigan to Selina, who nodded in agreement. It hadn't occurred to him that what he was experiencing was any different to the way other people felt magic. How could it have?

"I don't know," he said quietly. "I . . . I died twice. Maybe that has something to do with it. No. Three times." He was already losing track. "The Lover keeps sending me back."

Silence sat between them as they considered the repercussions of that. The sun was nearly below the horizon, and it was Brach who broke the contemplation.

"If we don't get back to the gorge soon, we're going to have the night crawlers out here to deal with."

Reigan gave Eaon back his staff, and he used it to pull himself up to his feet, trying and failing not to whine as his body protested the movement.

"Maybe it would be worth contacting the Sparrow Coven after all," Selina said quietly as they began their descent. "See if they have any information about witches who are brought back from the dead more than once. Or if there was ever a case of the Lover sending someone back of their own accord. Maybe they know about sentient magic."

There was nothing Eaon wanted to do less than have anything to do with those heretic, wicked pieces of shit. Except, perhaps, hurt someone by accident. Reigan had called him her friend. He remembered that very clearly.

Only Dearmead had ever called him that. And Cinn. And Selina, actually.

Did Tomaii think of himself as Eaon's friend? Did Killian?

Not important right now, dumbass, Eaon scolded himself, placing his feet carefully as he made his way down the mountain.

"You could ask Kaelean to inquire on your behalf," Selina suggested after seeing the grimace on Eaon's face.

"She hates them even more than I do."

"But she would do it. For you, she would."

Eaon frowned, looking across to her. "I think you're confusing her obsession with Cinn with—"

"No," Selina interrupted him. "I'm not. You, Eavha, Cinn and Dearmead are special to her more so than anyone else in Wyldeden. We all know it. You brought her back home."

She had called them her coven. Eaon had heard her say it, though none of them had agreed to such a thing. No ritual had taken place, no oaths sworn. Yet she had called them a coven all the same.

"I can't think about this. I can't think about any of it." Shaking his head, the jumble of loose threads wouldn't untangle themselves. "I just want to sleep. I want quiet."

"I'll get you a proper tonic, even if I have to steal ingredients from the brewers myself," Reigan grumbled.

"We didn't get your salamanders." Eaon suddenly remembered. That had been the whole point of this expedition.

"Pardon me if I don't have a fuck to give about that right now," Reigan snapped. "There was a monster the size of a horse crawling around up here. My cousin nearly died. I could have died. Killian could have died. But you were here. You put yourself through all that pain to save us. So I don't care about my salamanders, Eaon, I'm going to find you a fucking tonic."

Brach stopped walking. The rest of them went on high alert.

"What is it?" Selina hissed.

"Nothing," he said. "Nothing, I just . . . If there was one monster like that out here, there could be more. The missing scouts."

Reigan raised her eyebrows. "We'll talk to Miika when we get back."

Eaon let out a slow breath, focusing on his feet. Too much. There was too much to think about, and he was so tired. His knee buckled, but he gripped his staff to keep him upright, the wood bowing under his weight.

"You alright?" Selina asked, gloved hands hovering close by. She could touch him, but he didn't want her to. Didn't want to risk it.

"I'm fine," Eaon lied. "I'm fine."

CHAPTER FORTY

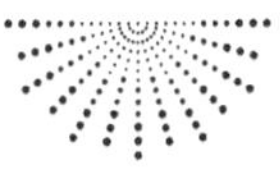

EAON

Despite insisting all he needed was rest, Reigan and Selina forced him to see a healer. It was a relief to see Tomaii looking better, laying on a cot on the floor of the healer's clinic, his upper arm and shoulder in bandages, smiling wearily as Eaon came limping in.

"There's our hero."

Killian gave Eaon a nod as he sat on another cot, grimacing once more at the ache in his body as he lay down. Killian was sitting beside Tomaii, a contraption wrapped around his arm. A similar one was around Tomaii's, a thin glass tube between them running red with blood.

"Are you alright?" Eaon asked the both of them.

"Better than you by the looks of it," Killian muttered.

His face had bruised from falling on it, and no doubt the color blooming under his eyes and across his cheekbones looked as bad as it felt. Reigan opened her mouth to tell them about the past few hours up on the mountain, but Killian's older brother came storming into the healer's clinic, murder etched on his brow.

"What kind of utter nonsense have I just been hearing? Twelve-foot salamanders? Have you lot been smoking again? Taking mushrooms?"

"No!" Killian snapped.

"Well, not today," Tomaii corrected.

"We weren't hallucinating," Reigan insisted. "It really was that big. I swear it on Ignatius's bones."

The healer ignored Miika, stepping around him to bring Eaon a poultice for his face and a bowl of broth. As if someone had warned her, leather gloves adorned her hands as she used a brush to apply the sticky green paste.

"I didn't see it, but I saw the tracks. And the, uh, remains," Brach said, the only one of the group Miika was likely to believe. "I'm no scout but that thing was enormous. Unnaturally so."

Miika looked to Eaon and narrowed his eyes. "Twice now, a beast has shown itself just to be struck down by your magic."

"Get that suspicious look of your ugly face and don't talk to Eaon like that," Killian snapped again. If it weren't for the glass tube delicately balanced between him and Tomaii, Killian might have stood up to get in his brother's face.

Reigan had moved to Killian's other side, slipping her hand in his and Miika looked down his nose at them.

"Lose the attitude, Kil. I am your elder now—"

"I don't care if you're the high priest himself, *do not speak to my friends like that*."

"If you want me to leave the gorge, I will," Eaon said, sipping his broth. "But it's not my fault you live in an area highly populated by beasts. If you have scouts out there facing mutations like the one we saw today, it's no wonder they're going missing. They need guardians with them."

"And who are you to tell me how to run my division?" Miika snarled. "No Wyldeden wimp—"

"Hey!" Brach interrupted. For Selina's sake. The insult rolled off Eaon's back like water from the hot pools—tepid and weightless.

"Eaon has a point," Reigan spoke up, a steadfast pillar among the rising tempers.

Miika crossed his arms. "Fine. I'll send out a scouting party with some guardians to see if there's any trace of the missing witches around this so-called giant salamander's lair. I'll even send an Igni-blessed one."

"Wow. Miika taking advice. A true miracle," Killian spat.

"As soon as you're done here, you can go with them," Miika sneered. "Since you're so fucking tough."

"Gladly. I'll even bring back one of the beast's teeth, just to prove we're not lying!"

"How petty that you're still fixated on that. Since when do you care if I think you're lying or not?"

"Fuck you."

"Grow up."

"Just go, Miika," Reigan warned.

"Gladly. I have more important things to do than squabble with a bunch of stoners anyway," Miika jabbed, then turned to storm out of the healer's clinic.

Killian sat there, seething silently as he watched his brother's back. Even Tomaii had gone quiet.

The healer came to remove the tube, pressing down on the wounds before bandaging them tightly.

"That should do it," she said quietly. "Stay a little longer, have some broth, then you should be fine to go home."

"Both of them?" Reigan asked. "All of them?"

"Yes." The healer spared a smile, then went to busy herself restocking bandages.

Reigan looked at Killian, anguished. "I don't want you to go back out there."

"I can't not go. Not after that," Killian countered, unashamedly squeezing Reigan's hand. "I'll be fine. I'm out there all the time. It's not different."

"I'll come," Eaon said, placing his empty bowl of broth beside the bed.

"Absolutely not," Brach, Selina and Reigan all said at once, stunning the other males into silence.

Which is when Reigan explained how Eaon had almost lost control over his magic, and how once she had got the cuffs back on, it had clawed at him for hours. The way Eaon had described it as having feelings. A temper.

"There's no reason he should have to put himself through that again," Reigan finished.

"Our guardians are well trained. They'll be plenty," Brach added.

Killian and Tomaii were both staring at Eaon with mixed expressions of horror and awe. Eaon just sunk back into the mattress and found a part of his nail to chew on.

"Offer stands," he mumbled.

"Come on," Selina said, coming to his bedside and passing him his staff once more. "Let the mountain clan sort it out. You need to rest and we need to draft a message to Kaelean."

Selina had a point. Despite how he cared for these three witches, he was not a part of their clan and this was very much a clan issue. Miika already thought Eaon was at fault and interfering further could cause bad blood between their two peoples. He had almost forgotten his role here. As a traveler, it was his job to keep the peace. To know his place.

Taking the staff, he grit his teeth again as he got upright.

"Sleep well, Eaon," Killian told him sincerely.

"Wake me if you need me," Eaon insisted.

Then with a nod to the others, Eaon followed Selina back out of the healer's clinic.

After another hot, satisfying meal from Killian's ma, Eaon retired once more to his lonely room. Physically drained, mentally exhausted, there was nothing he wanted more than to sleep. Reigan had dropped off a tonic she said was not the one she had hoped to get for him, but it would put him out for a few hours, no matter how manic he was.

So after washing the poultice from his face, he drank the lot and laid down, listening to the quiet chatter beyond the curtained partition, waiting to go under.

Waited, and waited, and waited.

Eaon woke up gasping. He didn't remember falling asleep, which made the dreams he'd had of surging through his cuffs and killing the entire mountain clan too real. But, beyond his room, he could hear an argument being had between Killian's sister and ma.

Everyone was fine.

He hadn't had dreams that bad in a while. Hadn't feared himself quite so much since before Cinn had come along. Fiddling with the button strung on his new twine necklace, he sighed deeply, almost imagining he could still feel the kinner lying beside him.

Cinn, who didn't want him the way Eaon longed to be wanted.

The way Tomaii wanted him. The way Dearmead used to want him.

Eaon sighed, closing his eyes against the emptiness he couldn't shake.

Eavha had asked him once what his favorite place in Nir was, and despite being unable to answer her at the time, he knew it was here. The Northern Mountain Clan had built a place so wild and free that, for just a little while, he could forget who he was.

It was nothing like Wyldeden. The witches here spoke Terranian with a few Igni phrases mashed into the language, but that was where the similarities ended. There were no firm clan roles, no tests to designate them, nor any hierarchy based on access to magic. People did what they wanted, and somehow everything still got done. Individuals living for themselves, but with a strong enough sense of community to know that jobs needed doing if they wanted to stay that way.

The people here had welcomed him, and it had taken him so long to realize why he was so enamored; there was no disdain, no mockery from them when they learned he was lowly blessed. They didn't care. They still treated him like an equal.

Even now, saddled with deadly magic, none of them had gone out of their way to make him feel uncomfortable. And Tomaii . . . Tomaii still wanted him. Wasn't afraid of him.

It was stupid to think of it. Of him, and the way just his presence, his closeness, made Eaon's head go quiet. The way he had taken Eaon by the hand in their youth and shown him true freedom. In that moment, he would have followed Tomaii into Ignatius's realm and happily burned for eternity if he had asked. Would have sold his soul to hang onto the feeling of being desired. Of being worth such things.

"Still in bed, you lazy rogue."

Eaon opened his eyes, shuffling to hide the hard aching his reminiscing had elicited, drawing a shaky breath to soothe the heat spreading beneath his skin.

Tomaii slipped inside, letting the curtain over the doorway fall closed.

"What's wrong?" Eaon asked, sitting up awkwardly.

"Nothing." His voice was low and easy, his steps relaxed as he came to stand by the hammock. "Just bored shitless. Killian left and Reigan is too busy worrying to play."

"Killian left? What time is it? How long have I been asleep?"

Tomaii chuckled. "Like, all night. Then all day."

"What?!" Eaon sat up, realizing the muscles in his body had mostly recovered. Thirst hit him, but Tomaii was already passing him a canteen of water.

"You obviously needed it."

Leather gloves encased Tomaii's hands, just as they encased Eaon's. The Ignatius-blessed witch smiled as he caught Eaon staring, reaching over to brush a thumb across his dry lip.

Eaon jerked back. "Don't."

"Why?"

Too many reasons. Not a single one felt good enough.

"The gloves are no guarantee," he said lamely, taking a long drink.

"What have I ever done to make you think I'm afraid of a little danger?" Tomaii grinned, leaning over until Eaon could smell the whiskey on his breath.

"I'm not in the mood for whatever you have planned," Eaon warned him, finishing the water.

"We could just stay here."

Tomaii's voice had gotten lower, the words coming out husky. The tension was suddenly thick between them and Eaon had a hard time getting his next words out.

"You should go home."

"Look me in the eye and tell me you don't want me to stay."

It would be a lie. A lie Eaon knew he should tell because it was the right thing to do. He was too dangerous, and Tomaii had no self-control—never had. Here in the mountains was one of the few places Eaon had ever been able to lose control too. But that was not an option anymore. Not with so much at stake. Keeping Tomaii safe, telling him to leave, was the only good choice.

Yet, as he met Tomaii's heavy stare, Eaon couldn't make himself say it.

"You're an idiot," he said instead, breath hitching as Tomaii grinned, reaching over to once again brush his thumb against Eaon's face. "A reckless, stupid fool."

"Keep talking." Tomaii crawled into the hammock, holding himself over Eaon until it stopped rocking, then gently easing himself down. Eaon couldn't breathe as he sunk back into the fabric, Tomaii straddling him, grinning wickedly as he felt what Eaon could no longer hide.

"I don't know why you're grinning," Eaon muttered. "This isn't going anywhere."

But even as he said it, his hands found Tomaii's knees on either side of him, smoothing their way up the outside of his thighs. Even with the gloves, with the pants between them, being like this again calmed something ravenous inside him. It wasn't quite the touch he craved, but he would never have that with anyone again. This, right now, this moment, was as good as it would get and he would have to get used to that.

"You lack imagination," Tomaii grinned, grabbing Eaon's wrist and moving his hand to the inside of his thigh.

"Tomaii?!" A voice called from the hall. Reigan. "Eaon?! Are you here?!"

There was panic in her voice. Tomaii swung his leg back over, tumbling from the hammock just as the curtain pulled back. Reigan came running in, face bleached. She didn't seem to care about the scene she was walking into.

"Killian's gone."

Eaon and Tomaii both stilled.

"Gone?" Tomaii's voice cracked. "Like . . . Like the others?"

Reigan nodded. "It only just happened. He was scouting with Aniqa and as soon as she realized he was missing she came running straight back to report it. They're putting together a search party."

Eaon was already moving again, every scrap of arousal dissipated. Snatching his staff from the corner, he blew past Reigan and ran through the caves toward the warren. Tomaii and Reigan followed, exchanging quick bursts of questions.

"Does Miika know?"

"Who do you think is organizing the search party?"

"What did Aniqa say? Was there a fight? Anything?"

"No. He just disappeared."

"Shit. *Shit.*"

In the main cavern, five witches were already suited up in sandy brown leather, strapping daggers and spears over their bodies. Aniqa was giving them clear directions to where she had last seen Killian.

"I'm coming," Eaon announced.

The hall went silent, looking between the three of them.

"Not a ch—" Miika started.

"I wasn't asking." Eaon walked forward, looking each of them in the eye.

"You're not trained—"

"And Killian was. Yet he's missing now. Maybe the five of you can take whatever's been stealing your scouts, but if you can't? Trust me, you want me to come along. One look at whatever is taking your scouts and I'll turn them to buzzard food."

He was already picturing it. Already imagining the bliss that would burst inside him as he took the soul of the beast. Let it pass through him on its way to the Lover. His mouth watered, fire burning through his veins. He was too awake. Too alert. He wanted to lay his bare hands on something.

"I am immortal. I am death. I'm a fucking god. I could kill everyone in this room, everyone in this gorge if I wanted to. And you want to leave me behind?"

It was laughable. The rising hysteria was almost orgasmic.

Everyone was staring at him, part in revulsion and part in fear.

Even Reigan.

Even Tomaii.

He didn't care. Pure energy pulsed through his veins, fortifying his bones. He was no longer on their level. He no longer lived by their rules. Anything he wanted, everything he wanted, could be his.

"In fact," Eaon continued, smirking at them all, "maybe you should all stay here. I'll go alone. That way I don't have to worry about any of you getting in my way."

Tomaii cleared his throat. "You're probably right, Eaon. You would be very useful out there. But I think it'd be best if you took one of your tonics first."

Eaon scoffed, and the magic in his gut, his chest, his hands and throat and mouth, roiled at the insult. He didn't need a tonic. He didn't need anything. He was beyond medicine; beyond food and water and air.

"I don't think so."

"Does he have the cuffs on?" Reigan asked in what she probably thought was a whisper, but rang like bells in Eaon's ears.

He'd been stupid to tell them about the spellmarks to dull his magic. Weak to assume he needed to be contained. Pulling back his sleeves, he began unbuckling the cuffs.

"Eaon, no," Tomaii snapped at him.

The guardians all put hands on their daggers.

"No? *No?* Tell me, which one of you are going to stop me?" he dared them, glaring around.

"Eaon." Tomaii stepped forward, voice hardening, still wearing those leather gloves. Reigan made to grab him, but he shrugged her off. Even now, he was not afraid of him. "Focus. You're wasting time. Killian—remember?"

Killian.

The heat of Tomaii's stare made Eaon frown, blinking through the pounding in his ears, trying to remember what the problem about Killian was. Why they were all gathered. If he even cared.

That thought hurt. He did care. He cared about Tomaii. Reigan. Killian. Looking around the room, he cared about all of them. This clan had given him more than he could ever explain and . . . had he really just threatened to kill them all?

"I . . . I do need my tonic, don't I?"

"Yeah," Reigan said, backing toward the caves. "I managed to find one. I'll go get it for you."

"I'm sorry." Rubbing his head, he struggled to look back at the witches still staring at him.

"Two minutes," Miika said. "If you can pull yourself together in the next two minutes, you can come with us."

Eaon nodded.

Running back, Reigan handed him a vial, and even though he didn't want to take it, even though the sense of grandeur he felt was thrilling and empowering and made him want to conquer the world, he remembered now—he needed to find Killian.

He drained it quickly, cringing at the strange taste before forcing himself to face Tomaii.

"Thank you. I'm sorry."

Every other witch in the room seemed to breathe for the first time in a minute, oblivious to the way Eaon still strained against the raging magic inside.

"You've got this." Tomaii squeezed Eaon's gloved hands, then turned to Miika. "We're coming too."

"No. Absolutely not." Miika shook his head. "Eaon I can agree with, but neither of you are combat trained and the clan can't risk losing an Igni-blessed witch. You're both staying."

"But—" Reigan started.

"I said, no!" Miika shouted at them. "We're leaving. Now. And if I scent either of you following us I'll stake you both."

The two cousins blanched, stepping back.

"It's fine," Eaon told them. "We'll find him."

Reigan jutted out her chin and kept her mouth shut. But her bloodshot eyes told Eaon everything she wanted to say.

Bring him back to me.

CHAPTER FORTY-ONE

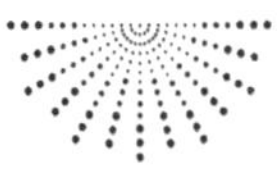

EAON

Tomaii hadn't been joking when he'd said Eaon had slept an entire night and day; the four guardians and one scout that Eaon accompanied ventured into the early night, armed to the teeth.

He should have gone with Killian to begin with. Should have pushed back against Reigan and Selina and Brach's worry. Should have smacked some sense into himself, thinking this wasn't his problem.

Stupid brain.

The scout took them out of the gorge and up a familiar path toward the bleeding mountain. It was a good few hours walk to where the salamander's lair had been, and in the dark it was twice as perilous. But the closer they got, the more Eaon could *feel* something wrong. The wilderness was too quiet. Had his magic hurt more animals than he'd thought? Or did the smell of it linger, scaring everything away?

The guardians and the scout began to fan out, taking deep breaths, scenting the area. A few of them crouched low, dipping their fingers in the soil to taste it, or pressing their hands against boulders and shrubs, feeling for whatever it was that Terranian witches could feel. Eaon didn't know. He couldn't do what they did.

So he did what he could do.

Please, play nice, he begged his magic.

Closing his eyes, he let it bubble to the surface. Let it peer through his eyes, looking for signs of life. He'd felt it before, after consuming a soul, when he would become hyper aware of all the other souls around he could take. He wanted that information now, and for once, he and his magic wanted the same thing.

He sensed the five witches with him, bright pulses of energy moving silently through the brush. In the sky, far above them, he sensed a lone falcon circling, looking for dinner. Tiny critters, bugs and mice, moving around among the bushland, but nothing larger than that.

But there was still a pull. East, farther into the Northern Mountains, something beckoned.

When he opened his eyes, there were colors everywhere.

He blinked in awe before groaning. This was not a good sign.

"What?" one of the other witches asked.

"Nothing," he said, trying to look at their face instead of the colorful threads of light protruding from their head, shooting straight up for a good few feet before breaking into frayed edges.

He didn't feel grandiose, the way he had earlier. He didn't feel scattered and full of unending energy, or fitfully irritable the way he had been for weeks on end now. He felt calm. Almost normal, or what he thought normal would feel like. Yet the colors were a clear indication that he was about to have a full-blown episode.

And one of those threads, shimmering like pearl across the midnight sky, thicker and brighter than any of the others webbed over the world, was tied to Eaon, shooting away toward the east.

"What are you looking at?" one of the other witches asked, following Eaon's gaze. "Did you see something? Killian?"

"No." Eaon shook his head. Killian. He didn't have time for this. And yet . . . "I think we should go east."

"Why?" they asked him.

He didn't know. "I just do."

The guardians all exchanged glances, but they weren't mocking him. They were *considering* it.

"The trees are singing toward the east," one of them said. "And there's no other sign."

"What are they saying?" the scout asked.

"Nothing I can interpret. But it's joyful."

"That can't be it then. Probably fae."

"The fae might know something. It can't hurt to ask them."

"Yes it can," another snorted. "Have you ever tried talking to the fae? They'll walk away from the conversation with promises from all of us and we still won't know any more about the missing scouts than we do now."

Eaon wished he could hear the trees. Wished that when he laid his bare hand on it, the dryads spoke to him instead of cringing away.

"You want to go back and explain to Miika that we didn't look for his brother properly because we were scared of the fae?" one of the others challenged. "If the trees say east, and the Wyldeden witch says east, then that's enough for me. There's nothing else here."

Eaon was already walking.

They walked the entire night, then most of the following day. Eaon found berries and bark to eat while the others shot birds out of the sky to roast over a fire. They still hadn't found any tracks, but the guardians said the trees were getting louder, urging them onwards. Eaon had been relieved when the colors faded into the day and he could sit down to rest for a while. As much as the urgency to find Killian fueled them, their bodies could only go so long without rest and food. And water. Eaon had been in too much of a hurry to pack his own things, but the others didn't resent sharing their canteens with him.

Wyldeden guardians would have let you die of dehydration before sharing their water with a laborer, his brain whispered to him. *Let alone now, with a soul-eater.*

He hated that his mind was drifting back there. To Lorelei, virtually unpunished for breeding such hate among their people. Having her magic bound, being forced to labor—Kaelean had punished the ex-high priestess by turning her into *him*.

Selina said the witch cared about him, but she didn't. She couldn't, if that was what she thought was a fitting way to handle the situation.

"*Eaon Nemuse.*"

Startled, Eaon looked around for who had called him. Two of the hunting party were awake, keeping watch, but everyone else had gone to sleep.

"Something wrong?" he croaked, coughing to clear the mountain dust from his throat.

The witches both flinched, turning to look at him. "What?"

"Did you call for me?"

"No?"

Eaon frowned, but shrugged. He probably needed to sleep, but he was still far too aware of sounds and smells. His skin was sensitive to the dry grass scratching his bare feet, so there was no way he was going to be able to get comfortable enough to sleep. But he lay down properly and tried anyway.

"*Eaon.*"

Stilling, sure the voice had come from right beside him, Eaon glanced over to the nearby bushes. The voice was familiar, but he couldn't quite place it.

Or was he hearing things again? He knew he was close to a frenzy. He was used to hallucinating colors and lines, but he'd never imagined voices before. Was his illness getting worse?

"*Eaon, quick.*"

Sitting up, Eaon clutched his staff.

"Who's there?"

"*Quick, come.*"

The urgency in the voice tugged at his heart as if there was a literal string tied to it.

"Everything okay?" one of the other witches asked, looking over with a hand on his dagger.

"*Don't tell them,*" the voice whispered.

Blinking, Eaon nodded and called back, "Everything's fine."

"*Come.*"

"I'll be back in a minute. Just . . . business," he lied, rising to his feet.

The blackberry bush to his left. That was where the voice was coming from. The voice he knew but didn't know. The voice that pulled on his heart in an irresistible way.

"Leave the wand. You don't need it."

He dropped it and wandered into the forest.

Dusk had arrived again and the farther from the campfire he went, the more complete the shadows seemed to wrap around him. There was a shape in the bushes, a creature as high as his shoulder, darting along, trying not to be seen.

"Who are you?" Eaon asked, stepping carefully so as not to leave tracks.

"I know where your friend is," it called back. "This way. Quick."

Something itched at the back of Eaon's brain, but he couldn't focus on the thought. Everything had become less tangible, his thoughts nothing but dust in the wind. But his heart—his heart knew what to do.

He followed the creature farther and farther into the forest. Through gaps in the canopy, the pale moonlight bounced off the creature's green skin and bulbous black eyes. Strands of wheat swayed in the gentle breeze instead of hair. A nymph of some kind. Fae.

Frowning, Eaon wasn't sure why knowing that concerned him. The nymph glanced back, realizing he had fallen behind.

"Quickly now. It's not much farther."

Another sharp tug in his chest and all the worry went out of Eaon's head as he followed the nymph.

"Killian is here?" he asked.

"Yes. Killian. He is this way."

The trees began to thin, and a ring of shiny red-capped mushrooms lined the perimeter of a large meadow. The air felt warmer there, and a sick feeling began to churn in Eaon's gut as he neared the clearing.

"Come on. In here, little witch."

"Is . . . Is this a trick?"

Fangs gleamed as the nymph broke out into a gleeful grin. They couldn't lie, he remembered. Killian had to be close by.

"Come in. It will be fun."

"I . . ."

"Don't ever engage with the fae." How many times had Kailevi warned him? *"There are so many rules and their magic will bind you to a life of servitude before you've even said two words."*

What had he said? What had he done that could ensnare him? He'd studied faerie law but his brain wouldn't work properly.

The nymph was watching him, practically salivating.

The only thing he could remember right then was that it was unwise to offend the fae. Had he unwittingly agreed to something by following the nymph to this faerie circle, or did the law of neighborliness only begin once he was inside?

"Is Killian inside the faerie ring?" he asked.

"Yes. He is having fun with the others."

He should be wary of how easily the nymph had answered him.

"How did you learn my name?" The tug in his chest . . . he'd never felt it before, but he'd read about what a faerie could do if they knew your true name.

"The mountains have ears. Now come."

Another tug, and whatever else Eaon was trying to think about emptied right out of his head again.

He stepped over the ring of mushrooms surrounding the empty clearing and into a savage revelry. A huge bonfire burned in the middle where at least a hundred fae were dancing. Euphoric music stole the breath from his lungs as sprites and nymphs and pixies whirled and crowed in feral joy. And among them, witches. Not many, but they stood out among the oddly colored creatures.

A red-haired female was so drunk on faerie wine her eyes were rolling in her head, two goblins holding her hands as they dragged her around and around the fire in a crazed dance. Somehow, her bleeding feet didn't miss a step. A burly blond male lay nearby with two nymphs, who laughed and caressed him as he begged for the golden fruit in their hands. And across the field, on a pile of boulders, kneeling at the feet of two goat-headed fae, was Killian. He'd been leashed, eyes glazed, gold smeared across his face.

Eaon wasn't entirely sure where he was or what he was doing, but he knew he had to get these witches out.

"Fuck your faerie rules," Eaon hissed, shucking off his gloves and throwing them in the dirt. They couldn't bind him in magic if they were all dead.

The blessing in his soul writhed with glee.

"Drink."

A cup of wine was shoved in his face. Eaon pursed his lips, but the green-skinned nymph tipped the cup anyway, the potent liquid flooding his nose.

Wrenching his head away, coughing and spluttering, the nymph only laughed.

"Drink more, Eaon Nemuse."

Reason emptied out of his head, and as the nymph held a second goblet out to him, Eaon took it and drank greedily.

The taste . . . sweeter than any wine any witch had ever made. No grape given by Terra could have made something like this. The party seemed to slow, the joyful faces of the dancers pulling a grin onto his own. He wanted more wine. He wanted to dance.

"Come," the nymph grabbed his hand.

And immediately started screaming.

Eaon laughed as the nymph tripped over its own foot, staring at the skin of its hand, its arm, as it began to rot and peel away.

"What are you!?" it screamed, the pitch of it growing higher and higher as the rot spread quickly over its entire body.

Many of the other fae nearby had stopped to stare, the revelry dying off. Whispering in a language Eaon didn't understand filled the field, but he didn't care. He wanted more wine.

"You killed him," one of them spat as Eaon stumbled toward a barrel.

"I did not," Eaon argued. "He killed himself."

"Your magic did it."

"He didn't ask about my magic. That's not my fault."

The sprite arguing with him turned beetroot red as the solidity of Eaon's argument became apparent. Eaon laughed again, finding a goblet to fill with wine.

A black hand came out of nowhere and grabbed his wrist just as he placed it under the barrel's tap. Eaon flinched, waiting.

Nothing happened.

Eaon stared at the hand, letting his magic lash out at the creature, but it was no use.

Slowly, he raised his eyes.

One of the goat-headed creatures had come to him, eyes glowing a buttercup yellow. Its body was that of a male, albeit strategically covered in fur, skin as dark as the Lover's void. Only its head was that of an oversized goat, two huge curling horns protruding from his forehead.

"What is your name," the creature demanded.

Eaon opened his mouth, but closed it quickly. Even as drunk as he was already, he knew not to say it.

The goat fae tightened his grip and yanked him closer. At least a foot taller than Eaon, the creature was the most intimidating thing Eaon had ever confronted. It was touching his skin and did not seem bothered.

"I said, what is your name."

"What is yours?" Eaon managed to ask.

The goat's nostrils flared, and as it stepped back, Eaon realized its legs were twisted the wrong way, hooves clopping over the earth instead of feet.

Dragging Eaon across the field, the other faeries got out of the way. With a snap of his fingers, the goat man ordered the music to resume. The dancing started again, and soon the encounter seemed to be completely forgotten.

As they reached the pile of boulders, the second goat, even taller with horns that spiked instead of curled, released the clasp on Killian's collar.

Killian.

Swallowing, Eaon shook his head, trying to clear it. He was here for Killian.

"Go dance, my sweet little witch." The taller goat shoved Killian toward the bonfire, and without even a glance of acknowledgment at

Eaon, Killian went to join the other fae. "Well, well, what do we have here?"

"Nothing you can play with," the goat holding Eaon's wrist warned, taking a seat and pulling Eaon down sharply. Landing hard on his knees, he caught himself with his other hand, wincing at the strain in the wrist the fae still held.

Surrendering all control, he let his magic loose.

The goat fae laughed. "That tickles. Do it again."

Eaon bared his teeth, but the effect was dulled by the fact his face was going numb, the potency of the wine he'd drank only now really hitting him.

"Share," the other goat demanded, leaning over for Eaon's other wrist.

To his surprise, the goat holding him let her.

With his magic already unleashed, she didn't get time to scream. As soon as her rough fingers touched the back of his hand, she became ash and scattered on the rocks.

Nobody seemed to notice, or care.

"How fascinating. It's been a while since I had something like you to play with."

"How?" Eaon managed through gritted teeth, pulling uselessly at his wrist. Without having his name held over his head, clarity was clearing the fog away. "You're not Kinner."

The goat flinched at the word, then began laughing so hard it rocked back on the boulder. Its guffawing was so loud the fae nearby stopped to stare, laughing too, though they didn't know why.

When he finally settled, his yellow eyes looked down at Eaon with an abundance of curiosity.

"And what would you know about the Kinner?"

"Let me go and I'll tell you."

This was dangerous. Stupid and dangerous, to bargain with a faerie. Especially one he couldn't kill.

The goat seemed to consider it, then huffed hot air out of his long nose.

"No. But if you can guess how I can touch you when nothing else can, I will let your friend go."

Eaon needed his brain to start working. Now.

"If I can guess why you can touch me, you release all the witches from all magic binding them to this faerie circle and let them return home without harm."

"I'll let you choose one witch."

"All of them."

"One. Remember, I don't have to bargain with you at all. It simply amuses me to watch you try."

Eaon bristled, blinking the haze out of his eyes. He still wanted more wine. Wanted to let it ruin him until none of this had to be his problem anymore.

Killian. He had to think of Killian, and the other witches who had been here for weeks.

"Release all the witches, and I will tell you what I know about the Kinner, too."

The goat grinned, exposing thick canines as sharp as any faerie fang.

"All the witches, except you."

Damn it. "Fine. Deal."

"Deal."

A heavy magic settled between them, snapping against his sternum. He was lucky to have gotten out of that without losing anything else. He had not offered eternal servitude; he could bargain for his own safe return later.

"Okay," Eaon sighed.

He also hadn't been restricted on how many guesses he was allowed to have. Really, he'd expected better from a faerie this strong.

"Take your time. We have a lot of it," the goat fae chuckled, keeping his grip on Eaon's wrist. "Would you like refreshments while you think?"

"No." He held his tongue on saying "thank you." It was Kaelean's warning that popped into mind this time. *Do not show them gratitude. You'll only indebt yourself.*

For a few minutes, he watched the fire. The fae dancing around it, drinking and eating, diving into debauchery and depravity everywhere he looked. This was a far cry from the beautiful ritual he'd seen in the

Northern Spine when traveling with Kailevi. These were not the fae in the soft paintings he'd seen in the city galleries. No, these were the fae that had battled the beasts during the First War and won.

A bell chimed in his head at the thought, but the connection slipped away before he could catch it. Too many sights and smells and sounds. His heart was beating too hard, his skin itching and sweating, his knees aching on the stone. Inside, his magic seethed. Its wrath was comparable to the way it raged at Cinn.

The goat fae laughed again, clacking his hooves on the stone.

"You can keep fighting like that if you like. I won't punish you. It gives me all kinds of interesting feelings."

Eaon wrinkled his nose, trying to rein in the magic. The last thing he wanted was to be giving the stupid faerie any more satisfaction than it was already getting. Without his staff though, it was difficult. Sucking in sharp breaths, the expected pain from trying to leash his blessing slid down his spine, sweat quickly soaking the back of his shirt.

The unleashing of his power hadn't been as catastrophic as it could be, and he wondered what would happen if he put actual effort into it instead of just letting it loose. But Eaon didn't want to force it. Not now. Didn't want to risk making himself sick or passing out at a time like this. Besides, the stupid faerie seemed to like the pain.

"Stop," Eaon muttered at himself, lowering his head to the rock so he could use his free hand to grip the back of his hair. He was getting sidetracked. Distracted. He couldn't think when he was like this under normal circumstances.

He looked for the witch with the bleeding feet, still being dragged around the bonfire in a dizzying dance. She had vomited since he'd last seen her, and yet still, her feet pranced on.

If she died while he knelt here, because he couldn't focus through his own stupid illness . . .

He wanted to smash his head on the rock. The impulse came on so strongly, so terrifyingly suddenly, Eaon sat up. As far as he could anyway. His control on his magic slipped and it went crashing into the solid presence of the goat fae once again.

This time, he didn't laugh. "You have no control over it, do you?"

Eaon grit his teeth, panting and tugging at his hair.

Useless. Pathetic, useless excuse for a witch.

He was spiraling. He knew he was, but he couldn't stop it. He needed more tonic. He needed Eavha, or Dearmead, or Cinn. Even Kaelean would do.

Could he call for help again? Like he had at the Copeland farm?

No. He'd struck a faerie bargain. Not even she could get him out of it. He should have thought of it earlier, but he'd underestimated how unwell he was going to get.

What he needed was a new brain.

Or a spell that would fix his one completely.

Wonder if a Kinner mark would heal him.

Wonder if a Kinner mark would counter the Lover-blessing.

No, no it wouldn't.

Kinner mark.

The faerie was not a Kinner because he was a faerie, but aside from the spellmarks he'd learned, there was nothing else that could nullify his magic like one.

Colors burst across the field again, like a web between every living creature in the field. Flowing lines of red and blue, green and purple, bright like fire but transparent like smoke. Slithering like snakes, but dancing like the fae themselves. The air seemed to sing with the beauty of all the colors and Eaon went slack, staring at the web.

At the purple line between him and Killian, now dancing with a dryad. The pearlescent one between himself and the phouka holding his wrist.

Phouka.

The word came out of nowhere.

"You're a phouka," he said stupidly.

The goat-headed faerie chuckled, watching Eaon curiously. "Yes, but that's not why."

"No, but . . . your kind is rare. Yet you let the other one die."

"She was getting annoying anyway."

Why were the phouka rare?

Hunted.

Why?

Enemies of the beasts. Half-beast, half-faerie hybrids, but chose the faeries' side during the First War.

The First War.

"The Kinner are humans who were given a witchmark to help them fight the beasts," Eaon said distantly. It was part of the bargain to tell the phouka what he knew about the Kinner anyway.

He didn't expect the look of surprise on the faerie's face. "That is not widely known information. How do you know that?"

"But they weren't the only ones fighting. They weren't the only ones to receive the witchmark. There were fae fighting alongside them, too."

Despite the colors, despite the music and the wine and the floating feeling taking over his body, dread hit Eaon like a rock in the gut. Pulling his eyes away from the lines of fate dancing through the crowd, Eaon looked up at the phouka.

"You wanted me to figure it out, didn't you? You let me have an easy deal, because you wanted me to figure it out."

"What are you?" the phouka asked with a frown, but Eaon shook his head.

"I'm just a useless Wyldeden witch, but you . . . you're fae with the mark of a Kinner, aren't you? You're one of the Old Ones."

For a moment, the phouka sat on the stone and stared at Eaon, stunned. Then he smiled and snapped his fingers. "Illia."

A pale blue nymph left the circle dancing by the fire and ran to the phouka's side.

"Fetch all the witches," he told her. "Clean them up and take them home safely."

"But . . . there are still five more nights of—"

"Do it now, or I'll ask someone else, and you can be the new entertainment."

The nymph squeaked and dashed off, stealing the bleeding-footed witch from the goblins with only a minor scuffle.

"Well done, witch. You're right. I did want you to learn what I was so you would be appropriately afraid. I am also bored of the other witches anyway, so I had no qualms of letting them go early. I would, however, like to know how you came to that conclusion so quickly."

Eaon looked away from him and watched the blue nymph collect a total of seven witches, including Killian, and lead them out of the faerie ring. He should feel relieved, but he didn't. The mix of dread and euphoria were making him dizzy and nauseous.

Vision blurring slightly, he looked back up at the phouka and whispered, "Your eyes look like the moon."

The phouka didn't ask him any more questions. Or perhaps Eaon just couldn't hear them. Couldn't hear anything beyond the music thrumming through his veins, the pain clawing down his spine, and the singing of colors lacing the sky in a pattern Eaon would never really understand.

CHAPTER FORTY-TWO

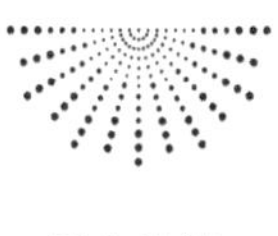

EAON

THE SUN WAS RISING ON THE FINAL DAY OF WHATEVER THEY HAD been celebrating, the fae finally winding down. Many had gone to sleep on the ground, likely for the first time in weeks, while others dragged their failing bodies into the shrubbery and promptly vanished from sight.

The phouka stayed on the boulder, continuing to sip at wine and watch the others with an insipid expression. From where he lounged on the rock by the faerie's feet, Eaon looked up to the phouka. The Old One had released its grip on his arm some time ago, but with the speed with which they glanced in his direction every time Eaon moved, there was no doubt in his mind that should he attempt to leave the phouka's side, he would not manage to get very far.

Sighing loudly, Eaon rolled onto his back to watch the dawn dull the stars. The fear from five days ago, when he'd first found himself in the faerie circle, had dissipated completely, replaced with a boredom that made it difficult to remember why he had ever been afraid at all. Since being brought to the boulder, he had not been commanded to do anything. Not even to stay still.

Sighing again, Eaon crossed his legs and propped his head on his wrist.

"Is something the matter?" the phouka asked with the same lack of interest he showed the remaining fae.

"I'm bored."

"Bored?"

"Yes, bored. You won't let me drink the wine, or eat the food. You won't let me dance. I'm not entirely sure why you haven't just told me to go," Eaon shrugged.

He didn't expect an answer. Every time he'd tried to start a conversation, the phouka had ignored him. Perhaps a little wary of Eaon finding a way to bargain his way out again.

Slowly, the faerie leaned back, spreading its long legs and turning its face up to the sky. Those large, heavy hooves were uncomfortably close to Eaon's head.

"You want to know why I'm not letting you go? It is because I am old. I am so old that I doubt your tiny witch brain could wrap your head around how old I am. I have seen all there is to see. I have done all there is to do. Tasted all there is to taste." At that, the phouka looked down at Eaon as if wondering exactly what Eaon would taste like. "The problem is that when you live for an eternity, things become rather . . . dull."

"Not as dull as this story," Eaon grumbled. As soon as the words were past his lips, he winced, preparing for a hoof to the head or stomach.

The phouka only chuckled. "When you grow a reputation so profound that the farmers in villages you've never been to leave out a phouka's share of their crops, just in case, terrorizing them loses its appeal. But there was this one day, I met a witch. And she was absolutely fascinating. In all my millennia, I had never met anything like her. Alas, like all mortal things, her life was fleeting. But what she gave me was not. I had hope that, perhaps, I had not seen all there was to see after all. Had not done and tasted all there was to do and taste. So, every so often I go to one of these repetitive, *boring*, revels in the hope that maybe this time, or maybe next time, I will meet someone like that witch."

The phouka sat up and leaned over his knees to look down at Eaon.

He couldn't explain what it was about the stare of those vibrant yellow eyes that made him still like a hare caught in the sights of a fox. The phouka smiled, as if it could smell the fear freshly aroused in him.

"And then you came strolling in. Once this party is over, I think you will find things much less boring, young witch."

Heart in his throat, Eaon threw every ounce of control he had into directing his magic into the phouka's face. Could he kill it? No. But he knew from Cinn that his magic could still hurt. Could still be crippling.

Rolling to his side, Eaon set his sights on the border of the faerie circle and prepared for the run of his life.

A large hand gripped the hair at the back of his head, yanking him up and backward until his back was against the phouka's knees, forced to arch as he pulled his head even farther.

"That was rude," the phouka growled.

"The party is over. I'm no longer a guest. Keeping me here against my will is rude." Eaon gasped, grabbing the fae goat's arm to try to lessen the strain on his back.

"Do you truly not wish to stay?" the phouka asked.

Eaon couldn't read the tone. There was a trap in the question, he knew it, but the grip in his hair was growing tighter, pulling tears to his eyes.

"No," Eaon gasped again.

"Then tell me what you really want."

Eaon didn't need to read the tone in that sentence; he felt it in his core. The stranglehold the command wrapped around his mind was absolute. That the faerie could do this without knowing his name was the single most terrifying thing Eaon had ever encountered.

"I want you to fill me up with faerie wine until I forget how alone I am."

The words weren't true, and yet they had to be.

The phouka blinked, releasing his grip in surprise. The hold on Eaon's mind slipped as he crumpled down onto the boulder.

"You are barely grown," the phouka said coldly. "What would you know about being alone?"

Eaon shook his head, unable to shake the terror gripping his heart again. He didn't know why he had said that, yet in that moment nothing felt truer. His parents were dead. His sister was on the other side of Nir, building her own life. His clan resented him; always had, always would. Even Kaelean only tolerated him because he was Eavha's brother. Cinn's friend. Cinn, who had left. The mountain clan had taken him in, but he was still an outsider. Proven by the fact that he had rescued the others days ago and nobody had come back to try and rescue him. He was a bit of fun for them—Killian, Reigan, Tomaii. Eaon knew that, didn't expect anything more than that from Tomaii, which only made his trying so hard to get past the barriers between them more hurtful.

Then there was Dearmead . . .

He didn't matter to any of them. Not the way he wanted to matter to somebody. Anybody.

The faerie circle had gone quiet. Eaon sniffed and turned his head. The small number of lingering fae were all staring at him.

Frowning, Eaon looked down at himself. At the skin that had turned ashen, the veins beneath darkening. The phouka reached down to grab his face and hissed at the contact. But, like a salve, the contact sucked the heaviness he hadn't realized was descending on him away. He breathed, and realized he hadn't for at least a minute.

"So powerful, and yet so unrefined," the phouka muttered through labored breaths. "Barely grown, but grown all the same. How does that happen? How does a witch get to your age and have such little control over a blessing of this magnitude?"

Eaon didn't care to explain. Didn't care for anything. Whatever he had just tapped into, he felt more at one with his magic than he ever had before. It wasn't separate to him, clawing to get out. No. Now he had the claws.

The screams from behind him as he eased into his power only lasted a second. Then the circle was quiet for a whole different reason. The phouka bared its teeth at him, tightening its grip on Eaon's face, but Eaon grabbed the phouka's face back.

"Stop."

The word was primal, and, like a switch, Eaon's magic shriveled up and hid somewhere behind his spine. The command had Eaon's hands dropping to his sides, blinking in a daze. He could still taste the souls he'd taken on the back of his throat, the buzz of their energy humming in his veins. The cuffs had not been enough this time.

"That magic does not belong to you."

The pain in Eaon's face finally registered. The grip of the phouka on his jaw made it impossible to speak.

"That *thing* is not meant to be here. You will tell me how you have it. Now."

At the pained sound Eaon made, the phouka released his grip, only to grab the back of Eaon's head again.

"I am Returned, and the Lover won't let me die permanently. I am their pawn."

His jaw ached, mouth salivating as the high began to wear off. His magic hadn't gone far, and he was hyperaware of every life force near enough for him to take. Resisting it made his body ache, his head spin. He couldn't think past it.

More. More, more, more.

"In what game?"

"I don't know." Eaon's chest was caving in. Too low, too high, and now he was crashing down again. It was enough to make him want to scream. Instead, his eyes started burning. "Make it stop. Please. Take me away, lock me up, make me forget everything, I don't care. I hate magic. Take it away. Please. Just make it stop. Please."

Pathetic. Disgusting, pathetic excuse for a witch.

The phouka's grip on the back of Eaon's head eased. "If that was a wish I could grant, I would grant it. I would not even bargain with you over it."

Leaving Eaon kneeling on the boulder, the phouka stood and closed its eyes, fists curling at its sides. When it spoke, it was more to itself than to Eaon. "The High Spirits were always selfish, capricious things, but this . . . What is the Lover up to now?"

Wiping his face, Eaon shook his head. "That's an interesting choice of words for someone who fought for the Lover, for Mother."

The phouka spat. "I fought for our people. And when Mother and Death fell in love with their Balance, forgetting that we were still here, fighting against Chaos, it was Sanni I fought for. It is Sanni and the other Fair Folk that I honor."

Eaon stayed very still and very quiet. He wasn't a hundred percent sure he was following what the phouka was saying, but any information he could glean might help.

"I don't know why . . ." The phouka trailed off, his moon eyes widening.

Eaon had been wrong before. That all-powerful command had not been the most terrifying thing he had ever seen; this was.

The phouka was afraid.

"How many times have you returned?"

Eaon frowned. "Why?"

"Answer me."

The pull wasn't there, but he answered anyway. "Three."

The phouka sagged with relief.

"If I'm right . . . it is a nasty thing that Death has done to you, young witch. A nasty, evil thing."

"What?" Eaon pleaded. "What is it?"

As if debating whether or not to tell him, whether or not Eaon could handle the information, the phouka crouched down to Eaon's eye level. He was low, he knew, but the potential for information, the possibility of learning something had him clinging onto what little shred of stability he had left.

"What possesses you is no blessing, nor is it a curse, but a seed," the phouka said softly. "A seed that, if you feed it, will grow and consume you until you become whatever it is the Lover needs you to become. Your soul, your essence, will pass on, but your body will have become something not of here. A shell—a conduit for something *else* to use. To exist here in this realm in a way it normally could not."

A conduit for Death.

"Help me," Eaon begged. "I'll give you anything. Just help me."

"All you can do is stop feeding it."

"I . . . I can't." Eaon's voice broke. "I had no real magic growing up. I can't control it. I don't know how."

The phouka hung his head and sighed in resignation. "That's why they chose you."

Why? Why did Death want to come here? What did this have to do with the legend of Chaos? What the fuck was going on?

"Eaon!"

His head whipped around at the sound of his name. A mistake.

"Eaon?" The phouka tilted its head. "That's a Terranian name."

"Eaon! We're coming!" Killian's voice called out.

The phouka rose to its full height, dawn glistening off its horns.

"Don't." Eaon didn't even know what he was asking for. Just that he didn't want anyone else to get hurt.

The phouka looked down at Eaon again, another unreadable expression on its face. Then, with a loud *pop*, the goat-headed fae was gone, replaced by a black horse with the same yellow eyes and long curling horns.

Without a word, it turned and sprinted off into the bush.

It took only a minute of sitting alone on the boulder for his mind to start trying to convince itself he had imagined the whole thing. He might have, if it weren't for the piles of ash scattering in the morning breeze.

"Eaon!"

Killian and an entire band of guardians came trudging through the bushland, armed to the teeth with iron tipped arrows, knives and spears. One of them crushed a mushroom from the faerie circle, but the scene before them wasn't what any of them would have expected.

Killian looked around the clearing, then to Eaon, who sat in a daze on the boulder.

"Figures," he said, smiling through the stress tightening his face.

Eaon tried to get up, but his legs had become weak. His whole body, now that he was thinking about it. He had not eaten in days.

Killian jogged over faster as the guardians spread out through the clearing, looking for lingering fae.

"I'm sorry it took us so long to find you. We were all really scattered until the wine and the commands wore off," Killian apologized, crouching in front of Eaon. "You alright?"

No. Eaon was not alright. Not remotely.

"Phouka," he managed, looking around the clearing.

"Is that what they were?"

Eaon nodded. "Old One. I couldn't . . . it was immune. Tell them . . . don't look for it. Let it go."

"Old One?" Killian's eyebrows shot up. "Fuck. *Fuck*. Helva!"

Standing up, Killian chased after one of the guardians.

"Let it go," Eaon repeated to nobody.

It had let him go.

CHAPTER FORTY-THREE

EAON

KILLIAN WAS RIGHT. IT TOOK A COUPLE OF DAYS FOR THE EFFECTS OF the fae to wear off enough for Eaon to explain what had happened, but even then, he kept a lot of it to himself. He didn't want to scare them with what the phouka had said about his magic. The seed. He didn't want to hear them talk about it like it wasn't a part of him. He didn't want to think about any of it.

Lounging on a pile of pillows in the communal space in Killian's home, Eaon had his nose buried in a book. Killian had been given time off to recover, sitting nearby with a closed book on his lap, too deep in thought to even bother opening it.

"We need to chart the fae holidays," he said suddenly. "All this time, they were just a few mountains down, entertaining the fae. For a holiday."

"Mmhm," Eaon mumbled, not wanting to talk about it.

"I know they won't return to the faerie circle, but we should still be more prepared. Lover damn us, how stupid we were, tossing around names as if we were locked away and safe like in Wyldeden."

"Yep," Eaon sighed, turning the page.

"We should only use a sign language when we're outside the gorge. Like the southern mountain witches do."

"Sure."

"You could teach us, right? Like you taught your friend Cinn?"

Eaon sighed, turning to glare at Killian. "I'm trying to read."

Reigan and Tomaii would finish working soon and come to annoy them. Ever since being ensnared by fae, Killian and Reigan had been in each other's pockets. Eaon was one grotesquely adoring look away from telling them to go somewhere and fuck already.

He was about ready to tell Tomaii to rip out his own eyes so he would stop looking at Eaon the same way.

The words he'd said to the phouka about being alone, they were stuck in his brain like a splinter. No matter how much time passed, he couldn't seem to find his rhythm here with these people who could have been his friends. He wasn't like them. He wasn't one of them. He wasn't like anyone.

A loud commotion in the halls distracted Eaon from his ceaseless irritation. Both he and Killian got to their feet to investigate. Witches were hurrying through the halls, heading for the warren where shouting and loud hissing echoed through the caverns.

Pulling on his gloves, Eaon followed Killian, joining the throng and pushing their way through the crowd. Eaon halted as he watched at least six witches wrestling with a dark shape that roared with bone-shattering ferocity. Blood smeared the ground, both the mulberry color of the witches and a bluish-black color.

"I will kill all of you!" a familiar voice sucked the air right out of Eaon's lungs. He stepped back as the group passed by, dragging the dark faerie by an iron chain wrapped around its throat.

For a moment, their sights crossed as the witches dragged the phouka. Its nostrils flared wide, rage like a thousand dying suns burning behind its eyes.

"You."

The Old One would never forget his scent. Would hunt him forever if it escaped. The terror Cinn must feel on a daily basis at the possibility of being captured by someone who wanted to inflict severe pain, all the while being unable to escape through death, descended on Eaon like a bag of boulders.

Shrinking back into the crowd completely, he leaned against the wall before he could faint. A million possibilities ran through his head at once, but they all led to the same conclusion. Eaon had made an immortal enemy, and there was nothing he could do now to change that.

The next breath he drew was sharp and shallow.

Killian found him, a deep crease on his forehead. "Why are you freaking out?"

"The phouka."

"This is a good thing. We can't have something like that lurking near the clan." Killian grimaced as if he couldn't understand why Eaon was so upset. "The high priest already sent word to the Sparrow Coven to ask for advice on how to contain an Old One. You know, since they supposedly got rid of the mythical Kinner."

"Who did nothing wrong, by the way! And neither did this phouka as far as we know! You're a fucking idiot if you think you'll be able to keep him handled, and now he thinks I'm responsible for his capture. Did you even think of that? That you've made everyone here, including me, a serious fucking enemy?"

"Okay, first, let's not get into the politics of what the Kinner and the Old Ones did or didn't do, okay? And secondly, you're being really dramatic. Go home and we'll talk about it when you calm down."

"*First*, you're fucking disgusting, and *second*, fuck you." Eaon turned his back and shoved his way through the crowd to the hall, running his fingers through his hair and tugging at it, trying to make his thoughts slow down.

Going back to his room, he grabbed his staff and sat in the corner, taking deep, measured breaths to calm the creeping cold from spreading through his body any further. There wasn't time to deal with his blessing, and for the millionth time, he wished Cinn was here.

Later, he stood with Tomaii and Reigan in the warren while Killian stood with Miika up on the raised platform. The guardians he'd gone into the mountains with had returned his staff to him, and it was strapped to his back once more as the elders and the high priest gathered to discuss the phouka. Unlike in Wyldeden, the rest of the people in the clan could have their say.

The mountain clan's usual kill-first-ask-questions-later mentality was finding ways around the invulnerability of the phouka—already, a dozen ideas from the Sparrow Coven on how to contain the faerie had been debated.

Eaon couldn't stand to listen to it any longer. In his mind, they weren't talking about how much suffering they could inflict on the phouka. They were talking about Cinn. It was Cinn that Eaon was envisioning being bound in chains and mummified in molten iron, then tossed into the Heart Lake where nothing would ever free him.

Heathens. All of them.

But, as he slipped away from the others, an idea formed, hazy and uncertain. With his staff in hand, Eaon stalked through the cavernous halls deep into the mountain until he reached the prison.

The phouka's screaming echoed against the rock; agonized cries of desperation and rage. Shaking, Eaon walked silently down the hall until he spotted four guardians keeping watch outside one of the cells, each holding an iron poker.

Eaon whistled to get their attention, ignoring the churning in his stomach.

The guardians turned, tightening their grips on their pokers and spears. "What are you doing down here? This area is off limits—"

"Dana, don't you know who that is?"

The guardians appraised him again with less condescension, and Eaon straightened, trying to embody the confidence of the role the clan had put on him since freeing their scouts.

"They want all the guardians in the warren. I can watch the Old One," Eaon told them.

The four witches shared wary glances, but Eaon had a reputation. Not only as a Lover-blessed witch, or whatever he was, but as a traveler. He was not one to cause problems. He was a helper. A peacemaker. Trusted.

One of them passed him their iron poker as they left. Eaon waited until they were out of view before tossing it to the ground.

Behind iron bars, the phouka lay on the ground in his goat-man form, neck and wrists bound in chains, the skin blistering beneath the metal. He was breathing heavily though gritted teeth but found the energy to glare at Eaon with a promise of everlasting pain.

Eaon pressed his lips together. "I came to make a deal."

"I will feed you . . . your own . . . intestines."

"I didn't do this, and I came to let you out. So shut up," Eaon hissed, taking a hesitant step toward the bars and taking off one of his gloves.

"Let me . . . guess. You let me out . . . in exchange for my name." The faerie bared its fangs at him.

The value of a faerie's name was common knowledge; to speak a faerie's true name was to bend its will to yours.

"I do not seek to enslave you," Eaon muttered, nostrils flaring at the thought. "I only ask that you leave and never hunt, kill or torture any of the mountain clan in vengeance. Just leave peacefully."

He would have to be careful how he phrased this deal, but there wasn't time to go through every possible contingency. The guardians would find out soon that Eaon had lied. There would be a price to pay for this, but better the evil you knew.

"That's it?" the phouka asked.

"Forget they exist. Forget this ever happened. No loopholes, no tricks." It was far from iron clad. "Promise, and I'll let you out."

For a painfully long moment, the phouka stared at Eaon with marginally less contempt. When he drew his next breath, a dribble of blue-black blood slid from between his lips.

"I promise to leave this mountain and forgive the mountain clan for this encounter."

Good enough.

Eaon grabbed the iron bar, closed his eyes and focused on the unlocking spell he'd read about in his book *Elementary Magic*. The one he'd seen Eavha do plenty of times. But his thoughts spun like eddies of snow during a storm and he couldn't focus, hissing through gritted teeth with frustration. The cold in his gut churned, palms burning with skin-splitting ice as the magic pulsed. In his hands, the metal began to rust.

Eaon opened his eyes, staring in shock as the lock crumpled and the door swung open.

"That'll work, too." Eaon shook his head. Later. He would consider this later.

Slipping his glove back on, he crouched by the phouka and began unwrapping the chains around his neck. As soon as the metal was gone, the skin beneath began to heal and he quickly took the chains off the faerie's wrists too.

With a low snarl, the phouka flipped Eaon onto his back and wrapped its hands around his throat. Stupidly, Eaon realized he had forgotten to include himself in the deal. He was not mountain clan.

Hurrying footsteps echoed down the hall, and before Eaon even had a chance to worry about the phouka strangling him, the faerie *popped* into a small goblin shape and scuttled off into the dark hall. Holding his throat, Eaon got to his feet and ran.

There was no avoiding the fact that everyone would know he was responsible for letting the phouka loose, but he was done here anyway. Done with the mountain clan and their bullshit. He would find somewhere else to wait for Cinn to return.

"Stop!" someone shouted behind him.

Cussing under his breath, Eaon forced his body to move faster. He'd have to find a way to get a message to Cinn not to come back this way. He would—

"Ah!"

Eaon flinched back as the lanterns ahead of him exploded, flame ringing the corridor in flickering orange and blue. Too hot. Far too hot. Before he had a chance to weigh up his options, the whistle of a staff sung behind him. Something hard hit the side of his head and everything went dark.

The irony of being held in the cell beside the one he'd just sprung the phouka from was not lost on him. Neither was the fact they had chained his wrists and ankles together in the same irons he'd taken off the creature.

Nobody came to visit him except Selina.

"I sent a whispering leaf explaining everything that's happened to Kaelean," she told him.

"No."

"Too late for protests, I already sent it."

Eaon shut his eyes and banged his head against the wall, flexing his wrists to ease the pressure of the irons a little. "I messed up. I did this. I will deal with the consequences."

"You are not from here, Eaon. It's an inter-clan issue now."

"Exactly. The only way to salvage the relationships between the two clans now is to let them punish me. It's fine. It's not the first time I fucked up while traveling."

But it was the first time he had fucked up without Kailevi being there to take responsibility. The first time he'd messed up as a matured witch. His da would be rolling in his grave.

"It's more complicated than that," Selina argued. "Kaelean won't let them do anything to you."

Eaon snorted, rolling his eyes. "Kaelean poisoned me on my quarter-century birthday, had me arrested by Pirevian soldiers, then thrown into the Sparrow prince's dungeon. She's not going to storm the Northern Mountains to stop me from getting a slap on the wrist."

"It's more than a slap on the wrist they're talking about," Selina said softly.

"I know."

"You need to tell them why you let the faerie go."

"Why? They'll never understand. They have no compassion for anything but themselves," Eaon spat.

"That's not true."

"I get that you love one of them, but don't try to tell me it isn't true. They're as closed-minded about the Kinner and Old Ones as the Anfar Forest Clan is about magic-less witches. They might as well be fucking Sparrows."

Selina narrowed her eyes. "You're under a lot of stress, so I'm going to forgive you for saying that."

"Which part?"

"All of it."

Eaon bit his tongue, holding back the rest of what he had to say about both clans. He was angry at Killian and taking it out on Selina, and that wasn't fair. He knew that. But right now, he hated all of them. He hated everything.

"Besides," he said instead. "I'd have to tell them what Cinn really is. It would put him in danger when he returns."

"Eaon, you need to stop worrying about him. Right now, you're the one in danger."

He could stop worrying about Cinn about as easily as he could stop the blood from pumping through his veins. "I don't care."

"That's not true."

"Yes, it is. I don't care. I don't care what happens to me. Just go away."

"Eaon."

"Go away, Selina."

Silence lingered. When it continued to linger, Eaon looked up.

Selina was gone.

CHAPTER FORTY-FOUR

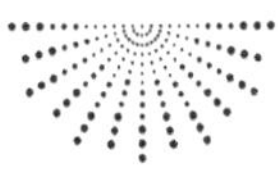

EAON

THEY DIDN'T BRING HIM OUT FOR SENTENCING. ONE OF THE guardians that stood outside his cell informed him upon rotation that the council had found him guilty of sabotaging the safety of the clan and that they now debated how he was to be punished.

Eaon didn't ask what kind of things were being suggested. He didn't ask if anyone had defended him. He didn't care.

He still didn't care when they unlocked his cell and unbound his ankles, hauling him to his feet by the length of chain they kept wrapped around his wrists. At least it wasn't digging into his skin. The cuffs he still wore padded them.

It wasn't until they had dragged him through the oddly empty warren, out into the gorge and all the way to the flat field above that the fear finally set in.

Everyone had gathered to watch. A bonfire had been prepared with a tall post standing upright in the middle of it.

Eaon had seen this done before. Sweat immediately dampened his skin.

Still, he didn't resist as they led him through the crowd. Didn't fight them as they walked him up to the stake and began to bind him to it in more chain.

There was nothing he could do except beg the Lover to let him pass this time, and let him pass quickly.

He didn't want to show them the fear that crept into his gut, but he couldn't stop from shaking, breath hitching wildly as the high priest stepped forward with the lit torch. The crowd watched stoically, silently, making Eaon's panicked breaths even louder in the clearing. Nowhere did he see a familiar face. Even if they had been there to scold him for his recklessness, he would have preferred it to being alone.

"Let Ignatius be your judge," the high priest said coldly.

Then he dropped the torch into the kindling.

A *boom* sucked the air out of the clearing as the kindling burst aflame, surrounding Eaon in an instant. He didn't care that a sob of panic broke from him, didn't care about the futility of it as he yanked at his chains.

Please, he prayed silently. *Please, please, please.*

Despite how quickly the kindling had lit, it had not moved closer to the larger pile around Eaon's legs. The heat from the fire was singeing his clothes, stray embers scalding his bare feet, but the flames themselves were not coming closer.

That's when he saw them.

Not among the crowd, but across the gorge.

Tomaii and Reigan were covered in ashy spellmarks, eyes closed and hands over a small fire they had lit on the cliff's edge. They were too far away to hear, but Eaon could see their mouths moving in sync. Saw the way the fire they prayed over held perfectly still, not even a flicker. Killian stood behind them, watching Eaon with a stern look on his face. Selina and Brach were with them, but the smoke filling the clearing blocked him from seeing their faces.

Slowly, Eaon's breathing evened out. A steady breeze blew most of the smoke away from Eaon's face. Enough to see one of the sky witches, Iniz, the one whose mount had died to the harpy, watching him, muttering under her breath too. Confusion broke out among the crowd as they realized the pyre would not burn, glancing around at each other in disbelief.

The high priest just stared.

"Seems Ignatius wishes to spare him," he addressed the crowd, even as his gaze never left Eaon. "So it shall be. Let the fire burn itself out and leave him for three days and three nights. After that, all is forgiven."

Eaon sucked in another shaky breath, his guts twisting.

Most of the crowd lingered, waiting to see if the fire really wouldn't spread. Perhaps it was out of duty to ensure the bushland didn't catch, or perhaps it was out of morbid curiosity. Eaon didn't care. The breeze didn't last and he had to focus on getting enough air. When the smoke was thicker, he buried his face in his shoulder, clenching his eyes closed. Blisters formed on his shins, the burn excruciating, yet he knew it was nothing compared to how bad it could have been.

Hours went by, but the five witches on the other side of the gorge stayed. When Reigan started to sway, Killian crouched behind her and held her upright so she could continue to do whatever magic she and Tomaii were doing to keep the flames from consuming him.

It was dusk by the time a ring of glowing embers was all that remained of the fire. The crowd had dispersed entirely, not even guardians left to keep an eye on him. Across the cliff, both Tomaii and Reigan had collapsed. Brach and Killian were preparing to carry them back inside.

He had betrayed them, and they had spared him.

Alone in the dark, wrists still bound behind the stake, Eaon let his exhausted body slide down to the ground and began to cry.

Just before dawn, Selina and Brach came to the stake. No beasts or fae had come to attack him during the night, and there had been no sign of the Old One either. He didn't know if he had them to thank for that as well, but he didn't have the energy to ask.

"Here," Selina's voice cracked as she crouched beside him and brought a cup of water to his lips.

Parched and caked with soot, Eaon drank greedily.

"I'm appealing this three days bullshit," Selina told him as she put the empty cup down and fed him pieces of mango and watermelon. "And I sent another leaf to Kaelean. They can't do this to you."

"Quick. We're not meant to be here," Brach whispered, looking around in a paranoid panic.

"You and the others are not meant to be here, but I'm Wyldeden too," Selina hissed. "I told you not to come."

Eaon ate, a heavy guilt setting into his chest. This was his own fault.

"I'll be back when I can. Just hang on, okay?" Selina told him, forcing a smile before standing up and following Brach back down into the gorge.

Eaon had been baking in the sun so long he could barely see. Everything was white and red. His body had stopped sweating but his clothes were soaked, the stink overpowering the taste of salt in his mouth. The trial by fire had failed, but the heat-stroke would kill him. Or he wished it would. Flashes of black kept dancing across his vision and, every time, he wished it was some beast come to finish him off.

But nothing came, and he continued to bake.

Water trickled over his chapped lips. Before he was even fully conscious his mouth was opening, searching for more.

"That's it." Killian's low timbre was recognizable, even through the haze in his head. "There's more where that came from. But you need to get up for me, okay?"

Get up?

Eaon realized he was laying on the ground, his wrists free from the chains, but not the cuffs. His skin was ablaze but inside he was ice, bones clattering from an impossible cold. He didn't remember going to the void again, but he must have. If only for a moment.

Cracking open his eyes, Killian lay on the ground beside him while Selina hovered nearby, holding his confiscated staff.

"Kaelean sent back a message, threatening to wage war on the mountain clan if they didn't stop punishing you," Selina explained. "She's really scary when she's mad."

Eaon closed his eyes, panting hard. He needed more water. Shade.

"You can rest with the others. It's not far, but I can't carry you," Killian said, regret lacing the words. Then he tipped more water into Eaon's mouth.

Heavy as a fallen oak, Eaon moved his arm. Rolled to his side. Shifted his legs until he got his knees on the ground, gritting his teeth as the burns on his shins pressed against the dry ground.

"That's it. You got it. You can do it."

Killian got up with him, and Selina let go of his staff as he took a hold of it. Inch by inch, he climbed to his feet, leaning so hard on his staff it began to bend.

Then there was walking. One foot in front of the other. Eaon focused on moving—not the pain he was in, not the worry about what relations between the two clans was going to be like now because of him. There was only walking and water.

Somehow, he made it inside the warren. Then he made it to someone's cave. A blanket had been put out for him to lie on, Tomaii and Reigan both passed out on the floor with damp cloths over their foreheads.

He looked at them, then to Killian, tongue still too dry to form words.

"They overheated," was all he said.

Eaon's head swam, knees buckling as he reached the blanket.

"I'll get something to treat those burns," Selina said quietly, ducking out of the room.

"Some of Reigan's salve is in my room," Killian called after her.

More water was given to him and Eaon drank fiendishly. It hadn't been much longer than a day, but the heat . . .

His breath hitched as it dawned on him how much longer he might have had to suffer out there if Kaelean hadn't intervened. This was not like when she had helped at the Copeland farm—Cinn was important to her, and she hated the Sparrows, and there had been so many reasons why he knew she would come to their aid. But this was just him. She knew he would not die, and he had made it pretty clear he was thinking about going wild . . . She had no reason to help him.

"It's alright. Lie down," Killian told him, anger underpinning his tone as he took the empty water container away.

"I'm sorry," Eaon croaked, wincing at the sound of his voice. Lowering himself as carefully as he could, Eaon eased onto the blanket and shuddered through another too-emotional breath.

He'd messed everything up.

"Don't you ever say that again," Killian hissed. "You were right to challenge them, and they're fucking animals for trying to kill you over it."

Eaon tried to frown, but his face hurt from the sunburn he no doubt had. Killian caught the expression anyway and sighed loudly.

"You think I'm mad at *you*, don't you? Your brain must be truly cooked."

The sweat-soaked clothes were growing cold in the shade of the cave, and Eaon was too busy trying to stay conscious as he began to shiver to think too much about what Killian was saying.

"Get some sleep, Eaon. You'll feel better when you wake up."

Then Killian waved a sweet-smelling cloth soaked in something dark under his nose and Eaon passed out once more.

CHAPTER FORTY-FIVE

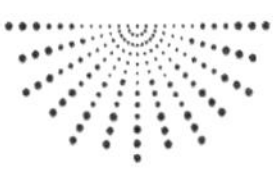

AISLING

AISLING WAS NOT AS BLESSED AS HER FATHER. NOT BY THE LOVER and not by Celeste. Opening a portal was taxing and opening one all the way to Dusarn to steal a vial of unicorn blood would drain her, at least for a few hours. After drinking a full liter of water, she packed a canteen and a pouch of food to help her recharge. Then she changed into dark clothes, including a cloak with a hood to hide her hair and pale skin.

"You could boost your power with the marks."

Davina's voice was quiet, her silhouette more shadowed than usual. It had only been ten hours since they had returned from Wyldeden, leaving Volya to be pampered by the stable hands, but in that time Davina had made herself scarce.

"You're still mad at me," Aisling said, strapping on a couple of thigh harnesses and tucking silver daggers into the scabbards.

"What makes you think that?" Davina asked, but she didn't deny it.

Aisling gave her a look. "You disappeared in Wyldeden after we got the diary, and aside from yelling at me you barely spoke to me. At least tell me why."

"I couldn't stand what you did to that Morvish witch."

Aisling shivered at the pain in Davina's voice. "Because she's Morvish, or because it makes me my father's daughter?"

"Both."

Aisling straightened and belted another harness around her waist, attaching pouches of salt and rowanberries. "Even before that, you weren't around. Not much since Eavha came to play chess with me."

"Don't," Davina snapped. "This is not about her. Eavha is lovely. She softens you."

"I would understand if you were jealous."

"Of course I am jealous, but that still has nothing to do with it. I told you that you needed to start practicing with the witchmarks, and you ignored me. I *died* for those witchmarks, died to protect you, Aisling. You don't get to ignore me."

"I'm doing everything you suggested. I'm following the plan, I'm playing the game. But I still have a city to run, and I am tired, Davina. I will practice, but I can't just drop everything to do what you want."

"You wouldn't be so tired if you stopped drinking."

"Don't start."

"The fate of our entire land rests on your shoulders—"

"Why do you think I drink?" Aisling hissed, shouldering her bag.

A knock on the door interrupted them, and Eavha didn't wait before sticking her head in. She was wearing that pretty pink ensemble again, highlighting the blush in her skin and offsetting the golden tones in her eyes.

"Oh, you're going already?"

"No time to waste, remember?" Aisling forced a smile.

"Give me a minute and I'll change. I'll—"

"No," Aisling interrupted her. "Not to Dusarn. It's far too dangerous."

"What if you're hurt?"

"I'll portal out and you can heal me when I get back."

Eavha frowned and crossed her arms. Aisling couldn't help but notice what the pose did for her breasts.

"I cannot allow you to risk yourself," Aisling continued.

"I understand." Eavha placed a hand over her sternum. "You alone must bear the burden of fighting Chaos's inevitable return. I shall languish by the lake and await your noble sacrifice."

"Are you mocking me?"

"Thoroughly."

Aisling smiled softly. "Please. Wait here."

Dropping her arms, Eavha sighed deeply and looked toward the open balcony doors. "Alright. I'll wait right here."

"Thank you." Pulling her hood up, Aisling gave her arm an affectionate squeeze before turning toward the window.

Taking a deep breath of the cooling end-of-summer air, Aisling stirred her Celeste-blessing. In the center of her sternum, right between her own breasts, were tattooed Marks of Concentration. The ink Davina had used was laced with all kinds of insidious things that had left her ill for days after each tattoo, but they turned the simple mark into something far stronger than it was ever designed to be.

She knew Davina was right. She ought to be practicing wielding them, but she was afraid. Of what, exactly, she wasn't sure, but the anxiety every time she thought of trying one of them made her deeply nauseated. But she didn't need them now. When the time came, that fear would be gone.

Reaching forward with her destination in mind, Aisling offered her intentions to Celeste. The air rippled at her fingertips, smooth as a curtain of ultraviolet silk that merely needed to be parted. Grabbing a hold of the filmy edges, the magic coursing through Aisling's veins speared out, ripping a tear into the sky realm. Pure light blinded her, a blast of wind whipping her hair back, but she trusted as she stepped into the tear that the Spirit would take her where she needed to go.

As she took her first step, someone grabbed her arm and pushed.

***

Aisling fell out of the portal, Eavha landing heavily on top of her. The rip in Celeste's realm closed, vacuuming the air as the two of them lay panting on the ground.

"You absolute lunatic!"

Aisling shoved Eavha off, but the priestess was too busy staring at their surroundings to bother with her rage. Blasted sands as bleached and gray as a corpse peaked and dipped in dunes as far as the eye could see, only broken by the strange shrubbery that spotted the crests. The full moonlight glistened off obsidian leaves, fat bloodberries hanging heavily from the low-hanging branches of shrubs. Muted green-and-pink succulents grew between them, some as large as a goat, their thirsty flowers arching for the cloudless sky.

That anything could grow at all in the barren landscape had always impressed Aisling. In the wet seasons, the storms that blew through the Sparrow Coven's homeland were so wild and fierce the rain fell sideways, barely dampening the sands and forcing the sparse trees to grow at strange angles.

This close to the walls of Dusarn, the fae and beasts that roamed freely through the territory kept their distance. A moat of rock salt surrounded the towering silver and iron walls, the bridge itself carved with wards warning the bravest of creatures that they were not welcomed here. It didn't stop all of them, of course, but the few who still managed to slither their way inside the city walls didn't usually last long.

Aisling got to her feet, dizzy from the magic, and brushed the fine gray sand from her knees. Then she offered Eavha a hand. The pink outfit that was so cute a moment ago was now a liability.

"What happened to staying in Hyrsch?" Aisling hissed, keeping her voice low as she peered toward the ridge of the city walls. Guards patrolled there, armed with silver and iron-tipped arrows, but their pace had not faltered; she had not been caught yet.

"I lied."

"Obviously."

Eavha righted her skirt as she wriggled her toes on the strange sand. Loose enough to lose your toes in, yet firm enough to walk without sinking. "I will not let you do this alone. I told you that."

Aisling scowled, grabbing Eavha's elbow and dragging her behind a nearby bush, its leaves glowing neon black.

"You're a fucking beacon. Here," Aisling hissed, shrugging off her cloak and wrapping it around Eavha.

"Ugh, why is it so hot?" Eavha whined as she sagged beneath the extra fabric.

"Because it's Dusarn," Aisling said bitterly. "If I'd known you were so stubborn I would have made you change."

"Well, now you know." Eavha sniffed, entirely unapologetic. "Why did you come out here? Why not inside the city?"

"They might not be as good as the ones surrounding Anfar, but the wards that keep fae out of the city do a good job of repelling other kinds of magic, too. I . . . I'm not well-blessed enough to do it."

Again, she thought of Davina's scolding. Her frustration with Aisling for not using the marks tattooed on her skin. She could have easily had the portal lead directly into the apothecary if she activated just two of them, but then what? She was still getting her head together after the magic she *had* used to jump this far; more would not be better.

Which is what the practice was meant to prepare her for, she supposed. As always, Davina was right, and Aisling was being a coward.

"Even with your Blessing Charm?" Eavha asked, eyes roaming down to the concealed feather tucked between Aisling's breasts.

"This is not the time for this discussion," Aisling warned, peering back over the bush. "Follow me. And try not to make any loud noises."

Eavha raised a brow. "You're telling me to be quiet?"

Aisling grimaced. That was pretty stupid.

Silently, the two of them crept through the dunes toward the moat of salt. Rather than lead Eavha toward the bridge, she took her around to a cluster of blown-over ghost trees. The angle they had grown at leaned away from the wall, which was the only reason they hadn't been removed. There was no way anything could use them to get over the moat. Aisling had also argued that the Coven ought not to disturb the wilderness more than absolutely necessary. Though they did not worship the elemental spirits after Passing, denying their existence was impossible and so respecting what little of Terra's dominion thrived in Kerveda was wise.

Her parents had agreed, for once, and let the cluster be.

As they approached, Aisling reached into her satchel and pulled out a handful of salt. Among the pale wood, tiny white lights blinked to life. Wisps the size of Aisling's pinkie finger watched them approach in eerie silence, broadcasting their whereabouts for all to see. Aisling flung salt at them, which they danced and dodged, prattling in their tiny voices in a language impossible to understand. But they didn't scatter.

Eavha chuckled as one perched on the back of her hand.

"They're so friendly."

"They'll get us caught."

Shooing them a little more urgently, Aisling dragged Eavha behind the thickest trunk. She used to think these trees were spooky and strange, but after being in Anfar they had lost their allure. The scraggly roots clinging to the sand, straining to keep the tree from toppling over, obscured an odd rise in the sand that, when she brushed it away, revealed a trapdoor. Ungloving her hand, she used the one mark she was comfortable with to unlock the iron-and-silver-laced wooden door and pull it open.

Eavha peered down into the dark tunnel. Barely wide enough for a body, the tunnel was at a slope subtle enough to allow someone to climb it, or to slide down it.

The wisps were already crowding in, curious.

"Go," Aisling shoved Eavha, who squeaked as she slipped into the tunnel.

Aisling went in after her, pulling the door closed and muttering the locking spell aloud. Only after she heard the clunk of it did she release the handle. Metal bars and planks of wood kept the sand at bay as she slid down the slope after Eavha, who had covered her mouth to contain her screeching. The dark was absolute, but Aisling knew this tunnel well enough not to need light. As the slope petered out, the tunnel widened enough to let them turn around. Aisling put a hand on Eavha's back and urged her to crawl forward.

"This feels like a very convenient flaw in Dusarn's defenses," Eavha muttered as she led the way through the dark.

"Well it should. I dug it myself," Aisling whispered back. "We're under the moat now. In about ten minutes there will be a rise. At the top will be another trapdoor. We might have to switch so I can open it. We will come out into the cellar of an old friend of mine within the city walls."

"And from there?" Eavha asked.

"From there, we will make our way to the apothecary. Stay close and don't touch anything. I'll steal the unicorn blood and we will get back out the same way."

"You can't just ask for it?" Eavha asked.

Aisling sighed. "The Coven is not as generous as your high priestess."

They went along in silence for a while before Eavha asked another question.

"Why did you make this tunnel?"

"To escape, obviously."

"But why?"

Aisling twisted her mouth as she considered what to say. In the end, she decided on honesty. "I wasn't always sure I wanted to undertake the Passing. But if I didn't, only Nevan would be eligible for the throne once the king and queen passed. And even all those years ago I knew I couldn't let that happen without a fight. There's something intrinsically wrong with him, as if he was born without a soul. If you think the ruling of the Sparrow Coven is cruel now, it would only be worse with Nevan at the head.

"So even though I didn't use this tunnel to escape the Passing, I still used it to get out of Dusarn sometimes. Davina and I would escape in the middle of the night and catch wild horses, riding them through the dunes until I was sure I would see my final Passing. It was . . . fun. Such things are limited for a princess, you know."

Eavha continued to shuffle forward, eventually saying, "Makes sense."

They reached the upward slope and conversation stopped. In the narrow space, Aisling managed to squeeze past Eavha, trying not to notice the easy give of her body, the softness of her as they were briefly pressed together. How little fabric the priestess wore.

It wasn't an easy climb, and Aisling was relieved to reach the top, unlocking the trapdoor and pushing it open.

She poked her head out and stilled. Two royal guards stood at attention, watching her.

Within a second, she was pulling one of her many masks on. Her face went blank, as if she was not remotely bothered to see them, clambering out of the tunnel and promptly shutting the trapdoor behind her. Standing on top of it, not trusting Eavha to stay hidden, Aisling clasped her hands before the guards and lifted her chin.

"Well don't just stand there," she snapped, lowering her voice. "I'm tired from the journey. Some water."

To be honest, she was a little surprised when one of them turned to climb the stairs back to the main house. The other, a large female she did not recognize, dipped her chin.

"Your Highness."

Aisling offered nothing. No explanation. No excuses. They would only make her look guilty of something.

The guard returned with a pitcher of water and a crystal glass. After pouring it full, he sipped a little before handing it to her. Aisling waited to see if he would react to a poison before drinking deeply.

"Well," she said as she placed the empty glass down on a nearby wine barrel. "Is an escort waiting for me? I don't particularly wish to walk to the castle."

"Of course, Your Highness," the second guard said.

Not an ounce of hostility or suspicion. They were playing the game, too.

Enunciating clearly, Aisling cast the locking spell over the trapdoor before stepping off it and following the guards up to the city above.

CHAPTER FORTY-SIX

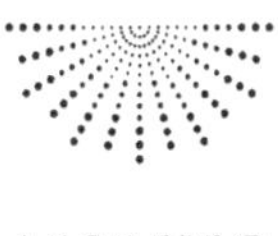

AISLING

Of course, it would be distasteful to present herself to the Sparrow Coven in the state she was in, so the guards led the way to her old rooms to clean up. As she marched through the familiar halls of her childhood home, servants and courtiers stopped to stare. The gray body suit, dusted with sand, and the windswept braid in a pillar down her spine was so far removed from the polished princess they remembered that some of the easily startled ladies even squeaked at the sight.

Everything was the same. The black wallpaper with gilded sparrows patterned across it covered the halls, the floor covered in rugs with literal gold threads running through it. Chandeliers and sconces crusted with crystals held balls of everlight, made by a few of the Igni-blessed witches who'd come to Dusarn wishing to join the Sparrow ranks. Most were turned away, but not before they had given their gifts in an attempt to buy a place.

Tapestries and paintings of each member of the Coven, both old and new, lined the walls in jeweled frames, watching her. It wasn't all in her mind. Her Lover-blessing let her see which of Coven members had remained in the void after their final Passing, wandering the halls or standing by their portraits, listening to what people had to say about them. Aisling pretended she didn't see them, lest they begin to follow her.

Only Davina was different. She had returned again, standing in the corner of Aisling's old rooms as the guards put her inside and locked the door.

"Is Eavha okay?" she asked first.

Davina nodded. "I believe so. This was a foolish plan."

Aisling went to her window first, opening the glass until the hot night air brought in the scents of the city below. The sprawling mass of it was twice as large as Hyrsch, its population twice that again. Homes were squashed together and overcrowded, a cesspool of infection and disease. Only those who lived within the castle knew luxury, and only those deemed fit to take the Passing were permitted in. Witches came from all over Nir, hoping to be allowed to Pass. Healers were brought to test their skills and train in necromancy, while others who worshipped Balance simply wished to stay near the Lover's temple, to be close to the High Spirit of Death and the birthplace of the Sparrow Coven, believing it the holiest of places. The rest of the city was human, too frail to face the fae and beasts outside the city walls in order to find somewhere else to live.

As for the demi-kin, Dusarn was a birthplace of sorts for them, too. It was the first city to be taken by the Coven during the Second War with the Kinner. The first city of the new era, ruled by Balance and what was thought to be justice for witches everywhere. Humans were reminded that they only lived because of the sacrifices magic wielders had made in the First War, and the Kinner were reminded of who it was that gave them immortality in the first place. Their half-breed offspring would pay an eternal price for what their ancestors had done to witches, and so Dusarn had become the birthplace of slavery.

For as long as she could remember, her teachers had drummed on about the righteousness of the Sparrow Coven. Their bravery and justness. The Kinner were more than myth inside the palace walls, but to speak of them outside the classroom was blasphemous. Again, as a child she had not understood, but after reading Sanni's diary it was making sense. The Kinner, or as her teachers described them, "those rotten, selfish, ungrateful leeches," had been happy to take from magic, but had turned their back on it during its time of need. And then they wondered why Death themself took the witches' side.

She had listened and absorbed it all, and yet when Nevan would take her to play with the demi-kin he'd bought in that dark, cold room below the palace, she had not enjoyed it. She looked at those people with their metal collars and concaved cheeks and been unable to see how they deserved it.

Then Davina had come.

"Aisling," she called, coming to stand beside her once more. "You need to use the marks I gave you. Portal to the apothecary right now, then go right back to Hyrsch."

The apothecary was only a block away; a squat, domed building that took up an entire block, gilded spikes piercing into the night. The Coven's flag sporting the Sparrow crest lay limp from the tallest spire, the night's flat heat without a lifting breeze.

"What about Eavha?"

"She wouldn't even be a problem if you'd gone straight to the apothecary. You wouldn't have been caught. Your mother would not be waiting for you in her rooms. It is too dangerous to linger here. One wrong word, and everything could unravel."

"Your lectures are becoming tiresome."

"Then listen to me!" she screeched, and Aisling felt a waft of impossible cold brush over her skin. Davina's frustration was pushing through the veil between realms.

"Okay," Aisling hissed. "Enough. When I get back to Hyrsch I will practice. But here and now is not the time to test things for the first time."

The hair on the back of Aisling's neck rose a moment before a bronzed hand shot up in the window, clinging to the sill. Aisling flinched back, reaching for her dagger before recognizing the soft grunt of effort coming from outside.

"Lover take me," Aisling hissed, rushing forward to grab Eavha's hand. The Wyldeden witch was a limpet on the outside of the castle wall, toes on holds Aisling could not see. Hauling her in through the window, she stared at Eavha with her heart in her throat, stomach in her boots. "Are you insane!"

"Thanks," she panted, pulling off the cloak and shaking her fingertips. "That was much harder than your palace in Hyrsch."

Aisling was sure her eyes were about to fall out of her face as she continued to stare at Eavha. Never in all her life had she met a witch as ridiculous and absurd and stupid.

"Oh, calm down before you burst that vein in your forehead."

"How did you get out of the tunnel?" she hissed.

"You think I don't know how to unlock a spelled door? I'm a little offended."

She hadn't said as much in the tunnels when Aisling had squeezed past her.

"I am a bit worried about your guards though. I followed the carriage all the way to the castle and they didn't even notice."

"On foot? Bare foot?" Aisling shook her head, looking down to Eavha's dirty feet.

"Well I certainly didn't do it with your stupid feet traps on. And then once I saw you brooding out your window, it was just a matter of climbing up."

Aisling looked out the window to the eight-story drop into the gardens. How long had she been staring out at the city to not even notice? How had the guards not even noticed?

"You are . . ." she started, but didn't know what exactly she wanted to call Eavha.

"I know." She grinned and flipped her hair over her shoulder. "I would have just gone straight to the apothecary, but I actually don't know what unicorn blood even looks like."

Davina was staring too, but unlike Aisling she had a little smile on her face. "You could learn something from this one."

Aisling huffed, then turned for her wardrobe. "My parents are expecting me. I'll take care of them while you . . . clamber your way to the apothecary."

It wasn't ideal, but clearly she had underestimated Eavha. The Anfar witches were as wraithlike and spooky as their forest. If she could cross the city and climb the palace wall without being spotted, perhaps she would be able to get in and out of the apothecary on her own.

"The blood is not hard to identify. It will be locked in a glass cabinet and spelled ten ways to the void, but look for something similar to liquid mercury, but pearlescent."

"Like Cinn's mark," Eavha said, rolling her eyes. "Of course. Obviously. Stupid Eavha."

The name made Aisling blink, but she quickly buried the nausea and pulled out one of her old black-and-gold pleated dresses.

"Are you sure you don't want me to come with you?" Eavha asked as she watched Aisling unbraid her hair and begin brushing it out.

"How exactly would I explain that?"

"True."

Still, Eavha lingered. Aisling ignored her as she washed her face from a bowl of rosewater a maid had left on the vanity. Grains of sand fell from every pore. She had only been in the dunes a few minutes, but the itch of it was everywhere.

Leaving her bodysuit on, Aisling pulled the formal gown over the top. It was too hot, but she didn't want to risk not having a chance to return and change back.

"Go, Eavha," Aisling said as she twisted her hair into a coronet. "Davina is with me."

"I'll meet you back at the tunnels," she said softly.

When Aisling finished her hair and turned back, Eavha was gone.

She hadn't even heard her open the window.

Halfway to her mother's room, Aisling and the two guards that had found her were stopped. A man dressed in the royal black-and-gold armor of the Sparrow Coven stepped in front of them, raising his square jaw with a hand on his sword.

"I need to speak to the princess."

Aisling eyed him, sure he was familiar, but it was Davina who placed him.

"He was at your Imsa. One of the king's guard."

The guards argued for a moment, but regardless of whether she was being considered suspicious for sneaking into Dusarn in the manner she had, she was still Princess Aisling Aurnia, and it was high time she remembered how to act like it.

"Enough," she hissed. Immediately, they all fell silent. "I will speak with him."

"Your mother insisted you be brought straight to her," the guards from the cellar argued.

"And I am insisting that I speak with my father's guard," she snapped, letting her eyes glitter with vicious cold.

She had a reputation in Dusarn. And the guards knew it. They stepped back, and Aisling followed the king's guard down a ways until they reached a private alcove. The other guards were still watching intently, so she made the king's guard stand with his back to them, hiding herself behind his tall frame.

He sagged with relief as soon as his face was hidden.

"Princess, I've been trying to reach you for some time."

"Does this have to do with my father?"

"Yes." He swallowed, glancing around nervously. "Though, I . . . I'm not here on his behalf, princess. I'm here to warn you."

She sneered, lifting an eyebrow. "I may be young, but I am no fool."

The guard took a steadying breath. "Your father has been conspiring against you because you are right. You are right about Chaos and he knows it. They all know it."

Aisling's face darkened as she glared up at him. "Be very careful what you say next."

The guard looked around once more, but they were alone. Still, he softened his voice even further. "There are a few of us here who have been trying to get word to you, but the Sparrow Coven is onto us. Chaos has the queen's ear. She told the king he had to stop you from gaining allies at Imsa, or kill you."

That, she had not expected. And she didn't know whether she could take what the guard was saying at face value.

"I'll investigate this," Davina said, disappearing.

"What you are saying is treason," she warned the guard.

A muscle in his jaw twitched. "What is a bit of treason in the face of Chaos's return?"

"I could have you executed for lying about the Sparrow Coven. They could have you executed for sharing Coven secrets."

"Then do it."

She liked him. "What is your name?"

"Foley, Your Highness."

"Foley. You want my advice?"

"Please," he practically begged.

"Gather whoever is brave enough to dissent and get them out of this city. Get them to Hyrsch as fast you can. You will be protected there."

"Protected? Your Highness, we want to stop this."

She didn't expect it to hit so hard. This man standing before her in her parent's colors, her coven's colors, wanting to help her. The ache almost made her do something stupid, like smile. She would not trust this. Not yet.

"I appreciate that, Foley. But we are dealing with a primordial deity here, and you are human. We need people in Hyrsch, so if you want to help, go there."

He seemed disappointed, but nodded. "I'll meet you there, Your Highness."

He bowed deeply, then walked away. The other guards came to get her.

"What did he want that was so important?"

"To ask about my recovery after Imsa," she lied. "Now, take me to my mother. I assume she has something important to talk to me about."

The queen's rooms were at the highest point of the castle, across the hall from the king's suite. The door was open, warm light spilling out from the fireplace and oil lamps burning on the wall, all of which were unnecessary in the middle of Dusarn's hottest season. By the time the guards guided her in, Aisling was sweating profusely.

"Ah, my daughter."

Queen Tallula lounged awkwardly on a settee, putting down a bowl of some strange dark porridge. Across the room, as far from the fireplace as he could be, King Phineas leaned against the wall with his arms crossed over his chest. The guards waited outside and closed the door, leaving the three of them alone. Or as alone as her parents ever were. Servants, all human of course, worked around the queen, keeping her plate full, the fire burning hot.

Aisling stood frozen in the threshold. She had not seen her mother in five, almost six years, since leaving Dusarn to take over control of Hyrsch, but she did not expect her to be so changed.

"Don't tell me you never heard the rumors," Queen Tallula teased as she rolled to a slightly more upright position, passing her bowl to a servant as she held her enormous swollen belly.

"I had not," Aisling lied. "You're pregnant."

Davina materialized beside her once more, holding back whatever she was about to say when she saw the queen.

"That's not normal," Davina told Aisling, "There must be four babies in there."

"I am." Tallula smiled, oblivious to Davina's presence. "Due any day now."

"Congratulations," Aisling managed, folding her hands in front of her. "I'm sorry to have disturbed you during such a precarious time."

"Disturb me?" Tallula chuckled darkly, looking to her servant, who instinctively knew to bring the queen a goblet of some kind of sweet-smelling juice. The instant, almost psychic bond between them reminded Aisling of how she used to be with Edwina. The comparison revolted her. "You were trying very hard not to disturb me, weren't you? Caught sneaking into the city through your old tunnel like a mischievous child. Yes, obviously I knew about that. Why you didn't just come through the gate is bewildering."

The tone her mother used was light and amused, but Aisling knew better than to trust it. After all, it was from Tallula that Aisling had learned how to don her costumes. Through all of this, Phineas remained still and silent across the room, watching the interaction as one might an intense game of chess.

"I didn't want to cause a scene with my arrival," she said truthfully.

"That's new for you," Tallula smiled around her goblet as she drank deeply.

"Careful," Davina said. "The other ghosts speak of Tallula's bloodthirstiness lately. Many servants and guards have met an early passing. They speak of monsters prowling the underground levels at night, and strange people with beast-like features roaming the halls."

Aisling nodded, both for Davina and her mother.

"Yes, but you see, I still have the heir of Wyldeden at my palace in Hyrsch and only meant to be here briefly. It is not ideal to leave our old enemies alone in my city for long, but I knew if I came in the gates you would insist on seeing me, which you did anyway, and this meeting is already taking longer than I truly wish to be away from home."

Mention of Eavha brought the king a step closer, hands falling to his sides.

Tallula cocked her head as she gave Aisling a once over. "You're bolder than you used to be."

"Ruling changes a person. You always said you wished me to show more spine."

Davina hovered closer, her transparent hand reaching for Aisling's, as if she could comfort her. Pandering to the queen would not please her, so Aisling hadn't bothered for many years before leaving for Hyrsch. Being pleasant now would only rouse suspicion.

"I suppose." The queen looked once more to her servant, who returned her bowl of mulberry-dark porridge to her. "But please, don't tell me you've taken another idealistic lover in this heir. A Qiri witch is one thing, but Anfar? Ugh. I can't stand to see you corrupted any further."

Aisling bristled, cheeks heating. "No, mother. We are just discussing an alliance."

"Still?" King Phineas finally said.

Aisling narrowed her eyes in his direction. "Despite your best efforts. You did say it would be wise regardless, didn't you?"

Phineas said nothing as Tallula sighed, rolling her eyes. But there was a sudden tightness in the queen's shoulders as she rolled the word around in her mouth. "An alliance. And you sanctioned this?"

Tallula acknowledged Phineas's presence for the first time. He gave a single nod. "It would be a mistake to close any avenues to procuring the land."

Tallula snorted, then winced as she adjusted her position on the settee. "What was your first lesson with me, Aisling?"

"We don't make deals—"

"—with peasants," Tallula finished in tandem, looking down her nose.

Thank the Mother Eavha wasn't there to hear that. Aisling wasn't sure what the Wyldeden witch would have done, but she doubted it would have been good.

"Say nothing," Davina warned her, watching Tallula like a hawk watched a mouse. "She is trying to bait you."

Aisling stood silently until her mother finally narrowed her eyes. "I—"

"It was my call, Tal," Phineas interrupted. "I stand by it."

The hostility her mother cast toward the king was unprecedented. "We will discuss it later." Then to Aisling, "Tell me, what is it you needed from your true home so urgently that you could not spare a single moment to speak with me?"

"Just an old necklace," she lied. "A gift for the heir."

"Wouldn't a new one from one of the artisans in that city be better?"

"Would you think so, if I gave you a human-made trinket?"

"Fair enough," Tallula chuckled. She looked Aisling over once more. "But please, next time just use the door. It is unseemly to have the princess crawling around in the sand like a worm."

"May I ask"—Aisling ignored the insult—"what happened to the porter who used to live there? Why were there guards waiting for me?"

Tallula finished her porridge and handed it to her servant, patting her lips clean before answering. "A breach in Dusarn's security was not to be taken lightly. The porter was appropriately punished for allowing such a thing to develop. As for the guards, they've been there the entire time since your little escape route was discovered. The porter told us it was you who dug it, but I was curious to see if you were still using it. Now that I know, I'll have it closed up."

Shit. Eavha.

"I left things in the tunnel. Has it already been collapsed?"

The queen eyed her, thin brows puckering. "Surely anything left behind can be easily replaced."

Aisling nodded. "True."

Inside, a storm was brewing. Panic chilled her bones as she tried to figure out how she was going to get Eavha out of this city without using her tattoos.

"But for what it's worth, I have not yet made the order. Go and collect your things before you leave. And I promise not to waste your time with pleasantries the next time you deign to visit me."

Aisling bowed. "Thank you. I did not mean to offend you."

"Of course you did. But it matters not. I am tired, so you can go to find your necklace. Darrington will escort you."

"I remember the way back to my own room."

"I know." Maybe she couldn't find a flaw in Aisling's lies, but she did not trust her to roam the castle alone.

Aisling curtsied. "Send my regards to Nevan if you see him."

"Bah. Idiot child. I hope I don't." Tallula waved a hand, rubbing her belly with the other.

That was possibly the biggest surprise of all. Nevan had always been Tallula's favorite.

But now she wanted a new heir. That much was clear. One to fit with the new regime she wanted to see come in. Which means she thought Nevan would not be suitable. Or, if what the guard said was true, he would not support Chaos. Which would have been a very interesting bit of information had she not already sent Nora and Owen to Pirevia to deal with him.

With a final glance to her father, who was staring with an intensity Aisling didn't understand, she allowed the guards to escort her from the queen's rooms.

CHAPTER FORTY-SEVEN

EAVHA

As heavy and uncomfortable as Aisling's cloak was, it helped her blend into the strange sandstone buildings as she clambered down the castle walls, then up the side of the apothecary. Her fingers were bruised, nails chipped and bleeding, as were her toes, but she didn't complain as she crept along the windowsills of the apothecary, looking for somewhere to climb inside.

Well, she didn't complain out loud. She was going to be incredibly sore for the next few days, her legs and arms, her core, her everything already aching in protest.

But she had told Aisling she would not have to do this alone and she meant it.

Once, she had watched the female guardians in Wyldeden training and been jealous of the strength and power of their bodies. In her mind, she imagined she was training to be one of them. Imagined them below, watching and judging her, and she refused to fail. To fall.

Finally, she found an empty treatment room. Holding all her weight on her toes, biting her lip through the further tearing of her ruined feet, she clawed at the window frame until she had enough of a grasp to pull it open. Then she hauled herself inside, collapsed on the floor, and covered her face to mask the sob of relief.

Giving herself a moment to catch her breath, she looked around the room from where she lay on the marble tiles. Cabinets lined the walls, laden with jars of things Eavha didn't recognize and was fairly sure she didn't want to know about. A steel table with a drain in it sat in the middle of the room, a large bucket underneath. The kind of table that probably wasn't used for living patients.

Sitting up, she held her bloody fingertips to her mouth and muttered a self-healing spell. It was still strange, needing to verbalize spells, but her Blessing Charm was not strong enough yet to cast everything wordlessly again. Bandages and balms would have helped, but she doubted she was going to find anything like that in here. When her fingers were better, she took another moment to hold each of her feet, reciting the spell over and over until the pain had eased enough to let her walk.

Despite doubting she would find unicorn blood in a room like this, she searched the cupboards anyway. She did find a cloth to wipe up the smears of dark blood she'd left on the white floors, removing any obvious evidence that she had been there before going to the door. The clacking of shoes on the corridor tiles gave away that it wasn't safe for her to wander yet, so she waited until there was only silence before cracking the wooden door and peeking out. Sconces holding candles lined the halls, casting flickering shadows that made her flinch. But the hall was empty.

Creeping quickly, she counted the doors that she already knew were occupied from her spying through the exterior windows. When the hall turned, she began listening again; one ear to the door, the other hoping nobody came down the halls behind her.

Sanni guide me, she prayed silently as she moved to the next door, taking her Blessing Charm from beneath her chest binding and clutching it delicately. *If it is your will to help me, show me where to find the unicorn blood.*

She repeated it in her mind, over and over, until she stood outside a door and felt a shiver run down her spine. Listening carefully, she didn't hear anything from inside, so she turned the handle and slipped in.

Empty. And there against the wall was a glass cabinet, hosting five vials of glimmering pearlescent liquid.

"Thank you," she whispered, kissing the charm before approaching the cabinet.

Opening herself up to the magic clinging to the glass, she felt the threads of the different locks and alarms that had been cast over it. Unlike the generic locking spell on the tunnel door that Eavha had been able to undo with half a thought, too many of these ones were made with Lover-blessings that she would not be able to get past.

There wasn't time to wait around for Aisling to figure out she needed help, nor were there any leaves to send a message with.

"What would Eaon do?" she asked herself. Eaon, who without magic for most of his life, had managed to do things on his own just fine.

Chewing her lip, Eavha flicked her hair over her shoulder and looked around the room for inspiration. The idea that came to her wasn't subtle, but it would have to do.

Trembling, she went to the window that faced the opposite side of the city than that she had approached from and pushed it open. The building wasn't quite tall enough to let her look over the streets, but she had a rough idea of where she needed to go. Then she went back to the door and cast a Terra-based locking spell. It would give away what kind of witch had been in their city, but it wouldn't be traceable to her or the Anfar Forest Clan specifically. It would also slow down anyone alerted by the spells on the cabinet when she took the vials.

Along another wall was a long desk with an intricate diffusion system slowly dripping some kind of solution into a beaker. She wasn't interested in that, but picked up the heavy stone-bound book beside it and weighted it in her hands.

"Sorry about this," she whispered to it.

Counting to three, she heaved the book over her shoulder and smashed it against the glass cabinet. As it shattered loudly, a pulse of nauseating magic burst through the room. But she had felt that kind of magic before, able to ignore the way it prickled against her skin and churned her stomach, only gagging slightly as she took all five vials of unicorn blood and slipped them inside her chest binding.

Already, she could hear the noisy clacking of multiple sets of feet running through the hall, so she ran to the window and leaped, praying to Terra the whole way as she plummeted the four stories down. The black-leaved bushes below responded, softening her fall, their branches catching her in a hammock. Still, she would feel the bruises tomorrow.

Pulling the cloak over her head, she clambered out of the shrubbery and ran.

It was hours before Aisling met her in the tunnels. The guards had not returned, so she'd been able to slide back down into the darkness to wait, glad for the coolness of it on her sweat-soaked skin. When Aisling arrived, the awful dress she had been putting on back in the castle was gone.

"Thank the Mother," Aisling sighed when she found Eavha waiting for her. "Are you alright?"

"Better than alright," she answered, pressing her hand against the cool glass vials against her chest. "I've got them."

"How much?"

"Five vials."

It was hard to see in the shadows, but Eavha thought she saw Aisling nodding.

"Five vials. Five kinner."

The witchmark in Sanni's diary had given an exact quantity to use for the spell, but Aisling was right. Judging just by eye, there would likely be enough for one casting per vial.

"Five kinners are better than no kinners," Eavha told her. Volunteer kinners, too, she added silently. Not ones that had been violently convinced to help against their wishes.

"We will have to hope it is enough."

"Were you followed?"

"No. Were you?"

Eavha snorted, then flinched as Aisling laughed. She wasn't sure she had heard the princess do that before and was surprised by the light, girlish sound of it.

"I really need to stop asking such stupid questions," Aisling explained before squeezing past Eavha to take the lead down the tunnel.

***

Dearmead was waiting for them in Aisling's room when they portaled back, his arms crossed over his muscular chest, seething.

"When are you going to stop disappearing without a lick of warning? I'm going to have a heart attack."

The air behind them closed again with that odd sucking sensation, and both Aisling and Eavha collapsed onto the chaise by the balcony. Her face heated at Dearmead's glare, but she managed to find the energy to snark back.

"I didn't realize you'd notice, since you spend so much time with Clayton doing anything but guarding us these days. What have you two been up to, anyway?"

Dearmead shook his head. "Keeping an eye on Edwina and Radley, if you must know. What exactly have you two been up to?"

Exhaustion was settling in quickly and Eavha made a mental note to have Dearmead give her a fitness regime. Not even Aisling was as puffed as she was, though the princess was laying back, pinching her nose as if she had a headache coming on.

Pulling the vials from her chest binding, Eavha showed Dearmead. "Unicorn blood. For a spell." She realized he didn't even know they had been to Wyldeden. "We found Sanni's diary at the Sanctuary back home. We're going to make new kinner for when Chaos comes."

Dearmead stared at her for a long time. She waited for his questions, or even a lecture about running off on her own. But as his gaze finally lowered from her face to the vials, throat bobbing before looking back up again, there was only desperation in his eyes.

"Make me one."

It was Eavha's turn to blink. Even Aisling had opened her eyes, turning to look at him.

"Dea," Eavha said quietly, forcing herself to get up on her shaky legs, tucking the vials back against her chest. "There's a lot to do still. A lot to think about. I've never done magic like this before, and there's no guarantee I'll get it right. Really, I ought to run trials, though I'm sick at the thought of wasting even a drop of this. But, Dea, even if I do manage it, it's a permanent change."

Nothing she said seemed to dull the pleading in his dark brown eyes. "Trial it on me."

"This is about Eaon, isn't it?" she asked, the ache in her heart growing until it rivaled that in her arms and legs. "You can't take a risk like this in the hopes you can be with him, Dea. We need this for people who will fight against Chaos—"

"Which I will do. I would have done so anyway. Please, Eavha."

He began to drop to his knees, but she grabbed his arm, voice cracking as she held him up.

"Don't beg."

"Let him do it," Aisling said, rising from the chaise. She was giving him a once over, assessing all six feet of hard, leather-clad muscle. "He is a warrior. He's exactly the kind of person we want for this anyway."

Eavha frowned, watching Aisling. Something niggled at her, but she wasn't sure what it was that made her uncomfortable.

"We can talk about it. Let me make the decantation first."

Dearmead made to argue, but Aisling nodded. "You can use my prayer room to work." With a tired smile, she petted the spot on the chaise beside her. "Dearmead, come and sit."

"Actually, I need some rest before I can start working," Eavha interrupted, tightening her hold on Dearmead's arm before he could go to Aisling. "We all do."

The sun was just bronzing the skyline, but she really did need at least a couple of hours to sleep, as well as a healing tonic and some time to pray before she could begin working on the decantation. But she also needed to clear her head so she could think about why she was suddenly so nervous.

"You're right," Aisling said, yawning deeply. "It's easy to get carried away. Meet me back up here for lunch?"

Eavha nodded, handing over the vials before looping her arm in Dearmead's. As if he could sense how tired she was, he helped her walk out of the tower, each step down to their own rooms sending a sharp jolt up her bruised feet.

"What is it?" Dearmead asked once they were out of hearing range. "Your hesitation isn't just worry for your own ability, is it?"

"She was too eager to use you," Eavha muttered.

"I thought you trusted her."

"I do," Eavha insisted. "I do. Mostly. But I think it's best we talk to Kaelean about this before we go any further."

With a frown, Dearmead nodded.

CHAPTER FORTY-EIGHT

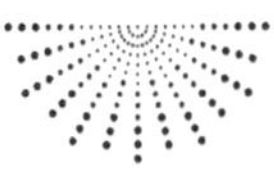

EAVHA

MILNOVA WAS PACING AS DEARMEAD HALF DRAGGED EAVHA BACK into their suite. With only a look, the elder keeper managed to wither what little strength Eavha had left, her knees buckling. Dearmead got her sitting in one of the foyer armchairs before sending another guardian to find some food and water.

"Dearmead already yelled at me," Eavha grumbled.

"Well I'm going to yell at you again," Milnova said as she ceased pacing. "You cannot run off like that. You are not a healer in training anymore; you are the heir to all of Wyldeden. Our reputation and our safety rests on your shoulders here, and you absolutely cannot just run off wherever you please without telling anyone. Without taking guardians and precautions. Without getting advice."

Sighing, Eavha looked over her shoulder, hoping something to eat was nearby. She had been scolded more often than she had been praised in her life, and Milnova was hardly as intimidating as some of her old Heads of House had been. Elder or not.

"I know what I'm doing."

"I highly doubt that. I am the Keeper of Law and Lore for our clan, and that you would take political risks by gallivanting around with the princess without consulting me is beyond irresponsible."

One of the human servants that worked in the palace followed the guardian back into their room with a tray of food and a large pitcher of water. They all waited for it to be placed and the servant to leave before continuing.

"Can you tell her?" Eavha asked Dearmead, pulling the lid off the plate. "Ew, tell me that's not meat."

"It's seitan. We had it earlier while you were—"

"Gallivanting, yes, of course," she muttered, grabbing the knife beside the tray and digging in.

As she ate, Dearmead filled Milnova in on what he knew about Eavha's activities. The impromptu trip to Wyldeden where they had found Sanni's diary, then the trip to Dusarn where they had gotten the unicorn blood needed to cast The Healing Mark of One Unending. Eavha filled in the gaps as he talked, bored with having to go over and over things.

When she finished eating, her legs steady enough to walk on her own, she got up and went to the bathing room. Glad she had seen plumbing before in Kaelean's Pirevian den, she ran a cold bath and poured salts from her stash in the water, speaking another healing prayer as the porcelain tub filled.

Dearmead and Milnova followed her, unperturbed as she stripped out of the cloak and her clothes, leaving them in a dusty pile on the floor before sinking into the water.

"Lover have mercy," she muttered as the cold bit her skin. But it would help with the soreness and bruising that would undoubtedly come.

"Did it ever occur to you that it was a bad time to be going to Dusarn?" Milnova said once Dearmead finished. "The king is not on good terms with the princess, and he could have taken that out on you."

"That's it?" Eavha raised her brow as she sank deeper, letting her curls spread out in the water around her. "You have nothing to say about the fact that we now have confirmation that Sanni made the Kinner during the First War? That her diary seems to be the first instance of witchmarks ever being used? That we now possess the ability to make our own invulnerable army against Chaos?"

"What did Kaelean think about this Chaos business?" Milnova ignored her questions.

"She is cynical, but not closed to the idea, apparently. She is willing to work with Aisling regardless," Dearmead chimed in.

"But I want to talk to her again," Eavha said. "As soon as Dearmead volunteered to be my test subject, Aisling . . . changed. It was disturbing, and I don't know why."

Milnova pulled up a stool and sat, removing the shawl from around her hair and folding it in her lap. Unfolding and refolding, unfolding and refolding.

"Tell me everything she has said these past weeks. Everything she said only to you, I mean."

"Everything?" Eavha whined, but put her head back and closed her eyes.

For over an hour, she detailed every conversation, every raised brow and tilted head between her and Aisling. Without knowing why, her eyes began to burn as she did. It felt like betrayal, sharing this. Aisling had been . . . not a friend. But almost. Could be. She was someone who knew what it was like to be different, to make bad choices in a position of power. It was different, of course. Eavha had never tortured anyone, but she couldn't help but wonder if her indifference to Eaon all those years wasn't like a form of torture.

"It's Eaon," Milnova said once Eavha stopped talking.

"Eaon?" both Eavha and Dearmead said as she sat up in the water.

"The Morvish prisoner said her prophecy only foretold that a Nemuse witch would be the downfall of Chaos. There are only two of you left, and she knows that. Aisling has you, clearly, but she wants to secure Eaon as well. Having you on her side might be enough to convince him to help her, but if Dearmead is a part of this too . . ." Milnova shook her head. "This is why you should be including me in everything. It's why Kaelean sent me with you, for Mother's sake. Don't bother her with this. It's obvious when you've spent a century or three watching those in power play their games. Aisling isn't subtle."

Yet both Eavha and Dearmead were staring as if she had solved the riddle of life itself. Eavha had been so foolish. Of course they were not friends. Aisling was preparing for war. Possibly the biggest war since the First. Eavha shouldn't be so surprised that the princess was scheming. She was just another pawn.

Climbing out of the tub, she let the water drain and wrapped one of the soft wool towels around her tired body.

"Well," she sniffed. "I'm going to try and get a few hours' rest, then go and have a chat to Aisling about her little side plans."

"Talk to me before you do. And for Mother's sake, don't go alone," Milnova scolded once more, preparing to give Eavha some space. "And as for you, Bayfield. I would think about exactly what it is you're signing up for. By becoming Kinner, you are making yourself an enemy to the Sparrow Coven. That the species is hardly even remembered outside knowledgeable circles is not a coincidence, nor is their disappearance. Whatever fate the Coven left them to . . . death would be kinder. Ask your friend Cinn how bearing the mark has worked out for him in his short life thus far. Love is a strong motivator, but spend a little time with logic, too."

Dearmead shuffled uncomfortably but nodded as Milnova left them.

"You don't need to touch someone to love them," Eavha tried.

It wasn't that she wanted to convince him not to do this, it's just that, well, she would prefer if the first person she tried to change wasn't someone quite so important to her. If something went wrong, if Dearmead was hurt, Eaon would never recover. Never. And she couldn't live with herself hurting him like that.

"You do if it's Eaon," Dearmead said, closing his eyes. "You could talk all day, but he won't hear you. It won't get through. And I've tried, but I can't. I can't stop loving him."

Untangling her hair with her fingers, Eavha took a moment. She didn't know Dearmead was capable of articulating like that. Hadn't fathomed how serious things actually were between the two of them.

"Do you want to talk about it?" she offered.

"No," Dearmead sighed. "I took your advice though. I've been writing things down. It helps."

Eavha smiled, glad he had found an outlet that worked for him. Leaving the bathing room, Eavha left her towel to dry in the morning sun and climbed under the covers of the too-soft bed.

"I'm not going to tell you no," she said as Dearmead made to leave the room. "Just make sure you think it through. Don't make this decision because you miss my brother's dick."

Eavha smirked as Dearmead choked, shooting her a reproachful glare.

"No offense, Eavha," he snapped, and Eavha stilled as she realized she may have gone too far. "But if I wanted opinions about my love life, I wouldn't ask you."

"Well that's rude," she scoffed.

"Who have you ever actually loved?" he asked, rhetorically, apparently, since he then promptly stomped out the door.

"Harsh, Dea!" she shouted back, but he was already gone.

Aisling's maiden, Larissa, stood outside the princess's door when Eavha eventually woke and went back up to find her. Apparently she was still sleeping, so the maiden let Eavha into Aisling's prayer room instead. The five vials and the page they had copied from Sanni's diary sat on the large mahogany desk, but she didn't go to it right away.

The map on the wall loomed over her once more, a sparrow painted in place of Dusarn at the very top left corner. She had traveled that far. Not the way Eaon traveled, but still, she had seen another part of the world. It still shook her to the core to know that it just kept going. Walls and borders meant nothing because there were always more out there.

Scanning the western edge of the map where Kerveda simply ended, Eavha wondered what lay beyond. Who decided that was where the map ended? Where was the western border of Kerveda and Bernt? What was beyond Nir? Another land?

Shuddering, she reached up to brush her fingers over the boab marking Wyldeden. Maybe it made her a coward, but there was still a part of her that would prefer to go home and never find out just how far beyond the edge of the map the world went. Adventure was fine, as long as she could return to where she belonged at the end of it.

Leaving the map and dragging out the plush seat at the desk, Eavha sat and stared at the page in front of her. The older the spell, the simpler it was in design, and that held true for The Healing Mark of One Unending. She had forgotten parts of the spell since closing Sanni's diary, but looking at the copy scrawled on regular parchment now, she began memorizing the procedure. Unicorn blood, a paste of mallow from the marsh, and blood of the turned, poured into the mark carved over the medulla oblongata with a blade of clear quartz and bound with Sanni's magic. Simple. There was no need to wait until a certain phase of the moon, or a week's worth of incantation to do over the ingredients to prepare them. Still, she found a clear quartz blade hiding in one of the many drawers and a jar of moon water to cleanse it.

Simple didn't mean easy. Messing with the medulla oblongata, even at just a skin level, was tricky work. The smallest mistake could steal his body's ability to regulate his heartbeat, his respiratory functions. Could leave him paralyzed, or dead. The irony was that stressing about it wasn't going to help.

When she was satisfied with the quartz, she went back to the chair and began to work on herself. From her crown to her root, she manifested clarity and power. She needed to be sure. To trust in herself and her knowledge, her ability. Doubt was a plague of its own and there could be no room for it in what was coming. She would cast this mark, and she would do it well.

Adding a few more hairs to her Blessing Charm wouldn't hurt either.

Which is how Aisling found her sometime later in the afternoon, praying over her charm and winding hair around and around.

"I don't think my prayer room has seen so much attention in a long time," Aisling said once Eavha was finished. "It feels lighter."

"I don't think Dearmead is going to change his mind."

"He is a good candidate."

"Because he will secure you my brothers aid?" Eavha asked.

Aisling looked to her, the gray of her eyes clearer than Eavha thought they'd been a few days ago. When was the last time the princess had a drink? Before or after Eavha had made her say Cinn's name?

"Would it bother you if I was?" Aisling answered.

"No," Eavha admitted. "It makes sense, objectively, and I can't hold that against you. I just wish you'd told me. You can be honest with me, you know."

"Forgive me if that is still something I'm trying to grow used to. Davina was the first and only person I have ever trusted wholly and look how that turned out."

"She didn't die because you trusted her."

"Didn't she?" Aisling smiled sadly.

A knock on the door interrupted them and Larissa poked her head in.

"Your Highness, the other Wyldeden witches are here. And Clayton."

"Thank you," Aisling told her. Then to Eavha, "I hope you don't mind. I summoned Dearmead, and your keeper insisted on coming. Clayton informed me that Edwina and Radley still aren't ready to come back to the palace, and I asked him to stay for this. If Dearmead does change his mind, I would like Clayton to consider being the first Kinner."

Eavha nodded, rising from her knees and collecting the ingredients.

"Would you do it?" she asked, suddenly curious. "Would you wear the mark?"

Without sparing a moment to consider it, Aisling shook her head. "One day I wish to join Davina in the after realm, if the Lover will embrace me. Us. Would you?"

Eavha shrugged. "I don't think I could cast it on myself."

"But if you could. If someone could cast it on you, would you want it?"

To live forever. To have an eternity to learn and practice her craft. To find out exactly what she was capable of.

"If I could stay in Wyldeden, I think I would. But not if I had to be out here. Not to fight or be hunted. Eternity is only worth it if you get to choose your life, and unfortunately, if there's one thing I've learned, it's that people rarely do."

Aisling nodded. "That's true."

Taking fresh mallow blooms from a drawer as well as the mortar and pestle, Eavha led Aisling from the prayer room to the foyer across the hall where there was enough room for everyone who'd gathered.

"Close the door, please," Eavha asked in thickly accented Nirnish, and Larissa complied.

Milnova stood by the window, praying quietly as Eavha placed the ingredients down on the little table someone had brought in and began to grind the flowers into a paste.

"There is no shame in changing your mind," Aisling said to Dearmead.

Clayton nodded his agreement, giving the guardian a once over, but Dearmead only lifted his chin and locked eyes with Eavha.

"I'm doing it. Yes, for Eaon. But also because I believe in what's coming. If bearing this mark will give us a fighting chance, then it will be both an honor and a risk worth taking."

Eavha nodded. "Then come put your blood in the bowl."

Unlacing his vambraces, Dearmead exposed the blemished skin of his forearm, a history of injuries left unattended puckering in pale ridges. Taking the clear quartz blade, Eavha nicked his arm and let enough blood flow out to make a decent paste.

"Don't waste energy healing it," Dearmead said, pulling away as Eavha reached for the cut. Larissa brought forward a bandage and pressed it to the wound, watching wide-eyed as Eavha nodded and uncorked the unicorn blood. The pearlescent color overwhelmed the blood, refusing to dull as she poured the entire vial into the mortar and mixed the ingredients to a creamy consistency.

One vial gone. If she messed this up, there would only be four more chances. Only four kinner to bring to the fight.

When it was done, she stared at the mortar for a long moment. It didn't seem like it should be so simple.

Warmth spread through her, an easy presence that called to her soul. Eavha closed her eyes. She had not gotten better at reaching into the spirit realms, but Sanni had come to her this time. The veil between the Mother's realm and Sanni's was thin enough to feel the warmth radiating from the Spirit of Healing.

It is ready. I allow this. You have the power.

Trembling, solid hands grabbed her arms to hold her up as the words echoed in her mind. This close to Sanni, her magic began to swell, singing through her veins in the presence of its master. It was more than a gift. This blessing was a thread that tied them together through the realms, through space and time, as if the two of them had been born to be bound together. Bubbling brighter, the magic rose to heights inside her unlike anything she had ever felt before. What would happen here today was not the meeting of Eavha's will and Sanni's permission; they were of one mind on this.

Opening her eyes, she reached for the blade. Milnova had collapsed to her knees, panting hard as the magic in the room battered her. Aisling clutched her chaise, a hand at her gut. Even Clayton and Larissa had backed away.

Dearmead knelt before her, holding her steady even as he trembled.

Moving his braid to the side, she let Sanni guide the blade in her hand. Two *S*'s, mirrored and overlapping, the ends turned like the caps of an hourglass. Then she took the mortar in her hands and scraped the contents over Dearmead's neck, slathering the wound. He jerked, his grip on her waist failing as he braced himself on the ground. Gathering all that magic writhing in her veins, Eavha tunneled it into her palm and lay it over the mark she had carved. Her scarred, ruined palm that would give its own kind of blessing today.

CHAPTER FORTY-NINE

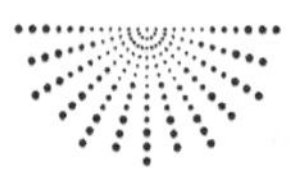

DEARMEAD

H E EXPECTED PAIN. A S THE POWER IN THE ROOM BECAME
unbearable, his very bones rattling from the force, it would only make
sense for there to be pain as Eavha lay her hand against the nape of his
neck. But there was only warmth.

Vision seared in white, Dearmead lost track of everything except
the heat coursing through his body. Not a burning, but as if the Spirits
themselves had come to wrap him in their finest wool. Every fiber of
his being, from his skin to his bones—there was no part of him left
untouched.

The magic ebbed, but the warmth lingered. Aside from that
though, Dearmead didn't feel any different. Didn't look any different,
as his vision cleared and he looked down at hands that were still
calloused and scarred from years of training. He raised his face just in
time to see Eavha's eyes roll back in her head, her Blessing Charm in
tatters around her neck.

"She's going to—" he started, but Aisling was already lunging for
her, catching Eavha before she could hit the floor.

Milnova still couldn't stand, but Clayton rushed forward to check
Eavha's pulse, sighing in relief.

"She's alright."

"She's not alright!" Aisling snapped, wiping a dribble of blood from Eavha's nose with her thumb. "She nearly burned herself out. Again."

"She tends to do that," Dearmead grumbled. Slipping an arm under her, he lifted Eavha and took her to Aisling's bed. Limp as a dead doe, he tucked her arms and legs beneath the comforter. "Let her sleep. And when she wakes—"

"Ginseng root. I know." Aisling stood by the door, wringing her skirt.

They stood for a moment, watching Eavha breathe, before Dearmead slid a hand over the back of his neck. That holy heat had gone, and the skin felt the same as it always had.

Aisling came to stand beside him, one of her long fingernails tracing a pattern on the back of his neck.

"It's stunning."

Dearmead stiffened.

"It worked?"

"There's a mark."

He was almost sick from the hope that rocked through him. Aisling drew her dagger and handed it to Dearmead, who took it with quivering hands. As he had done a hundred times, until Eavha had told him off, he put the blade in his palm and closed his hand around it. A sharp tug and an awful flash of pain left hot blood pooling in his hand, dripping off the blade onto the rug beneath.

Aisling watched, her chest rising and falling as fast as Dearmead's own.

When he opened his palm again, the wound had already healed.

PART V

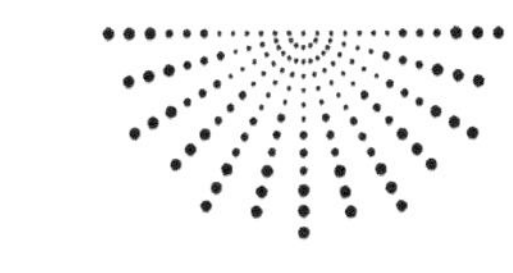

WATER OF THE WOMB

CHAPTER FIFTY

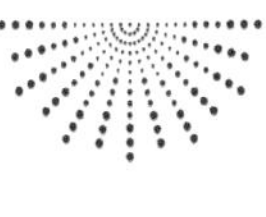

AISLING

T HE BALCONY DOORS WERE OPEN, A WARM SUMMER BREEZE BLOWING
the sheer curtains as Aisling and Eavha sat on the floor with a wooden
chess set, practicing openings. For two days, Eavha had slept, rousing
only to be spoon-fed ginseng root tea and porridge. But she was up
now, washed and lounging in one of Aisling's robes, soaking in the sun.
She had performed a miracle, and with her curling mousy hair aglow
with threads of molten honey, skin bronzed to perfection, she was a
goddess. One Aisling dreamed of worshipping.

And her guardian, Dearmead Bayfield, was a kinner. When he
wasn't up here checking on Eavha, he was training with Clayton,
teaching himself to fight with less fear of injury.

"Checkmate," Aisling said with a smile.

"Already?" Eavha scowled as she tipped over her wooden king.

"You were too focused on your own moves, you forgot to pay
attention to mine," Aisling explained, resetting the board. "Again?"

"Sure."

A knock on the door interrupted them.

Aisling waited for Larissa to answer it, then remembered it was her
maiden's day off. She no longer had a second entrusted to take care of
things for her. Grumbling, Aisling climbed to her feet and cinched her
robe tighter at the waist. She had refused to leave Eavha's side these

last forty-eight hours, sleeping fitfully beside her, not worrying about propriety as she'd stayed only in her satin robe.

Opening the door a sliver, Aisling frowned at the expression on the messenger's face.

"What."

"A parcel was delivered by horse rider. It's from your brother. It's . . ."

The messenger swallowed, averting his eyes.

Nevan. Still alive, then.

She counted the weeks in her head, trying to figure out how long Nora had been in Pirevia now. Long enough to have enacted the plan? Her soldiers waiting for the signal had not sent word yet, but surely it had been long enough.

"It's what?" she snapped.

The man's breath shuddered as he said, "It's leaking."

Fear hollowed her chest.

"Aisling?" Eavha asked quietly, having followed her to the door. "What's wrong?"

"Give it to me." Aisling's voice sounded vacant, even to herself.

It had been a risk to attack Pirevia this way. One she'd thought worth letting Nora take.

It might not be about that, she reminded herself. It could be entirely unrelated. Another attempt to bend Aisling to his will. Perhaps he had managed to kill the babe their mother carried, and this was his way of bragging.

The messenger crouched down to pick up a wooden box. Sure enough, liquid had dampened the corners, one of them dripping slowly. The putrid smell tainting the air was too familiar.

"Thank you, Walter. You may leave," Aisling said as she took the box from him.

"Are you sure?"

"Yes."

Stepping back, she closed the door with her foot.

Eavha's face paled as she stared at the box in Aisling's hands, but as the heat of the day worsened the smell, she didn't recoil. Didn't cover her nose or step away.

"You don't have to look," Aisling said quietly, eyes fixated on the wooden lid.

"I am not afraid of death," she answered, stepping closer. "But if you want to be alone . . ."

Aisling took the package to the chaise and placed it down carefully. Since she had not told her otherwise, Eavha came to stand beside her.

Endless possibilities. It could be anything, yet her heart was already steeling itself for the worst. Cold stilled her body, her mind, as she reached for the lid.

Opened it.

Nora's decapitated head stared back at her.

Eavha gasped, then screamed as something in Nora's mouth moved.

Aisling whipped her hand out to catch the striking viper midair, ignoring the dripping venom from the hissing snake's long fangs. But her eyes stayed on Nora.

"Eavha, pass me my knife."

Silently, the Wyldeden heir found Aisling's dagger, slipping it into her free hand. In one motion, Aisling cut the snake's head off and dropped its coiling mass to the floor.

"Who is that?" Eavha asked quietly.

Aisling couldn't answer. With steady hands, she reached for Nora's face, closing her eyes.

Show me, she asked Death.

And so Death did.

Shadows, and then bright white sand.

The screaming of a rowdy crowd high above.

Standing in the middle of Nevan's barbaric arena was Owen, gaunt and horrified.

"No," Nora sobbed. Turning, she looked up to the royal box where Nevan and his consort sat stoically. "Rhosyn! Please!"

The consort stared down at her coldly.

Owen ran to Nora and pulled out a tiny blade.

"No," Nora hissed, grabbing Owen's wrists.

"It's better to do this quick."

"No!"

"Whatever they do to you, just hang on. Aisling will come for you. You know she will. You're going to be a wonderful mother, my sweet Nora."

"Aisling will come," she repeated.

There was a kiss, and Nora's vision blurred.

"I love you," she told him

"It'll be alright, my love."

Another lie. But there was one thing she could do to ensure that, maybe one day, something might be alright.

"When Aisling comes, tell her I love her too."

Owen frowned. Too late did he realize Nora had taken the blade from him.

"Nora—"

The crowd disappeared as she opened her throat.

Aisling let go and found herself stepping back without meaning to.

"Easy." Eavha was there, grabbing her waist as she felt herself tilting. "Easy."

Lowering her to the floor safely, it wasn't until Eavha wiped at Aisling's cheeks that she realized she was crying. Bewildered, Aisling touched her own face. A different cold spread through her body, one that made her shiver instead of still. The rot in the air churned her stomach like nothing had before.

Standing by the table, Davina looked at her with pity. Not even her Morvish lover had said that to her. Nobody had. Aisling had never said it either. Wasn't sure she'd ever been loved; not that the lack of it had ever bothered her.

So why was she crying?

"I'm so sorry," Eavha said softly, tears reddening her own eyes as she cradled Aisling's face. "Whoever she was to you, I'm sorry."

Nora had been the only demi-kin to come to her throne room after she had abolished slavery in Hyrsch. The only one to tell her that it was not enough. That until there was a demi-kin in a position of power, to advocate for them authentically, there could never truly be freedom for them. Her advisors had told her to execute the brutalized female for her insolence, so of course she had hired her instead.

"She saved me," Aisling's voice cracked, the tears becoming hotter as they spilled down her cheeks. "And I sent her to her death."

"This is not your fault." Eavha shook her head, pulling Aisling close. She didn't know what to do with the affection, so she sat there and endured it.

By the time Eavha let go, Aisling had reined in her pain. Standing up, she tightened the knot of her robe with a sharp jerk before going back to the door where she knew the messenger still lurked. As the door opened, the man flinched back, cheeks blushing at being caught eavesdropping.

At the sight of Aisling's face, his blush bleached. "Your Highness?"

"Gather my advisors in the council room. Edwina and Radley, too. I'll be there shortly."

With a nod, the messenger raced off.

Eavha watched as Aisling stalked to her dressing suite and shed her robe, pulling a brush through her tangled locks. The aged mirror reflected a version of her she did not recognize. She had lost before, but this was different. The toll it was taking was more than she had to give.

"What are you doing?" Eavha asked, approaching as one would a rabid wolf.

"Getting ready."

"For what?"

"War."

Aisling didn't turn for Eavha's reaction, pulling her hair into a sharp ponytail before collecting undergarments.

"I thought you said you needed to stay in Hyrsch. That Davina's visions said they would come from the southwest, and—"

"I did," Davina said as she appeared beside her, watching with concern as Aisling pulled a plain black dress from the wardrobe and shimmied into it. "If you're not stationed here when they pass the spine—"

"I don't care," Aisling answered them both. "They could arrive tomorrow or in two months, but my brother needs to die now."

"You said there wasn't time for civil war," Eavha reminded her.

"There will be nothing civil about what I will do to him."

"Aisling," Davina snapped. "This is what he wants. You cannot afford to be distracted. I know Nora was important to you but—"

"But *nothing*!" Aisling hissed, making Eavha flinch back. "I *dare* Chaos to approach me before I kill Nevan. I fucking *dare* him!"

"You cannot deviate from the plan—"

"You don't get to die and then tell me what to do!" Aisling shouted back at her.

Deep down, she knew Davina was right. Chaos would come from the south, and Aisling needed to stop him before he reached the womb. It was the only way to avoid what else Davina had seen.

But Nora was dead.

Davina looked to Eavha, as if the Wyldeden witch could see her and would take her side. But Eavha, in nothing but a gauzy robe, her mousy brown curls a messy halo around her head, was not an advocate for peace right now. There was nothing soft about her expression as she took in Aisling, now dressed in sharp black satin, fastening daggers to the hidden pockets inside her skirts.

"I'm coming with you."

"What?"

"When you go to kill your brother, I will come with you."

"Absolutely not." The sheer panic that fluttered through her chest at the thought was the only thing that slowed the murderous rampage in her heart.

"If you are hurt and I am not there, you will scar. Taking a risk by leaving Hyrsch is one thing, but to risk Davina's work is just reckless. I'm coming with you."

No arguing about whether or not Aisling was making the right decision. No fretting and worrying, like Davina was doing.

Whirling around, Eavha went to collect her gown from the floor beside the bed. "I will get Dearmead."

Blinking once, Aisling nodded.

"This is a mistake," Davina continued. "Taking Pirevia was always going to be helpful, but it is not essential to your success. Leave it. There is too much at stake—"

Pushing down the Lover's-blessing that Aisling usually let roam free, Davina disappeared.

Dressed, Eavha hurried from the room to find her guardian, leaving Aisling alone in the silence to pack a duffle bag and put on her heels. One last glance toward the chaise, sun shining off the black scales of the dead snake.

"I'm sorry," Aisling whispered. Then strode from the room, leaving Nora's decapitated head behind.

CHAPTER FIFTY-ONE

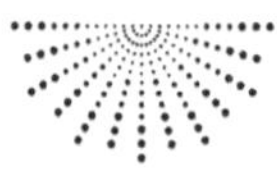

AISLING

Sitting on her chair in the council room, Aisling waited until everyone was gathered. Clayton stood to her left, Edwina to her right. Radley hovered by his sister, growing tenser by the second as the Sparrow advisors marched in. Dearmead and Eavha waited behind Clayton in their finest Wyldeden gear.

The advisors muttered among themselves, but Aisling waited until there was utter silence before turning to Edwina.

"I know you are not my servant anymore, but as I have not yet replaced you would you be so kind as to fetch us some wine?"

Radley bristled, but Edwina only looked at Aisling with equal frigidity.

"We will probably need two bottles," Aisling continued, glancing around at the number in the room. "Perhaps the Faritty forty-two."

The only sign of Edwina's surprise was how still she was.

"The one in the drawer?

"Yes. Please."

Edwina left, a couple of the advisors giving her smug looks as she did. They likely thought it proof that Aisling still adhered to some sense of hierarchy, sending the demi-kin instead of one of them.

"We're to have a toast," Aisling explained, crossing her ankles as she managed an unnatural calm. "I have learned that my mother is with child, so before we discuss what sort of celebration would be appropriate I would like to pray for her good health."

There were enough surprised expressions to know that some of them already knew and had not told her, while others were clueless.

"You are not bothered by this news?" the one named Orla asked suspiciously, words muffled by the awkward way she held her mouth and the red scar across her lips.

"Of course not. We all know that my politics are not suited to the Sparrow Throne, and I have not made it a secret how much I dislike my brother's ideals. So another option suits me fine."

Edwina returned with a cart, two decanters of wine and eleven glasses.

"I do hope to be invited to Dusarn more regularly so that I may have a positive influence on the child, of course," Aisling went on, trying to distract them from watching Edwina too closely; the way her new Second carefully poured the wine from one decanter in the glasses on her left, the wine from the second into the glasses on the right. "Which means I will be leaving Edwina in charge regularly. I know my decision to promote her over one of you was not agreed with, so I thought it also best to set some rules in place before any conflict can arise."

"Though we may not all share your fondness for the half-breeds, we can and do respect your orders, Your Highness." Pierre dipped his chin, taking the glass Edwina offered him with a strained smile.

"Call us half-breeds again and you'll have half a tongue," Radley spat.

Aisling didn't reproach him.

Finally, after everyone had their drink, Edwina handed Aisling a glass before resuming her place. She too had a glass of wine, which she raised.

Of course, it was Orla who narrowed her eyes. "How do we know this isn't poisoned?"

Quiet muttering broke out again, but Aisling only tilted her head.

"What a strange suspicion to have. Why on earth would I poison you?"

"She gave us all wine from one decanter, and all of you wine from the other."

"If your eyes are so keen, you would have noticed that I have the same wine as you do," Aisling lifted her glass. "Don't believe me? Trade with me."

Silence fell once again as the other advisors looked between Orla and Aisling. The old crone stuttered as she debated what would be worse, being poisoned or expressing enough distrust to trade glasses with the princess. Apparently, the disrespect she was willing to show knew no bounds. Orla slid her glass closer to Aisling, who happily slid her own back to Orla. Raising the glass, Aisling lifted her chin.

"To the blood of the covenant, and the water of the womb."

"Blood of the covenant, water of the womb," they all echoed back.

Aisling drained her glass first, the sweetness stinging her lips. The others all drank as well. As the quick bite of poison hit them, many rose in panic. Clayton moved to guard the door.

Even as bloody froth coated her tongue, Orla managed to look outraged. Aisling grinned at her, wincing as she choked on the bile bubbling in her own throat as poison corroded the flesh. Edwina moved closer, holding the vial of antidote with the same cold expression on her face.

"I heard about Nora. I never liked her, but I know Owen and Siobhan well. They will grieve for her. Are you going to kill Nevan?" she asked quietly.

Eavha stood up to help, but Radley drew a blade, pointing it at her.

Slowly, Aisling let go of the mask she'd kept over her rage and managed to nod.

Uncorking the vial, Edwina tipped the contents up Aisling's nose. Looking mildly disappointed, Radley lowered his blade.

"I should think so," Eavha snapped at him, indignant as she rushed to Aisling's side to lay a warm hand over her throat. "A little warning would have been nice. I almost had a heart attack."

The antidote was acting quickly but would still have taken most of the day to rid her entirely of its effects, except for Eavha clinging to the tatters of her barely functioning Blessing Charm, eyes closed as itching warmth repaired the seared flesh within.

"Careful, Eavha," Dearmead warned her.

It hadn't been that long since she had recovered from turning him. In fact, she soon became unsteady on her feet. Dearmead's spear clattered to the floor as he caught her, holding steady until she collapsed against him.

"Thank you," Aisling said, only a mild ache straining her voice.

"Why now?" Edwina asked, moving her wine glass to the center of the table as she looked at the bodies slumped across it.

"Because when I kill Nevan, the Coven may declare war. The advisors here would have overpowered you and taken control of the city. Now they cannot." Aisling stood, surprisingly steady. "As of now, Edwina, you are the Lady of Hyrsch. Keep an eye on the southern passages through the spine. At the first hint of trouble, send a raven and I will return to deal with it. When the threat has passed, I will not linger."

Edwina blinked, lips parting soundlessly as if only now truly understanding what her position meant.

"We will hold the city." Radley spoke instead. "And . . . we'll clean up."

Aisling held his gaze and nodded. Pulling her own Blessing Charm from her pocket, she tied it around her neck.

"You should stay and rest," Aisling told Eavha, who stood, taking deep breaths.

"I am coming."

"This is not a good idea," Dearmead muttered. "Milnova will be furious. And what would Eaon say?"

"Oh, Lover spare me, Dearmead." Eavha rolled her eyes.

Aisling glanced from Eavha to Dearmead, lifting her chin at the latter. "I can't stop her."

Understanding, Dearmead nodded.

"Correct. So—" Eavha's gloating was cut short when she stepped forward and Dearmead grabbed her arm.

Rallying her Celeste-blessing, Aisling winced. "I'm sorry."

"No. Don't," Eavha gasped, pulling at her arm. Dearmead held her tighter. "Stop it. Let go of me. I'm coming with you, Aisling."

With a sharp pull, Aisling tore open a narrow portal that would take her straight to Pirevia. Despite the joyful call of the wind in her veins, there was nothing to take away the weight of Nora's head in that box. Nothing else could matter until vengeance had been taken, and there was no price too high to pay for it.

She had murdered six Coven members in cold blood. Was about to wage war against her own brother—against the entire Sparrow Coven if necessary.

She would not have Eavha anywhere near it.

CHAPTER FIFTY-TWO

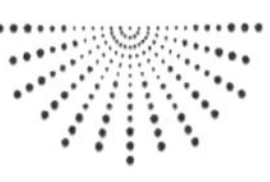

EAVHA

"No! Aisling, no!"

The harder she pulled against Dearmead the tighter he held her. Livid, she clenched her fist and swung at him. He had not expected it, yet he did not loosen his grip on her arm as her blow glanced off his shoulder. In fact, her hit only made him wrap his other arm around her and pull her snugly against him.

The last thing she saw before Dearmead pushed her face into his chest was Aisling stepping through the portal. Alone.

"You rogue! Let me go!"

"Eavha, stop. You can't go back there. Not now. Not for this."

They thought she would get in the way. Thought she would be no help. Maybe Davina's visions had Aisling convinced she would live long enough to face Chaos, but that was no guarantee. Even less so that she would be in any shape to do so and win. Survive it.

Stomping on Dearmead's foot, she shoved him back as hard as she could. His balance shifted just enough to get an arm loose, and she slammed her fist into his groin.

He flinched, grabbing a hold of the nearest chair to keep himself upright as he hissed breathlessly. "Eavha, stop it!"

She was loose, but too late.

Aisling was gone, the portal closed.

"She'll be alright—" Clayton began, but Eavha didn't wait to listen to whatever they said. None of them had even tried to go after her. Help her. Cowards, the lot of them. She ran for the door, fleeing through the halls faster than she had ever run before.

Through the foyer, out the doors and into the gardens, Eavha retraced her steps all the way to the stables. To the guarded building behind them.

"Out of my way!" Eavha shouted at the guards stationed outside. They recognized her, glancing between each other in hesitation.

Eavha didn't wait for them to decide whether or not to let her pass; she blew past them and into the stable. Directly to Volya.

She hadn't heard Dearmead following her but wasn't at all surprised that he had.

"Is that . . ." Dearmead came to a standstill as he took in the winged horse, eyes widening.

"Get out of my way," Eavha repeated, voice thick with unfettered desperation as she opened the gate and stepped up to Volya.

She knew. Volya knew why Eavha was here and did not fret as the saddle was awkwardly fitted to her back.

"Eavha, please, just stop."

"What is wrong with you!" she hissed at him.

"Do you not remember what Pirevia was like when you were there? The state I found you all in? You could have died, and I can't just let you run headfirst into that kind of trouble again. Aisling will be fine—"

"And what if she's not? I won't sit here and twiddle my thumbs while she risks herself and everything she has worked for."

"She doesn't want you there."

"That's not true. She's just trying to protect me."

"And rightly so!"

"Eaon was right about you." The words were past her lips before she could think them through. Words she knew would make him do whatever she wanted. "You're a coward."

She didn't see him flinch, but she felt it.

Securing the bridle and pulling the reins into place, Eavha guided Volya from her gate before mounting. The wind would be brutal against her bare thighs, her chest, arms and face. It would hurt, and it would be cold, but she had been freezing and in pain before. She was not afraid of it anymore.

"Get out of my way," she said again, stony faced.

The way Dearmead's chin jutted out, eyes hooded, gave away how much she had hurt him. Worse, he believed the words were true. Tapping the weapons he always had strapped to his side, his spear once more on his back, Dearmead took a shaky breath and met her gaze.

"If I can't stop you, can I at least come?"

"If you hurry up."

He spurted forward and leaped onto the saddle behind her, running his hands over Volya's soft hide.

"Hold on tight," she warned him. Then to Volya, "Let's go. She needs us, even if she doesn't know it yet."

With a snuffle of agreement, Volya galloped from the barn and spread her wings.

CHAPTER FIFTY-THREE

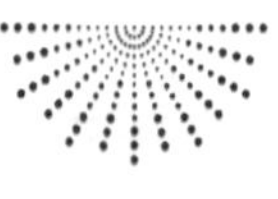

AISLING

WHATEVER GATHERING NEVAN HAD BEEN HOSTING IN HIS THRONE room came to a stunned silence as Aisling stepped through the portal, dressed in finery and wrath.

Davina appeared beside her as Aisling's grip on her blessing slipped, nervous but close. "Mind your temper."

"How dare you." Aisling spat on the ground as she glared at her brother.

Nevan blinked in mock innocence, a golden mask concealing the left side of his face. "My darling sister. What happened to your face?"

As if he cared about the scar on her cheek. As if her blistering rage was less noticeable.

"You sent me her *head*?!"

The courtiers and advisors gathered in the room shuffled anxiously, backing toward the exits.

"You're interrupting my party planning," Nevan said coolly.

Slipping her hand between her skirts, Aisling gripped the dagger hidden in her pocket. She could throw it, sink it into his neck and watch him bleed out on the marble. From where she stood, she would not miss.

The glitter in Nevan's eyes told her he knew exactly what she fantasized about.

"I am glad you got the invitation though," he continued. "It's going to be a mighty affair."

"You killed—"

"The demi-kin you sent to my city as punishment for betraying you? Yes. Is that a problem?" The amusement in his tone was more annoying than the smug smirk visible on the right side of his mouth, tenfold.

"Easy," Davina begged, hands raised as if she could calm Aisling with the gesture alone.

Gritting her teeth, she tried. As angry as she was, she was not stupid enough to step into her own grave.

"You may do what you please in your own city, but you clearly knew who she was to me, and you *sent me her decapitated head*!"

"I take it you didn't like your present, then." Nevan grinned, gaze rising above her.

Carefully, Aisling turned just enough to see what he was looking at. The rest of Nora was strung up by her ankles over the doorway, a bunch of mistletoe stuck in the cavity of her neck.

"Perhaps you would like a moment alone with your sister," one of the waiting men said quietly.

"A wise suggestion," Nevan acknowledged, but the words were barely audible through the pounding in Aisling's ears.

She was going to be sick.

Only once they were alone did she dare to turn back to him. The arrogant smirk on his face was gone.

"You tried to stage a coup in my city."

"Prove it."

"You want to play games, Aisling? Let's play games. Let's play like we used to when we were witchlings."

Aisling drew her knife. And found one at her own throat.

"Hello, Rhosyn," Aisling sneered, knowing exactly who must have stood behind her.

The consort had never sought Nevan's attentions, the position more of a punishment than an honor. A punishment Aisling thought the human woman would have wanted to end, enough so to help Nora in the plan to dethrone him. Clearly, yet another mistake.

In one swift movement, Aisling flung her glove off and pressed her palm against Rhosyn's side. Magic pulsed, a shock of frigid air against the thin fabric of Rhosyn's dress, making her jerk back and giving Aisling room to do the same. The blade at her throat might still have cut her open but Rhosyn was slow, even for a human, and Aisling slipped her own knife between her neck and the blade, pushing back.

Free from her, Aisling spun and grabbed a fistful of Rhosyn's strawberry blond hair, switching their positions until she had her blade at the consort's throat instead.

Nevan was still as stone.

"Seriously? You thought your human pet could best me?"

The pretty little thing was supposed to be the key to taking the city, but apparently her loyalty to the prince ran deeper than Aisling thought. Why, she would never understand. He treated her worse than he did the demi-kin, and that was saying something.

"You're drunk half the time, so it was possible," Nevan chided.

"Come here and take her place."

"I'd rather not."

"Please," Rhosyn begged, trembling against Aisling like the lamb she was.

Aisling snarled in her ear, "You picked the wrong team."

"I couldn't help her," Rhosyn cried.

"And I can't help you."

Pressing harder, the tang of fresh blood in her nose, the bright red of it oozing beneath the blade.

"Do it," Nevan said with a stiff shrug. "I'm bored of her anyway."

"No!" Rhosyn sobbed. "Please!"

"Aisling," Davina warned. The bloodlust was blinding her. She knew it, but she couldn't see what she was missing. "That he wants you to do it should be enough to still your hand."

That he said he wanted her to do it was a ploy. What he really wanted was for her to second-guess herself, to stay her hand. Or was it a level deeper than that?

Nevan laughed. "You should see the frown on your face. If only you'd thought that hard about your stupid little plan before sending your rats here on your behalf. You don't have the brain or the balls to take my city. You don't have—"

Aisling shoved Rhosyn away, sending her sprawling across the white marble floor. The decision seemed to confuse Nevan, the mask shifting as he raised his eyebrows.

"Interesting."

"There you go." Davina smiled. "That's my Aisling."

"Consider it a gift for whatever stupid holiday you're celebrating," she said, eyeing Rhosyn as she scooted across the floor, the vibrant red of her dress catching under her heels. "I suggest you get as far away from me as possible, because the next time I lay eyes on you I will make Death themself take pity on you."

Rhosyn got up and ran.

Aisling turned to her brother.

It was one of his first lessons from when they were children, learning how to be awful together in Dusarn. No witnesses. Rhosyn was hardly objective, but she was something.

"We are not witchlings anymore, Nevan. I don't want to play games. You've tried a hundred times to kill me, and I you. Don't deny it," she interrupted as he opened his mouth. "So let's be done with it. One round, one fight to end them all. In front of your entire city, so there are witnesses who can speak to the truth of things."

Nevan considered it, then, "You came in here all brimstone and fire, and now you're almost calm."

Aisling said nothing. That was the second lesson he taught her. Emotions made you stupid. She was very skilled at putting hers away when she had to. At least for a moment.

"Fine." He nodded. "I can hardly turn down an opportunity to put you back in your place. First thing tomorrow morning."

"Why wait?"

"I will need time to choose a champion. And I suppose you will need time to find someone willing to represent you."

Aisling shook her head, snorting in derision. "How pathetic. No champions, Nevan. You and me."

Nevan blinked, as if this surprised him. "Mother and father would disapprove."

"Won't matter. Neither of us will see the throne anyway. Why do you think they bothered to sire a third?"

And that got more of a reaction than the death threat to Rhosyn ever would. Nevan's face reddened.

"There won't be a third."

"There will," she assured him. "They will sire a thousand children before they let either of us rule. I am too soft, and you are a little fish in a big pond."

She knew how to hit him. Knew his theatrics were a cry for attention. Ever since her birth, he had been trying to prove how special he was, how unnecessary her addition to the royal bloodline had been. Snarling at her, his mightier-than-thou demeanor slipped even farther.

"You and me, Nevan," she continued. "It's time to grow up. I want this to be over. You win, you're free to go after the throne. But unless I'm dead I will continue to undermine you."

"I don't need to face you in a public spat to kill you," he snapped. "I could do it right now."

Yet he didn't stand from the throne. Didn't reach for the rapier at his waist. He sat there and seethed, and Aisling was tempted to make the first move. To attack him right here in the throne room where Nora's body would be their only witness. She wanted it so much she could already taste his blood on her tongue, or maybe it was hers, jaw clenched so tightly her gums had to be bleeding.

"You could, but that would be awfully suspicious, wouldn't it?" she sneered, taking a tentative step forward and enjoying the way he stiffened at the movement. "First you try to blackmail me into killing our soon-to-be-born sibling, then you murder me without cause? Do you think being the only option will make our parents appoint you as heir?"

"I'd say you attacked me."

"You forget that we are Sparrow. You cannot hide the cause of death."

"There is The Mark—"

"The one you never could cast correctly?" she mocked.

Nevan's face reddened further, nostrils flaring wide.

"But," she continued, taking another step toward him. "Make it public, make it a game, and then it's justified. I consented to the duel, and you are free to do as you please."

"And if I say no?" he managed through his own gritted teeth, fists curling on the arms of his throne.

"I'll make you regret that decision every day for the very short number of them you have left," Aisling promised. "Because you crossed a line today, Nevan. Maybe I sent the rebels here for punishment, but Nora was my friend first, and you sent me her head. After everything I went through with Davina, you did that to me, and I will ruin you for it."

At that, Nevan rolled his eyes. "You are so fucking dramatic. Get over it, Aisling."

"Take the day to consider it," she offered, knowing he would give in. "One way or the other, I'll see you in the morning."

With a cold sneer, she turned for the ornate doors to the throne room and passed beneath the rotting wreath on her way out.

Alone on the balcony of the suite she had claimed as her own, Aisling released the emotion she had suffocated earlier. Hot tears dripped from her chin as she watched the rowdy celebrations going on in the streets. Some kind of parade, and a chant she couldn't hear properly from so high up, no doubt boorish and obscene.

The still night left her hair hanging limp down her back, a light robe wrapped tightly around her otherwise bare body. She resisted the urge to reach for the untouched bottle of wine on a nearby cart, the humidity clouding her head already. It would be a good night for drinking, though as the alcohol was yet to solve any of her problems she was sure she would regret it come morning.

"I'm proud of you," Davina said softly, the glow from the city below shining through her mirage-like body. "You were very convincing. I thought you were really about to lose it for a moment."

"I almost did lose it." Her voice fell flat, even to her own ears.

It had been Nora's plan to take the city, and Aisling had been too caught up in the larger game to make sure Nora's part went smoothly. She never should have allowed this to happen. Pirevia would be an ace in the sleeve, but it wasn't worth all of this pain.

But now, she would take it out of spite.

Davina hummed lightly, cheek dimpling as she said, "Eavha's had a good effect on you."

A stone clacked on the balcony and Aisling whirled, pulling a dagger from her thigh. Eavha clung to the wall above the door, grimacing at the poor placement of her foot. Dearmead was a few feet above her.

"No," Aisling gasped, dropping the blade. "How!"

Hair a nest of knotted curls, body flushed and pale, lips chapped, Eavha huffed as she dropped onto the balcony. "Look at my hair, Aisling. How do you think?"

Dearmead didn't look much better, his braid loose in places, stray hairs tangled around his face.

Looking up to the roof far above, Aisling spotted Volya settling like a crow in a roost.

"You're insane."

Despite her wobbly legs, Eavha managed to storm up to Aisling with enough ferocity to rival a wild beast. "Then we make a good pair."

Dearmead dropped down behind her, making his way to the railing to frown deeply at the marching crowd.

Aisling leveled a glare at him. "I thought you and I were in agreement."

"I tried," he grumbled.

"Not very hard, apparently."

"I was very mean to him," Eavha said, turning shyly to her guardian. "And I lied, Dea. Eaon never said that about you."

Dearmead's demeanor did not change.

"I'm taking you back. Right now," Aisling spat. She was tired, but with her Blessing Charm she could find the strength to portal again.

"No!" Eavha planted her feet and snatched the charm from around Aisling's neck, yanking it free.

"Don't argue with me on this. Please. I'm fighting Nevan in the morning and I can't concentrate with you here."

"Really? Because in the training room with Clayton you seemed to focus better after you knew I was there."

"I was showing off."

"So show off again. I will not let you be alone. I won't do it."

"And I won't let someone else I care about get killed." Aisling took Eavha's face between her cold hands. "There have been so few people in my life that I have cared about, and doing so is starting to feel like a punishment because they keep being taken from me."

"Then let's go back together."

"I can't."

Eavha knew that. She had to.

"Then I stay. I'm staying, Aisling. You can't get rid of me."

Aisling sighed deeply, the shakiest of smiles pulling at her lip. "No matter how hard I try, apparently."

Another tear slipped down her chin as Aisling leaned in and kissed her. Just for a second.

Dearmead was going inside, but she barely noticed as Eavha stared at her, wide-eyed and frozen.

"Sorry," she whispered, letting her go. But Eavha grabbed her wrist.

"Do it again," Eavha breathed, brushing away the dampness on Aisling's face.

So Aisling did.

They did not linger on the balcony, because though Aisling did not care, Eavha was aware that Dearmead was waiting inside. As soon as they came in, hand in hand, Dearmead started asking questions from where he leaned against the wall with his arms tightly crossed.

"What's happening in the morning?"

"I'm settling things with Nevan. He wants a duel fought by champions, but I will walk into his arena myself and he will have no choice but to face me. Then I will kill him, and the laws of our people will see it as a legal conquering. The city and its people will belong to me. Nora wins."

Sort of. Not really. And the last part was a lie. There was nothing legal or honourable about killing another Sparrow. The Coven would come for her unless she could figure out how to convince them not to.

"It's risky." Dearmead shook his head. "You should fight with a champion and send me. I cannot die. It's a sure win."

She had thought of that, but had not expected the offer from the Wyldeden warrior. Being kinner made it a sensible choice, but the thought made her nauseous. Not one more person would fight on her behalf. Not one more person would bleed for her. She'd had enough.

But Eavha started at the idea. "It's perfect."

"It's not. Your people are pacifists. I cannot let Nevan live," Aisling explained.

Dearmead looked down at her, his chest expanding as he took a deep breath.

"I will kill him for you."

Eavha gasped, the shock in her voice palpable. "Dearmead!"

"I appreciate the offer, Dearmead, but it would only make more problems than it's worth," Aisling said, shaking her head. "Witnesses would see that it was Wyldeden that killed him, and the Coven could blame your people. Anything could happen, and I need as little resistance as possible. Owen is still here somewhere. The other demi-kin. If nothing else, I have to get them out."

"What if I do it as a rogue?"

"Dearmead, enough!" Eavha let go of Aisling's hand to take Dearmead's. "I'm sorry I called you a coward. It was a lie. Stop suggesting these reckless things trying to prove something. It's not you."

Dearmead looked ready to argue, but his shoulders drooped and he hung his head instead. Whatever had transpired between them during their journey north clearly bothered him.

Eavha sighed deeply. "Becoming someone you aren't will not win him back."

Sucking in a sharp breath, Aisling didn't expect the words to hit her so hard. Not for the same reason they made Dearmead turn his head in shame, but because Aisling realized she had only ever been someone she was not.

The pampered princess. The cruel Sparrow witch. The kind liberator.

They were a part of her, but they were not who she was. Tomorrow would change that, because after tomorrow, there would be no more masks to hide behind.

CHAPTER FIFTY-FOUR

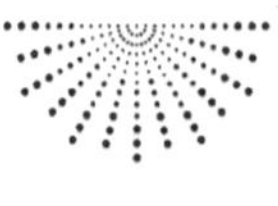

EAON

Eaon sat holding the washbowl as Killian cooled Reigan and Tomaii's foreheads with an icy cloth. There was an ache in his chest tainting the overwhelming gratitude for what they had done for him, and it was more than resentment that he couldn't do more to help them in return. It was resentment at being indebted to them. Which wasn't fair, he knew, but he couldn't help it. Too many times while laboring had he needed rescuing and had that debt dangled over his head like an axe.

"They should have just let me burn," he said quietly, scratching the still healing spots where the embers had burned him.

Killian gave him a strange look. "You're ridiculous."

"I would have lived."

Probably. He hadn't wanted to, but now that his mood had somewhat stabilized he doubted whatever plans the Lover had in store for him had come to pass yet.

"Yeah? In what condition?" Killian challenged. "I don't know what things are like in Wyldeden, but here in the mountains we don't let our friends burn to death, even if they're fucking idiots."

"If you're trying to make me feel better, it's not working."

But there was that word again. Friend. His stupid brain couldn't find a reason why the three of them would put themselves through this that didn't lead back to friendship. And it was trying. Really trying.

A too-familiar tiredness made it hard to lift his head, even as Tomaii groaned, trying to roll to his side.

"You're alright. Sleep," Killian said to him.

"Eaon?"

"He's here. He's fine."

Eaon clenched his eyes closed against the pain watering his eyes. He didn't deserve them. Not when he was one bad mood away from obliterating everything.

His head grew heavier.

Impossibly heavy.

Unusually heavy.

Blinking, sucking in a deep breath, he tried to straighten but found that his whole body had become as useless as stone.

Was he about to surge? Was he having some kind of episode? How could he get away from everybody? How could he contain it?

His hands lost their strength and the washbowl clattered to the ground.

"Eaon?" Killian's voice cracked as panic washed through him too.

Unable to move his mouth, the room fading to darkness, there was nothing he could do as he collapsed in a heap on the ground.

"Eaon, don't do this to me right now," Killian whined. "Fuck. I can't pick you up. Are you conscious? Are you alive?"

He was, but he had the distinct sensation of his mind, his soul and essence, slipping from his body. The world blurred into a swirl of color and shape he couldn't comprehend, movement flashing by in ways that didn't make any sense.

Only one other solid thing existed, and he did not recognize her.

Because we've never met, she said, as if reading his mind. *I'm sorry I had to drag you here when you've had no training, but it's urgent.*

She came forward, but as Eaon looked down he couldn't see his body. It didn't exist anymore, and the sensation was familiar. It was like being in the Lover's realm, except he was not dead and this place was all color and dizzying motion.

Another Spirit, then.

No, she answered his unasked question again. *My name is Moyra Thorne. Cinn is here in Ahrenhale with me. I am Morvia-blessed and I have seen something in the stars that Cinn said you needed to know urgently. It's about Eavha.*

All thoughts emptied from his mind as he stared at the witch, so close he could have touched her if he had any hands.

She's followed Aisling Aurnia to Pirevia to fight Prince Nevan. Dearmead is with her. The stars show a massacre.

Eaon froze. The words wouldn't sink in. Eavha did not fight, and she would not assist Aisling after what she had done to Cinn. It made no sense. It made no sense why this Moyra witch even knew or cared about his sister.

I know it is a lot, and it is confusing. I warned Cinn this might be too much for you, so try to put this out of your mind. When we meet, I will explain as much as I can. Just focus on Eavha. She needs you. Dearmead needs you. And Aisling. You must protect her at all costs.

Moyra was starting to fade, the manic colors slowing as the world began to take shape again. His skin was tingling . . . his skin. His body. It was back now.

Opening his eyes, Eaon took a moment to remember how to move. How to breathe and speak. It had only been a minute, but his body felt foreign and heavy and material in a way he almost resented. The colors of the cave seemed dull in comparison to the realm he had just come from.

A blanket was placed over him, Killian's muttering straining against the disconnect still lingering between Eaon and his body.

Focus on Eavha.

Eavha. In Pirevia. With the Sparrow princess.

"Shit," he hissed, the sound of his own voice shattering the glass wall in his head. Moving his arms, his legs, Eaon pushed himself onto unsteady feet.

"Whoa, are you alright? What happened?" Killian asked, half crouched by Reigan, who had begun to stir.

"I have to go."

"What?"

"Eavha is in trouble. I need to get to Pirevia."

He didn't wait for Killian's questions, ignoring his insistence that Eaon sit down for a second, to drink some water, as he pulled a set of discarded mountain clan leathers from a pile on the floor and tugged them on over his clothes.

The more he moved the more of his strength returned and soon he was barreling down the cavern's passages faster than ever before. Pirevia was two weeks away at least, and on the other side of the Vein. He needed a horse, but the nearest human town was in the wrong direction and he had nothing to trade. He thought of the sky witches' moths, but they would never lend him one. Stealing one would take too long, and if he was caught he would be in even bigger shit. If he could even ride one without killing it.

Kill them, his magic whispered. *Kill them and take what you need.*

For Eavha, for Dearmead, he would. And that terrified him.

Footsteps echoed behind him, but Eaon didn't slow down enough to see who was following him. Bursting out of the caves, the clear night sky illuminated the gorge.

"This way," Killian panted, taking off toward the path that led topside.

Eaon sucked in a breath and followed.

With Killian alongside, the guardians patrolling the gorge didn't stop them, only shouting to ask if they needed help. Neither bothered to respond.

Just before they reached the top of the gorge, Killian darted to the left and into a nook almost entirely hidden by bamboo. Again, Eaon followed, blinking back his shock as he took in the stables. Horses. He hadn't known the clan had horses.

"Take Daani. She's fastest."

"You have horses?" he couldn't help but ask.

"The elders do. This is Miika's."

Eaon went to grab the reins from the hook on the wall, then paused. He couldn't touch the horse without killing it. But Killian was already moving, throwing leather blankets, a saddle and reins over the patient animal.

"She understands verbal commands, so you shouldn't need to touch her," Killian continued, dragging over a stepping stool so Eaon could climb onto Daani carefully.

"You just . . . believe me?" Eaon asked, frowning deeply as he settled into the saddle, gripping the reins tightly.

"Of course I do."

"Kil, you'll be in trouble for this. Miika—"

"Miika can bite it."

Eaon shook his head as Killian smiled, then gave the horse a smack, sending them off into the night.

He'd made it to the bottom of the mountain, racing along grassy planes at the speed of a comet, when he heard it. Hooves.

Risking a glance behind him, hoping the clan was following him to help and not hinder, Eaon nearly choked on the unexpected sight. A horse with no rider, coat black as a starless night, eyes shimmering in buttercup yellow and long horns curling up and away from its face.

Eaon braced himself, wishing he'd thought to grab a weapon besides the staff strapped to his back. He didn't have time for this nonsense with the Old One.

As the phouka caught up, its hot breath warming the back of Eaon's neck, he turned pleading eyes to the faerie horse.

"Please. Not now . . ." Eaon panted. "My sister . . ."

"I know. Get on."

"What?"

"GET ON!"

He couldn't think, but the command was too powerful to resist. Rising in the saddle, careful where he let his bare feet find purchase, Eaon readied himself to leap between the speeding animals. The phouka was faster, keeping pace with a slightly panicked Daani as they came to run side by side. Eaon jumped, barely able to keep a hold of the black horse without a saddle or reins. Daani veered off, whinnying loudly as she turned back for the clan.

"Why?" Eaon panted, righting himself and gripping the horse's long whipping mane.

"You said I had to leave the mountain, but not that I couldn't come back. I waited for a chance to kill you, and I saw what they did. A favor was owed," the phouka explained. "Now hold on."

Eaon clutched the faerie tighter as they reached the crest of a hill and the horse leaped into the air. For one fleeting moment, the faerie disappeared with a *pop* before reappearing beneath him. The size of the bird he'd changed into was twice as large as the horse, black feathered wings flapped hard, pulling them into the sky.

"Holy Mother." Eaon clutched the bird and lowered himself flat across its back as the wind roared fiercely overhead.

At the contact between his bare palms and the phouka, the deadly magic tried and failed to rip into him.

Chuckling, the phouka shivered. "Mmm, tingly. I like it."

"Shut up."

Another laugh. Then, flapping his muscular wings, he added, "I hope you're not afraid of heights, little witch."

CHAPTER FIFTY-FIVE

AISLING

One look at Dearmead in his Terranian guardian leathers, all muscle and sternness, the spear strapped to his back and rows of stone daggers along his thighs, and Nevan undoubtedly believed he was here to fight for Aisling.

Her brother lounged in his royal box, that ridiculous mask on his face again. Aisling didn't understand it, and she didn't care to. The consort, Rhosyn, was nowhere in sight, but a burly man with twin swords at his sides stood in full armor, waiting.

A man to fight a witch, and still, Nevan had the nerve to look cocky.

Aisling, Eavha and Dearmead stood in the section of the rows across the arena that had been cleared just for them, shade cloths draped in an attempt to make it look like a second royal box. Guards stood along the edges, keeping the crowd at bay.

As the man in armor and Nevan exchanged a handshake, Aisling gave Eavha's hand a final squeeze. The human climbed down a rope ladder from the royal box into the arena, more guards quickly pulling it away.

Aisling began untying her skirt.

"Get my corset off, would you?"

"It's not too late. I will still fight for you," Dearmead offered, even as Eavha began to loosen the straps at the back of Aisling's dress

"I appreciate that. You don't know how much I appreciate that. But this is my fight."

She threw her skirts away and tore the corset off, ripping the pins and curls from her head.

"Don't hate me for asking, but are you sure? Can you really fight—" Eavha was fretting. It was sweet of her.

"Eavha, darling. Not only can I best that brute, but I'm going to make my brother regret not suffocating me in my cradle."

Beneath the dress, she had worn her supple leather body suit, her feet clad in steel-capped boots she'd had customized specifically for her feet. She felt more herself than she had in a very long time.

Nevan was staring across the arena in a state of shock as Aisling braided her hair and began strapping on her harnesses. Once all her weapons were in place, she gave Eavha a brief, sweet kiss.

"If for some reason this doesn't go my way, promise me you will go back to Hyrsch and rally whatever forces are left." Aisling caught Eavha's warm gaze and held it until the pretty little witch nodded.

Vaulting over the wall, Aisling jumped into the arena. Behind her was the caged door to where she knew Nevan kept his demi-kin fighters. The entertainment, as he called them.

How many demi-kin slaves had walked through that door? Down that hall of slick stone and stinking refuse that assaulted her even from where she stood? How many had been forced to fight each other, or some beast, to entertain Nevan and his barbaric people?

Nora had been in this arena. Had died in this shithole in the name of strategy.

A mistake.

Never again would she risk another's life.

The city had crowded into the stands to watch, children perched on the shoulders of men and breaking into screams of feral anticipation at the sight of Aisling standing in the muddy sand. It had been dampened on purpose, but she was used to fighting on a surface like this.

Nevan rose to his feet, still staring at her.

"Don't tell me none of your friends would stand for you?" he taunted, but there was a little panic in his eyes too.

"I don't need them to," she spat.

She didn't wait for the trumpets, drawing two daggers and making a beeline for Nevan's champion.

He smirked, stepping forward to meet her. Pulling free one of his swords, he swung.

So slow. So human.

Aisling pivoted around the blade, ducked under the male's large arm and, faster than he could ever hope to be, rammed her blade into the gap in his armor between the chest and abdominal plate. It wouldn't be enough to kill him, so with a sharp tug she ripped the armor clean off his body and used her other blade to slash open his gut. Hot blood spewed across her as the man staggered, staring down at where his intestines were falling in a slopping heap on the dirt.

The crowd was silent as he finally collapsed.

Aisling raised her chin at Nevan.

"I think your people were expecting a better show, brother. Why don't you stop being such a gutless coward and get down here."

For a moment, she wasn't sure Nevan would do it. But her brother had never been one to let her best him. Letting his cape fall from his shoulders, he leaped over the balustrade and landed in the mud in front of her. No armor, no battle suit.

"You want to play?" he asked, cocking his head. "What will mother and father think of this petty little squabble? Over a handful of vermin?"

Not waiting for him to finish his taunt, she kicked low to swipe his feet from under him. They had fought too often for the move to catch him off guard, but she didn't expect it to, turning into the spin and lashing out with her blades. He raised an arm to block, but she was stronger than she'd been when they were spatting witchlings in Kerveda, the force of her blow knocking him down. It wasn't only Nevan out of practice fighting against witches though. She was too slow to get out of the way as Nevan grabbed a hold of her braid and pulled her down with him, kicking the blades out of her hands as they landed hard in the mud.

A mistake she wouldn't make again. In the same breath, she rolled back to her feet and drew her axe, whirling it down on him.

Nevan had done the same, pulling the rapier at his waist. A delicate weapon compared to hers, but he had the strength to block, to shove her back and send her sprawling across the ground. He lunged, but Aisling was quick to her feet, dancing out the way.

"Clever trick," he said as he began to circle her, twirling his weapon in a pompous display.

The crowd screamed for her head, but she barely heard them as she fixed her grip and went on the attack.

Her strikes were quick, but so were Nevan's blocks. She couldn't get past, but he couldn't get her on the defensive, either. He wouldn't mind that though. He would be relying on her tiring herself out.

Which was happening. She was slowing, and finally he launched his first attack.

She dodged, turning directly into a rising knee that knocked the breath from her.

Stumbling back, she heard Eavha's scream of terror from the stands.

Aisling almost smiled. It was cute how little faith Eavha had in her.

Sensing weakness, Nevan went for the kill.

A vicious snarl escaped as she swung up with the axe, knocking his blow aside and opening up his left. Stepping in, she smashed her head into Nevan's nose. The crack that preceded the spray of blood across her face made her grin, and as Nevan stumbled back, she heaved her weapon over her shoulder and brought it down toward his head.

Nevan moved, but too slow.

The axe clipped the golden mask and sent it flying across the arena. The sudden waft of rotting flesh was the only warning she had before realizing half of her brother's face was missing, sinew and decaying meat exposed to the brutal sun.

Too shocked, she could only stare as Nevan's hand fluttered to the damaged side of his face. But it was too late to hide it.

"And you had the nerve to mock *my* face," she scoffed. "What the fuck happened to yours?"

Now he was angry.

"The Anfar cunt you brought with you would know."

Aisling flinched but hid it with a smirk. Since Eavha and her brother's escape from Pirevia last spring, Nevan had been *ill* she remembered.

"Got a habit of biting off more than you can chew, don't you?" she mocked, glad for a moment to catch her breath.

"As if you're any better," he spat, pus oozing from the wound in his face. "If only your army of rats could fight as well as you do, the ones you sent to storm my city might have been there to rescue your half-breed bitch instead of fertilizing the swamp."

Damn it. She had wondered what had happened to them.

"But don't worry," he added. "You'll be joining them in a minute."

He lunged, striking faster and harder than before, and Aisling found herself on the defensive. Silently, she begged Celeste to give her air. To keep it from her brother. To give his weapons resistance.

The Spirit listened.

"Bitch," Nevan spat, realizing what she was doing as he gasped for air. "Fucking bitch." Then a familiar word that stopped her heart. "*Vallhassanan.*"

Instinct dropped her to the ground, axe abandoned as she threw her arms over her head. The marks on her skin chilled as she forced the air to harden into a shield that absorbed the bolt of deathly magic spearing for her.

Again and again, her brother hissed curses at her while swinging his weapon until she was too busy rolling and ducking away from the steel, trying to keep her shield up against the bursts of magic, that she could no longer think about how to attack.

"What's wrong, Aisling? Don't want to play anymore?" he teased, stopping for a moment to catch his breath, soaking in the gleeful screams of the city surrounding them.

She felt it a moment before Nevan. The tremble in the earth beneath them.

But while he snarled and glared at the Wyldeden witches behind him, Aisling leaped for her daggers, half buried in the mud where the weapons had fallen.

Sensing her, Nevan whipped his head around. But he couldn't lift his feet, mud swallowing and hardening around them.

"Cheat!" he began before Aisling lunged, ramming a blade through his neck.

The venom didn't leave his face as he glared down at her. Why would it, when he believed the Lover would soon embrace him.

"I have prayed every day since I first learned of your cruelty that Death will deny you an embrace when I inevitably killed you," she told him. "Enjoy eternity in the void."

He only had a second for the fear to sink in before his eyes dulled and his body began to slacken. Aisling removed the blade and watched him fall. Heard the rattle of his final breath echo like a thunderclap in the otherwise silent arena.

Straightening, she looked up to Eavha.

Eavha, who was watching the crowd.

The shock and horror and rage that found its voice in the high tenor of a child.

"Kill her!"

CHAPTER FIFTY-SIX

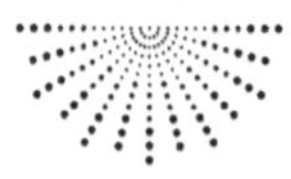

DEARMEAD

"Kill the bitch!"

The words rang through the arena, rousing the spectators and guards back to life.

"We need to get out of here," Dearmead said, reaching back for Eavha.

Who was gone.

Heart in his throat, Dearmead turned to look where she had been sitting a moment ago only to find her mid-leap over the barrier, dropping into the arena.

"Oh, fuck," he hissed, chasing after her.

Fuck.

Fuck, fuck, fuck.

The crowd was standing up, guards moving down the stairs carrying ladders. The ones closest to the exit gates blocked the way with swords in hands and there was more violence in their stillness than any fight that had ever taken place in this cursed arena.

Telling Eavha to run was pointless—there was nowhere to run to—so as Dearmead reached where she stood with Aisling, he put her between them.

"Can you portal us out?" Dearmead asked through clenched teeth, unlatching his spear from his back.

"I need a few minutes to recharge," Aisling panted, swaying slightly.

From every direction, men and women climbed down into the arena, armed with those human-forged blades that had cut right through Dearmead's leather last time.

The slightest pressure at his thigh stole his attention for a second. Eavha had taken one of the stone daggers strapped to him, but the steel in her eye was sharper.

"Last chance," Aisling warned the oncomers, exuding a confidence that couldn't be real. "Spare yourselves. Surrender the city."

"Witches or no; the three of you cannot take this city alone," one of the guards called back.

Dearmead knew how to pick a losing fight when he saw one.

This was it.

They would die today.

High above them, an earsplitting screech shattered the tension. Cries of alarm rippled as heads swiveled, searching the clouds for the source of the sound.

Dearmead nearly dropped his spear as he witnessed the beast descending from the clouds; a bird large enough it could have carried horses in its talons, shaped like a falcon but black as a crow. It was coming down fast, and the guards on the ground braced themselves as the creature's enormous wings sent wave after wave of downwind into the mud. The muscle in the creature's legs could have crushed a man's skull as they bunched under the weight of its landing.

"Oh, wow," Eavha breathed.

From the creature's back, Eaon carefully slid down into the arena. Wrapped in foreign leathers, his staff strapped to his back, Eaon bared his teeth at the Pirevians surrounding them. A chilling aura swelled but held dormant.

"If I have to reach for my staff, every human in this arena will die today," he warned them.

Aisling sucked in a sharp breath. "How . . ."

For one eternal second, hope fluttered through Dearmead's stomach.

From the corner of his eye, he spotted the slow movement of a guard pulling a throwing dagger from his belt, eyes trained on Eaon.

Not again.

Dearmead shifted his weight and threw his spear. It cracked the air like lightning as it streaked for the guard. His aim was perfect. The man's head split open with a spray of blood, the knife in his palm dropping harmlessly to the ground.

The screams of horror preceded the roars of battle by an ant's leg of a fraction. Drawing two more stone knives from his belt, Dearmead kept his back to Eavha as he watched the swarm descend upon them.

"Eaon!" Eavha screamed a mere second before he was out of sight. Panic knotted in Dearmead's throat, but he could not go to him. He had promised to protect Eavha, and Eaon would hate him forever if he abandoned her now.

The enormous falcon screeched before popping out of existence and reappearing as a black-furred goat-headed man, disappearing into the fray.

And then the Pirevians were upon them and Dearmead's head went silent.

He plunged one blade into the belly of a man just to rip it out and whip his fist into the head of another. Spinning, he swiped a leg across the ankles of two men approaching from the sides, sending them to the ground. But he couldn't just disable them. These people were here for blood.

The next time he threw a fist, he put his full strength into it and felt the skull of the woman crack beneath it.

Hot wetness sprayed across his neck, but he ignored the blood as he slashed another throat. Keen ears picked up the whistle of an arrow, and in the split second he saw it slicing through the air he knew it would hit Eavha. Pushing Eavha behind him, he knocked the arrow out of the air with the back of his arm. The leather where it brushed against him was hot, but the archer was already knocking another. Dipping and rolling across the soil, he stabbed up into the belly of an attacker before picking up the arrow, spinning to fling it back toward the archer. Messy, but effective as it sank into the man's face.

Screams swelled and rippled through the crowd just to be cut short.

In the blink of an eye, all the people between the three of them and Eaon melted into puddles of gore.

Dearmead spared a glance across the arena, but quickly wished he hadn't.

Eaon was bleeding, but his eyes had gone darker than night. Staff in hand, he aimed it at another guard and unleashed that terrible power living within him, a feral grin of ecstasy breaking across his face.

That was not Eaon.

Behind him, Eavha screamed.

Dearmead turned, already picking up his dagger again. Eavha was sprayed with red, her blade sunk into a man's side. He'd grabbed a hold of her hair though, pulling her away from the protective circle of Dearmead and Aisling, who was elbow deep in battle with three guardsmen.

There was no room to worry about anything except the kill.

Dearmead took the three steps needed to reach Eavha and plunged his knife through the man's back. He wasn't wearing armor. A civilian, so wrathful he had come to take his pound of flesh.

As the life bled from him, he let go of Eavha, who stumbled back wide-eyed, looking for her next attacker. Dearmead stayed close, turning to block the blows of a woman who'd come at him with nothing but her bare fists.

There were so many people still swarming in from the pews.

Dearmead knocked the woman to the ground just in time to block another, but too slow to stop the third from landing a punch to the side of his head.

Dearmead reeled but used his shifting weight to shove the human to the ground. He needed his spear back. That was where his strength truly lay.

Just as he spun back, braid whipping behind him, an arrow pierced the skull of another man, the shaft still aflame.

A new wave of terrified screams alerted him to more arrivals from the sky.

Four giant moths fluttered above the arena, two witches on each. The one in front was veiled while the one behind held a bow. Pulling another arrow from a quiver, the witch blew on the end of it, setting it alight.

Ignatius-blessed witches.

Two, at least. The other two shot regular arrows into the fray.

Dearmead sensed the change in the Pirevians. Many of the civilians were turning back, trying to climb back into the pews or through the single gate leading out of the arena. The guards were not as smart.

Sinking his blade into the weak spots of the human armor, he ducked under the swing of a long sword, rolled into the man's ankles and sent him sprawling. A punch to the throat disabled him and Dearmead took the blade.

It was far heavier than anything he knew how to fight with. What little practice he had done with Clayton was not enough.

Abandoning it, he threw one of his daggers into another archer taking aim at Aisling, then reached for his spare.

The spare Eavha had.

Swearing, Dearmead dodged another swing of a sword.

Nearby, the air tingled with a sickening magic, so Dearmead took a leap backward, rolling again to pluck a steel dagger from the belt of a fallen soldier.

The weight was still strange, but not unmanageable.

"No!"

The scream came a breath before the pain.

A burning poker in his back.

Instinctively, Dearmead grabbed the wrist of the woman who'd stuck a knife in him to stop her from twisting it or pulling it out. Her arm disintegrated in his hand as the guard melted into a pile of guts so quickly there wasn't time for her to scream.

"No."

Eaon's face had lost all color and the air began to prickle. The churning in his gut warned him of the scale of magic about to cascade through the arena.

Fuck.

Dearmead took a deep breath and, against all his training, pulled the blade out of his back, shuddering at the searing heat flushing through him as he did. It didn't linger. An itch a thousand times worse than the fire ants consuming his skin from Eaon's magic pulled at the wound.

There wasn't time to wallow. Lunging forward, Dearmead grabbed Eaon's hand and yanked him forward. Pulling him into a hard embrace the way Cinn used to do, the prickling on the outside becoming as intense as the itching inside.

"No!" Eaon screamed again, writhing in Dearmead's grip, trying to get away. "What are you doing?!"

Dearmead thought he knew pain, but he knew nothing. Compared to the death sinking into his every fiber, ripping him apart as fast as his new body could put itself back together, every wound he'd ever received in training, every beating he'd taken, was nothing.

As his knees buckled, vision spotting from it, Dearmead made sure he held onto Eaon. Made sure the surge of power pouring from him could hurt nobody but him.

The whistle of an arrow and the dying gurgle of the last guard somewhere behind him was the final sound before the rapid beating of Eaon's heart became the only thing Dearmead could hear.

Breathing hard, the acid eating at his body slowly began to ease. Eaon stopped trying to pull away, becoming heavy as his shaking hands found their way to Dearmead's elbows.

Warily, he loosened his grip. Eaon's eyes were wide, lips parted as he stared. Swallowing the ragged stone that had somehow found its way into his throat, Dearmead reached up to push a stray piece of Eaon's hair away from his sweaty face, curling it around his fingers as he did. Eaon held perfectly still as he let Dearmead's fingers trail slowly down the side of his bare neck.

Closing those empty, void-black eyes, Eaon shuddered.

"How."

"Eavha made me kinner."

Eaon opened his eyes again, the amber in them alight.

For the first time since Eavha had jumped into the arena, Dearmead breathed.

"For you." His mouth went dry. Too many times, he'd held back what he'd really wanted to say. Too many times, it had nearly been too late to say them. "I love you."

Eaon flinched. Reaching up to cup his cheek, Dearmead hated seeing the light in Eaon's eyes flicker in disbelief. The hum of magic against his palm was pleasant now, the way it was to lie on Eaon's chest and feel his voice vibrate.

"I always have and I always will."

Hand trembling, Eaon held Dearmead's palm to his face, leaning into the contact before kissing him in a homecoming more healing than any spell. The axis of the world righted itself once again as Dearmead parted his lips, tongue rolling against Eaon's for too brief a moment.

Pulling back, Eaon rested his forehead against Dearmead's as he whispered, "I love you too. Always have. Always will."

The warmth that spread through Dearmead's body at those words was unexpected; he grinned giddily as he kissed Eaon again, gently.

"If you two are finished sucking face, I'm waiting for my thank you."

Eaon turned to glare at his sister, whose cheeks had dimpled from the force of her smile.

"How about I thank you by not strangling you for jumping into a Pirevian arena!"

Eavha's smile disappeared. "I'll take it."

"And you." Eaon stepped away from Dearmead entirely to stalk toward Aisling, whose gray hair was soaked in red. She wiped streaks of blood from her face as she returned her axe to the harness across her back.

Everywhere, the bodies of Pirevian soldiers lay bleeding. Only the dead were left, the living having fled entirely. Before Eaon could take another step closer toward Aisling, to add her body to the pile, the black fae creature grabbed a hold of him.

Dearmead flinched, waiting, but it did not seem affected.

"You are not under control yet," it said to him in a voice like two rocks being ground together.

"I'm fine," Eaon snapped, trying to shrug out of the faerie's grip.

Around them, the four giant moths were landing, their passengers disembarking.

"Eaon, you alright?" one of them asked, threading his bow over his arm and jogging toward them.

"Killian," Eaon breathed, shaking his head. "What . . ."

Eaon made to step toward his friend, but his knees buckled. If the fae hadn't been holding him he'd have gone down into the mud and filth coating the arena floor.

Dearmead ran to his side. "You okay?"

"Yeah," he panted, but his arms were shaking.

"We need to get somewhere safe to rest," Eavha said, looking around. "Before they come back with reinforcements."

"Someone open the gates," Aisling panted, pointing toward the one that would lead to the demi-kin.

Dearmead doubted they knew who she was, but one of the sky witches jogged for the gate, unlocking it quickly with a muttered spell.

"Would someone mind telling me what the fuck is going on?" Another of the witches asked as he strode from one of the moths. "It's not often Killian comes running to me, begging for help, but I didn't think this was what you were dragging me into. Dragging our clan into!"

"Miika . . ." Eaon started, but he was getting weaker. Dearmead pulled his other arm over his shoulder to help the fae keep him upright.

"We were on the brink of war with Wyldeden because of what you did to Eaon," Killian snapped. "Saving their heir might just settle things down."

"At the cost of getting into a war with Sparrows?" Miika's voice became high pitched.

"No," Aisling interrupted. "I am Sparrow. You will not be punished for aiding me."

The relief on Miika's face was short lived as Eavha stepped forward.

"What did you do to my brother?"

The same question was on Dearmead's lips, grip tightening on Eaon's waist.

"Nothing, Eavha. Don't worry about it," Eaon panted. Then forced a smile. "It's good to see you."

Fists clenched, soaked in dirt and blood and sweat, Eavha managed to smile back at him.

"Put your grievances aside for now," the faerie said. "I sense discord. I think it wise if I investigate. But you," he looked down to Eaon, yellow eyes blazing. "No more magic. Not another lick of it until we have a talk."

Even Dearmead felt the power in the command. Eaon nodded, a little dazed.

Taking Eaon's weight, Dearmead watched as the faerie stepped back and popped once more, turning back into the enormous bird and taking to the skies.

From the southern gated archways, the sky witch came back. Behind her, demi-kin emerged. Most of them looked around the arena in states of shock. One female began stomping on the head of a dead guard.

One male stopped walking, staring at the princess of Hyrsch.

"Owen," Aisling said, so softly the male didn't likely hear.

Still, he dropped to his knees and buried his face in his hands.

Ignoring Eaon's glaring, Aisling walked past him toward the demi-kin. Knelt beside him.

"Nora's husband," Eavha explained gently. "Let them grieve."

Running a hand through his hair, the witch who'd shouted at Miika looked around at the empty pews. "We should get somewhere safe before another riot breaks out."

"You're right." Eaon nodded. Then, "Killian, this is Dearmead. Dearmead, Killian. My friend from the Northern Mountain Clan."

Dearmead nodded at the mountain witch before suggesting, "I remember the way to Kaelean's apartment. We should—"

"We should go to the palace," Eavha interrupted. "Whether they like it or not, the guards there are employed by the Coven and must guard Aisling. At least until the king and queen says otherwise. As long as we stick with her, we'll be protected. Plus, there is the consort and the advisors to deal with, and Aisling will—"

"I'm sorry," Eaon stopped her, raising his eyebrows. "I was under the impression we were getting the fuck out of here now that you're not about to be the victim of mob brutality."

Eavha straightened her shoulders. Dearmead doubted this conversation was going to go well, and here, now, was not the time or place to have it.

"We all have a lot to talk about, I think," he said before they could start fighting. "Let's secure the palace. We'll fill you in on the princess and my new mark, and you can tell us all about your new friends."

The word carried every ounce of threat Dearmead could put into it. If this Miika figure had done something to hurt Eaon . . .

Behind them, Aisling had removed Owen's collar and helped him to his feet. The demi-kin was in a state of shock and could barely walk.

There was much to be done.

CHAPTER FIFTY-SEVEN

DEARMEAD

DEARMEAD WOULD HAVE LOVED NOTHING MORE THAN TO SLIP AWAY
with Eaon immediately, but he was the closest thing to a guard Aisling
had as they took Nevan's palace.

News that the prince had fallen had spread quickly, and the guards
at the palace were in fighting stances when they arrived. One look at
Aisling's blood-soaked face, at Eaon and his phouka friend who had
already returned from a quick flight around the city, and the pack of
murderous demi-kin beside them, had most of the guards throwing
their swords on the ground.

A few fought. They quickly died.

And ever since his first kill in this city all those months ago, the
visceral grief Dearmead felt as their souls left their bodies slowly begun
to numb. He would still pray for forgiveness later, would still think
about them for days or weeks afterward, but his stomach had
hardened. Just the way his ma had always said it would.

Owen was a shell of a man, but he led the other demi-kin toward
the stairwell that would take them down into that awful prison
Dearmead had rescued Eaon, Eavha and Cinn from last spring. There
were others to be liberated, he overheard someone saying—demi-kin
who had never seen the sky a day in their lives.

But Aisling did not follow him, powering ahead to the grand castle and whipping her blade across the throats of anyone who didn't bow. No mercy, no pity warmed the stony wrath on her face as she carved a path of death through the halls. For the first time, Dearmead worried about their alliance with her.

"Where is she?" Aisling hissed to one of the guards who had gotten on his knees before her.

"Wh-who?"

"Rhosyn. Nevan's whore."

The guard swallowed deeply. "Her room, most likely."

Aisling kicked him, then stormed toward a staircase, calling over her shoulder as she did. "Find whoever calls themselves an authority in this fucking shithole and have them meet me in Nevan's throne room."

"I should keep things in order there," Eaon muttered, having regained enough strength to walk on his own.

"Be careful," Eavha pleaded.

With a short nod, Eaon and the phouka strode after the Pirevian guards. It took every ounce of Dearmead's self-control not to follow him, but he went with Eavha and Aisling up the long spiraling stairs to a pretty suite where a plump woman in silk robes stood trembling, her blond hair in limp curls.

"Pr-princess," she stuttered, backing away quickly.

"Nora's death is your fault," Aisling spat, raising her axe.

"Aisling, slow down," Eavha said softly.

Aisling ignored her. "After I kill you, I'm going to hunt down your precious demi-kin lover and slaughter him and everyone he loves, just to spite you!"

"No!" Rhosyn sobbed, darting around the bed, crawling across it to keep away from Aisling. "Please! I was cursed! I had no choice but to turn her in!"

"I don't give a fuck!" Aisling screeched, any pretense of the proper princess she had been in Hyrsch completely gone.

"It's not her fault!" Eavha snapped, throwing herself in front of the human woman. "You're the one who concocted a plan that hinged on a stranger's love. You're the one who sent Nora here!"

Dearmead stiffened, trying to move silently enough that Aisling wouldn't notice him putting himself in position to attack. He didn't want to kill the princess, but he would not let any harm come to Eavha.

Aisling stopped chasing the human, incensed, her eyes and nostrils flaring.

"How dare you."

"It's not untrue. Killing this woman will not take the pain away, Aisling. Neither will torturing her, so get that look off your face." Eavha left Rhosyn and stepped up to Aisling, putting one steady hand on the hilt of the bloody weapon, the other on Aisling's shoulder. "Nora would not approve. Now is not the time to make decisions."

Like the sway of a willow's braches when the wind suddenly died, Aisling sagged. Then turned her poisonous gaze back to Rhosyn.

"I'm taking the city. If you don't want to lose your head, I suggest you stay in your room until summoned."

"Alright," Rhosyn whimpered.

Aisling kept it together until she slammed the door closed. Collapsing against the wall, she dropped her weapon and took a shuddering breath.

"I only said those things to make you stop," Eavha promised as she took the princess's face in her hands.

Dearmead kept an eye on the halls as Eavha continued whispering sweet words, pulling the breaking pieces of Aisling back together until she found the strength to stand again.

Over the next few hours, the phouka took routine flights around the city and reported back on how the people rioted, marching in the streets and calling for Aisling's head. The mountain and sky witches left to gather reinforcements, leaving only the ones named Killian and Miika behind.

None of them were required as Aisling sat in the throne room, arguing with the Pirevian advisors. They would not dare harm her, and Dearmead had no doubts that she could handle them if they tried.

Instead, he and the rest had settled in the infirmary. Eavha was organizing the demi-kin, treating the most unwell first; the ones from the arena were battered and bruised, but those who'd come up from the prison were barely alive. Finding a space, Eaon gathered fresh water and food for the ravenous prisoners while Dearmead blessed bandages and mixed simple salves to tide the less injured ones over until Eavha could get to them.

Killian and Miika were arguing with the guards outside, trying to get them to cooperate, but without Aisling present many of them were beginning to question how loyal they planned on being.

"I still think we should go while we can," Eaon muttered. "Leave the princess to her mess."

"You are biased because of her history with Cinn," Dearmead spoke quietly.

"And that should be enough," Eaon hissed. "How could either of you stomach being near her, let alone work with her?"

Dearmead took a deep breath. "Well, firstly, I'm pretty sure Eavha's in love with her."

Eaon shattered a glass between his now-gloved hands, nostrils flaring wide as he turned toward his sister, mouth opening as if planning to chastise her right there and then. Dearmead grabbed his arm, ignoring the way Eaon flinched.

Looking down at the contact, Eaon shook his head. "I'm still not used to that."

"Secondly," Dearmead continued, before he could fall into the trap of telling Eaon exactly how used to it he hoped they could become. "I know you've heard about the First War, but I'm not sure how much stock you put into it."

"What does that have to do with anything?"

"It's real, Eaon. Chaos is real and he's coming. Aisling is the only Sparrow who seems to believe it, or care. That's who Aadya's master is. That's who turned her into whatever she is now, mutating her into something impossible."

Doubt began to crease Eaon's brow, but then he stilled, eyes darting side to side the way they did when he was figuring about a puzzle.

"I've seen some strange, rather impossible things up in the mountains recently," he said quietly. "But . . . no. No, that's ridiculous."

"I don't think it is. Neither does Eavha, or Kaelean. She sent us approval to stay and investigate. Becoming kinner was a part of that."

Turning away, Eaon began cleaning up the broken glass littering the counter. Dearmead could see his mind working, trying to process it. Trying to grasp the enormity of the problem.

"Well, shit."

"That's what I said."

"I . . . I had this weird dream. A dream that wasn't a dream. Moyra Thorne, the witch Cinn went to find, came to me and told me about Eavha coming to this place. That she needed me. And that the princess had to be protected."

Nothing really surprised Dearmead when it came to Morvish witches anymore. They were the least understood of all the Spirit-blessed for a reason.

"I know you hate her—"

"You have no idea how deeply I hate her."

"—but I think you need to take that as a sign."

"I'll take it as a sign not to kill her on sight," was all Eaon promised. Then he wrinkled his nose, shaking his head. "Her and Eavha? Seriously?"

Dearmead shrugged. "It's weird."

"That's a word choice I wouldn't have made."

Smiling, Dearmead reached out to brush his fingers against Eaon's leathers, simply wanting to touch him again. "You're surprisingly okay with all of this."

"I'm in a weird state of semi-frenzied delusion right now, so I'm not convinced this isn't all a really bad dream."

He said it as a joke, but Dearmead knew how Eaon could get sometimes. The stress of the arena, the pressure of it all, the adrenaline, the fighting . . . it would make sense for Eaon to be off, but there was a wildness coursing through him, blazing behind his eyes, that was too familiar. He blinked too much, teeth gnashing.

"I know it's a lot to take in, but are you alright?" Dearmead asked.

"Yeah, yeah," he said distractedly.

"Is it because of your magic?"

"No. I mean, that's . . . a bit, but I'm just, you know."

Dearmead nodded. "Do you have any of your tonics?"

Eaon snorted and didn't elaborate.

"Eaon."

"They haven't worked in months, okay? I had it looked into at the mountains, and Kaelean sent me to a dodgy brewer who didn't like me. My tonics weren't being blessed, and the ones I could get in the mountains were weird. They worked, but they were weird, and I'd already gone through the withdrawals so I didn't see the point—"

"Wait, what?" Dearmead frowned, a familiar anger brewing in his gut. "That's bullshit. They can't do that."

"Is that really what seems the most important thing right now?" Eaon asked, turning to look at him. "I'm alright."

And there it was again. That fire in Dearmead's belly that never truly died flared with vibrancy, along with the insatiable desire to touch him.

Eaon must have seen it, because he cleared his throat and mumbled, "I'm going to get this food out."

"Yeah, alright," Dearmead sighed, returning to the bandages.

***

The sun had set, but the city was finally under control. The phouka had gone to find a nearby friend to help patrol the streets, keeping the civilians in line, while the reinforcements from the North Mountain kept guard of the palace.

In one of the grand council rooms, so very different and yet also similar to the ones in Hyrsch, Dearmead and the others had gathered once more. Aisling sat at the head of the table, an open bottle of wine on the table, her hand limp around the neck as she stared at the ceiling, utterly exhausted. Eavha sat beside her, chin on the table, eyes blinking heavily.

Miika and Killian had insisted on joining them, representing the mountain clan's involvement in this coup, but neither of them had the energy to stand up. Dearmead sat beside them, struggling as well, but he was also busy watching Eaon, who paced the length of the room over and over.

"It's simple," he finally said. "We find out where Chaos's army is gathering, I walk in and let loose. War averted."

Eavha, Dearmead, Killian and the Phouka all said at the same time, "No."

"Why?" Eaon threw his hands up. "It's the most obvious solution."

"Because I've seen how it hurts you," Killian said.

"Because Chaos can just make another army. We have to cut the head off the snake," Eavha added.

Dearmead didn't have a reason, he just didn't like the idea of Eaon walking into an army of beasts.

"Because"—the phouka stepped forward—"it will feed the seed."

Everyone in the room turned.

"What are you even still doing here?" Eaon rounded on him. "You helped me get here. You helped in the arena, and you helped take the city. Your debt is paid."

"I am here because after seeing you in that arena, I cannot in good conscious leave you to continue to feed it. What you will bring into the world should never see the light of day."

"What is he talking about?" Dearmead asked.

"What seed?" Eavha sat up, rubbing her eyes.

"The Phouka is an Old One," Eaon explained. "And he thinks my magic is a seed. I don't know."

"You have blessings, that much I can smell on you. But where the death stems from is not a blessing. Death has planted a seed in you."

"What seed?" Eavha was zeroed in on that one part. Of course.

"There are plenty of Lover-blessed witches around. What makes Eaon different?" Killian added.

"Every time he takes a soul, you can see it in his eyes. Something *other* lives inside him, growing stronger. You feel it, don't you? Every time you kill, it gets harder to stop. Gets harder to find yourself again. The magic inside you is sentient, riling you up, making you crave what makes it stronger, but you weaker. One day, you will take a life and you will not come back. The thing inside you will take over. And if it is Death who put it there, then Death it will serve. Perhaps they wish to come to this plane themself. Face Chaos themself. Fight on behalf of Mother, as they never did before. You would be their vessel, lost to the

High Spirit that would take all you are and change you to suit their cause."

Silence sat heavy in the room before Eavha turned to Eaon.

"Power corrupts."

The words Yomra had told them the last time they were in this awful city.

Eaon paled as he recalled Yomra's instruction to him. "Stop fighting it."

No.

He had to fight it.

The expression on the phouka's face, on Eavha and Killian's, matched Dearmead's silent refusal to let this seed take root.

"Obviously," Eaon started, clearing his throat before continuing, "Obviously, I would prefer that not to happen. But, if that's what has to be done to stop Chaos, if that's how I am useful—"

"No," Dearmead snarled, rising from his chair and storming to where Eaon had finally stopped pacing.

There was resignation in his eyes that made Dearmead want to throw up. He was already surrendering to it. This so-called purpose that had been thrust upon him against his will. Again.

Dearmead took his face and put every ounce of command he could muster into his next words. "No. I cannot lose you again."

"I already have a plan against Chaos," Aisling spoke up, tipping more wine down her gullet. "Sacrifices have already been made for his defeat. It will be enough."

Eaon turned away, leveling a look of revulsion at Aisling. "I don't recall asking for your input, hag."

"We aren't going to solve anything else tonight." Miika raised his hands and stood wearily from the table. "I need to report back to my high priest. If war is coming, we need to prepare. But we can reconvene after a few hours' sleep and some food. I would like to hear about this plan."

Eaon scoffed, pulling himself away from Dearmead and storming from the council room. Exchanging a look with Eavha, Dearmead nodded and chased after him.

"Eaon."

"Every word out of her dumb mouth makes me . . . makes me . . ."

He rubbed his wrists, and for the first time Dearmead noticed the leather straps wrapped around them.

"Hey," Dearmead grabbed a hold of his arm to stop him from walking away. "What are those?"

"The cuffs? They're spell-marked. Stop me from surging. Not always comfortable."

Dearmead ran a thumb along the leather, feeling the magic sizzling. Then he raised Eaon's hand to his mouth and let his lips brush against the cool skin. Felt the buzz of that deadly magic touching him, and bouncing off harmlessly.

Moving the hand from his mouth to his cheek, Dearmead hummed quietly as Eaon's palm sent that buzz all down his neck and into his chest.

Eaon had stopped breathing, pupils dilated so wide the honey of his eyes was a thin ring.

"I know you're bordering on a frenzy right now," Dearmead said softly. "And I know there's a lot of water yet to pass under the bridge between you and me. And I want you to know that I didn't do this, become kinner, as some kind of attempt to convince you to forgive me, and you're not obligated to. But Mother of all, Eaon, I have fucking missed you."

"I can't. We can't." His voice was breaking, rage forgotten. "I . . . I need it too much."

To be close to someone. To feel their affection on his skin. A physical promise that he was not alone, not unwanted. Words had never been enough to comfort Eaon, but a hug, a kiss, a night beneath the sheets, usually did the job. These months of being unable to touch would have driven him mad, and it had never been clearer how badly he needed this.

"I know you do."

But simply needing something had never been enough for Eaon, either. Dearmead knew that, too often, Eaon had been required to put other's needs before his own. That he was of stable enough mind to hesitate instead of devolving into starved abandon at the promise of a warm body to entangle himself in was all the proof Dearmead needed this would not be a mistake.

With a shake of his head, Eaon warned, "I don't know what I think. I don't know what I feel."

"It doesn't have to mean anything," Dearmead promised.

"It will mean something to you."

"It doesn't have to."

Loosing a trembling breath, Eaon's resistance crumbled. He took Dearmead's hand and stalked down the halls, pushing open doors until they found an empty room. It probably belonged to a servant of some kind as it had only a single bed with a dusty old blanket, a toilet and sink in the corner, and a chest of drawers under a dirty window.

Closing the door with his foot, Dearmead leaned back against it, breathing ragged as Eaon stepped into his space. Carefully, his lips brushed against Eaon's. The prickle where their skin met was acute, somewhere between painful and pleasant. A low whine escaped, and what little space there was between them disappeared. Eaon's mouth moved hungrily, his hands pushing Dearmead's hips back against the wall. The heat relaxed every muscle in his body, any concerns disappearing. One hand cupping Eaon's jaw, the other found its way back to tangle in the wild hair Eaon had bound back in a knot.

"I didn't talk you into this, did I?" Dearmead panted, suddenly worried.

Eaon's mouth had moved to his jaw, teeth grazing against stubble before sucking on the tender flesh of his throat. Further words had completely dissolved in Dearmead's mouth, grip tightening as he held his head there.

"I missed you," he said instead, closing his eyes as Eaon's fingers found the buckle of his pants and began to loosen them. "I missed you so much."

"I missed you too," Eaon muttered, resting his forehead on Dearmead's shoulder. "I missed this."

Dearmead turned his face to nip at Eaon's ear, but waited.

"You promise this doesn't mean anything?"

"Swear."

Another whine and Eaon brought his head up, eyes wild with desire as he took Dearmead's mouth again.

"You look so weird in leather," Dearmead said stupidly as they pulled apart again so he could unbuckle the straps at Eaon's side.

"Thanks." Eaon rolled his eyes as he helped pull the blood-slicked gear over his head. Then the sweat-soaked linen shirt that probably used to be white but now was anything but. He flung the cloth across the room. "Better?"

Dearmead swallowed, eyes roaming over Eaon's bare chest. A painful squeeze of panic dulled the desire flooding his veins as he ran his calloused fingers over the fresh scars flecking bronze skin that had once been so flawless. The large jagged one over his sternum that Dearmead knew had a twin on his back was still red and shiny. The smaller ones, more than his blurring eyes could focus on, would also have copies.

"Hey," Eaon said softly, cupping Dearmead's face and turning his gaze upward. "I'm okay."

"I'm sorry." He didn't realize how heavy those unsaid words had been until he set them down.

"It's not your fault, Dea."

None of the anger and resentment he had seen lingering in Eaon's eyes the last time he saw him remained. Words had lost meaning entirely. He didn't know the right ones to explain what Eaon's forgiveness meant to him, or how it only made him more determined to make sure nothing bad ever happened to Eaon again.

Words had never been enough, anyway. Eaon had to be shown, and Dearmead planned on taking his sweet time making sure he thoroughly understood the way he loved him.

CHAPTER FIFTY-EIGHT

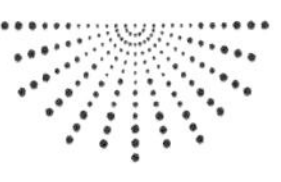

EAON

The window in the tiny servant's room wasn't large, so the morning light that filtered through was pale and dusty. It was still enough to wake Eaon from the best sleep he'd had in a very long time, content in the stuffy room full of stale air, the smell of their bodies thick in his head.

The two of them were tangled, crammed onto the small bed only wide enough for one of them to lay flat. Eaon looked down to where Dearmead had fallen asleep, head warm and heavy on his chest. Slowly, he traced the lines of his lips. Kissed his forehead, relishing the saltiness of his skin before pushing a damp piece of hair back into the braid falling apart across Dearmead's back. A back that rippled with muscle as Dearmead shifted, sighed, then settled once more, hot breath sending a shiver down Eaon's spine.

The familiar warmth calmed something that had been restless ever since being excommunicated, and yet at the same time that he wanted to lay in this bed with Dearmead forever, he also wanted to run. Familiarity was as frightening as it was comforting, and he quite suddenly knew that there was no part of him that wanted to go back to Wyldeden. There was no part of him that felt it was home.

"I can literally feel you overthinking," Dearmead mumbled sleepily.

"Sorry. Didn't mean to wake you."

"The sun woke me."

Eaon raised an eyebrow and smiled knowing that Dearmead had been awake, content to lay lazily across his chest. It was almost disappointing when he shifted, raising his head enough to meet Eaon's eye.

"Don't think. Just be happy."

"Wow, Dea. Why didn't I ever think of that before."

With a sigh, Dearmead gathered his long hair and twisted it up into a knot before pushing himself onto his elbows, hovering over Eaon's face.

"Want some help?"

A giddy thrill rushed through him as he craned his neck to reach Dearmead's lips. His throat. Grazing the kiss against his shoulder, Eaon shuddered at the feeling of being this close to someone again.

As Dearmead burrowed into his neck, Eaon took and kissed his wrist. It was there he noticed the strange callouses on Dearmead's fingers. "This is new."

Grimacing, Dearmead raised his head to see where Eaon rubbed his thumb against the hardened skin. "I've been . . . writing. A lot."

"Writing?"

"Yeah."

Eaon tilted his head, curious.

With a sigh, Dearmead settled back down and admitted, "I had some free time in Hyrsch and a lot on my mind, so . . . I was writing a story."

"Wait, really?" Eaon stopped rubbing Dearmead's callous and eased his thumb across the lines of his palm instead, massaging the places he knew his own hand cramped when he'd been writing too long. "What's it about?"

"It's just made-up stuff."

But Dearmead wouldn't look at him, pressing his mouth back to the base of Eaon's throat.

"Stop trying to distract me. What's it about?"

The kissing stopped, and it took a while before Dearmead found the courage to raise his face once more, inches away from Eaon's.

"It's about you, okay? And me. Except . . . not really. I wrote us both as human princes, and there's this stupid drama in it about a crown. It's dumb."

Eaon's eyes sparkled. "Can I read it?"

"It's in Hyrsch."

"But can I read it?"

The shame threatening to shut him down retreated as Dearmead took in Eaon's genuine excitement.

"Maybe when it's finished."

"I can wait. But can I have a spoiler?"

Dearmead's face twisted with so much heat and pain that Eaon stopped smiling. Again, it took a while for Dearmead to find the words. When he did, Eaon almost wish he hadn't.

"In the end, I stay. I stay with you."

Eaon swallowed. "Why?"

"What do you mean?"

"Why would you want to stay?"

Frowning, Dearmead took his chin. "You know why."

He had told him a thousand times why, from of the long list of people who'd ever expressed an interest in Dearmead, he had waited for Eaon. Still waited for Eaon. Yet he couldn't make sense of it.

"I haven't been well for a while, Dea."

"I know. I can tell. Do you regret last night?"

"Only in the sense that you should. Things are calming down in my head now, but the last few months . . . I'd have slept with Tomaii if I could have. I would have slept with Cinn if he wanted to. And I don't know how I feel about any of it, any of them." Eaon didn't want to talk about what he felt for Cinn. He wasn't even sure he understood it, or what point there was in feeling it. There was something there, but it was different. That was more obvious now than ever. "And then there's you . . ."

"Eaon, I know." Dearmead brushed a thumb along his lips, gaze trained on them. "How long have we known each other? And how many times have I told you that it's okay to want and need?"

Too often.

"And, to be perfectly honest, from what I know about Cinn and what you've told me about Tomaii, there are worse people you could choose. There are worse things you could be doing when the frenzy comes. And don't worry about me. I promised you this didn't have to mean anything. You needed this, and I . . . I did too. Even if down the track you choose Tomaii, or Cinn, I can live with that. We had this moment. A proper goodbye."

Eaon stared at Dearmead, empty headed for the first time in a long time.

Dearmead grimaced, shaking loose his long, silky sheen of black hair. "That got weird."

"No."

"It's the writing. It's helped me find my words."

Eaon smiled, skin tingling. "I'm glad. And thank you. I don't deserve—"

"Don't finish that sentence."

Eaon didn't, letting Dearmead's warm mouth find his again. But the mental silence only lasted a few minutes. He stopped Dearmead before things got too far again. There was one last thing he needed to say.

"Dea?"

"Mm?" Dearmead hummed from where his mouth was working its way down Eaon's chest. His stomach. Biting his lip, he closed his eyes. He couldn't let this go on. He had to say it.

"Once everything is sorted, I'm going to go."

Dearmead stopped, coming back up. One look at Eaon and he nodded, as if having expected nothing less. "Go where?"

"Back to the North Mountains to wait for Cinn, then once he's settled . . . I don't know. I don't know where I'm going, but I know . . . I'm going to go wild. Kaelean won't like it, but I think it's just who I am. I don't think I was meant to stay in one place."

He hadn't expected such a sad smile from Dearmead. "I think you're right."

His friend, his lover, his home, couldn't meet his eye. Last night, Dearmead had said something about sex not having to mean anything. That he hadn't become kinner with the expectation that doing so would win Eaon back somehow. At the time, he had been too overwhelmed to process the words or to reply with any kind of sense.

But it meant something.

"Would you come with me?"

Dearmead's gaze snapped to Eaon's, face slackening.

"You want me to come with you?"

"I'm not going to be mad if you don't want to. You have to live the life that's right for you, and I have to live mine, but—"

Dearmead closed his eyes, letting his head hang low. Low enough for Eaon to press another tender kiss against his forehead.

"I'll come with you. I'd go anywhere with you."

The relief shuddered deeply in Eaon's chest. The part of him that wanted to run rejoiced, as did the part of him that wanted to stay. He could have both. He could have everything.

Nevan's palace was bare of servants, of whoever else would normally be roaming the halls. The princess of Hyrsch may have laid claim to the city, may have cowed them into refraining from open warfare, but the humans had all abandoned their positions. They would not serve her. In the streets, Eaon could hear their anger. The mourning of the monster who had ruled them.

Hand in hand, Eaon and Dearmead found their way back to the council room where Aisling, Eavha, Killian and Miika were facing down a handful of Sparrow witches clad in blue and gold. The uniform was different to the ones who'd attacked the Copeland farm, but the sight of the crest was enough to set Eaon's blood boiling. Dearmead squeezed his hand. That he was even able to do so still made Eaon's head spin.

"This is unacceptable." One of the Pirevian advisors was foaming at the mouth as he slammed his hands on the table.

"He declared war on me, not the other way around," Aisling said calmly, grey hair still stained pink from yesterday's blood.

"The demi-kin you sent us tried to lead an insurgence. Do you really expect us to believe you had no hand in it?"

"They were rebels in my city. I sent them here for that exact reason. It is not my fault you underestimated them."

She lied so convincingly. Only Eavha's shuffling feet told Eaon there was more to this story.

"Your parents will hear about this."

"I suspect they already have. That they have not come to reprimand me should tell you all you need to know for now about their opinion on the matter."

"They will not let you rule half the Sparrow territories!"

Aisling curled her lip in an expression that was both amused and terrifying.

"If you don't leave this council room, you will not live long enough to find out."

The advisor stared Aisling down for a minute, but the others were backing out of the room. Eventually, he followed. The door closed heavily behind them.

"Holding this city is going to be a pain," Killian sighed. Then turned to Eaon. "Your friend found another Old One. They're collecting fae to help."

Eaon grimaced. He still had not had a chance to ask the phouka more about why he was still helping to hold a human city. The "good conscience" thing was bullshit. Fae didn't have a conscience, but manipulation was likely. He desperately tried to remember the faerie rules about favors, and if he had said or done anything to suggest he would have to repay some debt for this aid.

When he realized Eavha was watching him, looking at Dearmead and Eaon's joined hands with the most joyful smile on her face that Eaon had ever seen, he lost his train of thought entirely. Giving Dearmead's hand a squeeze, he smiled back at her.

"I need to return to Hyrsch as soon as possible," Aisling said, looking at a map of Nir spread over the table. "There is still so much to prepare before winter. But now that we have Pirevia, if we can get the people here to cooperate, our army will double."

"What is this 'we' business?" Eaon said, feeling the sting as his magic roiled.

He'd read more books on creation lore than he cared to admit, though he'd never gone so far as to believe any of it as truth. Some, perhaps, but stories were unreliable. Translation errors were always a possibility, as was bias perception and omitting things that didn't suit the narrative. But this felt real. He could accept that Chaos was real, and knew that something had to be done, but he would not accept working with Aisling. He didn't care if she had a plan.

Dearmead's hiss and the flex of his hand reminded Eaon to calm down.

"Your sister is onboard. Your boyfriend is onboard. So get onboard, Eaon," Aisling snapped.

His whole life, Eaon had been taught to do what had to be done. To not think of himself, but of the family. The clan. Their community, and how he could best contribute to it. He had never hated it as much as he did right then, because he could see the logic in what she was saying. If Chaos was returning, it only made sense to help the one person who knew what was coming.

But all he could think about were those months he'd spent with Cinn. The trauma that had ravaged him so completely he still couldn't speak. Couldn't sleep without nightmares. The way you could see how close to breaking, how close to insanity, the kinner really was.

Reaching for the new twine around his neck, Eaon rubbed the button threaded there.

"Do you know who I am?" he asked Aisling, voice stone cold.

The princess straightened her shoulders. "I do. You're a Nemuse. Eavha's brother, and the most powerful Returned I have ever heard of. Without even blinking, you could turn this entire city to dust."

Her flattery did nothing.

"I could also kill you. Just you. And I could make it slow. I could do it from right here. I could make you watch your body rot, your meat slide off your bones like a well-roasted pig."

He felt Dearmead's grip tightening, but Eaon didn't care.

Aisling didn't even flinch.

"You would make a formidable enemy, Eaon."

"I *am* and will always be your enemy. For now, I can consider being your ally, too. But I want a vow from you. I want your blood sworn vow that when Cinn returns, you will give him however many pounds of flesh he wants from you."

"Eaon . . ." Eavha said quietly.

Aisling put a hand on Eavha's elbow. Red burst across Eaon's vision. Dearmead's arm suddenly wrapping around his chest was the only thing that kept him from flying out of his seat to rip her hand off her body.

Still, the princess didn't flinch. "In the spirit of ally-ship, I will be honest with you. I cannot be bound by blood oath or vow. Not even the power of Imsa could keep me to my word. But I can promise that before this is over, the kinner will get his vengeance. I will get what is coming to me."

Eavha frowned, turning to Aisling.

"What does that—"

A warning screech silenced them just before the glass window shattered, the phouka in all its winged glory, swooping inside. With a *pop*, he transformed back into his goat-headed form, yellow eyes wild with panic.

"What's wrong?" Eaon asked.

"The forest," he panted. "The Anfar forest is on fire."

CHAPTER FIFTY-NINE

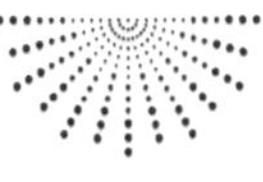

KAELEAN

THE ELDERS HAD ALREADY GATHERED IN THE PAVILION. KAELEAN ran across the field and leaped onto the stone, raising her voice over the panicked chatter of the other witches.

"How long until the blaze reaches the Boab?"

"An hour."

"We should have started evacuating immediately," another called out, making the rest break into argument again.

"Evacuate? *Into* the fire? We're safe here."

"What will happen to Wyldeden if the tree burns?"

Normally their stupid questions would have annoyed her, but she understood the panic. She felt it herself.

"Yvette, begin evacuating people immediately. Peera and Nuala, get outside now and start people moving south."

"But—"

"There is no choice," Kaelean interrupted, voice breaking. "If the bridge I made between Wyldeden and Anfar is still open when the tree burns, the fire will enter Terra's realm. If I close it while we are still inside, this pocket will collapse and we will die. I have to close the bridge, but everybody needs to get out."

"There isn't time. There's no way we can get everyone out within an hour."

"Every witch capable of casting a witchmark needs to get to the boundary and tear a hole in the realm."

"That gives us, what, three extra doors?"

"Four." From behind a pillar, Lorelei stepped forward. "Unbind me, Kaelean."

Kaelean ignored her. Peera and Nuala had already left. "Rally the most powerful earth-movers we have and send them out first. Have them clear the forest as best they can between the blaze and the Boab. Slow it down a little, maybe. I'll be there to join them shortly."

"What about the crystals? The animals? The books?"

"Leave them."

"We can't! A millennia of knowledge!"

"Leave them! And go!" she shouted, voice cracking once more.

Her usual aloofness was gone, and the elders stared as their high priestess began to cry. One by one, they turned to do what they had to do.

"Unbind me, Kaelean," Lorelei demanded again. "You will need my power."

"You have learned nothing," Kaelean hissed at her. "You can count yourself lucky I don't chain you to the outside of the Boab and let you burn."

"You're being petty—"

"Listen to me," Kaelean spat. "Your only job in all of this is to go and find Cinn's cat and make sure no harm comes to that wretched thing. Fail, and I will take far more from you than your magic."

The fear on Lorelei's face was only just concealed by her indignation as she turned on her heel and strode from the pavilion.

Crouching in the dirt, Kaelean wiped her eyes. Then she scooped up soil and began marking her face.

CHAPTER SIXTY

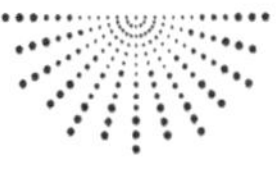

EAVHA

MIIKA PROMISED HE COULD KEEP A HOLD OF PIREVIA WHILE KILLIAN rode with one of the sky witches back to the North Mountains to find out what was going on and get help, which left Eavha and Aisling running from the palace to the stables, Eaon and Dearmead already atop the phouka.

Under other circumstances, it might have been fun to race Volya against the phouka, but as they got into the skies it became clear that something was very wrong. Black smoke billowed into the sky. Not a pillar of it, but a mountain's worth. The forest closest to the spine was lost in darkness and she couldn't see the Boab at all.

A streak of black went past, Eaon closest to the phouka's head, with Dearmead and his spear poised behind.

"Hold on," Aisling warned her, pressing Eavha down closer to the horse's neck before flicking the reins.

The beautiful snowy creature whinnied before beating her wings harder, racing toward the disaster awaiting them.

Eavha told herself it was the smoke making her eyes water as they flew over the Anfar forest. The mountains were completely obscured, the sky blackened until one could have been forgiven for thinking it was midnight. Head down, tucked in tight against Volya with Aisling at her back, who was using her Celeste-blessing to keep the worst of the smoke and burning wind off their faces, it was hard to focus on what had to be done. On finding the source of the fire. A part of her was screaming for the trees and the dryads caught inside. The animals fleeing their homes. Even the unbound witches who dwelled in the forest.

"It will be okay," Aisling whispered in her ear.

She'd started shaking, despite the oppressive heat beginning to ripple the air around them.

"Can you see it yet?" she asked, too afraid to look.

The Great Boab.

Aisling didn't answer. When Eavha began to raise her head, Aisling let go of the reins to push it back down.

"Don't look."

Pain lanced her heart, pulling out a soft sob. *Please*, she prayed silently. *Let them be safe.*

She hadn't ever managed to do it successfully, but she tried anyway; relaxing the tautness of her body, Eavha looked for a way to open herself to Terra. Before, already living and training inside the realm, the best she had been able to do was find the door. When she had tried in Hyrsch, there had been nothing to connect with. Yet, as she closed her eyes and calmed scorching breaths, letting her blessing swell inside her until her body was nothing but a cage, she found the door to Terra's realm was already open. The Spirit stood there in all her glowing ethereal beauty, waiting.

Are they safe? Eavha asked.

No. Come quickly.

With barely a thought, Eavha snapped back to herself and sat up quickly.

"What—" Aisling startled.

In the near distance to their left, the Great Boab was a pillar of flame rising above the inferno below, a torch in the red and black sky. Wind whipped the blaze into a funnel, sending embers spitting into the east to catch onto fresh kindling. But that wasn't where the tug in her gut was pulling her. Halfway between the Boab and the Dividing River, the trees were shifting, parting, as if to allow a great mass of people through at once. A trail of fire followed them in skips and sprints, spreading faster than any witch could outrace.

"There." Eavha pointed. "My clan. They need me."

She wasn't entirely sure what she could do. Perhaps if people were hurt she could patch them up enough to keep running, but—

"Keep going!" Aisling shouted into the wind.

Eaon frowned, but his new phouka friend nodded, flapping his great wings toward the darkest parts of the burning forest and disappearing into the rippling heat.

Without warning, Aisling shifted her weight and flicked Volya's reins. Gripping her saddle tightly, Eavha lowered herself again and grit her teeth against the onslaught of wind that not even Aisling could control as they plummeted in the direction of the shifting trees.

It took a few minutes to get ahead of the fire, but as they skimmed the treetops Eavha spotted her people fleeing desperately. Kaelean was in her lupanis form carrying three humans on her back. Cinn's family. She could not use her magic in that form, and as far as Eavha knew, Lorelei's was still bound. No one else had the power to clear their path the way it seemed to be doing, and yet the twisting roots of trees sunk deeper into the soil, low-hanging branches twisting up and out of the way as tens of thousands of witches ran for their lives. Between the kindness of the dryads in their final moments and Terra's will, thousands of witches used their blessings in unison, changing the very shape of the world around them.

The ones farthest behind were barely visible as thick smoke clouded the air, faces red and blistered from heat even with the flames still a mile behind.

"They're not going to make it to the river," Eavha cried, gripping the pommel of the saddle.

Tunneling into her magic, begging Terra to give her strength, Eavha tried to remember everything she knew about fire. Which wasn't much. She didn't know how to keep it back using just the earth.

"Save it," Aisling said sharply.

Screams were barely audible above the wildfire's distant roaring as

Volya's shadow flew over the Wyldeden witches. As they reached the front of the crowd, the winged horse transitioned between flying and running as smoothly as she had done the first time, though Eavha sensed the panic of the creature. It did not want to be on the ground where it was so vulnerable.

The lupanis continued to run alongside them, sparing a glance that somehow managed to look surprised despite its scaled canine features.

"Time to trust me, High Priestess," Aisling called, then pulled back on the reins, slowing Volya.

"What are you doing?" Eavha asked.

Streaked with soot, Aisling dismounted and shucked off her gloves. Two of the marks on her skin had deepened, no longer simple ink but black as the void.

Kaelean skidded to a stop.

Taking a deep breath, Aisling closed her eyes. Reaching forward, her fists clenched something invisible and the swell of magic that burst through the air was potent enough to make even Kaelean stumble back. With a vicious pull, Aisling tore open a portal. The power of the magic she was using sent her to her knees as she opened her palms and pushed it open wider.

Wider still.

Wider, until Eavha couldn't see the ends of it.

Without hesitating, Kaelean charged through. Without hesitating, the Wyldeden clan followed.

Eavha stared at Aisling, stunned. The princess held the enormous portal as an entire city worth of witches fled through it, exhaustion quickly caving her shoulders.

Only the sound of retching pulled Eavha from her shock. Turning, she left Aisling and ran to the back of the masses. The forest was gone, replaced by hot black smoke that scorched her lungs and left her stumbling blind. But there were a few stragglers too overcome to go on that Eavha hauled to their feet, blasting with enough healing magic to get them to the portal. Nothing sophisticated, just raw power commanded by a verbal spell that she could barely get out through her burning throat, leaving many of the stragglers screaming in agony. It was better that than waiting for death.

Only when the collapsed witches she found were beyond saving did she stop looking for them, silently promising to pray for their safe embrace once she got to safety.

Unable to see, she stumbled blindly until a gentle pressure against her back steadied her. Turning, a weeping dryad with sap dried into the cracks of their wooden face greeted her with a knowing smile. There was no saving them. Its branch-like arm guided her to where a second waited, pointing the way back out of the dark to where Aisling was waiting for her. Head bowed almost to the ground, her back rose in shallow breaths, arms shaking as she continued to hold the rapidly shrinking portal. The last of the witches had stumbled through, so, grunting with the strain, Eavha helped Aisling to her feet and dragged her through the failing portal.

On the other side, the clan was trying to cross the Dividing River but the single bridge into Oford had been drawn up.

Kaelean had shifted back, the humans standing silently nearby, terrified expressions on their faces as they watched Kaelean and Lorelei argue viciously.

"I'm sorry," Aisling panted as they reached them. "I couldn't send you farther."

The two high priestesses didn't acknowledge that she had spoken.

"I can do it, Kaelean," Lorelei hissed, fists clenched at her sides. "Are you really going to let our people die for the sake of punishing me?!"

"You've done nothing to make me trust that you would—"

"What's going on," Eavha shouted over them, demanding rather than asking.

That got their attention.

"Tell her to unbind my magic so I can get our people across the river," Lorelei snapped.

A part of Eavha still recoiled from being spoken to like that. Lorelei may have spent the past few months laboring, but it had not dulled the air of superiority she held. Had not curbed her distaste for being magic-less, nor the others born that way.

But that was not important right now.

Eavha turned to Kaelean. "Why are you even arguing about this? Just do it."

"She will turn on us."

There wasn't time to argue the point. "If you don't do it, I will."

Both Lorelei and Kaelean looked at Eavha like she had grown a second nose.

"You don't know how."

"Never stopped me before." Stepping forward, Eavha reached one hand out to place on Lorelei's head. Kaelean pushed her away.

"Ridiculous child," Kaelean hissed, then turned to Lorelei. "You will be bound again as soon as it is done."

Lorelei said nothing, eyes glittering as she stared Kaelean down. Muttering under her breath, Kaelean placed a hand on Lorelei's head and closed her eyes.

They all felt it as the binding on Lorelei broke. As power returned to her. She stood a little taller, smiled a little wider as she flexed her hands.

Without waiting for instruction, Lorelei pushed her way to the front of the crowd to stand by the bridge. Kneeling, she dragged her fingers through the dirt and quickly drew marks over her face before beginning an incantation. As she lay her hands on the wooden post of the bridge, a surge of power rocked through the clan once more. Many collapsed from it, more leaning over to vomit.

But the bridge was descending. Roots exploded out of the ground, crawling over the frame, twisting together in tight knots all the way across the dirty brown water of the river, widening it three-fold. Already, witches were desperately climbing over the new roots, leaping and running to the other side.

Eavha was both overwhelmed by the power of her old high priestess and utterly cowed by her own comparative lack. She could do nothing like this.

Kaelean watched with a scowl. "Go," she said to Eavha and Aisling. "There is one last thing to do. Make sure the Copelands get across okay."

Aisling was already leading Volya to them, tripping over her dragging feet as she did. "Come," she told them, helping Sarah on first.

"What do you need to do?" Eavha asked.

"The river isn't wide enough to stop a strong wind blowing embers over. So I'm going to widen it."

Eavha gawked. "Can . . . can you do that without burning out?"

Kaelean narrowed her eyes further. "We will find out."

Lorelei was on her hands and knees, panting hard, a slight dribble of blood leaking from her nose. Two laborers Eavha recognized from the Sanctuary stopped beside her, grabbing her and hauling her to her feet.

Kaelean turned away from the bridge. The sky was so dark that, as the witch took a few steps back toward the forest, she would have been lost to the haze if not for the red of her hair.

"Eavha," Aisling called from the bridge, slapping Volya's rear to send her flying over the river.

"Go," Eavha told her.

Kaelean looked back. "Eavha, go with the clan. I have to do this on this side of the bridge. I need the forest's power."

"I know. And I am staying with you. This clan needs you. I need you. I might not be able to open a portal to bring a city across the forest, or make a bridge out of nothing, or change the entire river, but I will do what I can. I will be here so if you burn out, I can bring you back."

There wasn't time to argue and Kaelean knew it. Dropping to her knees, burying her hands in the soil, Kaelean sent her magic tunneling into it. Beneath her feet, Eavha felt the earth stirring. Giving.

Rushing to Kaelean's side, Eavha knelt beside her and placed her hands on the high priestess's shoulders.

Keep her strong, Eavha pleaded to Sanni.

With the Spirit's permission, Eavha's magic swelled and spilled into Kaelean, who sucked in a sharp breath and spilled her own magic deeper into the ground.

People behind them were screaming, and Eavha dared to look back. The bridge was collapsing, the last of her people flinging themselves across it and onto the shore, hurrying away from the banks as they crept out, widening the river.

Kaelean's breaths were becoming wet and Eavha could feel her essence, her soul, beginning to fray.

"It's enough," Eavha said.

"A little more," Kaelean panted through bloody teeth.

The edge of the river was a few feet from their ankles now, twice as wide as it had been before, the water a dozen feet below the surface. The fire burned close enough that Eavha had to turn her face away, the smoke coating her lungs leaving her choking.

Kaelean went limp.

"Get up," Eavha coughed out the words, trying to lift Kaelean to her feet.

But the high priestess's powerful legs were shaking too hard to keep her up for long. Dragging her the last few feet to the sharp drop of the river's edge, Eavha only had the strength to wrap her arms around Kaelean and fall back, letting gravity plunge them into the water.

Their weight took them beneath the surface, the world blurring as water enveloped them. Too heavy to aim for the surface, and though she was not a good swimmer, Eavha kept her arms around Kaelean and kicked. The water was warm and filthy, brown with the Spirits only knew what, but there wasn't anything living around to bother them as Eavha struggled through the deep river.

She needed to breathe. The thin scrap of air she'd been able to hold in her soot-riddled lungs was not enough.

Above, a booming splash churned the water. Panic nearly made her drop Kaelean, but Aisling was suddenly there beside her. Grabbing Eavha's face, she pressed her mouth to hers and blew. Fresh air filled her lungs, a bubble of it expanding over her mouth and nose. As Aisling pulled away, one covered her face as well. Then the princess grabbed a hold of Kaelean and helped Eavha pull her to the surface.

Witches were waiting for them on the other side, holding roots and branches down the steep riverbank for them to climb out with. A number of guardians jumped into the water to help, climbing up behind them.

"Get to the city," Aisling panted as she rolled onto her back. "We will have refuge there."

"There's an entire forest full of beasts and fae between there and here," Lorelei reminded her. "They're not like normal animals, and the fire will have sent the rogues running too, both only making the fae more temperamental and the beasts more territorial. Can you portal us again?"

Aisling looked ready to faint as she shook her head.

Eavha took a deep breath. "I know it's scary. I know everything out here is more dangerous than anything most of you have ever faced." Her voice carried across the gathered witches, the ones farther back repeating her words for the others to hear. "But it is still Terra's realm. And we are still Terranian. Let the forest guide you."

Mutters of agreement and fear echoed through the crowd.

Eavha looked to Kaelean, who was breathing too hard, still too weak to stand on her own. So she turned to Lorelei, who was staring at her with curiosity. A nod of her head suggested she should continue.

She was heir. The high priestess could not rule right now, and though Lorelei had her magic back, she was deferring to Eavha.

"Scouts, listen to the trees. Keep us away from trouble. Guardians, stay closest to the perimeter of the group, or close to those most vulnerable. Everyone with the strength to do so, find a weapon. A stick, a rock, anything. We move toward Hyrsch and we stop for nothing."

People immediately began moving, elders repeating instructions, sending particular witches to particular areas. Aisling whistled and Volya landed. The humans got off and helped Kaelean climb onto the creature's back while Lorelei lifted her chin to the older human woman, who clutched a mangy looking cat.

"I will take it now," Lorelei said, taking the feline creature from the woman and tucking it under her arm.

"Are you hurt?" Eavha asked the humans in Nirnish, looking them over.

"We're okay," the pregnant one said.

"You're Eaon's sister," the man said. "Have you heard anything from him? Are he and Cinn alright?"

"Cinn is in Qiri," Eavha answered. "And Eaon . . ." She glanced back across the river.

"Eaon is in good hands," Aisling said softly. "We need to get to Hyrsch."

But the worry for Eaon didn't ebb. The reality of what was happening was catching up with her. Wyldeden was gone. Anfar was burning.

"Is this the start of it?" Eavha asked Aisling in Terranian. "Is this Chaos?"

"Chaos?" Lorelei interrupted, but they ignored her.

Aisling had gotten paler, her eyes growing darker. "It might be."

She'd thought they had time.

"Perhaps you can talk about this once we're safe," the pregnant human suggested.

Aisling turned and gave her a once over, somehow growing even paler. "You must be Siobhan."

The human stiffened, straightening her shoulders as if only now remembering how she had tried to gut the princess. The other humans moved slightly in front of her.

"I am."

"You look so much like Nora."

"Nora." Siobhan put a hand to her throat and coughed deeply. Then, "And Owen. What did you do with them? Are they alright?"

Aisling said nothing. Eavha stepped forward and put a hand on the pregnant woman's back. "Come. I will explain."

And with that, they joined the marching witches of Wyldeden into unknown territory.

CHAPTER SIXTY-ONE

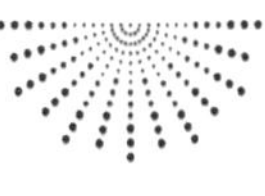

EAON

T HE SMOKE WAS A THOUSAND TIMES WORSE THAN WHEN E AON HAD been on the stake, and the closer they got to the womb the thicker it got until even the phouka had to veer back, flapping madly to get above it. Pulling his shirt over his mouth and nose barely helped to filter his breaths, and behind him he could hear Dearmead hacking hot soot from his lungs. This was going to kill them before they ever reached the flames.

"Is this the North Mountain Clan? Is this revenge for what you did there?" Dearmead croaked, barely audible over the blistering roar of the wildfire.

"Better not be," Eaon grumbled.

The thought that he could have done this . . .

Then he felt it. Magic.

The air around them churned, the smoke dissipating until it was only a light haze. To the right, from the mountains, a swarm of giant moths rode toward them, two riders on each. Eaon recognized the way the haze began to twist and twirl, up and away to clear the space above the fire. Ten, twelve, fifteen vortexes of black smoke rising into the clouds to expose the ravaging flames beneath. Flames that seemed to hesitate as the second riders, the Ignatius-blessed, did what they could to contain it from so high up.

They were not here to burn the forest. They had come to stop it.

"More of your friends?" Dearmead asked, awed.

Eaon spared a grateful smile.

A smile that shattered as a horrific inhuman screech bellowed from the mountains, so earsplittingly loud that the roar of the fire became white noise. Ahead, Eaon could make out the silhouette of the two towers on either side of the womb, a bridge suspended between them. It was the only way to cross the womb without facing the mountain clans, and was normally heavily guarded by Sparrows. Today, waiting at the very edge of the wards around Anfar, it had a different guardian.

A giant winged beast rose from the roof of the eastern tower.

"Um, what is that?" Dearmead asked.

"What in the Lover's realm have you gotten me into, witch," the phouka cursed, banking sharply away.

Eaon couldn't answer either of them as he turned his head to watch the dragon rise above the haze. The phouka's eagle form was large enough to carry the both of them comfortably, but he was only half the size of one of the dragon's yellow-black wings. The moths even smaller.

"It's going for the Igni." Eaon straightened as much as he could on the back of the phouka and began rousing the deadly power inside him.

"Don't," the phouka snapped.

Eaon paused. He had not had time to give any more thought to the phouka's warnings about using his magic. Restraining it in the arena had been impossible, only the fear of hurting Eavha and the others delaying his inevitable surrender to that bliss. He had lost his mind, and if Dearmead hadn't been there . . . hadn't been touching him . . .

Eaon shook his head. "It doesn't matter. I have to do it."

The phouka glided from updraft to updraft, using the gray haze of smoke as a cover to rise above the dragon still focused on the only witches capable of controlling the blaze below.

"No, you don't," Dearmead said as he braced himself on Eaon's shoulder, getting his feet under him to stand on the phouka's back. Shouting over the scream of the wind in their ears, Dearmead called to the phouka, "Get me as close as you can!"

"What are you doing?" Eaon hissed.

They were above the dragon now, a pigeon keeping pace with an eagle. The raw bone of the twisting horns jutting out from its snakelike temple were tipped in gold, as were the spiny ridges down its back and tail, each as large as a man was tall. Fixated on the sky coven and their Igni riders, it didn't seem to consider the possibility of a threat from above.

Neither did the thing riding it.

Like Aadya, the rider's body was mostly scaled, bar his hands and head. A forked tail whipped behind him as he stayed close to the dragon's thick neck, watching eagerly as they approached the sky coven.

Dearmead didn't answer Eaon's question, but he didn't need to. Crouching, palming two of his stone daggers, Dearmead gave Eaon a wry smile and a quick kiss on the temple.

"I'll be fine," he said.

Then he leaped off the back of the phouka.

The panic that swelled in Eaon's chest made him reach after him, but the phouka was already banking away, flapping hard to put some distance between them and the beast.

"Don't leave him!"

"I'm not!" the phouka snapped back.

He can't die, Eaon reminded himself as he strained to see Dearmead fall, body spearing through the smoky haze, aiming right for the rider. *He can't die, he can't die, he can't die.*

Dearmead's landing must have jolted the beast enough to draw the rider's attention, his head snapping around as Dearmead stuck his daggers into the dragon's back.

The beast didn't even notice. The weapons weren't made of silver.

"Shit," Eaon hissed. "*Shit.*"

With long claws instead of fingers, the rider dragged himself across the dragon's back to where Dearmead was waiting, his braid whipping behind him like a violent tail.

Before he could see what happened, Eaon lost sight of them as the world spun madly, the phouka folding in his wings and plummeting toward the dragon's face. Nearly jolted off the phouka's back as they struck, Eaon clung tightly as they immediately flapped away again, one of the dragon's ruby eyes hanging from the phouka's talons. The pained screech that chased after them burst something in Eaon's ear, heat spilling down the side of his face as a dizzying ringing reverberated through his skull.

Eaon looked back to where Dearmead and the rider wrestled, dark blood slicking the scales and staining Dearmead's feet. One knife still embedded in the dragon's flesh, anchoring him to the now furious beast, Dearmead had gotten his legs around the rider's waist, an arm around his throat, his other knife deep in the rider's shoulder. Thrashing madly, the rider lashed out with his thick claws and ripped open the leather of Dearmead's thigh. More blood spilled across the dragon's back.

The sky coven had noticed the dragon now, scattering apart, forcing the beast to swivel its head around to track them. The phouka turned, aiming for the dragon's other eye.

"Get the rider!" Eaon shouted, watching where Dearmead was finally forced to let go, the rider catching his face with those claws and ripping him apart.

"I have fought beside kinner before. He will be fine," the phouka huffed.

Sure enough, the wounds were already closing. Pulling the stone knife from his shoulder, the rider snarled and tossed it aside, toes curling into the dragon's hide to keep him upright. An advantage Dearmead didn't have, still anchored only by his other blade. Spitting blood, he pulled his spear from his back and whipped it around, keeping the rider at bay until his wounds had closed completely. As the rider neared once more, Dearmead thrust the spear, but the rider swerved as if his bones were liquid. Turning the missed thrust into a whip, Dearmead smacked the rider in the side with the staff and sent him careening across the dragon's back.

Eaon held his breath, but the rider sunk his claws into the beast's flesh and managed to hold on.

Then the phouka was diving again, and Eaon had to duck his head to stop from being blown off. The element of surprise was truly lost now though, and the dragon was waiting, flashing teeth as long as Eaon was tall. The snapping jaws grazed the phouka's feathers, drawing glistening opalescent blood. Crying out, the phouka flapped madly backward, the wound across its wing already healing.

Eaon looked back to Dearmead again and his stomach sank.

The rider had managed to get a hold of Dearmead's spear, grinning as he pulled on it. Dearmead had to let go of either the spear or the dagger, or risk dislocating his shoulders. To let go of the spear would be to surrender it to the rider. To let go of the dagger was to let go of the anchor keeping him on the dragon's back.

Dearmead let go of the dagger, using his considerable strength and grip on the spear to stabilize as he rushed forward. As if predicting the move, the rider tossed the spear away, leaving Dearmead unanchored, unbalanced.

The dragon banked.

Dearmead fell.

"No!" Rising up on the phouka's back, Eaon nearly jumped, as if he could sprout wings of his own.

With a screech that stabbed dully in Eaon's wrecked ear, the phouka tucked in his wings and dived once more. Swearing, he dropped and grabbed a hold of the feathery mane, stomach twisting at the impossible speed with which they shot through the sky after Dearmead.

But the dragon, too, was diving. And it was much closer.

There was nothing to be done as the dragon snatched Dearmead out of his plummet in one giant claw, spreading its wings for two sharp backward flaps, slowing their descent.

"DEARMEAD!"

The phouka continued to dive, but Eaon was done being a useless passenger on this ride. The magic inside him boiled over.

"Don't!" the phouka snapped breathlessly.

Too late.

It exploded out of Eaon in an arc of death.

For the first time, the rider looked up. Their gazes locked for a brief moment before the rider raised an arm, pushing the blast of power away. Redirected it, as inconsequential as a paper plane, right into the path of the sky coven.

"No!"

Desperately, Eaon tried to rein it in, but as the first three pearls of bliss hit him he knew he'd failed. Didn't need to see if the witches and their mount tumbled from the sky, grey and limp, or if they'd simply misted. Sinking against the phouka's back, eyes rolling in his head at the threads of pure ecstasy rushing through his veins, the thing inside him rejoiced as it reached for more.

"Snap out of it!" the phouka shouted, but the words seemed so far away. "Right now!"

Three more pearls of white heat burst behind his eyes, flooding his head, his chest, with the purest energy there was. Everything else melted away. He could sense them all around him, the souls waiting to be reaped. They would go to the Lover and receive their embrace, moving on to a place where there was only this bliss.

A bone-shattering screech of agony that threatened the break apart the entire Northern Spine made him lift his head. Caught in the dragon's grip, Dearmead had wedged another of his knives into the sensitive flesh of a cuticle.

"Dearmead," Eaon whispered, trying to shake the fireworks out of his eyes.

"Hold on, you stupid witch," the phouka spat.

Talons stretched, the phouka plummeted once more in an attempt to snatch Dearmead out of the dragon's grip. But the rider was still watching Eaon, shouting an inaudible command to the beast.

Banking left, arching its long serpentine neck, the dragon looked right at Eaon. Its one ruby eye glittered with wildfire right as it opened its giant maw.

"Damn it!" the phouka opened his wings and banked hard, but it was too late.

Eaon felt the heat before he saw the fire. Then the world tipped over and all he could see was smoke and clouds as he tumbled, limp with bliss, toward the towers far below.

Black feathers fell around him, still burning.

CHAPTER SIXTY-TWO

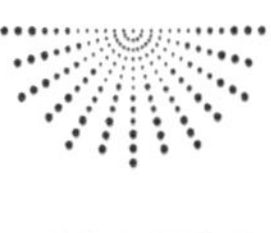

AISLING

There had never been so many people in the palace. In the city. Many of her people had opened their homes to the Anfar Forest Clan, but crowds still sat in the street, congregating on the steps to the theater and the museum, the banks and restaurants and clothiers. Coated in soot, burned and frightened, the witches were wary of the human healers that had come out to help.

Aisling watched them from where she sat against the stained-glass window in the throne room, too tired to even stand. Eavha had stayed down there to do what she could for her people, organizing the Wyldeden healers and sending them off with blessed bandages, but she would come up soon. So would the others: Kaelean and Lorelei, the Copelands and Siobhan, plus any elders who had survived.

Edwina sat on Aisling's old throne, eyes closed and breathing deeply. Her brother paced along the dais.

"This is the part where you tell us that ruling a city is not all it's hyped up to be," Radley snarled.

Aisling didn't have the energy to bite back.

The throne room doors banged open, bringing Radley to a halt. Eavha's torn dress billowed behind her as she stormed in, tears streaking the soot on her face as she pointed a finger at Aisling.

"I thought you said they would come from the south! I thought you said it would be winter!"

"That's what Davina saw," she answered, finally releasing the hold on her magic so the Morvish ghost could present herself once more.

Davina was a simmering ball of rage as well. "How dare you."

A few paces behind, Kaelean and Lorelei looked as exhausted as Aisling felt. They dragged their feet to the dais, looking between where Aisling was leaning against the window and Edwina sitting on the throne.

"Who is in charge?" Kaelean asked.

Aisling waved a hand at Edwina, who still hadn't opened her eyes.

"Demi-kin rule the city?" Lorelei asked, shocked derision in her voice.

Beyond the slight curling of her upper lip at the tone, Aisling was too tired to deal with Lorelei, either.

Luckily, she didn't have to.

"Did I say you could speak?" Kaelean snarled at the same time Radley snapped: "You got a problem with that, witch?"

Lorelei's nostrils flared as she raised her chin, looking down her nose at the both of them. She opened her mouth, but Kaelean interrupted her.

"I will bind you again right now if you even utter a sound."

Lorelei shut her mouth.

"Where are the Copelands?" Aisling managed to ask.

The name of the human farmers made Radley stop walking. Finally, Edwina opened her eyes.

"The humans are down in the street, helping who they can." Kaelean looked the two demi-kin over. "You know them?"

"Cinn," Eavha explained, struggling with the Nirnish. "This is his brother and sister."

Kaelean stiffened. Then the high priestess of Wyldeden—*No*, Aisling reminded herself, throat tightening. Wyldeden was gone now— the high priestess of the Anfar Forest Clan, bowed.

"I look forward to being better acquainted when the situation is not so dire," she told them, then rose, looking out the window. "Thank you for giving us refuge."

"As if we had a choice," Radley scoffed, throwing a hand out in Aisling's direction. "If it was up to me, anyone who sides with this bitch would be left out to die."

All three Anfar witches were instantly incensed, but before a fight could break out, Edwina stood up.

Her back was straight as a rod, shoulders back, chin high. A queen, in any other life.

Then she turned to Aisling. "I don't know what to do."

To be honest, neither did Aisling. She looked up to Davina, who was still fuming.

"You said winter."

The rage waned as Davina looked back out the window. "Look."

Aisling looked. A fine coat of white ash rained down on the city, coating it just like snow did during the early days of winter.

"I . . . I made a mistake. I misinterpreted."

They didn't have until winter. Chaos was here.

Aisling put her head back against the window and tried to still her mind. She wasn't ready. Not even close.

"Aisling," Eavha called. "What does Davina say?"

"What do we do?" Edwina asked.

Davina moved closer, sitting down beside Aisling, invisible to everyone but her. "I'm sorry. But I'm still here."

"I don't know what to do," Aisling whispered, so softly she hoped nobody else could hear.

"The game has begun. What's our opening move?" Davina prodded.

Whether she was ready or not, it was time to play.

Grunting, Aisling placed a trembling hand on the window and got to her feet. To Edwina and Radley, she said, "Get our soldiers ready to the west. The beast army will come."

"Our guardians will aid you," Kaelean added, then looked around the room. "Where is Dearmead?"

"He's with Eaon," Eavha explained.

"Eaon?" Kaelean reeled back. "What?"

"I'll explain later. Is our elder guardian still here?" Eavha asked Radley.

"Yeah, he and Clayton are keeping order down in the streets. I'll go tell them." At that, Radley excused himself.

"I'll fly back to Pirevia and get what troops I can rally and get them marching," Aisling continued.

"Through the fire?" Lorelei snorted.

Kaelean turned to glare at her, but Lorelei had a good point. The fire still blazed. There was nothing she could do about that.

"I'll go," Kaelean finally said. "I have a *relationship* with the Northern Mountain Clan. Their Igni-blessed will be able to help us get the fire under control."

"There were Northern Mountain Clan witches keeping Pirevia in check when we left," Eavha added. "Eaon's friends. They will help."

"I'm hoping to rally the energy to portal them," Aisling explained, flexing her hands. They were still trembling, her magic in tatters inside her. "I don't know how much time we have, but I doubt it's enough to travel by foot."

The conversation stopped when a clap of thunder broke through the room, a portal ripping open the throne room.

King Phineas Aurnia stumbled through, holding closed a gaping wound in his gut, intestines spilling through his fingers. Collapsing in a heap on the floor, his eyes searched out Aisling, who had frozen, reaching for her axe.

"Tallula," he croaked before coughing up blood.

Eavha rushed forward, her magic crackling.

"Don't," Aisling snapped at her.

"He's dying," she said, wide-eyed.

Aisling moved to stand over her father. "What about her?"

"Beasts . . ." the king managed, letting go of his stomach to point back at the still-open portal. "Chaos."

That one word tipped over the entire chessboard; her pieces, her plan, crumbling to ashes.

Chaos was in Kerveda.

"Kill it," the king gasped, clutching Aisling's boot. "Kill it."

Before she could shake him off, his fingers went limp as his eyes glazed over. The portal closed with a sputter as the magic died with him.

Edwina sat back down, a hand over her mouth.

"Eavha," Kaelean said, a knowing look in her eye. "Go to Pirevia. Rally who you can and take care of the fire. I'm going with the princess."

"No, I'm coming with you," Eavha demanded.

Aisling didn't know what was about to happen, but she knew parts. She knew she would face Chaos. She knew she would somehow end up on the bridge over the womb, facing him alone.

"Take Volya," Aisling rasped.

"I told you, I will not let you go into this on your own," Eavha snapped, stomping her foot.

"She's not," Kaelean said. "Trust me, young one. This battle is not the place for you."

That Eavha did not argue again, that she stood still as stone as a fresh tear rolled down her face, was all the evidence of her surrender she would allow.

"Do I have to bind you again?" Kaelean asked as she turned to Lorelei.

"No. I offer freely my vow of forfeit. Shall I do anything in your absence that you later disapprove of, I forfeit the entirety of my blessings permanently."

Kaelean nodded, then turned to Edwina. "Lorelei is the Wyldeden . . . Anfar Forest Clan emissary while I am gone. Do not trust her," she added, pointing a finger at Lorelei, who only raised her chin. "I will be back. Do not doubt it for a moment."

Aisling stepped forward, took Eavha's pretty face in her hands and wiped the dirty tears away. "Save my people for me."

Shaking, Eavha nodded. "Come back."

Aisling closed her eyes and rested her forehead against Eavha's, taking a deep breath that smelled of burnt peonies.

"For you, I will try."

Eavha placed her hands over Aisling's, sending a trickle of tingling magic to draw the tiny fragments of her magic back together. Aisling gasped, straightening as Eavha began to sag. Edwina leaped from the dais to catch her before she could collapse completely.

"What was that?" Aisling snapped.

"Just a little healing. Can't have you going to face Chaos on dregs." Eavha smiled, exhaustion lining her eyes.

Before the burning in Aisling's eyes could betray her, she turned to Kaelean who had already marked her sooty face in spellmarks and begun to shift into a lupanis.

Unbuttoning her blouse and rolling up her sleeves, Aisling let the world see the witchmarks covering her body. Sinking into her skin, they glowed with a neon darkness that made her bones ache. She could bear it knowing they would let her do what should be impossible.

With Kaelean on one side and Davina on the other, Aisling ripped open a portal directly into the castle in Kerveda.

The throne room of her parents' castle was slick with blood, yet empty of bodies. Only Aisling's mother lay on the dais, washed in the red glow of stained glass, her swollen belly far larger than should be possible. Elegant dress torn open, Tallula's body was on display where, beneath the near-translucent skin, something dark roiled and stretched. The queen arched off the floor in a spasm of pain, a bloody knife falling from her limp fingers.

Kaelean stalked to the dark corners of the sandstone room while Aisling warily approached the queen.

"Mother, where is it?" Aisling whispered once close enough.

Tallula's agonized gaze fixed on Aisling.

"Nevan," she gasped, blood spilling from between her lips.

"It's Aisling, Ma."

"No." The queen closed her eyes. "Nevan. I name Nevan king."

Of course. The shred of pity Aisling had mustered for her mother petered out.

"Nevan is dead," she said flatly. "I killed him."

The queen's eyes burned for a brief moment, words falling soundlessly from her lips as the blood in her mouth stopped bubbling. Her body sagged and the blaze died in her eyes, shit spilling over the dais.

Glancing around the room, it dawned on her that there was nobody else here. The knife on the floor, inches from the queen's fingers, was the beginning of a bloody trail that ended too suddenly. As if whoever she had cut had simply disappeared into thin air. Literally.

Kill it.

Her father's dying plea.

And for once, Aisling didn't need her blessing to know what had caused his death. Who. There was nobody else here. Whatever was growing inside the queen was not a witch, yet she had defended it with her dying breaths. She knew what she was bringing into the world, and King Phineas had realized too late that something was very wrong.

"What has she done?" Davina breathed from where she lingered by the wall, hand against her throat.

The thing in the queen's belly stretched again, bones cracking as the skin tore in a wet rip that sprayed Aisling with blood and globs of white like spoiled milk.

Drawing her axe, Aisling took a few step forward.

A skull-splitting screech made her flinch, the red of the room darkening as a shadow obscured the wall of glass behind the dais. With a thud, the room shuddered, bricks of sandstone crumbling to the ground in skull-sized chunks. The window shattered inwards.

Dropping to the ground, Aisling covered her head as glass rained down.

"No," she panted, sheer terror making the word a sob as shards of glass cut into her shoulders. A shudder ran down her spine as the power of two marks dwindled out. "No."

A bellow of beastly rage announced the enormous, scaled head that snaked through the broken window. The sight of the dragon with its one ruby eye left Aisling frozen on the floor.

Luckily, Kaelean was not as unnerved.

Vicious growl echoing through the chamber, she leaped for the dragon's remaining eye. Even without flame, the heat of its breath boiled the air as the dragon opened its maw, a pained bellow blasting through the room. Sucking down a dry breath, Aisling watched as the dragon tried to shake Kaelean loose. Its meaty neck slammed against the window frame and the entire wall began to crumble.

"Use your marks!" Davina screamed at her.

Aisling threw her hands up, shoving every scrap of magic that bubbled in her veins through the marks on her palm, pushing out a shield. Through the carnage, a figure scrambled over the horns along the dragon's crown and tumbled into the throne room, throwing himself over the queen's exposed body.

The dragon screeched, rearing back out of the throne room with the lupanis still attached to its face, ripping and shredding with gore-stained claws. As it fell away, Aisling caught sight of what lay beyond. The castle was in ruins, only one of the six other towers still standing.

Under different circumstances, it would have been satisfying to see her childhood home reduced to rubble, but the figure who'd protected the queen from debris was rising. A male witch covered in soot, forked tail whipping the air behind him, long claws in place of fingers and toes.

His feral gaze was locked on the thing crawling out of her mother's belly.

Aisling didn't understand what she was looking at. All shadow and mist, claw and fang, scale and fur, frills and spikes, there was no sensible shape to it.

Kill it.

She didn't need to be told.

As she raised her axe again, the dragon rider finally looked at her.

And grinned.

"So you're the one." His voice matched his swollen, bulging face perfectly, thick and warbled, like he had too many teeth in his mouth. "Do you like the new sibling your mother and I made? He will soon be your master."

"The marks, Aisling," Davina reminded her, trembling.

Aisling took a deep breath.

Celeste, hear my call. Let my will be yours, she prayed.

The mark on her sternum burned and the air against her skin tingled. With nothing but a thought, she slipped into the sky-Spirit's realm. Just for a moment. Crossing the room in the blink of an eye, she stepped back out and swung her blade toward the abomination now feasting on her mother's corpse.

With a wrathful roar, the dragon rider let loose a blast of

pressurized air that pushed Aisling off her feet. Before she hit the ground, she slipped back into Celeste's realm. Half a second to right herself and she dropped back out above the abomination, blade plunging for it.

Another blast sent her sprawling across the room.

The pain of her elbows scraping across the stone floor was secondary. Singularly focused, she slipped into the realm again and stepped out beside the abomination.

The rider was waiting, holding a stone dagger that looked familiar.

Instinct sent her turning back into the spirit realm before the rider could strike. Whirling around him, Aisling stepped back out and swung her axe for his neck. The rider blocked Aisling's axe with his dagger, and in the moment their weapons connected she felt the raw power coursing through him. A strength she couldn't match. Shoving her back, he kicked out with those deadly clawed feet, aiming for her gut.

Though the magic was draining her, Aisling spun out of range and called on another mark, screaming as the power of it burned her bones. All around the room, the scattered glass lifted off the ground, sharp edges turning in their direction. Aisling verbalized through gritted teeth as she cast another shield around herself before sending every shard of glass shooting for them.

Still, she felt it as the attack crashed against her magic. Felt the shredding pain of it, though not a scrap touched her. Unlike the rider, who was pummeled. Knocked to the ground by the force of the glass cutting through his body, he didn't try to rise as white-specked blood pooled around him.

Aisling dropped her shield, panting hard, body heavy with the weight of the marks.

Unaffected by the chaos around it and existing partly of mist, the abomination still feasted. Aisling's breath rasped as she took in the gnashing mess of shifting body parts, as if it had not yet decided what it wanted to be.

Glancing to Davina, her confusion was reflected in the ghost's face.

"I did not foresee this, but I think . . ." Davina swallowed nervously. "I think that might be him. Chaos. Or at least an embodiment of him, somehow."

Aisling would not lose an opportunity to end this force of destruction before it could gather strength. Blade of steel and silver, she stepped over the abomination and raised her heavy weapon once more.

A hand wrapped around her ankle.

"Aisling!" Davina screamed, but too late.

Yanking hard, the dragon rider pulled Aisling's leg out from under her, the axe skittering across the floor. Remnants of glass embedded itself in her hands. Her stomach and face. Behind her, the rider rose, plucking glass from his chest.

"A worthy effort," he mocked, stepping over her battered form to stroke the abomination's ever-shifting back.

Ignoring the pain, Aisling rolled, reaching for the axe's handle. The rider stomped down on her upper back, forcing glass deeper into her flesh. A pained whine cracked her throat as she tried to reach back. Hooking an arm around his ankle, she yanked, and it was enough to make him wobble. Enough to give her leverage to roll and clamber to her feet.

"For the Mother's sake, Aisling, *the marks*," Davina cried.

Gritting her teeth, Aisling delved into her magic once more. Another mark somewhere down her spine burned with cold as the axe shot into her hand. She was almost too tired to raise her arms, but she swung anyway.

The rider's blast of air sent her crashing back again with nothing but a flick of the wrist.

"Pathetic."

He must have been a Celeste-blessed witch before he was changed. The way Aadya was Morvish before she had become whatever she had become.

Climbing back to her feet, she spat blood on the tiles as the rider turned his back on her.

"You're not walking away from me, are you?" she mocked. To buy herself time to catch her breath, yes, but it did seem like he was about to leave as he peered out the gaping hole in the wall where the window used to be. The silence of the world outside suggested Kaelean was keeping it busy elsewhere.

"You're of little consequence, princess. If you can't best me, you certainly won't be able to best *him*. But it will be fun to watch you try."

That he had a point was more painful than Aisling cared to admit.

The rider scooped the shifting mass of flesh and mist into his arms, cradling it against his chest. If she had any hope of killing it at all it was now, not when it grew stronger, but she would have to get through the dragon rider first. With the splintering cold in her bones from the few marks she had used threatening to cripple her, she didn't know if she could.

But she couldn't let them leave, either.

"I have your friend," she tried, the words coming out in a pant. "Aadya."

To her surprise, the rider froze. Cold ire seethed behind his cat-slit eyes.

"*You* have her? You mean I burned the Anfar forest for nothing?"

Aisling said nothing. Gave away nothing.

The rider laughed a dark, dangerous chuckle. "Guess I will have to bring damnation to your city as well, then."

Aisling didn't dare glance to Davina, who gasped. Perhaps if she had not told him, the beast army would never come. But it was too late to take it back.

"Surrender that thing to me, and I'll let her go," she offered.

He paused. "You mean, she lives?"

That was hope in the undercurrent of his voice.

Again, Aisling said nothing.

Hope dissolved into a sneer as the rider shrugged. "Sucks to be her, I guess."

But the words were a lie. Tightness lined his eyes as he looked for his dragon again. When there still wasn't any sign of it coming, he moved for the door.

Aisling held out a hand and blasted it closed.

As the rider stilled, the abomination turned its head-like body part, two glistening red orbs peering out at her with something frighteningly close to intelligence. Knees quaking with the effort to keep standing,

Aisling felt its gaze roaming over her, memorizing her, and she knew in her bones right then that Davina was right. The King of Beasts was here.

Magic unlike anything Aisling had ever felt swelled in the air. The pressure of it was the final straw that dropped Aisling to her knees, bile rising in her throat as the throne room shook. Dampness seeped across her pants as the atmosphere flexed, her atoms expanding, and the intangible fabric of reality *rippled.*

The dragon rider screamed as his back bowed. Two fleshy lumps swelled from either side of his spine until branches of bones tore through, lengthening and twisting until wings of skin unfurled. The rider's screams became broken and bloody, and as the magic reached its crescendo, Aisling joined him. Pain scoured her to the marrow until the transformation finally ceased. The rippling in the world stilled, her body contracting before losing all strength and crumpling to the floor.

Drooling bile, the rider stood rigid as the abomination in his arms shuffled. Its red orbs slid to the gaping hole in the throne room, tendrils of mist snaking toward it. As if it were reaching.

"Tell Aadya," the rider croaked, wincing as he tested the new limbs protruding from his back, "I'm coming for her. That Byron intends to keep his promise."

Aisling couldn't answer.

Kill it, the voice in her head was screaming. *Now! Before it's too late!*

But that *thing*, barely an hour old, had done creation magic. The marks on her body felt like silly scribbles compared to that power.

She watched, stupefied, as the rider leaped from the broken window into the darkening evening sky, falling for a moment before figuring out how to flap his virgin wings.

Only after he was gone from sight did Aisling try to move. One hand planted flat on the floor, then the other, she pushed herself up to her knees. Dragged herself to her feet, swaying dizzily in the ringing silence.

She had failed.

Would fail.

As Davina appeared before her, Aisling expected to see the same desolation blooming in her chest reflected on her passed-lover's face.

Hoped for some words of encouragement as she trembled in the rubble, no clue how she was going to fight what was coming. But Davina looked down her nose stonily, a silent reprimand for all the days Aisling had delayed training with the marks on her pursed lips.

Spite coated the words as Davina's voice echoed through the ruined chamber.

"All hail the Sparrow Queen."

ACKNOWLEDGMENTS

If *The Mark of Things Unwanted* was my first baby step into the publishing world, then this has been a nose dive into the deep end. I have so much gratitude that I barely know how to express it toward everyone who's been with me on this journey so far.

You, first and foremost. The person who enjoyed the first book of *The Witches of Wyldeden Chronicles* enough to read the second. You make this thing I'm doing a hundred times more exciting than simply writing for myself, and I hope you're not too mad at me for leaving things the way they are for now. I promise, I'm already working on the next instalment and will get it to you as quick as I can!

As always, I need to take the time to thank my parents, my in-laws, and all the family I'm lucky to have supporting me as I chase my dreams. Without you, I would be nowhere.

To my dear friend AJ, who slogged through this beast of a book in its early drafts and listened to my exhausting to-and-fro about how to best tell this part of the story, I can't wait to see you in person again. You're a large part of why my sanity is quasi-intact and I love you very much.

And of course, Kat, my superb, wonderful, amazing, talented, intelligent (is that too many adjectives—not adverbs—?) editor, without who this book would still be unpalatable. In case I haven't told you, I am disgustingly grateful to have you on my team and hope you're enjoying a tall glass of fish wine right now.

And unfortunately, there are people I wish to thank who are not here to read this anymore. My nana, Lorraine, who I once told at the ripe age of five that I would "write big books" one day. Who encouraged my love of books with every chance she had, lending me a copy of one of her prized Stephen King novels when I was absolutely too young to read it. Thank you for being such an enormous part of my life, and I miss you very much.

Others, such as my godmother Leontina, and Aunty Beth, who gave me love and support through some of the hardest times, you will always hold cherished places in my heart.

And James. Always, James.

Lastly, but certainly not the least, my Sam. If for no other reason, I am glad I have written these books so that you can find your own love of telling stories. My notebooks are full of your own wonderful books, and one day I hope to learn your secret language so that I can read them. Until then, thank you for inspiring love in my heart every morning.

Rise and shine, baby.

ABOUT THE AUTHOR

Alex Clifford is an emerging author from the coffee capital: Melbourne, Australia. She has spent the past decade studying creative writing, interior design, sociology, psychology, and secondary education. As a neurodiverse, queer, widowed, single-mother, Alex is excited to bring her unique perspective to the fantasy genre for many years to come.

For more on Alex Clifford's upcoming work, visit:
www.alexclifford.com.au

You can find her on social media at:
    Facebook: facebook.com/AfsCliffordBooks
    Twitter: @AfsClifford
    Instagram: @almost_alex
    TikTok: @alexcliffordwrites